Drowning
In
Angst

David J. Pedersen

Odysia Press

Cover art by:
Alessandro Brunelli

Editing by:
Angela D. Pedersen
Danielle Fine

Acknowledgements

It takes a team of very patient and dedicated people to make one of these novel things happen. I couldn't do it without their encouragement and support. I couldn't do it alone and have to thank all of them! My wife, Angie, does an amazing job of editing the first, very rough draft. She patiently listens to me drone on about ideas, saves me dinner after late writing sessions, and encourages me to keep going when I don't feel like it. Speaking of patience, Becky, Matt and Mike provide invaluable insight and ideas as they review small handfuls of chapters that sporadically trickle in. Cristi not only provides excellent and colorful critiques for those rough drafts, she also models chainmail bikinis for me at cons – which I'm pretty sure is the real reason I sell books. Danielle Fine edits the final draft, challenging me in all the right ways. I truly believe she makes me a better writer. I also need to thank Alessandro Brunelli for his incredible cover art!

Finally, I thank you, my reader. It takes me a long time to write a novel, too long. I know that many have patiently waited, sticking with me the entire time. Your comments, reviews, messages, tweets—all keep me going. I couldn't be more fortunate, or more grateful! Thank you!

I've been waiting for five years to share this story, and I hope you enjoy it!

Books by David J. Pedersen

Angst Five Book Series:

Book 1: Angst
Book 2: Buried in Angst
Book 3: Drowning in Angst
Book 4: Burning with Angst
Book 5: Dying with Angst

Young Adult / Middle Grade Fiction:

Clod Makes A Friend

Map of Ehrde

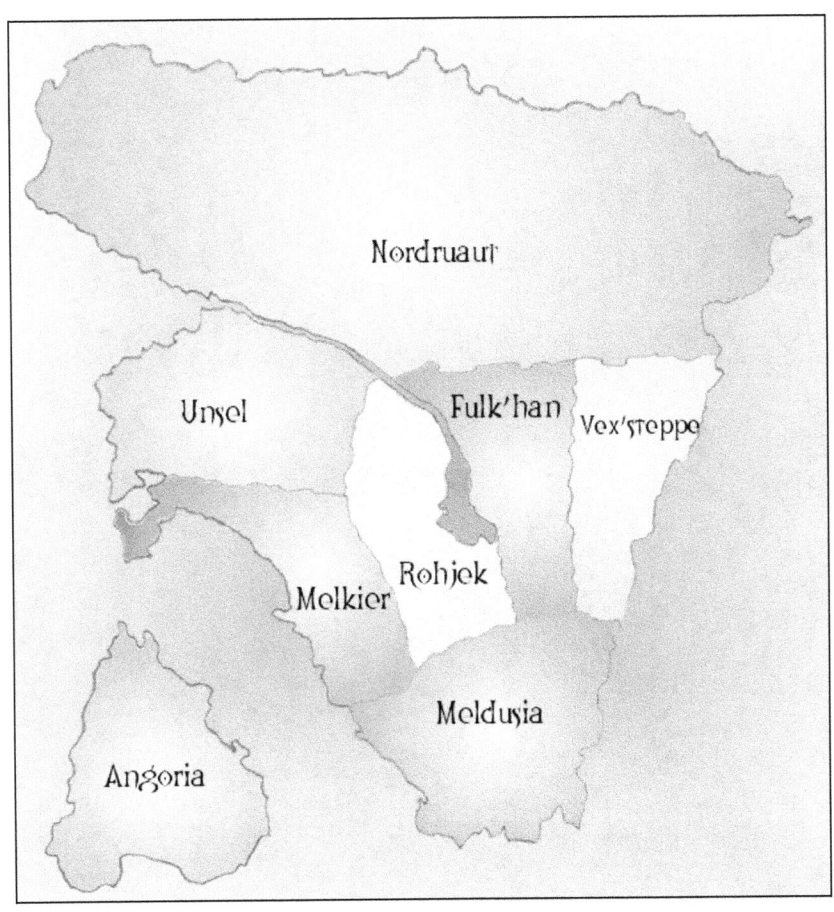

Prelude

Four months ago in Melkier

The princess hugged herself, squeezing tight for protection from the misery hovering over the harbor. A dense fog surrounded her, and the damp chill seeped into her pores. Like a low-hanging cloud, the fog hid the stormy waves until they were too close to dodge, breaking against the rock wall at her feet. She wiggled her toes and huffed in annoyance at their sogginess. This trip made her bitter, being a middle-aged, single princess made her bitter, and now her wet feet made her bitter.

Men had once come to her like these waves, begging at her feet to be let in before washing away. It had been fun, until it wasn't. How had it come to this? Her pale hair had few grays, she kept herself thin, and she was important. And yet, here she was. It wasn't just the cool wet between her toes or the thick-as-fur fog that made her shiver; it was embarrassment. She dreaded this so much she would've done anything to stay here and remain unmarried and unwooed. The old fool king, her father, wouldn't give in, insisting this suitor could be the one—which was exactly what he'd said last time. And so she waited with her cold shoulders and wet toes and embarrassment, wrapped in a blanket of bitterness.

"Your Majesty's ship will be leaving for Unsel soon," said the double-wide man with the formidable shoulders and beard to match. King Gaarder had handpicked her guards for this trip, so she trusted them, reluctantly, but this one made her uneasy. His

1

tiresome worry and constant attentions were unwarranted, and his gaze wandered up and down her body like a child picking out a new toy.

"The ship will wait until I'm ready," she commanded.

"Yes, Your Majesty." He bowed before suddenly jerking upright. The bearded man grabbed his sword. "What's that smell?"

"I smell nothing but fish." She tried speaking down to him in her highest of haughty voices, but when she took in a short breath, she caught the scent. "Smoke?"

The bearded man sniffed deeply and frowned. "Smoke," he agreed.

"Dragons!" screamed a far-off voice.

A stream of fire tore through the fog, crashing into the ocean only fifty feet away. Water boiled on contact and chunks of flotsam burned. Another barrage of liquid flame shot through the cloudy air, closely followed by dying screams. Like a curtain rising before a tragedy, the dragons' heat began lifting the nearby fog.

Every ship, from the smallest fishing boat to the king's pride, burned, listed, or was already sinking. Fires from the boats cast the dragons' long shadows onto the foggy backdrop. The princess stood awestruck as the scene unfolded to screams and madness and chaos. Survivors jumped from boats only to be snatched up by the large winged creatures. Dragons fought over the sailors, tugging like dogs over scraps of meat.

"Your Majesty," a man said from a walkway behind them. "You must run!"

"No need to run." The bearded man wielded his sword, gripping her arm firmly. "Stay behind me, Princess Nicadilia. I've slain many dragons."

"Many?" she pleaded. "Commander Loc?"

"That's Crloc, Your Majesty." He let go and gripped his sword with both hands. "Well, some."

A horned beast descended from the mist, flapping its great wings slowly. Ocean sprayed their faces as it hovered a short nightmare away. The diamond-shaped head of the dragon was bright red and covered in wet scale. A forked tongue danced hungrily along its lips before the enormous head reared back in a deep breath. The princess grabbed Crloc's arm and hid behind him, knowing full well that not even a dozen armored knights could protect her at this distance.

"I don't want to die!" Nicadilia cried.

Just as the blast began to engulf her, in that briefest second between pain and obliteration, everything stopped. She looked around to see that nothing moved, except for Crloc, who let go of his melting sword to wiggle what remained of his burned fingers.

An ageless man pushed through the smoke and fog, moving it aside to clear the air as though it were a curtain of silk. He was awkwardly tall, with a long face and protruding eyes. His cheeks were sunken, and dark shadows painted every curve and crevice. He was hairless, except for thin dark eyebrows that arched threateningly.

"Tsk, tsk, tsk." The man shook his head. "This is no way for a princess to die." He walked in front of the blast of dragonfire, which hung in the air like a decoration. "Is this how you wanted it to happen, Princess Nicadilia?"

"N-no," she stuttered.

"You don't have to die this day," he said. "Not completely. Not yet."

"What do you want?" Crloc demanded.

* * * *

Three months ago in Vex'steppe

The desert attacked with such ferocity, ANduaut expected the storm to wield daggers and bare sharp teeth. The roaring wind was deafening, and the abrasive sand pricked and bit at their arms and faces. ANduaut's dark skin was raw as layers were cooked off by the heat, but it still wasn't enough to make him give up.

"We can survive this." He pulled EnDaer by the hand, dragging his reluctant second through the onslaught.

"Please stop," EnDaer replied in his squeaky voice. "We can go back. Endure the punishment, not this slow death!"

ANduaut pulled EnDaer very close so his lips were against the other man's ear. "The punishment for loving another man is slow death, you idiot!"

"The Iroquia will forgive you," EnDaer cried out. "You are his son!"

"They will never understand you, me, *us*! Now go!" ANduaut kissed the ear, bit it, and then jerked his arm to follow. "We will heal and be whole together, free from my father and the old laws!"

ANduaut stopped believing his own words after only a few steps. They were already dead, or so near death he wondered if there was a difference. He wrapped his arms around EnDaer protectively, preparing to meet his death, but then the sand fell from the sky as though the very wind had given up. The heat, the painful heat, subsided to a gentle simmer. The men let go of one another, wiping sand and blood from their faces as they looked around in stunned silence.

"What...what was that?" EnDaer asked. "Are we free?"

ANduaut looked at his love's bright blue eyes, his dark, sunken cheeks, and receding light brown hair. He sighed in relief and nodded to himself. They lived. It had been worth all the effort.

There was a crunchy thud as something landed in the sand nearby. They spun about, EnDaer wielding two long, curved daggers and ANduaut twirling his stadauf staff in one hand. They faced dozens of small, dog-sized dragons. Foamy lava spilled from the beasts' mouths like drool, and they peered at the men with hungry, golden eyes.

"Stop," a familiar voice shouted behind them.

"What's this?" ANduaut shouted over his shoulder.

"How on Ehrde did the old man find us?" EnDaer spat.

"That way is death! Come back to me, son," his father yelled, still several hundred yards away. "Both of you, my sons. We

4

will find a way."

"It's a trick." ANduaut looked into EnDaer's eyes. "If we return to the tribe, we will never be together. They will kill us!"

They both nodded and turned to face the dragons.

"There are too many to fight," EnDaer cried out.

"There is no time to argue! Now!" ANduaut commanded, and the two men ran into the standing flock.

ANduaut struck out and sliced at every dragon he passed. EnDaer flipped and parried slashing claws, cutting with his mean daggers. Not a single dragon fell. As they approached the center, the dragons began to lift off. Within seconds, the storm of sand was upon them again. It was as if the very wind had let loose daggers.

ANduaut's body cooked in a blast of dragonfire. A jaw snapped shut around his arm, jerking away a mouthful of muscle. EnDaer gurgled, screaming through blood as flame ravaged his face and chest.

"*No!*" ANduaut roared. "I don't want to die!"

"Is that so?" said a man's high-pitched voice. "You don't have to die this day. Not completely. Not yet."

Time stopped. The burning flames and biting sands hung in the air as if painted on canvas. The dragons were still and silent. ANduaut felt no pain. He looked at EnDaer, who was still covering his face but no longer screaming. Outside their prison, beyond the sand and scales, his father appeared to be weeping. The very tall, ageless man walked to EnDaer and began wiping off his wounds like brushing away lines in sand.

EnDaer was whole again, but his face was filled with panic. "What do you want?"

"Funny you should ask," the bald man replied with a mischievous grin.

* * * *

Two months ago at Cliffview in Unsel

Duke Yardel and Lady Delora looked at Alloria with eyes that wanted to trust. She stared at the floor with a blush in her cheeks. She knew the blush appeared genuine, because she'd taken extra care with her makeup earlier that evening. The young woman squeezed her eyes shut and yawned uncontrollably. Her father also yawned, making her mother frown at him.

"We aren't that old." She slapped him playfully in the chest with the back of her hand. "You must make a presence. We are guests."

"Of course, dear," he said, swallowing a second yawn and facing his daughter. "You promised if we brought you to Cliffview, you would do as asked, and tonight we ask you to go to bed."

"I promise." She feigned disappointment. "I want to adventure, but I said I would stay, so I'll be here, bored."

"Honey, this place will be much more fun when you're grown. It's boring for children," Lady Delora said consolingly.

Alloria fought back the wince, pleading with her father with the biggest puppy dog eyes she could summon, if not to be set free from the confines of this inn then hopefully from the unwelcome and condescending prattle of her third stepmother. Her first mum, daughter to a baron, had died when she was too young to remember. The other two, a countess and a duchess, had both passed away suddenly. "Unfortunate circumstances to secure your future," he'd explained dismissively. "It will make sense when you are older."

"Yes, ma'am," she said with her best 'I'm only sixteen and not a full-grown old woman like you' smile.

Lady Delora looked momentarily sad before bristling. She stood upright and gripped her husband's arm tight. "We will be late."

"Yes, dear," he said, patting her hand. He faced Alloria with a dad-look of concern and cautious trust. "We won't be long, but no need to stay up."

"Okay," she said, kissing him on the cheek. "Have fun, Father. You too, *Delora*." She refused to call her mother.

Lady Delora shut her eyes slowly and grimaced as though preparing for battle, but the fight was interrupted by Yardel hastily leading her out of the room.

Alloria flopped onto her bed. The warm flannel nightgown a five-year-old would wear made her perspire, and not in the fun way. She looked down as she straightened it out, admiring her large breasts and wondering if the too-old wife number four felt like less of a woman when comparing her wasting, drooping figure to Alloria's.

After a whispered count to one hundred, skipping most of the numbers in the middle, she tore away the ugly brown flannel nightie to reveal a black corset cut so low and so tightfitting that little was left to the imagination. Her black leather pants fit her curves perfectly, and her heeled boots were thigh high. She sat up and ran a brush through her honey-brown hair, smiling at their foolishness. This wasn't a city for grown-ups; this was a city for fun and adventure—exactly why her friends had followed her here and were waiting at a brothel on the other side of town.

"You may only be sixteen, but what tavern would turn you away?" She looked at the mirror and smiled wickedly.

The room shook, making her gasp. According to her father, the occasional earthquake was normal for Cliffview. It wasn't normal for her, but as the quaking subsided, so did her concerns as she refocused on more important matters. Alloria added more makeup, heavy on the eyes and lips, ready to be the party. The room shook again, violently this time. Books dropped from shelves and a candle fell over. She tapped it out with her hand and licked the heat from her palm. The shaking stopped, and she took a calming breath.

Alloria left her room to find a busy hallway filled with men and women too concerned to notice how stunning she looked. Their loss, she thought, spinning on a sharp heel to stomp down the stairs in all her glory. She grabbed the rail as the inn shook again, and dust dropped from boards overhead. She stumbled to the front door and jammed her shoulder against it to force it open. People were screaming and running up the causeway.

"What's this?" she asked.

"Get out!" a cute, curly-haired blond man said, madly rapping a broom against doors as he ran past. "We're under attack! Get out now!"

She watched him, dumbfounded by his crazy. He ran along the cliff-side path to stairs leading to the next level, which he scrambled up. She jerked her head toward the loud wrenching of metal. The steel barricade that kept everyone from falling to their deaths collapsed as the cliff wall crumbled like pastry. Alloria leaped back to the inn as the path before her plummeted into the sea. A man behind her grabbed her shoulder to steady her, but the inn was already splitting apart. Floorboards tore, cracking like chips of ice and falling away.

"Please, no! I don't want to die!" she cried out as her feet dropped from under her.

A strong, cold hand gripped her forearm, and instinctively, she held tight. People and buildings and animals fell into the ocean like snow as time slowed without halting. The world continued to collapse—but seconds became minutes. Alloria looked up into the bulging eyes of an incredibly tall man. He was bald as if elderly, but his face bore no wrinkles; she couldn't begin to guess his age.

"You are already dead," he said. "If that's what you want?"

"Please, no." Alloria looked down. There was nothing underfoot. She hung by his hand and stared into calculating eyes. "What do you want?"

"Funny you should ask," he said. "Why, I want you, dear."

There had to be a way out! She had always been able to manipulate her parents, all of them. Could she negotiate her life like she got out of being grounded? "What if I say no?" she asked tentatively.

"Look down. I'll say it once more, you're already dead," he said. "But you can continue to exist. I will own you, you will serve nobody but me, my bidding will be your greatest desire, and to go against me will be to face an oblivion worse than death."

Her eyes stung as tears washed away her makeup. She looked around for help, but she was alone. More than anything, she wanted her father. Even her step-mum. Her heart wrenched, but what choice did she have? She swallowed her fear. "What do I get in return?"

"This is exactly why I chose you," he said. "You get everything you want. You will become queen of Unsel. Men will bow at your feet and follow your whim. You will be a harbinger of what is to come. You will not die. Not completely."

"Who are you?" she asked.

"I'm the glue that keeps it all together," he stated. "I am the Vivek."

"Done." She held out her hand to shake. *For now*, she thought.

"Very done." He took her hand and placed a ruby ring on her finger.

* * * *

One month ago in Angoria

It was a day of days. The sky was clear, the ocean calm, and the air cool. Her entire life, she'd wanted to travel, wanted to adventure, and the beauty before her was like a personal invitation. She glanced over her bare toes gripping the cliff edge to see a crowd of waiting women. Their people, her friends, were tiny specks from this height. Her stomach clenched, and she wrung her hands. It was going to be her first time for so many things.

"I hate that we have to leave, mother," the tall young woman lied nervously, her toes wiggling.

"Faeoris," her mother chided, brushing her daughter's long, fine brown hair with her fingers. "This is how we survive, how we continue."

"Yes, I know," Faeoris said sadly. "I guess I just worry for you. You're old, and this trip is so long."

"I'm not as old as that, young warrior. Not for a Ber-femmian," she said proudly. "And I am still the feather that launches the flock." She winked. "As you will be one day."

"Maybe I should wait until next year," she argued weakly.

"You're a woman, and there is no longer any need to wait." Her mother smiled. "It's time for adventure, your first of many."

"It's a long way down." Faeoris's eyes widened with antici-pation. "What if I don't do it right? What happens if my wings don't come out?"

"They will appear because we need them, you will see." Sla-lim took her daughter's hand, and they both went over the cliff edge. "Follow me, and we will get the others."

Hands clasped, they leaped gracefully, as if diving into the ocean. They hung in the air for the briefest of seconds before arcing downward. Faeoris glanced over her shoulder. Nothing had happened, nothing appeared.

"No!" Her mother's voice was panic-stricken.

Slalim's grip tightened as they rushed to the ground. The air bursting in Faeoris's lungs made her heart race, and she was un-sure which would explode first. Where were their wings? She screamed even as time slowed, and she wondered if this was a nightmare. Halfway between the high cliff ledge and the low sandy ground, they stopped.

"What is this?" her mother demanded. "We are supposed to be flying, not falling!"

"Or stopping," Faeoris couldn't keep the shaking from her voice. "I don't want to die."

"You can live this day," said a very tall, ageless man standing in the air beside them.

"Is this your fault?" her mother asked through gritted teeth. "I'll kill you."

The two women pushed themselves upward on an invisible platform. Slalim inspected her daughter before placing a hand on her cheek. Her mother looked incredibly old at that moment, as if the fall had aged her several decades. They both studied the man who stood a head taller.

"You have one chance to save your lovely daughter," he said, eyeing Faeoris hungrily. "Do you want to live?"

"What do you want?"

"Funny you should ask," he said. "Why, I want you, and your daugh—"

The older woman's foot met his jaw with a loud crack.

"Fine." With a flick of his hand, she fell through the platform, screaming in anger.

"No!" Faeoris reached out. "Mother!"

As she fell, a sliver of light left Slalim's body. Silver and gold, the oval hung in the air like a distant star.

"Now the choice is yours," the old man said in delight. "You are almost dead, but you can continue to exist by my will alone. I will own you—"

"Bastard," she spat before jumping into the air, kicking him in the chest with both feet and launching toward her mother.

"I've always hated Berfemmian," he shouted from overhead. "We will simply do this without you!"

Faeoris reached for the silver and gold light just beyond her grasp.

1

Angst was irritable. After all they'd been through, was it too much to ask for something to go right? How many monsters did he need to kill, how many foci did he need to bond with, how many women did he need to woo—well, that part wasn't so bad—before he got one solid night's sleep? Instead, he stood in an open field, smack dab in the middle of a dream. A foci dream.

"Angst, duck!" Victoria warned, shielding her head in a poor attempt to crouch.

A mountain peak zoomed by overhead and crashed into the ground, shattering a thousand feet away. Its passing showered the ground with debris. Rocks of all sizes pelted the earth like a hailstorm.

Victoria screamed as a boulder landed on top of Angst.

He shook his head and sighed. All the power that had come from bonding with his giant sword, Dulgirgraut, had not only saved his life, it had made him a hero. Again. He'd shared part of himself with the sword, and it had shared something with him. The bonding was intimate, and close, and a bit beyond his understanding. The sword wasn't a friend, or a lover, or even a pet. His foci was more like a partner who didn't always recognize that he might, possibly, have made his own plans. Like sleeping.

Angst drifted out of the boulder like a slow-moving cloud, his ghostly presence passing through the rock unharmed. He reached out to calm his friend but couldn't touch her.

"It's just a dream, Tori," he said soothingly. "We're okay. I'm okay."

She sniffed and wiped her cheeks. Her large green eyes were filled with worry and wet from loss. She pursed her pouty lips, struggling to hold back more tears, and tugged on a long strand of curly blond hair. "I should've figured when you changed into your armor."

Angst looked down in surprise. He was wearing the custom armor made for him back home in Unsel. The top half of his chestpiece was a cuirass that made him appear muscular, while the bottom half was chainmail that, fortunately, hid his gut. Black plate protected the front of his legs and part of his arms, but wide gaps kept zyn'ight armor, as Dallow called it, incredibly light so he could wield magic unencumbered.

"Hey, it's better than seeing me naked," he said with a grin. "Well, better for me anyway."

Victoria's battle gear made her look older than nineteen. Her riding boots reached over her knees, and low-cut black leather riding pants showed a pale, muscular midriff. Her top was the newly-acquired Berfemmian armor, a chainmail piece that barely covered her breasts while pushing them up and together. It was nice.

"I thought by now you'd be bored of seeing me partially clothed." She stared at him in warning.

"Nope." He grinned, wondering if she'd read his thoughts or if he'd just been that obvious.

"It was that obvious," she said as she looked around. "This isn't Unsel, Angst. Why aren't we in Unsel?"

"I don't know, Tori." He was more concerned with her well-being than where they were. "Maybe the dreams will take us there next."

"I'll tear us out of this dream if it doesn't happen soon!" She crossed her arms. "I need to know if Vars killed my mother and Tyrell!"

They'd shared a dream that had taken them all around Ehrde.

They'd seen a Nordruaut wielding an enormous battle axe, another foci, that left him coated in ice. Nicadilia had killed her father, or was it her red ring that had killed the elderly despot? A dark-skinned old man was slaughtered by his son in the desert. It appeared that Rohjek was now allied with the gray men and purple women of Fulk'han. Heather was safe, but Scar was in danger. And the very worst: it seemed Vars had killed Captain Guard Tyrell, and Queen Isabelle, Victoria's mother. Not only had she lost her mother, but Victoria, his best friend, would be Queen of Unsel, if it all proved to be true.

Too much had happened in one night for it to be coincidence, but still, they needed confirmation. After she'd recovered from the blow of seeing her mother killed, Victoria had wanted to dream again. He'd warned her that they needed to sleep apart and not share dreams, to get actual rest, but she'd been determined to find proof. This wasn't it, and he sighed deeply.

Tori crouched again, protecting her head. Angst turned to see a ball of fire hurtling toward them from the opposite direction. It was the same size as the mountaintop, and he instinctively tried to dive for safety. He never moved right in dreams, and, in the end, could do nothing but watch in awe as the small sun passed through them, leaving a blackened smoky path in its wake. He now hung at an awkward angle, an embarrassing reminder that, in spite of being an official hero, things never worked out like he planned.

"Your dreams always take us where we need to go," Angst suggested. "Maybe we need to see this first. It could be important."

"More important than my mother?" She swallowed hard.

"I didn't mean that, it's just…" As Angst righted himself, he looked off into the distance, taking it all in while she continued glaring at him. "Um, Tori? Where are we?"

They stood dumbstruck in the middle of a vast expanse, stunned and horrified by their surroundings. The field was miles across, a circular valley in the middle of mountains. To their left was a creature of raging fire, an exposed volcano shaped almost

14

like a man. Directly across from Fire stood a mountain with arms, legs, and a head—a crude rendering of the Earth maiden they'd watched die. South of Earth hovered a cloudburst— rain pouring from a dark sky to reveal a shadowy figure churning with power. A tornado whirled to the south of Fire, so tall it reached high up past the clouds, with spouts of dusty air protruding like arms. Each element was positioned at four corners of a square with Angst and Victoria in the center. It reminded him of a game or tournament, but on a scale he could barely fathom.

"Angst, what's that?" Victoria asked, pointing directly to the north.

A thick beam of white light shot from the ground and seemingly forever into the sky. It was so bright Angst had to look away, blinking dots from his eyes.

"It's like they're preparing to fight. That mountain, that fireball, were they just warning shots?" He stared at the tallest mountain, shielding his eyes from the white beam that had burned like staring at the sun. "I'd say that's Magic, but the beam that chased me was dark not light."

Victoria was now twisting her hair around her finger so fast, Angst was sure the entire strand would fall out. She tapped her toe at a frantic pace, making everything jiggle.

"Wait." He held out a warning hand. "We should figure this out."

"This is not *Unsel*!" Victoria roared.

"Tori," he pleaded. "We're here for a reason. The dreams always take us where we need to go."

"*No!*" She shook her head maddeningly, pulling at her hair with both hands.

"Don't do it!" he pleaded. "Don't wake us up! We need to know!"

Victoria slapped herself, and the field began to fade into a foggy haze. A woman approached them through the fog. She was petite, with tanned skin and a mane of brown hair. She was beautiful, but to Angst's surprise, she appeared the same age as him, or older.

"Aerella." Angst reached out.

"Angst, I have to tell you something. You need to know—"
Victoria bit down on her own arm and the vision faded.

"I'll find you, Angst." Aerella's husky voice trailed away.
"This is not over."

* * * *

"Get out!" Victoria screamed, pushing him roughly.

"What?" He scrambled to his knees. "This is my tent!"

"Now!" she shouted, throwing a tantrum unlike any he'd ever seen.

Angst grabbed his clothes, tripping out of the tent into a bright, snowy morning. He leaned against Dulgirgraut, which stood upright on its tip, and the cold air coaxed goosebumps from his arms and legs as he fumbled to find his pants. When his eyes adjusted to the morning light, he blinked away bleary sleep to see Hector, Tarness, and Dallow sitting nearby.

"You getting kicked out of the princess's tent is the first normal thing that's happened on this trip!" Hector said.

2

"Bad dreams?" Tarness chuckled. He rolled his muscular right shoulder until there was an audible pop.

"Bad vision." Angst hopped into his pants and tied the drawstring. He looked down at his belly and sighed. In spite of almost wasting away, he'd managed to retain a belly. It seemed...unfair, somehow.

"Was it another foci dream?" Dallow rubbed at the stubble on his chin thoughtfully.

"I'm more interested in why the princess was upset," Hector snapped. "I've never thought it was appropriate for you to share a tent with her, but gave you the benefit of the doubt."

Angst couldn't believe what Hector was accusing him of. He would never take advantage of Tori; she was his best friend. Hector should've realized that by now, but the older man seemed so upset that Angst wanted to check for hackles. He glanced at Hector's steady hand. No weapon. His thoughts rattled as much as his teeth, and he quickly slipped into his shirt and boots.

"Until now I assumed she was scared, and your twisted sense of chivalry justified your bad choices, but I knew something would happen," Hector growled. "Tell me, did you finally cross the line, loverboy?"

Angst's jaw set, and he hefted Dulgirgraut, placing it to hover behind his back as if resting the giant blade in a sheath. Hector

17

put one foot back, getting into a defensive stance. Did he really mean to fight?

"I need some time to think," Angst said dismissively. "I'll tell you what happened when you start making sense." He shoved past his old mentor.

"I'm not done," Hector snapped, grabbing his shoulder and spinning him around.

Angst raised his fists instinctively, anger building from the accusations. Hector instantly held up both hands and took another step back.

"Easy, buddy." Tarness stood from his fallen log. "Your eyes are glowing."

"What do you expect?" Angst shouted.

"What did you do to get kicked out, Angst?" Hector was now holding two long, thin daggers. Everything about them looked dangerous. "Crossed the line one time too many? The night her mother was killed?" Hector waved a dagger at his face. "If you did, with or without your foci..."

They stared at each other with all the exhaustion and bitterness two old friends could muster. He knew Hector hated his relationship with Victoria, and he despised Hector for assuming they were more than friends, but this was something more. He broke eye contact and looked around. His friends, all of them, were hurting.

This adventure should've been done. It hadn't wrapped up quickly in the happy ending of some hero story, and every nerve was stretched thin. Tarness was still recovering from his collapse on the battlefield. Dallow...it was like a hand gripping Angst's heart to see the blindfold covering his oldest friend's face where his eyes had been completely burned away by dragonfire.

In some ways, Hector must've taken it all harder than others. The old soldier was used to order and expected to be in charge. Their adventure had been a rock rolling down a hill, taking any available path. For Hector, this was madness, and Angst realized that Hector wasn't just upset at him—his friend was lashing out at all of it.

Angst took a deep breath and sighed with all his might. He met Hector's gaze again and let Dulgirgraut fall from his back. It landed in the sloppy snow with a noisy slap. Gently, Angst patted Hector on the shoulder until his friend relaxed then pulled the older man in for a hug. When he stepped away, the daggers were gone, but Hector wouldn't look him in the eye.

Angst walked to the small fire and rubbed his arms. "Tori wanted me in the same tent to see if her dreams were true."

"*Her dreams?*" Dallow cocked his head. "I thought these were supposed to be foci dreams."

"So did I," Angst admitted, "but all this time they've been her visions, not mine. We discovered that last night."

"And?" Tarness waved his hand encouragingly. "What did you see?"

"I don't remember." Angst's fist was clenched. "I hate this. I experience the dreams, but they fade away so fast!"

"That's all you've got?" Hector rolled his eyes.

"No! There's more, I just can't... Look, Tori was upset about her mother. We were trying to dream about Unsel, to confirm if Isabelle and Tyrell were really dead."

"I didn't know," Hector almost apologized.

"Of course you didn't." Angst smiled. "Tori pulled us out of the dream before we could see what it was about. And then she kicked me out of the tent."

"You aren't used to being thrown out of a woman's bed?" Tarness asked.

"It felt like I was home again." Angst winked.

"I'm not Heather." Tori crawled from the tent. She was already dressed, and wrapped tightly in her red cloak.

"I wasn't suggesting that," Angst said defensively.

She didn't reply, instead walking past Angst to warm herself by the fire. "We were in a vast field surrounded by massive versions of Earth, Fire, Water, and Air. There was also a beam of light that could've been Magic. We couldn't decide. Anyway, they were lobbing mountains and suns at each other."

"Warning shots?" Hector asked.

"Yes! That's what it looked like to me," Angst said as the cobwebs in his mind faded. "It's hard to explain. Everything was so incredible, so large. It was like the first time you see mountains. They're so big you think you're almost there, but you're actually far away."

"What else?" Hector encouraged.

"Aerella appeared."

"That's never a good sign," Tarness said.

"I disagree. It's like she's following me, trying to warn me," Angst said. "She was old this time, my age, but still beautiful."

"Imagine that." Hector rolled his eyes.

"She was trying to warn us about something," Angst continued. "That's when Victoria woke us up."

Angst looked to Dallow, trusting in his mnemonic ability to absorb and recall books for answers. His friend rubbed his temples as a bright white light shone through the blue kerchief the princess had given him to hide his scars. It was surreal, knowing his eyes were gone but seeing the light through their covering as though they still existed. The princess had said he would see again, but Angst couldn't imagine how, and the guilt was like quicksand. Dallow's eyes of light seemed to fix on Angst, looking at and through him.

Angst refused to look away but swallowed very hard. "Does any of this make sense, Dallow?" Angst asked quietly. "Do you see...I mean, have you found something we can use?"

Dallow smiled at the gaffe as though it were a bad joke. "While you guys are arguing about dreams, I'm trying to figure out how we can find Rose. You didn't dream about her, did you?"

"No." Angst shook his head.

Victoria stared at Dallow, her brow furrowed in concentration. She tore her eyes away and began patting Angst's arm as though looking for something in a dark room. "Search your pockets for rocks," she said. "Everyone."

Angst raised his eyebrows but immediately reached into every pocket. After some digging, he produced a glass-like stone that made Victoria nod in excitement. It was a piece of the memndus—the giant dome in Gressmore Towers. Dallow had found the remains during an expedition and gifted them to everyone before they left for Melkier.

"Dallow knows a spell," Tori explained. "He can use the rocks to find Rose!"

"Everyone give Dallow your stone." Angst beckoned them to hurry.

"I do not understand, Your Majesty," Dallow said as he held a hand out to take everyone's memndus stones. "I don't know any spell I can cast with these."

"You just don't remember yet," Victoria said excitedly. "Tell him, Angst."

"I don't know the spell either," Angst said.

"No," Victoria said, stomping her foot in frustration, "don't tell him the spell. Tell him where these stones really came from."

"That's not a good idea," Angst said. "That could hurt him, all of them. Aerella warned me that those memories should stay locked away."

"I don't think we have a choice," Victoria said.

"I'm not sure what you're talking about, Angst," Dallow said, gripping the stones tight in his hand. "But if it can help us find Rose, do it."

Angst looked at Hector and Tarness, and both men nodded.

"Brace yourselves." Angst took a deep breath and spoke carefully. "What I did changed time, and when I explain, you may feel a little ill."

"This should be good." Hector sat on a log.

"We didn't actually visit Gressmore Ruins. When we got there, it was an ancient mage city filled with wielders. Two thousand years ago, Gressmore Towers was attacked by dragons. To save them, Anderfeld cast a great spell, willing Dulgirgraut to protect them 'at all costs.'"

"That was the spell?" Dallow asked. "At all costs?"

"That's what Anderfeld said," Angst continued. "But it didn't work the way he'd hoped. Somehow, Dulgirgraut protected them by pulling the entire city out of time. They were safe from the wyrm attack, but forced to relive the same day over and over again."

There was a loud thud as Tarness landed face-first on the ground, unmoving. Hector and Dallow were pushing against their temples, struggling with the memories. Blood dripped freely from Hector's nose. Victoria rushed to Tarness.

"Aerella told me this would hurt because you've got two sets of overlapping memories," he explained. "You remember visiting a Gressmore Ruins that was destroyed by the dragon attack two thousand years ago. You also remember visiting Gressmore Towers, alive and thriving with people."

Hector cried out and clutched his head.

"Angst, stop," Victoria pleaded, wiping blood from Tarness's ear.

Angst replied, "They're strong enough. They can handle this."

Dallow nodded. Hector grunted, gesturing for Angst to continue.

"There was a magical device, called a memndus."

"*Nngg*. I," Dallow whimpered, "I remember."

"The memndus allowed us to see a living map of Ehrde," Angst spoke quickly, hoping to soften the blow. "I used Chryslaenor to control what we saw and focused in for a better view of Unsel. Remember, I was able to see Heather and Victoria, to make sure they were safe."

"Really?" Victoria asked in surprise.

Angst nodded. "The memndus was unfinished, and I accidentally destroyed it to see them," he blurted.

"I think I..." Hector rolled off the log with a grunt.

"You killed him," Dallow said, speaking faster as his memory returned. "Anderfeld. Aerella's father...he was bonded with Dulgirgraut, and you thought he had killed Rose. They did it to break the curse."

"Yes, Dallow," Angst said in despair. "Rose's death was an

illusion, but it was enough to make me lose control, and I killed him."

With all that had happened, he'd almost forgotten, and the memories rushed back painfully. He looked down at the ground in shame. Victoria put her hand on his arm, and his face went taut as he battled his guilt.

"They tricked me...he tricked me, so that I'd kill him." Angst swallowed hard. "An innocent man, with nothing but good intent in his heart. It was the only way to end the curse. I did, and it was all gone."

"I remember...the library. All those books," Dallow said as he dropped to his knees. "I remember...I remember all of it."

"As do I," Hector said slowly.

Tarness grunted, and pounded the ground with a fist.

Angst didn't know when the tears had started flowing or when Victoria took him in her arms, but it hurt so badly, he almost couldn't absorb it. He'd never killed a man, and Anderfeld hadn't deserved to die. Uncontrollable anger had washed over him like madness, and he'd wanted nothing more than to avenge Rose. He sobbed into Victoria's shoulder.

"Angst, we should make sure they're okay," she suggested. "I don't completely understand what happened, but it's obviously affecting everyone."

"They now have memories of two different realities, basically, and it's painfully confusing. Aerella was there to help me through it," Angst said, composing himself. "But if Dallow remembers everything he absorbed in the Gressmore library, maybe he can identify a spell to find Rose."

"You really broke the memm-thing to make sure I was safe?"

"I had to," he said. "I love you."

She hugged him tight before letting go and making her way to Dallow. Angst knelt by Tarness, whose head was on the ground. He waved Angst off.

"I get it, I remember," he said through gritted teeth, still lying face down in the snow. "I hate this crap!"

"Me too." Angst patted Tarness on the back and scrambled to

Hector. His mentor looked at him with bloodshot eyes that screamed the worst hangover in a century.

"I hate it too, but I get it," he said. "Dallow?"

Dallow was sitting upright as if nothing had happened, his eyes shining brightly through the kerchief. Victoria looked over at Angst, her eyes wide with surprise. Angst shrugged. Maybe Dallow was just absorbing the memories like he did all information.

"I'll hurt later." Dallow grunted. "Rose needs us...now. Let me see if I can find something to help us."

Like the eyes of a dreamer, the glowing remnants of Dallow's eyes shot from side to side as he sifted through vast catalogs of information in his mind.

"Found it," Dallow said excitedly. "I read most of the books at Gressmore Towers, but forgot them when time changed. Oh, hey, I know how to speak Acratic now too. It's all coming back, and just...wow."

"What is it?" Angst asked.

"So much lost, and I remember all of it," Dallow said proudly, holding out his hand.

The stones rose from his palm. They spun in a horizontal oval, faster and faster. "Angst, use the foci to create the map like you did with the memndus in Gressmore Towers."

Angst fought to remember what it was like to control the memndus—it felt like so long ago. He set Dulgirgraut down in front of him, resting the tip on the ground. A burgundy glow surrounded the great blade until an image appeared. It was like viewing a map of Ehrde from high above in the face of an oblong mirror. Blue and white lights appeared on the map like distant stars.

"We have map," Angst declared, grateful that Dulgirgraut chose to work this time.

"Do you see any markers?" Dallow asked. "Bright lights on the map?"

"There are four white markers," Angst said. "I also see three blue ones."

"One blue marker is right on top of us," Tarness said, pointing at it.

"Exactly what I was hoping! Anderfeld told us the white ones are mage cities. The three blue ones are residual magic from the memndus rocks. The blue light north of our location should be Gressmore. I would guess there are more memndus shards buried there," Dallow said hopefully. "The third one has to be Rose! Can you see her on the map?"

Angst sighed. "Yeah."

"What?" Dallow asked.

"There's one in the middle of the ocean," Angst said. "Right next to a mage city."

"In the middle of the ocean?" Dallow asked.

"Yup," Angst said dourly, his shoulders slumping.

"Why is that a problem?" Hector asked.

"Don't you remember what Earth said?" Tarness asked. "Water hates Angst even more than Magic does."

Dallow released the stones and they fell to the ground. Angst collected the rocks and gripped them tight. It was never easy. He tossed one to Hector and another to Tarness as they stood. Without thinking, he threw the last one to Dallow. The stone struck Dallow in the temple, making him sit upright.

"Dallow, I am so sorry." Angst rushed to his friend. "That was just...that was thoughtless."

"Quick." Dallow reached out. "Give it to me!"

Angst looked in the snow for the shard, finally finding it underfoot.

Dallow patted his shoulder, reaching hungrily. "Hurry," he pleaded.

Angst placed the memndus piece in his hand.

Dallow lifted the shard and set it against his temple. He began to hyperventilate and sounded ready to cry.

"What?" Angst asked. "What is it?"

"I can see!" Dallow declared.

3

Unsel

Alloria preened and peacocked, stretching and lounging so obnoxiously on the throne that she surely couldn't have been comfortable. She twirled her too-long honey-brown hair with a ring-laden finger while looking down to admire her raiment. Her large, young breasts billowed over the smallish, tightish black corset dress made fresh for her mourning.

Our queen, Vars thought, swallowing bile.

"We need to discuss the pending attack," he said.

"Hmm?" she murmured. "Oh, that. Send criers to clear out any towns remaining in the sinkhole's path and keep our troops close to Unsel. Those holes aren't the only threat we need to prepare for."

"What?" he snapped. With a deep sigh, the old man let his irritation shudder through him. "I'm sorry, Your Highness. It's just that I expected to go on the offense. Attack the gargoyle creatures."

"With what?" she asked. "Losing a hundred men wasn't enough? You heard what those creatures did in mere minutes. Don't be foolish. Our soldiers are no use to us dead."

"Then what does Your Majesty have in mind?"

"Angst, of course." She smiled wickedly.

"Of course." Vars rolled his eyes. "If he has survived, what do you expect your *daddy issues* to do?"

"My what?" She sat up.

"Your champion," he corrected himself.

"I'm confident *my champion* is alive and coming to rescue me," she said, now at the edge of her seat.

"You?" he asked.

"Well, and Unsel." She shrugged. "And maybe his wife."

"Speaking of which, do we know where she is?" Vars asked.

"She'll be here any minute." Alloria smiled, sitting up and reaching for something behind her.

"How could you possibly know that?" He hated having to deal with her. Perhaps he should have chosen death after all.

"Haven't you heard?" She blinked rapidly and pursed her lips as a knocking echoed through the chamber. "I'm the queen!"

"Right, and I'm sure they'll *love* how the queen mourns," he muttered to himself with a final glare at her inappropriate attire. He walked to the grand double doors and opened one wide enough for a young page to peek in. Vars fought the urge to close it on his head.

"Her Majesty requested the presence of Angst's wife, Heather, if she were to arrive in Unsel," the smallish page stated.

"Of course." Vars opened the door wider to view the muscular curly-haired soldier, Rook, a fiery redhead, and a distraught middle-aged woman.

"Please, come this way," Vars said, turning on his heel then stopping immediately as he caught sight of Alloria.

The lackadaisical, self-impressed sexpot had somehow transformed into a grieving niece. From nowhere, she'd produced a black lace shawl that covered her shoulders and buttoned below her chest. Her eyes were now tired, and incredibly sad. Her shoulders drooped, slouching heavily with the unwanted weight of Unsel. Her lips pulled back in a thin, forced smile as they approached.

"Your Majesty." Heather bowed, as did Rook and the woman. "I'm so sorry for your loss."

Alloria sat straighter with noticeable effort, as if gathering her composure to brave a conversation. Her bottom lip trembled slightly. "Thank you. This was a loss to all of us, and..." She looked around for some guidance. "Um, thank you."

Heather frowned with concern. "You summoned me, Your Majesty?"

Alloria stood from the chair and, with great reserve, walked to Heather. "We haven't formally been introduced. I'm Alloria." She curtsied politely.

"Oh, yes, Your Majesty, my husband speaks fondly of you," Heather said. "I'm Heather, and this is Rook, and my friend, Janda. They've been helping me in his absence." She patted her pregnant belly.

Alloria nodded in understanding, "How are you? How is your..."

"We're fine," Heather said, rubbing her stomach. "Thank you for asking."

"Thank you all for coming." Alloria sighed. "This may sound a little odd, Heather, but I miss your husband's counsel. He was so supportive after I lost my parents."

"No, that sounds about right," Heather said dryly.

"Have you heard anything from Angst?" she asked. "Unsel needs him now more than ever, as I'm sure you do."

"I miss him terribly, Your Majesty," Heather admitted. "We haven't heard from him, but I have good reason to believe he was successful in acquiring the sword."

"Oh." Alloria smiled, grabbing Heather's hand and bending slightly at her knees. "That's the first good news I've heard in days. May I ask how you know?"

"It's, well, it's magic-related, Your Highness." Heather looked sheepishly at Vars, who *tsk*ed his disapproval.

"Our opinions differ considerably, Heather." Alloria nodded toward Vars, still holding Heather's hand. "And my opinion matters, so please, feel free."

"Angst has a connection to our dog, Scar. The same malady that was affecting Angst when he was dying without a foci affected Scar too," she continued at Alloria's nodding. "Scar

28

seemed to die, but something happened and he came back."

"That's wonderful news." Alloria held her hands together. "Is Scar here?"

"No." Heather looked down and took a deep breath. "Scar turns into a, well, a giant monster dog when he needs to. After he came back to life, he became the monster and stayed that way. So, we left him at home."

"I...um. Oh." Alloria appeared dumbfounded. "Is there anything that I, that Unsel can do to help?"

"At this point, I believe it would be dangerous to bring him to the castle," Heather said gratefully. "I like to think Scar just needs Angst to return, Your Majesty."

"Don't we all," Alloria said, walking back to the throne and fwumping into it.

"The sinkholes?" Rook asked.

"Speak when spoken to," Vars snapped.

Rook whipped his head around, his teeth bared and gaze hot.

"Vars," Alloria snapped as if yelling at a pet. "These are friends. I invited them here for help and guidance. We can stand on ceremony later."

Vars's fists shook, but he nodded as he acknowledged her command.

Alloria covered her mouth and nose with her hand as though hiding and contemplating. After long, worrisome moments, she spoke. "Yes, Lieutenant Rook. The sinkholes are only weeks away from Unsel. Without Angst and his sword, I'm not sure what we can do."

"Evacuate the city, Your Majesty," Rook said without hesitation. "While there's still time."

Vars rustled in his armor. How dare this mere mortal give advice to the queen?

Alloria held a hand out to calm him. "That's a good thought, Mr. Rook." She smiled. "Go on."

"Why do you need Angst?" Rook asked.

"For his magics, of course." Alloria's brow furrowed. "I thought that would be obvious."

"He's not the only one in Unsel who wields magic," Rook said. "There are more than a dozen men and women who came to Unsel's defense when the monster birds attacked. Under the right leadership, they could defend—"

"That's enough!" Vars marched forward and gripped Rook's shoulder, spinning him about.

Rook dropped his hand to his sword. "I beat your son in every round we dueled," he whispered. "Care to have a go, old man?"

Vars smirked and reached for his own weapon. Heather and Janda slowly made their way to the door.

"Stop!" Alloria stood, pointing a finger at both men. "Vars! You go stand over there!"

"The corner?" Vars asked in disbelief.

Alloria's eyes darkened as she held up a hand and wiggled the fingers he no longer had.

Vars shuddered, his heart wrenching from the humiliation. He glared at Rook as he slowly made his way to the corner by the door.

"Lieutenant Rook," Alloria spat, "if you ever, *ever*, threaten Vars or another soldier of Unsel again, I'll see you in irons. Is that clear?"

"Yes, Your Majesty." Rook stood to attention.

"Heather, Janda, you weren't dismissed." Alloria put her hands on her hips.

The women looked at each other, stopping mid-stride on their way to the exit.

"Rook, you were suggesting a mage corps, like the old zyn'ights?" she asked.

"Yes, Your Highness," Rook said, sounding amazed.

"Stop being surprised." Alloria rolled her eyes. "I'm royalty. I've had more than a little education."

"Of course." He nodded appreciatively.

"Gather them, Rook, while there's still time," Alloria commanded.

"Right away," Rook said proudly, daring a smile at Janda.

"What?" Vars said from his corner, furious she would even

suggest the idea of a mage corps. How foolish could she be to put them in such danger?

"Were you talking?" Alloria snapped.

Vars grumbled to himself and partly turned to face the wall, still keeping one eye on them.

"Heather," Alloria said, her voice suddenly warm butter. "I would like you to stay at the castle. Your friend is welcome to join you."

"Oh, I was going to stay at—"

"You are staying here," Alloria continued. "I want to keep you and your baby safe. And if you find a way to communicate with Angst, I have to tell him how much we need him."

"Yes, Your Majesty."

"And I would appreciate your counsel, of course."

"Of course." Heather sighed.

"You can stay in Victoria's chambers, as they're currently unoccupied," Alloria said.

"Thank you," Heather said, sounding as if she'd gagged up the words.

Alloria nodded warmly, as if she'd given the greatest of gifts. "Rook, please let me know your progress. I expect to hear from you by tomorrow."

"Yes, Your Highness," Rook said proudly.

She nodded to dismiss them.

Rook bowed low with the others and led them to the door. They slowed as Vars opened it.

"This isn't over," Vars whispered.

"You're right," Rook said coolly.

4

"How?" Angst asked, rushing over to Dallow.

He held out a hand to keep Angst back and stood slowly, his forehead scrunched in concentration and the memndus stone pressed firmly against his temple. He took a step, followed by another, and another until he was walking around the campsite like a rat in a maze. A broad grin crept across Dallow's face, and Tori began to clap excitedly. He circled the campfire, tripped over a branch, and fell into Tarness's arms. The stone went flying. Hector caught it before it was lost to the woods.

"Neat trick," Hector said, handing it back to Dallow. "How does it work?"

"When I press it against my temple, it's like looking into the original memndus at Gressmore," Dallow answered between excited breaths. "Like looking at a map so I can see the top of everyone's heads. It's going to take some practice—"

"Hmm?" Angst lifted his head and stared off into the woods.

"What?" Hector said, sniffing the air and looking around.

"We have company." Angst remained seated.

Hector did not, brandishing a short sword as he stood. He tilted his head back as if his nose was squinting for a better view. "Nothing." He cocked his head to one side and cupped a hand behind his ear. "How can you tell before me?"

"Really?" Angst's eyebrows scrunched together.

"Oh, that." Hector nodded once at Dulgirgraut before Angst

32

could answer.

"Have a seat. It's not that kind of company." Angst stood, walked to the edge of the campfire heat, and dropped to both knees, resting on his feet.

"What is Angst doing?" Dallow asked, pulling the memndus stone away from his temple.

"I have no idea," Tarness answered.

"Come on out. It's okay," Angst called. He slapped his knees twice, like beckoning a pet.

The almost-human face of a gamlin popped out of the ground as if peeking out of a lake, making a small ripple of dirt and snow that flattened to leave behind no trace of its arrival. Gamlin were the foot soldiers of the element Earth—much like dragons were for Fire, cavastil birds for Air, and gargoyles for Water. Gamlin seemed to come in the same sizes as dogs, ranging from yip-yip to eating you out of house and home. The smaller ones were sort of cute, like hedgehogs but with rocky quill-like protrusions and humanish faces. Their cuteness was deceiving. They had long bear-claws instead of fingers, sharp teeth, and seemed to be invulnerable. Angst had watched them dive in and out of dragons as easily as the ground. Normally, he would've stayed away, but Earth's final words were, "The remaining gamlin are yours." He was starting to understand what that meant.

Angst smiled, holding out a hand.

The creature's nose scrunched in concern as it inched forward.

"You're not in danger. Not from me anyway," Angst promised.

The gamlin reached him, leaning forward to lick his finger.

"Be careful, Angst," Victoria called out.

His new friend looked at Victoria in panic and dove back into the ground. Angst frowned at the princess over his shoulder. She shrugged dismissively but then her eyes suddenly widened and she pointed. Angst faced forward to see four gamlin around him, all within arm's reach. Three more popped out of the ground. The sixth gamlin bumped into the seventh, who immediately pushed the other, for all the world like a rock-covered toddler.

"Hey, that's enough of that," Angst warned, and they stopped.

"They're listening to you," Victoria said, now directly behind him, placing a hand on his shoulder.

"Should she be there, that close?" Hector worried aloud.

"Yeah, she's fine," Angst replied. He whispered to Victoria, "I think you're fine."

"I'm fine." Victoria dropped to her knees beside Angst and coaxed the smallest gamlin closer. It crawled forward and sat on her lap. She oohed, which made Angst smile. Victoria reached to touch it, jerking her hands back nervously every time it moved. It was the size of a small cat, and looked up at her with an innocent smile. Victoria touched its cheek with the back of her fingers and it closed its eyes at the affection.

"I want one!" she declared.

"Figures," Hector grunted, sheathing his sword into nothingness and sitting on the fallen log.

"I don't think they're house-trained," Angst teased.

Tori petted the gamlin's back. "They're too cute, Angst. When they aren't trying to kill us and— Ouch!" She jerked her hand away, blood covering the tips of her fingers.

The gamlin looked at her nervously, glanced at Angst, and dove from her knees into the ground, quickly followed by several more.

"Are you okay?" Angst took her hand and inspected the cut.

"It stings, but I'll be all right," she said, pulling her hand back. "The quills on their backs are like razors."

"We should remember that. Why don't you have Dallow heal—"

She placed a hand on his arm. "Angst?" Tori nodded for him to look.

Three gamlin were standing before him. Two held the smallest one captive, and pushed it forward. Without warning, it screamed in a high croaky voice as the two gamlin holding it began plucking quills from its back.

"*No!*" Angst commanded, jumping to his feet. "Stop now!"

They all stopped, their beady eyes looking at him nervously.

"What were they doing?" Victoria took his hand to stand.

"They were punishing him for harming you," Angst said. "I think they meant to kill him."

"Why?" She frowned. "Wait. How do you know that?"

"I think...I can sense what's going on. What they want... It's hard to explain." He shook his head.

"You can sense all of them?" Tori touched his cheek. "How many are there?"

"Seven hundred and eighty-two," Angst stated. She pulled her hand back. "I think."

"You think?" she asked in surprise. "How could you even guess?"

Angst didn't have an answer for something he didn't understand. He returned his attention to the gamlin. "Let him go," Angst commanded.

The small one pulled free, smiled at Angst then returned to Victoria's lap for more attention.

She smiled and held her hand over its back, trying to figure out how to pet it.

"Do you control all of them? All seven hundred and eighty-two?" Tarness asked.

"It's not exactly about control—" Angst began.

All of the gamlin sat upright, like deer listening in the woods. They dove into the ground, the smallest licking Victoria's hand before departing.

"What is it?" Hector looked around. "Isn't your sword supposed to glow when we're in danger?"

"Are the gamlin attacking?" Dallow asked.

"Not us," Angst said calmly. He walked to the others and wielded the giant blade. "I can feel movement in the ground five hundred yards away. Someone's riding toward us. Maybe soldiers?"

Everyone readied their weapons.

Angst grinned wickedly. "I want to try this foci out in a normal battle," he said excitedly.

"You have no control over that thing," Hector admonished.

"I've got this," Angst assured him, smiling.

In a blur, he tore off in the direction of the gamlin. Something felt off. He rushed past trees, seeking the fastest path through the woods, and suddenly there it was. With a loud crack, he careened off a large tree, spinning out of control until crashing into another. The tree creaked painfully as it wrenched from the ground and fell onto the road. There was a loud cry in the distance and the crunching of metal followed by abrupt silence. Angst lay still, sprawled in his armor like a turtle on its back.

"Is he okay?" Victoria asked frantically, running to Angst's side. She dropped to a knee beside him. "Are you okay?"

"Did we get 'em?" Angst said weakly.

"You did great, hero." Hector laughed, tears streaming down his cheeks.

Angst sat up then lay back down. The world was spinning, and he couldn't catch his breath.

"I can't believe you lived through that," Tarness said. "You knocked over that tree."

"I thought I ran around it," Angst wheezed. What happened?

"Angst, guys, you need to see what your gamlin did," Dallow said in concern. "This isn't good."

"Help me up." Angst reached weakly for a hand.

Tarness lifted him and threw Angst's arm over his shoulder. "Short people... This would be easier if I carried you."

"Please don't," Angst pleaded with a whimper. He wasn't sure what hurt worse, his chest or his pride.

They followed the tree to the road, Tarness half-carrying a wheezing and limping Angst. When they arrived, Victoria covered her mouth and looked away. Tarness whistled, and Hector glared at Angst accusingly. Bodies had been crushed under the tree, and his heart raced to catch up with his thoughts. Had he accidentally killed innocents? Angst stared until Tarness patted him on the shoulder and pointed at the gamlin.

The little creatures were red, soaked in steaming blood, and looking at Angst like dogs waiting for approval. Five armored soldiers lay motionless on the snowy road with gaping, gamlin-sized holes in their chests. Cored like apples. The dread that had begun to clutch at his heart washed away in a wave of relief. The gamlin, his gamlin, had probably just saved them.

"Hey, what do you know? The soldiers are taken care of." Angst looked at everyone proudly, only to see shocked faces. He frowned. How could his friends not appreciate what the gamlin had done for them? Angst certainly appreciated them, and continued smiling at the gamlin until he could no longer avoid the concern in Hector's eyes.

"What now?" Angst asked.

"Angst, how did they know the men were soldiers?" Hector asked.

"The armor." Angst frowned. "They were wearing way too much armor for farmhands or traders."

"You're making that up." Hector pointed at the gamlin. "How could these new pets of yours even begin to tell the difference...?"

"I don't see what you're so upset about." Angst pulled away from Tarness and knelt, holding out his arms to the anxious gamlin.

"These could've been innocents," Hector said. "You don't even know if they were after us."

The seven gamlin inched closer to Angst. He petted each of them, careful to avoid the sharp quills.

"Good job, boys," Angst said, ignoring Hector. All the man did was complain! What happened to being his mentor? He frowned, wiggling a loose tooth with his tongue. "Guard the perimeter. Let me know what's coming."

The tallest gamlin nodded in response. He horted loudly, turned with the others, and they leaped into the ground, disappearing from sight.

"Good thing they were here," Angst said loudly. "Makes me feel a little safer."

To Angst's surprise, Hector face appeared more concerned

than upset. In fact, all of his friends seemed worried. What had he done wrong? Were they really so upset about the gamlin killing Melkier soldiers, who were probably hunting them down?

"What?" Angst asked with a sigh. "What else?"

"Why did you almost kill yourself attacking that tree?" Tarness asked.

"I'll figure it out." Angst shrugged, not wanting to explain what he really didn't understand.

"Sooner would be better than later," Hector admonished. "Before we're in real danger."

"You know, that judgmental stare really loses its punch when you're always upset at everything I do," Angst said.

"You're going to continue deflecting, aren't you?" Hector looked Angst up and down, concern still in his eyes. "We should get out of here in case others come."

"I'm sure we'll be safe," Angst said.

"I wasn't worried about us," Hector said.

5

Angst wanted to complain, but he could tell that Victoria wanted to complain more. She tromped through the wintry forest with all the delicacy of a Nordruaut bookeen mount, and Hector's face twitched with every crunchy step and cracked twig. Her sigh was loud enough that Tarness looked at Angst as though it were one of his. Angst tilted his head toward the princess, trying not to roll his eyes at her.

"What?" she snapped.

"Sometimes this is part of adventuring," he said patiently.

"This is not adventuring," she snapped. "This is walking."

"I can just ride with someone," Dallow said, his face wrenched in concern. "I don't need to practice walking. We are wasting time. We need to hurry and save Rose."

"When you learn how to walk without tripping, we can ride," Hector said. "When Angst can make Dulgirgraut work right, we'll ride faster."

"What?" Angst asked. "My sword works fine."

"Maybe it does, but you don't." Hector's bushy eyebrows frowned. "Sometimes you kill dragons, sometimes you run through trees. Not to mention, you've got seven-hundred-something gamlin in your head now."

"Seven hundred and eighty-two," Angst corrected. "Hey, seven hundred and eighty-three!"

"Exactly!" Hector shook his head. "Speaking of, where are

the little monsters?"

"Around," he said with a shrug.

Angst didn't want to admit that he was unsure, only to hear more of Hector's accusations. The gamlin wanted to help them, he could feel that much. And Dulgirgraut had come through when it was time to kill the dragon. Everything had a way of working out…Hector just couldn't see that.

"Wouldn't the road be better?" Victoria whined as she kicked mud from a boot.

"I'm not in any condition to fight," Tarness said with an exhausted sigh, "and we don't want the gamlin, wherever they are, killing innocents."

Angst was impressed to see Dallow slow for a small outcropping of rock; he was already figuring out how to maneuver in spite of seeing everything from a map view, top down. Dallow stepped over it, but his foot clipped the tip of the rock, throwing him off balance. Tarness gripped one arm while Dallow drove his staff into the ground for support with the other, grunting in frustration.

"You're doing better, Dallow," Tarness said in soothing tones, and Dallow took a deep breath.

"Thanks." He smiled. "It's just that every time I trip, my view starts at the beginning. The 'map' in my mind gets smaller, more distant, and I have to refocus close enough to see us."

"That's exactly why we're taking time for you to practice." Hector smiled. "I'm glad at least one of you is trying."

"What am I supposed to be doing?" Angst frowned. "It'll work when we need it. We handled the dragon just fine."

"Have you tried talking to it?" Victoria asked.

He'd tried that with Chryslaenor, and it had never worked. And Chryslaenor had liked him. With Dulgirgraut, the idea seemed ludicrous, but he knew better than to say that out loud.

"You shouldn't have even thought it." Her eyes narrowed.

There was no winning when she could read his mind. "No, I haven't tried since fighting Fire or the dragon. It's a different sword. Maybe it doesn't work the same."

"Sure," Hector said.

"Uh huh," Tarness said.

"Really?" Victoria crossed her arms. "Hector's right. You're just being stubborn."

"Thank you." Hector stretched his arms out triumphantly, placing his hands behind his head.

"You're just taking his side because you're angry with me," Angst said in resignation. "You're always angry with me."

There was an annoying buzzing in his head, and he waved at the air like swatting a fly. The high-pitched whine quieted, and Angst thought for a moment he heard the distant guttural horting sound of a gamlin. Were they trying to communicate with him?

"Quit being a baby," Victoria chided. "I'm not angry. I'm right."

Dallow tripped over a leg-sized root hidden by snow and leaves. Tarness missed his grab, and Dallow landed on his knees. He took in another deep, calming breath before clapping dirt off his hands. He stopped suddenly.

"You okay?" Angst asked.

"Shush." Dallow hunched slightly, his head bowed, and the memndus stone pressed firmly to his temple.

Hector was sniffing the air and cocked his head to listen intently. After several moments, he shook his head. "I don't hear anything."

"Shhh," Dallow whispered. "Quick, with me."

Angst and Hector looked at each other, shrugged, and followed their friend behind a nearby thicket. Dallow maneuvered to nestle between tall bushes, crouching low enough to be mostly hidden. Everyone huddled around him, struggling to see the thin, wooded path through the thicket.

"What is it?" Angst frowned.

Hector smiled knowingly, and then a red bear the size of a cottage ran by, his enormous paws thundering with every step.

"Looks like dinner." Hector began to stand, but Dallow jerked him back down.

The ground shook with thuds too loud and violent for the bear to make. Crisp snow hopped and dead leaves that had clung onto autumn branches fell from the shaking trees. The bear roared as a great dragon mouth wrapped around its red body and shook it side to side like a dog playing tug-of-war. With a loud snap, the bear went limp, and the dragon let it fall to the ground, its slender tongue flicking the edges of its mouth hungrily.

The red-scaled monster was much smaller than the giant mother-of-all-dragons Angst had killed, but it was still larger than two houses and apparently hungry enough to eat both. Angst grabbed for Dulgirgraut, which was locked onto his back like a knife stuck in a tree. He tugged it several times without success before finally giving up. At least his friends were watching the dragon prepare for its feast instead of him fumbling with the foci. Maybe no one had noticed.

Scales on the dragon's neck stretched and contracted until it belched a glob of wet fire onto its prey. It turned the bear over several times until the fur had burned away then picked up the freshly-cooked carcass and tossed it into the air, catching it in one bite. The creature's throat bulged as the bear made its way to the dragon's belly. After a smoky burp, it spread its wings wide and began to flap, throwing up enough snow and dirt that everyone winced or covered their heads. Branches fell as the beast broke through the canopy and flew off. They remained quiet for several minutes to ensure it was far enough away.

His friends looked exhausted, each several shades paler than normal with wide eyes or dropped jaws.

"Well, I'm not hungry anymore," Angst said, exhaling deeply.

"That makes one of us," Tarness said. "I was looking forward to some steak."

"Thanks, Dallow." Hector patted the tall, thin man on his arm.

Dallow nodded and smiled before returning to their path.

Hector spun about with an angry finger directed at Angst. "You two need to figure out your problems before you get us killed!"

Angst looked at Victoria, who shrugged.

"Hector, what are you talking about?" Victoria asked. "How could problems between Angst and me—"

Hector cursed under his breath. "Not your problems." He pointed between Angst and Victoria. "I don't even want to know what that's about. I'm talking about *their* problems." He gestured at Angst and Dulgirgraut.

"What problems?" Angst stepped out of the thicket and away from his friends.

"The sword didn't warn you they were coming, Angst?" Dallow grimaced. "It would be better not to count on me. It doesn't work if I pull it away." He held the memndus shard at arms length.

"No warning, but like I said, maybe this one works differently," Angst said. "And you did amazing."

"Nothing from the gamlin?" Tarness asked.

"Maybe, I just..." Angst was overwhelmed by all the things he was supposed to be doing. "I think they tried to warn me."

"You couldn't even wield it," Hector said in a low, dangerous voice. "You and that sword are the only defense we have against the monsters, Angst! How are you going to defend the princess if you can't even pull it from your back?"

"I don't know," Angst said, kicking at the ground.

"We can't save Rose if it doesn't work," Hector continued, his voice getting louder. "And you were going to hide this from us? Not knowing puts us in more danger than we can handle."

Angst stared at him, unsure of what to say. Hector gripped Angst's fancy chestpiece and pointed a finger at Dallow. "How much more danger are you willing to put them through?" Hector shoved Angst and turned away to help Dallow the rest of the way to the path. "Go figure out your crap while we find a place to set up camp."

Angst clutched his stomach as the guilt wrenched in his gut. He would never forgive himself for what had happened to Dallow. Dulgirgraut fell from his back, landing with a loud thud and a crack as it had split a fallen tree in half. Everyone stopped to look back except Hector. His old mentor merely looked down at the ground and shook his head. Victoria frowned and inched toward him as if debating whether or not to follow.

"He's right, I need time alone." Angst tried not to sound choked up and avoided eye contact.

"I believe in you, Angst," she said. "Go make things right with Dulgirgraut."

That was why she was the perfect friend. In spite of it all, she worried enough to care and encourage him to succeed. She smiled at his thought and sprang forward to catch up with the others.

Angst sighed out everything, bent over to lift the hilt of the foci, and dragged it deeper into the woods.

6

Unsel

Closing the door behind Heather, Rook, and Janda, Vars felt a pinch as his chainmail shirt plucked at his hackles with every deep breath. The breaths weren't at all calming, and he wondered if he was going to start hyperventilating like a young soldier on the front for the first time. She'd humiliated him in front of *wielders*, and the embarrassment flowed hot through his veins. He marched stiffly to the throne.

"Your Highness, as your Captain Guard, it's my duty to remind you that we aren't to utilize wielders." He almost bit his tongue on the last word, it filled him with such rage.

"I have a busy day ahead, Vars," she said airily, completely ignoring his warning. "I have a funeral to plan. The sooner I bury Isabelle, the sooner I can officially take the crown."

"Alloria, please," Vars cautioned. "The Vivek made that very clear. The only wielder even allowed to help is Angst...if he survives."

Alloria slammed her fist on the armrest and stood abruptly. The movement was so sudden, her eyes so wild, Vars took a step back.

"Your problem, Captain Guard, is that you assume everyone else is a fool or an idiot." She stepped down from the throne with a finger aimed rigidly at his face. "If you would actually advise me instead of just telling me what you want me to do, we could accomplish something. You don't know all the pieces in play—I don't even think *he* does—but before I can make any decisions, I need to know what's going on."

She was out of control. He had to put a stop to this before they were both killed, but there appeared to be no reasoning with her.

"Your Majesty," he said, still rubbing his hands behind his back. "Consider what I've told you, or there will be consequences."

Alloria arched her back and stared down her nose. Her face was cool as the wildness in her eyes turned to something more analytical. She spun on a heel, giving her back to him. He wanted to crush her skull with his bare hands, and his fingers twitched anxiously at the thought. Seven of his fingers. The missing three had been magicked away, presumably by the Vivek as punishment for threatening Alloria. His chest felt tight at the thought of losing another body part, but she needed to be put in her place. How could he do it without the risk of retribution?

"You were going to debrief me on the other nations," she reminded him, the anger gone from her voice, but her eyebrows furrowed. "Now advise me, or someone else will."

Vars took a deep breath, attempting to unlock his stiff muscles and set jaw. He sighed. "According to the Vivek, Melkier is neither a threat nor an ally. Angst and his friends destroyed most of the capital city, and King Gaarder is dead. Their defenses have literally been stripped away. Their armor and weapons are once again vulnerable to magic and fire. Unless they find a miracle, they are both harmless, and useless."

"Angst destroyed the capital city?" Elation filled her voice and her eyes were hungry. "How much power does that man wield?"

"Too much," Vars whispered.

"What of the Berfemmian? What of Meldusia?"

"No word on the Berfemmian, but as long as they're stuck on Angoria, there's no concern. If they got loose, not even the

Nordruaut hordes would survive," he said. "The Meldusians can be forgotten. They seem to have gone missing. All except for Jintorich, who you'll be meeting with tomorrow, along with the Nordruaut Ambassador Maarja. It would be wise to keep her happy."

"Agreed," Alloria said, waving him on to the next report. "What of the Nordruauts, the Vex'steppe tribes, or those bastard Fulk'han?"

"Those nations are a hornet's nest, each their own cataclysm." Vars couldn't keep the worry from his voice. "If those storms were to meet, it would be the most devastating war Ehrde has seen in thousands of years."

* * * *

Nordruaut

Stone shards and dust sprayed like sparks from frosty stone mugs smashing together. It was a hardy brawl of booze and fellowship as Nordruaut men and women washed away the cold with strong, warm ale and talk as tall as their gigantic bodies. Two men faced one another across a gray slate table, a stack of empty stone mugs resting beside each like growing trophy collections. They drank, and the room went silent. The younger man listed further with every gulp of mead, to the warning oohs of the crowd. When he placed the mug on the stack and seemed to steady himself, everyone cheered. His opponent was older, much older, his strong body wrinkled and his thinning hair white as frost. He drank his ale so slowly that several viewers let go of their held breath. As his chin and chest became drenched in frothy warm spirits, everyone laughed. He dropped the partially-filled mug to the table.

King Rasaol grabbed the white-haired man by the scruff of his mangy gray pelts and tossed him into a chair, where he either passed out or was knocked unconscious. The king stretched his muscular bare arms to display their full power, purposefully flexing as he lifted the largest stein in the room to his lips. It was great enough that he should've held on with a second hand, but didn't dare, and hoped no one noticed the slight quiver. Standing opposite each other, they tipped back and drank in giant gulps.

"Go...go...go," echoed throughout the long hall as their audience pounded on tables and stomped the stone hall floor.

Shouts from sixty Nordruaut revelers echoing between the walls of Owenqua would be enough to make a human go deaf, or frighten full armies into surrender. It made the old king smile behind his keg.

A bevy of younger Nordruaut maids oohed at the king's stamina as he downed the contents of his mug. The tiniest trickle of dark brown ale dripped along strands of long braids and beard to wet his bare chest. The king wore a light leather vest too small to close around enormous pectoral muscles, providing a full view of overlarge abdominals that shuddered with every deep gulp. He looked a Nordruaut of a mere two hundred instead of a ripened three hundred and seventeen.

The king squinted as he finally emptied the bucket shaped like a mug. He took a deep breath that rattled his chest, and his hand was shaky—had anyone else noticed these signs of aging? When he was absolutely certain the brew would stay under his belt, he lowered the mug to boisterous cheers. Rasaol wiped ale froth from his mouth and chin before squeezing it out of his long dark red beard and braids. His opponent coughed ale back into the half-full mug to the bellows and rowdy laughter of their audience. With the strength to uproot a small tree, Rasaol threw the stone mug to the floor. He hoped they wouldn't see the worry on his face. It had to break; it was the tradition and showed strength. Several gasps followed the mug as it slid across the floor and stopped under the boot of a Nordruaut who'd just entered. The stone mug shattered against the visitor's raised boot and sprayed across the floor like an icicle on a frozen lake. Cheering hid Rasaol's deep sigh.

The visitor closed the tall wooden door to the hall, brushing off chunks of mug, remnants of ale, and frosty winter. Tiny balls of ice dangled from the furs he removed in layers then placed onto a maiden's outstretched arms. The disrobing revealed a tan, muscular body with arms almost the size of Rasaol's. The king smiled as the snow mask was removed, and marched over to him.

"Jarle, you came." Rasaol clasped arms with the other man.

"By your request." Jarle's lips thinned in a careful smile.

Rasaol reached out and grabbed at the air until he held a flask of mead. He handed it to the old Nordruaut. Jarle hastily downed the entire contents and set it on a table, unbroken.

"Eh," Rasaol grunted at the discarded tradition. "Welcome, we have much to discuss."

Men and women stood and nodded respectfully at Jarle as he passed. "Impressive," he said with raised eyebrows. "It looks like you've gathered every leader from eastern Nordruaut. Am I the only one from the west?"

"The only one we need. They will listen to you," Rasaol said. "If you will listen to me." He then yelled so all could hear, "There are stories to tell!"

All went silent inside the walls of Owenqua as King Rasaol paced before the raging fire. Nordruaut men and women, old and young, hunters and soldiers, sat with crossed legs and slouched shoulders, each clad in the barest of leathers. They were spread about the enormous round room, holding their collective breath until their king began his story. The bonfire in the center of the room snapped loudly, making several jump as the flames rose to the spacious hole in the stone dome overhead, battling cold air with embers and ash.

Rasaol's face was a mask of anguish and pain. He held a finger out dramatically, pointing at each of them. "Most here are too young to remember the war my great-grandfather survived, the war that changed Nordruaut. When you hear this, you will believe as I do that we may have changed too much.

"You have all heard stories of the terrible war of elements that raged across Ehrde, and how the great hunter protected us from them. Just as the elements battled, there was also a war of men across all nations. The barbaric Angorians, Mendahir of the woods, creatures who lived in the ocean, and humans from all corners of Ehrde battled with vicious ferocity."

He sought their faces, trying to make eye contact with everyone in the hall.

"We were hunters, just as we are today, and no match for the combined forces of the Mendahir and the Angorians. The beast, the deceiver, the all-powerful Magic tricked those powerful nations into an alliance. Together, they destroyed our homes and our lands. It was almost our end and the decision was made." He began to shout, raising a fist in the air, "We marched to those drums of war."

He paused to see some eyes wide with surprise, and many nods of excitement.

"The Nordruaut marched to protect our lands, to protect our people. We are here today because we won that battle!"

Rasaol's voice fell to a whisper and he looked down.

"But the cost of this war was too high. Water again reigned as champion, but spends her days seeking to free her people, lost and alone. One of the most powerful races on Ehrde, the Mendahir, was destroyed so entirely even their ghosts are almost gone. Because of this, it was agreed that, to protect Ehrde, the barbarians of Angoria would be divided, separating the men and women forever."

"The warrior Nordruaut agreed to become hunters once again, watching over Ehrde just as the great hunter guards the Vivek. The Vivek who keeps balance over the elements for thousands of years until the moment Magic finds freedom and the war begins anew."

His eyes widened as he stood up straight. "This war is upon us now! We have seen the magics of the Vex'kvette, heard tales that the dragons have returned, and seen the birth of an Al'eyrn! We will not wait to be defeated, nor will we be killed off like the Mendahir. Nordruaut will fight as one to protect Ehrde, even if they don't want it."

He lowered his head in finality. Together, sixty Nordruaut chanted, "And so it is said, and so it must be told."

One Nordruaut did not chant. Jarle stood at this revelation. "No! How do you know this to be true?"

"That my father said it should be enough." Rasaol thumbed his chest proudly. "We need to come under one roof. All of Nordruaut needs to gather, to prepare for the monsters and the war that is coming."

"Monsters?" Jarle said in an uncertain tone. "We have hunted the monsters from Vex'kvette. Few remain."

"The real monsters, Jarle, the ones with power," Rasaol continued. "The wielders. Especially the one with the sword."

"Angst?" Jarle asked. "Angst and his friends are powerful, but they are not enemies. Their hunt was true."

"Of course you believe this, you were with them," Rasaol agreed. "But if you were on the march? If we were to defend against Unsel, would he champion them? Would he face you in battle?"

"Yes," Jarle said. His lips were pressed together in a tight grimace. "That sword he wields is more power than we can face."

"Do you say we cower and hide?" Rasaol looked around the room. There were mumbles.

"No," Jarle said. "The hunt becomes the march."

The fretful mutters of eastern tribal leaders accompanied the stomping of feet. They smacked the ground together, the sound of an army marching to war.

"Unsel may not be our enemy, Jarle, but Fulk'han is!" His voice raised once again. "They have already sent killers to our home."

"What?" Jarle snapped. "But the zealots are a meager people."

"No longer. They are changed by the Vex'kvette and worthy of the hunt!" Rasaol could see the wild look of concern in Jarle's eyes. "You have much to learn, my friend. Together, we must prepare to face champions," Rasaol pleaded.

"But how?" Jarle asked.

The feet continued their vehement cadence as Rasaol led Jarle around the fire to a shadowy, cold corner of the room. The gray stones were dark from wet, and the darkness met frost as if it battled the bonfire. Frost-covered stones crunched underfoot and chilled the air until Rasaol breathed fog, and his joints stiffened.

"Unsel has Angst and his sword," Rasaol declared. "Now Nordruaut has a weapon." His torchlight danced over the giant war axe Ghorfjend.

"You found another," Jarle said nervously, reaching out but hesitant to touch the blade. "And you have an Al'eyrn?"

"We have a champion," Rasaol announced.

The sound of mugs pounding and feet stomping could be heard for miles.

* * * *

Fulk'han

Dusty snow clouded the air as Guldrich's stallion skidded to a halt. More steam huffed from his nose than from his mount's. He'd barely stopped during his three-day ride home to the capital city of Fulk'han, and he was sore. Late afternoon shadows fell across his gray arms, hiding the kill marks, and bringing a chill to the already-wintry air. He dismounted, patting the horse in acknowledgment for not dying.

Guldrich had much to tell the new emperor about the traitorous queen now ruling over Unsel. Fulk'han had assisted and supported her, and, finally, in trade for their help, the bitch had turned the tables on them. It was the worst deceit—Unsel should've already been a part of the Fulk'han empire. Instead, it was a raggedy mess ruled by a young girl and without the protection of that wielder.

It wasn't like anyone needed a reminder of their hatred for Unsel, but it rose from the heart of Fulk'han like a wound. The giant tree-like remains of their Takarn-Ivan spread deep roots throughout the coliseum. Guldrich stood before the husk and stared at its enormity. Long tentacles reached high into the clouds like branches attempting to touch all things. Fulk'hans knew this was their Takarn's last message, a call to expand. That they were destined to extend their reach, amassing an empire for his return. With a deep breath and clenched fist, he strode past the faint glow emanating from Takarn-Ivan's carcass and into what remained of the castle entrance.

The castle had been destroyed by Ivan, reformed into the arena where he'd battled Angst. Days after the fight ended, it was decided to create the new headquarters for their empire directly under Takarn-Ivan's remains. The Fulk'hans had aggressively excavated around root-like tendrils, digging out rooms and hallways. Their work was hasty, and shoddy, but had potential for greatness and was enough to host a war room and house an emperor.

Two smaller gray men smashed their chests with closed fist in salute as he entered, and he nodded in reply. The war room was a square, twenty-five feet from end to end with a single entrance. An oval table rested in the center, covered with a map of Ehrde. Three gray men hovered over the map—General Arbeter on the left, Sergeant Advisor Beld on the right, and, in the middle of it all, their new emperor, Gath. All looked up at his arrival. Gath shrugged off a purple woman who'd been rubbing his shoulders, and her long tail slapped the table at the rough dismissal.

"Tell us about your failure," the emperor demanded. "This should have been easy without their wielder and his weapon."

"There were other wielders, and they ousted us before we could begin," Guldrich growled defensively. "All is not lost. The queen is dead, as is Tyrell."

"Tyrell?" General Arbeter asked. "That must've been a fight. How did you take him, and the queen, but not the kingdom?"

"It was deceit." Guldrich's thin gray lips curled. "Just as Alloria took the crown, she brought forth her team of wielders—a well-trained militia that killed everyone. But they set me free, proving they are weak."

"Angst and his companions are still missing?" Gath asked.

"Yes," Guldrich said.

"We have time to strike!" General Arbeter slammed his fist

on the map. "We send in more men!"

"How many do you need?" the emperor asked.

"All of them, Your Majesty," Arbeter said, rubbing his hands together.

"They have other wielders," Guldrich snapped. "And Angst is rumored to return soon. We've missed our window. We can't go without our own champion."

"I thought *you* were our champion?" Beld asked, his eyes narrow.

The three gray men and the purple woman all looked to Guldrich, who shook in anger. He clenched his fists, and lowered his head.

"We will determine your fate at a later time," Emperor Gath stated darkly. With two fingers, he beckoned for guards to escort Guldrich from the room. "There is more important work to be done than dealing with your failure."

As the two gray men wrapped their arms around his, Guldrich made eye contact with the purple woman, who winked seductively. It didn't help.

* * * *

Vex'steppe

ANduaut struggled against the ropes, blood dripping from an open cut on his cheek. He lay on the floor of his tent, his hands and legs bound behind his back. He heard the tent flap pull back and could only assume death was coming. Pale bare feet beneath flowing dark robes took two steps before the man kneeled. He *tsk*ed noisily and snapped his fingers. The ropes began untying.

"What happened to the guards I left with you?" the Vivek asked.

"Those weren't guards, they were birds," ANduaut snapped. "I told you they wouldn't be enough."

"Birds?" The ageless man rolled his large eyes. "Not just birds. They were Cavastil birds, the same ones you couldn't defeat."

"Yeah." ANduaut rolled to a sitting position, his numb arms flopping helplessly.

Vivek sighed impatiently. "And?"

"They ate them." ANduaut winced as he flexed blood back into his fingers.

Vivek gripped ANduaut's neck and lifted him up with one arm, bringing the young man to eye level. "They what?"

"My tribe, my ex-tribe, ate them before binding me," ANduaut choked out. "Your five guards lasted about five minutes. What did you expect?"

"More than five minutes! They weren't even mine. I had them on loan." He dropped ANduaut, who landed lightly on his feet. "No human could've survived a battle with those things."

"We aren't exactly human," ANduaut said, rubbing his neck with his hand. "Where did they come from anyway?"

"I borrowed them. It was a trade." The old man tapped a long finger to his lips.

"It's only been two weeks, and my people already hate me." ANduaut wrung his hands together behind his back. "The only reason they haven't stripped the skin from my bones is that I carry my father's stadauf."

"Why am I underestimating everything?" Vivek muttered under his breath.

ANduaut picked up his father's twin-bladed wooden staff, twirling it like a toy. Sharp stone blades whisked the sand floor of his tent with every turn. He stared at the stadauf and wanted to cry. It couldn't have been for his father; he felt no guilt for killing him. He must still be mourning the loss of his love, En-Daer—one of the few things in this life that had brought him happiness. He wanted, more than anything, to be left alone, but he'd promised to stay and lead in order to live.

"Of course they hate you." The ageless man rolled his bulging eyes. "You sent away their sex. I'd hate you too."

"You said the Berfemmian weren't on our side." ANduaut was confused. "Of course I sent them away."

"It was the right thing to do, you'll see." Vivek looked him up and down. "Did you really want to mate with a female?"

"Of course not." ANduaut grimaced.

"You weren't the only one. There are a few more like you," the old man said then replied to his silent surprise. "What did you expect in a country without women?"

"What about the rest of them?" ANduaut said. "They won't follow me!

"Sometimes change requires sacrifice," the man said.

"Haven't I sacrificed enough?" ANduaut asked.

"No," Vivek replied dismissively.

"But, how do I do this without EnDaer?" he whined. "They'll just try to kill me again."

Vivek stroked his chin thoughtfully. "Why do you have to do this by yourself?"

"Well, I just thought—"

"Stop thinking already!" he snapped. "Before you destroy us both."

ANduaut gripped the stadauf with both hands, feeling the dark, red ring dig deep into his finger. A constant reminder that the Vivek ruled over his every action.

"I may have a new second for you," the ageless man said. "A champion."

"Really?" he asked hungrily. "How is he a champion?"

"Not he," the Vivek said. "She."

"Oh." Disappointment weighed heavily on his shoulders.

"Remember? Sacrifice," he said. "If my plan works, she may be the most powerful human in Ehrde."

"And if that doesn't happen?"

"I'm sure something will make its way through that thick skull of yours." The ageless man rapped a knuckle on ANduaut's forehead. "Now, follow me. You're of no use here, especially if they do decide to kill you."

Vivek waved an arm casually. Light and color spun in front of them, blending into a black oval that hovered inches above the ground. It was like a window into dark waters, taller than both men. Vivek walked through, unconcerned, as if merely crossing the room. He disappeared in the blackness, leaving a ripple of wobbly color behind. ANduaut placed a reluctant hand into the void and pulled it back nervously. He wiggled his fingers and hesitated to test the waters again. Reaching out from the void, a hand grabbed ANduaut's wrist, abruptly jerking him through.

They appeared in a dark, cold place that smelled of stale air and fish. It took several minutes for ANduaut's eyes to adjust, and even when he could see, it wasn't very far. They stood on a stone patio that was too many stories high to see the dark ground below. Gently glowing moss on seashell-covered walls barely allowed him to make out the Vivek.

"What is this place?" he asked, rubbing his arms for warmth.

"It's called Azaktrha," Vivek answered. "It's an ancient city."

"I don't want to be here," ANduaut said firmly.

"Can you swim?" Vivek asked.

"Not well," he said with a frown.

"Then you won't be leaving any time soon," Vivek said. "Do your job, and I'll bring you home."

"Fine," ANduaut huffed. "What is my job?"

"There's a young woman here that you need to find, and save."

"Why am I saving her?"

"You're saving her for me," he said with a broad grin.

7

"Nice work, Your Maje...Victoria," Hector said with a nod. "Thanks."

She shook mud and snow off her hands before taking a final look over the two tents she'd set up for herself and Angst. They stood on opposite sides of the campground. She hated this—the thought of tenting it alone made her shudder, but she didn't want to share his dreams. Couldn't share them. It felt like his foci dreams were now intruding into hers. She hoped the separation would give her a clear vision of what had happened back home. Had her mother truly died? Was Tyrell really gone? Was she Queen of Unsel? It was everything she could do not to crumple into a ball of remorse and fear, but if her mother had taught her anything, it was how to set...no, more like *shove* emotion aside.

"I'm going to hunt for dinner," Hector said, avoiding eye contact as he turned to stalk off into the woods, quickly disappearing in the dusk.

He was lying. He guarded his thoughts very well, and he was already too far away for a clear read, but that brief flash of his immediate future didn't include hunting.

"I'll check on Dallow," she said to no one with a sigh.

Dallow sat on a dryish patch of dormant moss under an tall fir tree. The tree was old and broad, with long branches that drooped to the ground beneath heavy snow. Like an elder watching over its children, it seemed to hover protectively over the several smaller trees surrounding it.

He smiled as she approached, brushing light blond bangs from his forehead. He'd removed the blue kerchief she'd given him. Tori sucked in her lips as she braved the sight. Dallow's missing eyes were horrific, two dark sockets surrounded by a raccoon mask of freshly-healed burn scars. As if he could read her mind, he fumbled on the ground for his kerchief.

"I'm sorry, I didn't even think to put it on when I heard you approach." He grabbed the cloth and held it over his eyes. "Sometimes they itch."

"Then leave it off." Victoria ducked under a branch to kneel beside him. "You came here to be alone. I wanted to check on you, but I'm intruding."

"Not alone." He paused. "Well, I guess there's no room for little lies if you read minds."

Victoria took the kerchief from his hand and placed it on his leg, patting it so he would know where it was. "It's not exactly reading minds, not for most. I certainly don't see everything, and I try not to intrude." She looked around and found they were somewhat hidden. Under the weighed-down branches it felt like a child's fort. "This place just makes it a little obvious. Are you okay?"

"Mostly. I need to practice and thought it would help to hide. The map I see in my head doesn't always do what I want. It always starts out high above," he explained. "When I focus, I can see closer, but the view is directly overhead. So I'm trying to see if I can view other areas of Ehrde, like Unsel."

"That would be great," she said encouragingly.

He nodded. "But it's not working. I can't control it like Angst did."

"Didn't he have to use a foci with the memndus?"

"I think so. Those memories are cloudy. That would be a valid reason why it doesn't do what I want." Dallow's shoulders drooped like the tree branches. "I guess I'm fortunate I can use it at all. But I'll still try."

"Is there anything you need?" Victoria asked.

59

"My eyes." Dallow grimaced. "Sorry, that was uncalled for."

"I'd be upset too," she replied quietly, looking down.

"What's wrong?" Dallow asked. "There is something troubling you, beyond what you saw last night."

"It's nothing." She looked at the ground.

"I think there is a lot on your mind," he said. "Obviously I can't help you with your mother, or Angst, but is there anything else?"

"Angst?" She tilted her head to one shoulder.

"What else is bothering you, Princess?" he said softly, ignoring her question.

"Well, since you asked, there is one thing." She braced herself. "I thought I wanted to be an adventurer, like Angst. Like all of you. But I'm exhausted. I feel like, well, like I'm getting old or something. That sounds silly, but is this all adventuring is? Is it all work and no wonder?"

"Is that why you are here?" he asked. "For the adventure?"

"I'm here for lots of reasons, Mr. Dallow." Her voice was very quiet.

Dallow smiled knowingly. "While I do not consider myself an adventurer, I do think what you are asking is a fair question." Dallow pushed himself up to his knees and picked up his staff. "Please take a few steps beyond the tree branches."

"Okay," she said hesitantly, inching out from under the canopy to stand in the nearby clearing. "Here?"

"That will do," he said. "Don't be afraid."

"All right." She looked around, suddenly feeling very exposed.

"Hold out your arms."

"Like this?" She felt like a child trying to fly. "I feel a little silly."

"Perfect." He sounded excited. "Are you ready?"

"Um. Sure?" She frowned.

Dallow held his long hardwood staff horizontal, took a deep breath, and swung it hard. The staff struck the trunk of the fir tree with a resounding crack. There was a loud rustling, the sound of a gentle wind rushing through a valley. The snow covering the fir branches lifted and fluttered as a thousand soft wings flapped.

Victoria squeaked with alarm.

"Snow moths," Dallow reassured her. "Just keep your arms still."

Victoria breathed rapidly as her arms grew heavy. She was surrounded by giant fluttering snowflakes as the moths sought a new perch. Wings as large as her face and as small as her iris brushed her hands and cheeks. The panic passed as they settled on her outstretched arms. A particularly big snow moth landed on top of her head, its tiny legs gripping her forehead. She struggled to decide if the hairy bug-eyed creatures were cute or creepy, but they were, indeed, wondrous. Wings moved up and down gently as they rested, tickling her arms. When they finally stopped flapping, brown patches on the moths' wings turned the color of her cloak, her hair, or her hands. Her arms looked like they were partially covered in snow. She stared into the moth's large, dark eyes and frowned. An orange, string-like tongue flicked out of its mouth to inspect her eyebrows and nose.

"Hold still so I can focus in closer and see everything," he said. "There. Isn't that something? They have the ability to camouflage themselves during the winter."

"Are you sure they're safe?" she whispered.

"Mostly," he said. "Until they start to burrow and lay eggs."

"What?" she screamed and flapped her arms.

Even as she stomped and waved her arms like a threatening bird, she could hear Dallow's bellowing laughter. When her convulsions stopped, and the moths had finally departed, she waited for him to catch his breath.

"Sorry, but that's exactly what I needed," he said between chuckles.

"Glad I could help," she replied dryly.

"But don't you see, Your Majesty?" Dallow took deep breaths to calm himself. "The wonder is out here, you just have to look."

"Maybe I need to stick to the boring...or the danger," she said, brushing moth dust off her arms. "They were pretty amazing though."

Dallow lifted an arm and pointed a long finger northwest. "Angst is a quarter mile in that direction."

"I...I just..." She frowned. "Now you read minds too?"

"I do not need eyes to see the obvious." Dallow smiled. "Thanks for checking on me, and thank you for the laughter. Now go look in on him for both of us."

"Thank you, Mr. Dallow." She curtsied.

"You're welcome, Your Majesty." He bowed his head.

Victoria walked through camp on her way to Angst, brushing the tickle off her arms. Tarness was stoking the fire by a pile of freshly-collected wood. He glanced at her sheepishly, nodded, and continued his work. The unasked question hung on him like a sign, and she sighed inwardly. He wanted to know his future. This had to be the best reason not to tell anyone what she could do. She stopped right beside him and looked up. The man was seven feet of blubberous muscle. Thick, steel plate armor covered his chest and back, worn leather straps straining to hold it together. His plate leg guards had been replaced with more comfortable leather riding pants. His light brown eyes smiled beneath the permanent frown of his thick brow. His receding hairline gave him a tall forehead, which looked odd with so much bushy hair. Victoria reached out and took one of his giant hands in two of hers.

"You realize that I see all futures, and don't always know which one will actually happen," she reminded him. "I can sometimes pinpoint which one, but not always."

"You don't have to... Uh, I didn't ask you to... I just... Thanks." His fumbling words trailed off to a whisper.

She nodded as much to acknowledge his gratitude as to shush him. "Your shoulder won't get better unless we save Rose. You'll see Maarja again, but not right away, and it's possible you'll find love." Her words gradually became quieter. "Oh!"

"What?" he said excitedly, his face alight.

"Not just love, not just with her," she said. "Ugh. I think you'll find some loving sooner than you expect."

"Really," he said hopefully.

She pulled her hands back and hid chagrin with a false princess smile. "If what I saw was even close to what happens, you won't be disappointed. But most importantly, you have to keep Angst safe. He's going to need us." She hadn't seen that, but figured it wouldn't hurt.

"He always does." Tarness's grin was ear to ear, his burdens apparently lifted. He raised an arm and pointed into the woods. "I'm pretty sure Angst is thataway."

"That obvious?" she said quietly.

He lowered his head and smiled warmly. "The only one who'll never know is Angst," he said. "Unless you tell him, and that's not something I suspect a princess does. Anyway, he's there, go find him. Don't worry about getting lost, Hector can track you."

"Thank you, Tarness." She hugged as much of Tarness as she could.

"Thank *you*, Your Majesty." He patted her gently before she ran off into the woods.

8

After dragging the giant sword behind him for fifteen minutes, Angst felt alone. He couldn't hear the others and pulled Dulgirgraut in front of him, resting the foci on its tip. The woods were silent, aside from a nervous squirrel. He took a deep breath and exhaled steam. Angst circled the blade, staring at it with concern.

Was it him, or the sword? When he'd finally bonded with Chryslaenor, the foci had seemed brimming with enthusiasm. It couldn't share enough, like a child anxious to please a parent. He'd had to ignore the onslaught of information from the sword because of the chase to Unsel. Dulgirgraut, however, was the reluctant guardian, unwilling to reveal its secrets, as though unhappy to be here. Since he hadn't done anything different with the second foci, he was convinced it couldn't be him.

"What?" Angst asked as he continued to circle, his voice filled with challenge. "What is it with you?"

The sword was monstrous. Obnoxious. The foci hovered vertically over the ground, its tip inches from the dirty snow. The blade was identical to Chryslaenor: a ridiculous five feet tall and two feet wide across the flat. A thin handle rose from the base, almost silly in comparison to the great beast. A riser down the center made Dulgirgraut appear slightly rounded. It was so enormous, it should've been too heavy to wield—but Angst was Al'eyrn.

CHAPTER EIGHT

Angst was bonded to the magical sword in a way that went beyond holding hands or heavy petting. It had merged with him, his consciousness, his very self. It should've been a once in a lifetime connection, but he'd done this once before with Chryslaenor. Their brief bonding had given him incredible power and the knowledge to use it. But to save everyone he loved, Angst had been forced to remove that bond, ripping it from his mind. It had worked, he had successfully trapped Magic, but the cost was almost his life. That forced separation had left behind a hole intent on eating him alive, and the only cure had been to bond with another foci.

But Dulgirgraut was different. It was like a distant second wife who'd married you for money and gave you mediocre sex. It provided no comfort or support. He had all the power, the vast, unfathomable power that gushed from the foci like a waterfall—without a single ounce of the knowledge to wield it. Using this sword to fight was almost like having his hands cinched to his waist, forcing him to awkwardly swing at a bully with his shoulders.

"I asked you a question!" Angst shouted. "So give it up. Are you just going to sit by while my friends and I throw ourselves into danger, or are you going to actually help?"

Dulgirgraut did not budge or undulate or glow or hum. Angst stretched his neck to one side until he heard a pop.

"I don't think you're just a hunk of metal. Somehow, you're alive in a way I can't imagine. I think you're even intelligent, though maybe not smart." Angst scoffed. "So, if I'm right, that makes me wonder: do you feel?"

Still nothing. The blade remained stoic. Angst stopped circling it, facing the flat, and raised a hand to slap it.

"Stop!" Victoria said.

"What?" Angst spun about, his heart skipping a beat. "I thought I was supposed to be left alone."

"Pardon?" she replied haughtily.

"Don't princess me right now." Angst ground his teeth together. He pointed back and forth between the sword and himself. "Hector said it, we need to work this out before things get messy again. I can't...I can't have another Dallow. If that were to happen to you, I'd—"

"Were you going to slap it?" she asked accusingly, stomping forward to face him.

"Well, yeah." Angst thought he saw a slight red glow from the sword. "I'm trying to get a reaction from it."

"Is that how you get me to react?" she asked.

"Of course not," Angst said then, under his breath, "Not yet."

"Very funny," she said. "Even when things are bad between us, like they are now," she paused to let this settle in, "we're still close."

"Well, yes," Angst said meekly. "Always."

"Your bond makes you closer to that thing than you'll ever be with me." She winced but walked up to him, pressing her chest against his, her lips mere inches from his. "Do you still love me, Angst?"

He took a deep breath of Victoria, his heart racing as he felt her warmth. He closed his eyes. From the beginning, there'd been a connection between them he couldn't explain. She was his best friend, one who often walked a tight rope between appropriate hugs and inappropriately crawling into his bed naked. When she'd invited herself along on their mission, he'd been relieved. His health had been failing fast, and she'd chosen to stand by him.

But then she'd spent most of the trip to Melkier using magic to secretly communicate with Jaden, and hadn't even told Jaden to let Heather know he was alive. When, soon after, she'd discovered that her cousin, Alloria, had kissed him...well, they still hadn't quite recovered. If only he could figure out how to put things right between them.

"Of course I do," he said, then teased, "Most of the time."

"Would you really strike me to get what you wanted?"

"No, I could never hurt you," Angst snapped. "Never on purpose."

"Why do you treat me with kindness and not Dulgirgraut?"

Victoria asked. "Because I have boobs?"

"Seems like a good reason to me." He glanced down at her chest.

Victoria sighed and stepped back. "I hope you aren't missing my point."

"Don't slap you if I want something." Angst frowned mockingly. "Got it."

"Look, for both our sakes, until you work things out with your sword, the three of us aren't going to share a tent," she said.

"What if I promise not to slap you?" he said without thinking.

"Ha ha." She rolled her eyes. "I need my own dreams. I need to know if what happened is true—and you two are getting in my head. Until you fix things with the sword, and with us, I'll be staying in my own tent." Victoria spun about and ran off toward camp.

"But I never asked you to sleep with me," Angst said to nobody. He looked at the sword innocently hovering over the snow. "Now I really want to slap you."

There was a gentle burst of burgundy glow from the sword.

"Was that a chuckle?" Angst asked hopefully. "I just want to understand. Why are you so reluctant to help?" He placed his hands on the base of the blade and reached up to each side of the hilt. He lowered his head reverently and pleaded, "Please tell me."

"At least it's a reaction," Hector said from above.

Angst yelped, gripping the sword tightly to keep from falling back. "I hate it when you do that."

Hector leaped from a tree branch fifteen feet overhead, his arms out and his body straight as he flipped in the air to land soundlessly on the ground. Angst had never completely understood Hector's connection to magic, but was always amazed by it. Strong and agile, yet thin and wiry, the man could climb trees like a monkey, move silently as a cat, and fight like a cornered badger. Even watching him kill was beautiful, in a twisted sort of way. And all the weapons he could wield at a moment's notice...what was that about?

His friend peered after the princess with his gray wolf-like eyes. He drew his thumb along a thin scar that ran the length of his chin. When she was out of sight, Hector placed both hands on his hips and arched his back until it popped noisily. He rocked his muscular arms back and forth then lifted one leg at a time as if warming up for a run.

"Tarness, Dallow, come on out!" Angst shouted with a hand cupped around his mouth.

"Why do you think Tarness and Dallow are here?" Hector looked around the nearby wood.

"I thought everyone was going to leave me alone, but so far I've seen Tori and now you," Angst said. "I figured everyone else would follow."

"I wasn't expecting her to be here," Hector admitted. "That's why I hid in the tree. She's bright, that one. I think she'd make a good queen."

"Good, because I think she already is one," Angst said, his heart heavy for his friend. "Wait, so you don't hate her anymore?"

"I never hated her. Not in the least. I just didn't think she'd be safe—and still don't," Hector said. "I also can't tell if she's good for you. You're happier with her around, but conflicted. Like you're a teenager with a crush."

"So you came out here to give me girlfriend advice?" Angst was dumbfounded.

"Is that what she is now?" Hector crossed his arms.

"No." Angst crossed his arms.

"Right." Hector shook his head.

"If I can't get some alone time, I'll head back to camp." Angst reached for Dulgirgraut. "I can figure this out later. Arguing isn't going to help."

Angst grabbed the handle and marched away, letting the foci drag behind him.

"Wait, Angst." Hector caught up, placing a hand on his shoulder. "I didn't come to argue."

"That's new," Angst snapped. "What is it then?"

CHAPTER EIGHT

"Do you remember your sealtian?"

"I remember that you tried to teach me," Angst said, chuckling at the memory. "You said I was better at dancing. I'm awful at dancing."

"You're right, you *are* a terrible dancer." Hector cracked a smile, and Angst wondered if it hurt. "What do you remember?"

When he was younger, he used to watch Captain Guard Tyrell use sealtian to teach the queen's guards how to fight with swords. They would spend hours practicing the choreographed moves with their blades, repeating the stances over and over until they blurred together in, well, a dance. Tyrell used to tell them they'd have to master all thirty if they ever wanted to beat him in a duel.

"I recall being embarrassed that I was so bad at it," Angst said, his cheeks warming. "There seemed to be a lot of falling, and sword dropping."

"That's all you got out of three months of training?" Hector asked.

"I could probably do the first two," Angst said, hesitant to admit it. "Maybe."

"Want to do the first?" he asked, pulling his arms in awkward stretches over his head.

"Now?" Angst looked around, hoping Tori was back at camp. "You're serious."

Hector reached behind his back and pulled a longsword from neverwhere. He held it out, studying the edge before nodding in approval.

"How do you do that?" Angst asked. "Wielding weapons when you have none."

"Deep back pocket." Hector winked. "You never completely understood the purpose of the sealtian, how they taught you to make the sword another appendage, like an extension of your arm."

"That's how Chryslaenor felt," Angst said, remembering how amazing it was.

"You've mentioned that these things might be alive. If that's true, the princess is right. Slapping won't help." Hector ran his hand along the flat of his blade. "They seem to be more than weapons, Angst. Dulgirgraut and Chryslaenor are like companions. They need to be wooed like women and treated like friends. Taken care of like you take care of your own body. Well, maybe more like I take care of mine."

"That sounds really odd," Angst said hesitantly, ignoring the jab.

"The sealtian is the only way I know to make weapons a part of you," Hector said, now facing Angst. He let his legs bow slightly and held his sword out, palm down and perfectly horizontal. "I try to do these every morning...when you're still cuddling, of course."

"Cuddling?" Angst raised an eyebrow.

"Er, sleeping." Hector winked.

Angst smirked and shrugged. He lifted Dulgirgraut horizontally with one arm and balanced with the other, following his old mentor's lead. A gentle red hue surrounded the blade. He could do this. He had to. Tori would keep him away, keep pushing him away until he did. She— The glow flickered out. *Crap.* Taking a deep breath, he tried to refocus, lifting the sword vertically over his head until both hands met. A red light surrounded the sword once again. It didn't help that she kept yelling at him. Pushing him. She was starting to remind him of his wife. *Heather...* He missed her, he wanted to see how pregnant she was, and hold her in his arms without being yelled at. Angst shook his head and concentrated on the sword, reaching out to it with his mind as he lowered it in front of him until it was horizontal to the ground. This was useless. And a waste of time. They should've been rushing to Rose instead of doing calisthenics. He certainly hadn't had to exercise with Chryslaenor; it had just worked. The top of the blade touched the ground, and Angst sighed deeply.

"It was a great idea, Hector," Angst said apologetically. "I really appreciate it."

Hector ignored Angst, lifting one arm over his head and curling the second to create a crescent shape. He bowed his legs and bent over fluidly, stepping onto the ball of his foot. Hector had made him follow these moves hundreds of times, but he was too distracted, and it just didn't feel right.

"Thank you for trying," Angst said. "But it can't be this simple. I'm sorry, but I need to find my own way."

Hector barely nodded in acknowledgment, and Angst knew his old friend wouldn't stop his sealtian out of respect for old ways he didn't completely understand. Angst headed in the direction Tori had run off, feeling guiltier now than when he'd arrived.

9

Azaktrha

More than anything, Rose wanted to sleep, but the cold, moist hand on her bare shoulder made her shiver. She moved to wave it away and screamed in pain. Her arm had to be broken; it felt far worse than a dislocation. Pulse racing, she tried to clear the fuzziness from her brain, tried to remember how she'd got here, or where here was.

One arm still seemed to work. Shakily, Rose struggled to push herself from her gritty stone bed. Heavy eyelids tried luring her back to slumber, but that annoying wet hand remained. Rolling over to escape it was a big mistake. Everything hurt, even her mouth, which wouldn't close. Rose began to shiver, feeling feverish flashes of hot and cold.

"What ih goig ohn!" she said. She coughed, and orange splattered onto the ground.

Like a surprise tsunami, the hunger reached out from her core and sought her next meal. Her body wanted to heal, and it was so overwhelming, she worried it would eat her alive. Rose whimpered, and an unfamiliar little voice in her head echoed the whimper. That echo frightened her far more than the pain she was just becoming aware of. She allowed a trickle of life force from the clammy hand to feed her. Cool darkness filled her core, fighting that pain. When the whimpers became a whisper, she

72

stopped.

The hands tugged weakly, insistent without being rough. Still, the pain surged again, and she wanted to yell at them to stop, but her jaw had locked up and wouldn't move. It had to be broken again. This was how it had felt when Vars struck her at Ivan's funeral. Frustration and agony squeezed tears from her eyes. Rose reached up to her chin and set her jaw back into place with a muffled cry. The warmth of healing quickly numbed the pain, but it was using up her reserves. She knew her snack only teased of a full meal. After several minutes and more than a few tears, she could move her jaw.

"Get your hands off me. You're not safe," she said roughly to her unknown companion.

She repositioned to sit and heard a loud scrape, as a bone sticking out of her right thigh caught on the ground. Shock had hidden the pain, until now. It was so overwhelming she didn't even scream. Her stomach wrenched, trying to vomit, but only more of that lovely orange goop came out. Why was everything orange? Her spine ached, and she was grateful she couldn't see it, too.

What had happened to her? Memories flashed of her captor, a creature the size of an island, that had brought her to a hole, right into a hole in the middle of the ocean. She remembered jumping. How far had she fallen? Why was she not dead?

Slowly looking up, she saw a dark sky without end. The air was stale and smelled a little like fish. Their fall had created a small crater, and the big dumb sword was lying next to her in it. Rose wiggled her fingers and smiled—at least it wasn't attached to her hand anymore.

"I hate you," she said darkly. "I absolutely hate you. I wanted an adventure with friends. I never asked to be a hero, or whatever it is you're trying to make me. You were supposed to be for Angst, and I really want you to leave me alone."

Wet feet slapped the ground as her pesky companion hopped around to face her. She wanted to roll into a protective ball and go back to sleep, but even the slightest twitch brought more pain.

Her hunger was growing—the snack had been like trying to appease a lion with a cracker, and her healing required so much more. In spite of this, somehow she was in control, though just barely. Enough to make eye contact without devouring it. And it was definitely an it. The creature looked sort of like a deflated gargoyle. Blue fish scales covered its entire body, save for a foot wide swath of pale skin that stretched from torso to chest. It had a humanoid face, with enormous black eyes and a sky blue circle on its forehead that looked like a birthmark. Its ears were tall fins that waved gently with every breath from the gills along its neck. Its inappropriately pawing wet fingers were webbed and seemed too long, with the ends thicker than the base. It was scrawny, weak after she'd stolen its strength, and didn't appear threatening. Until it smiled.

"Stop smiling." She shuddered. "Those teeth."

It quickly clamped its lips over its teeth and looked down.

"I'm sure you can't help it," she said. "I just have a thing for gross teeth, and you have a lot of them."

It nodded in agreement.

"You understand me, but you can't talk?" she asked. "I wish you could tell me where I am."

"Azaktrha," she heard in her mind.

Its mouth hadn't moved, and it pulled at her healthy arm.

"Was that you?" she asked. "Did you speak in my head?"

"Yes," it replied.

"Don't you *ever* do that again!" she screamed, making it scurry away in fear. "Ever!"

It inched forward, its large eyes looking sad. Up close, she noticed a blue, oblong circle on its forehead, as if someone had spilled a dollop of ink. It was careful not to touch her, but waved for her to follow.

She presented her destroyed leg and arm with her good hand, as if they weren't obvious enough impediments. "I'm not going anywhere fast, not until I heal, which means eating."

It jumped back.

"Not you. I think you're even smaller than Angst. Obviously

not enough of a snack for the mess I'm in."

Over the creature's shoulder, torchlight flickered against shiny buildings. Why were the buildings shiny? The creature now seeming unwilling to grab her hand but still urged her to follow with desperate waving movements.

"I know, you want me to come with you," she said. "I can't. I don't even know if I'll ever heal from this."

As her eyes adjusted, she made out more buildings, a lot of them, as if they were in a city. Five smallish figures approached from a long street. Her companion hopped up and down as it waved its long, webbed fingers. She tried to move again, but the broken bone of her leg crunched and pressed outward.

"Ahhh," she cried out and stopped moving.

It scurried away to hide behind a nearby building. Torchlight reflecting off its beady eyes.

"Very sneaky," she called out. "I'm sure they'll never find you!" She whispered to herself, "Creeper."

The figures stopped to wield weapons.

"Maybe you guys can help me," she said. "Where am I?"

They rushed toward her, scrambling on all fours, daggers and sticks with hooked ends clacking on the ground with every stride. She swallowed hard. Maybe staying had been a mistake. Not that she'd really had a choice. Five fish-men arrived, appearing healthier than the one who'd woken her, though not much larger. They wore an assortment of shells that shone like the sides of the buildings. The tallest one in the center leaned forward and inhaled deeply, his thin tongue flicking against her cheek.

"Great, you're all creepers," she groaned, pushing his face away from hers.

The creature chomped down on her good hand, and Rose screamed, pulling back. Her hand was gone. Orange blood sprayed from the stump, as if she were spewing Vex'kvette.

They leaped forward as she screamed, "You bastard!"

An arc of black lightning danced from Chryslaenor to her body. It poured from her eyes to cover both arms. Blessed numbness masked her pain as she rose into the air. The five fish-men jumped back in fear as the dark lightning lifted them with her. They hovered helplessly, their feet wheeling as if they still touched the ground, marionettes on strings of angry black light.

"I hope this hurts," Rose cried out.

The creatures threw their heads back in silent screams, shrinking as if punctured. Rose's back straightened with a frightening crack. They scratched and clawed at their throats as her hand grew back and arm reformed, slotting cleanly into its socket. Their legs flailed as her bones noisily mended. Rose licked her lips with the satisfaction of eating any seven-course meal while dusty remains sifted into tiny piles. She winced cautiously when her feet touched solid ground and was grateful to feel no pain. Closing her eyes, she took a deep, reviving breath.

"This place stinks," she said to Chryslaenor. Flexing the fingers of her once-mangled hand, she added, "I guess I don't completely hate you."

She lifted the giant sword with her right hand and successfully transferred it to her left. Her heart skipped a beat; she was no longer tethered! She was finally in control! Rose swung the foci over her shoulder to set it on her back as she'd seen Angst do. Unwilling or unable to lock in place, the sword fell to the ground—crashing loudly as it dug up chunks of dirt.

"But I still hate Angst," she grumbled.

* * * *

Unsel

Alloria stretched lazily, arching her back and yawning like a cat. A nearby fire crackled loudly as it battled the cool morning air, catching her attention. She turned her head, staring into the fire and contemplating how the day would reward her cunning. The pieces in play fit so very well together, but she was clever enough to realize that timing was everything. Keeping Vars occupied, without upsetting the wielders, while waiting for Angst to get here before the sinkhole attack and whatever disaster followed…it was a lot to keep track of.

She needed her hero to come fast. Vars was up to something, she knew it. But what if Angst didn't make it? What if the wielders couldn't protect her from Vars? She would need more people on her side. She lifted the covers and looked at her naked body with its full breasts, youthful curves, and fair skin. How could she not find support with all of this?

Anxiety crept into her heart, and its beat quickened. She sat bolt upright and blood rushed to her head, her scalp tingling and numb as if it had fallen asleep. She suddenly felt like she'd tackled several bottles of mead by herself, and smacked her lips to check for dry mouth. It wasn't booze. Flopping back to the bed, she hoped it wasn't illness—there just wasn't time for that nonsense.

Alloria pressed on her temples with the palm of her hands, trying to relax. She brushed through strands of hair with her fingers and was surprised to feel skin. Her full mane of unkempt curls felt shockingly thin. She drew her hands back, and chunks of honey-brown hair stuck to her fingers as if glued.

Alloria's heart raced once again. She gasped as she pulled hair from her scalp like freeing cobwebs from blades of grass. It kept coming, and she kicked off her blankets to roll out of bed and find a mirror. The cold air enveloped her nudity in a chilly cocoon, but she ignored it.

Alloria whimpered in panic, unable to catch her breath at the sight in the mirror. Patches of her glorious, beautiful hair were gone. She looked back to find piles on her pillow, her bed, and a trail on the floor leading to her feet. Her reflection confirmed that she had four distinct, grotesque bald patches, each showing an inch or more of scalp. Another handful of hair came out as if her scalp were disease-ridden. She stared at the fistful of hair in her hand and screamed.

* * * *

Vars paced the length of the queen's study, surprised he hadn't worn a path in the floor. He'd been waiting for forty minutes, and had sent the page to check on Alloria twice. The youth was curtly dismissed, but reported that he'd heard sobbing, and there was a stampede of handmaidens frantically scurrying about the hallway. Vars smirked. She'd needed to be punished, and he longed to know the result. It would be worth the wait.

The wooden door to the queen's study opened, and Alloria walked in. Her back was arched proudly, but worry clouded her face. There wasn't enough makeup in Unsel to hide the despondent droop in her eyes or quiver in her chin. She wore her sadness like a chip on her shoulder, and that chip appeared to weigh a ton.

She passed him without making eye contact, bumping her thigh on the corner of the desk as she rushed to the high-backed chair. She wore an old-fashioned crown that featured a velvet inset, covering her scalp. His shoulders lightened, his burden lifting as the taste of sweet revenge renewed his spirits. Her hair barely showed beneath the crown. The teasing curl that usually dropped over her eyebrow was gone, and the long flowing mane now replaced by a thinnish ponytail the width of two fingers.

He hadn't known what to expect when he'd complained about her poor decisions, but couldn't have asked for anything better. Almost anything. She breathed in deeply, which was easy to see in her lower-than-usual corset. She must've hoped her breasts would distract from her baldness. For him, at least, they did not.

"Is something wrong, Your Majesty?" He did his best to hide the smirk in his voice.

"No, Captain Guard. Please report," she said in a quiet voice.

"It seems the holes are advancing faster than anticipated," he said, leaning to one side for a better view of her profile.

Alloria frantically tucked several hairs back into their velvet cage.

"I anticipate that we have only ten to twelve days before they arrive." He took several steps to the side of the greymaul desk for a better view.

"The towns in the sinkhole's path, have they been evacuated?" she asked, inching her chair around noisily in a vain attempt to keep up with his advance.

"Your Majesty, it seems something *is* wrong." He tapped his chin thoughtfully with a nub. "I just can't put my finger on it."

Her eyes instantly grew wide and she gasped loudly. "What did you do?"

He merely raised his thin eyebrows.

"You stole my hair!" she screamed, standing and pointing at him. "I'll have you quartered for this!"

"Not me, Your Majesty," he warned. "Him."

"Him?" She sat roughly. "The Vivek? But why?"

He raised both hands in front of his face, though the missing fingers left one of his watchful eyes uncovered. "You wished to empower wielders, to make a militia." He shook his head. "Not only is that a disgusting notion, but against his wishes. You realize we are working for him, that we follow his orders."

"You really think that was my plan?" she challenged. "You are a fool."

"You told Rook to gather them, Majesty," he said mockingly.

She sank deeper into the leather chair, pressing two of her fingers together and tapping her chin as she pondered. He had hoped for more. Apologies, compromises, total submission. Anything but pondering. The young woman ruled with her cleavage, and those breasts couldn't possibly be that intelligent. She was only seventeen, what could she know? She launched from the chair, smiling broadly.

Vars stared in surprise at this sudden turnabout as she passed him without word and made her way toward the door.

"Your Majesty," he said. "The ambassadors from Meldusia and Nordruaut have scheduled a meeting—"

"It will have to wait," she said. "Please give them my sincere apologies and reschedule like a dear, would you? I must fix something."

10

After another day of marching through thickets and skirting the roads, Dallow seemed almost graceful in comparison to his first day with the memndus stone. He hopped up onto a snowy log and lifted both hands, one holding his staff horizontally for balance. Victoria and Angst clapped at the sudden performance, which made Dallow smile. Without further warning, he summoned his gazelle swifen. It seemed carved from wood and shone as if freshly polished.

"What are you doing?" Hector snapped, looking around the woods as if they were surrounded.

"You said when I could handle walking, we would ride." Dallow mounted the swifen as if his eyes had never been taken. "Let's ride."

"There's another problem that needs resolving." Hector's gaze slid over to Angst.

"That could take forever!" Tarness said. "Are you planning to walk all the way to Rose?"

"Hey!" Angst shot Tarness a glare.

"Don't blame Tarness for your problems with your sword." Victoria smirked.

Dallow and Tarness laughed.

"No, I mostly blame you," Angst replied.

"Kids..." Hector interrupted Victoria's quickly arching back.

"Tarness is right," Dallow said, scratching under the blue

kerchief covering his eyes. "Whatever is holding you back from properly using the sword is going to take a lot more than a walk in the woods. Whether you're alone or not."

Hector shook his head as the others summoned their swifen. Victoria squeed when her pink flying unicorn appeared and hugged the forlorn creature.

"I know how she feels," Angst muttered.

Victoria ignored him as she mounted.

Angst's ram appeared far healthier than before. It was now solid steel and reinforced with more muscles, as if it had been lifting weights for a year. He grinned; something about it gave him hope, and for the briefest of moments, he thought he heard a distant song. Was that Chryslaenor reaching out or Dulgirgraut finally saying hello? It was too quiet to identify, but it was something. His ram reared back onto its hind legs. He looked over his shoulder at Hector.

"Coming?" He grinned.

* * * *

The cold went from bitter to biting as a dank wind picked up from the nearby ocean. The distant sound of waves crashing on the shoreline grew louder as the crunch of gravel slowly became sand. Angst knew sheer stubbornness kept Victoria from riding with him. Her teeth were chattering loudly enough to be heard, in spite of Dallow acting as a buffer between them.

"You know," Angst said across Dallow, "you'd be warmer if you put on your riding gear instead of the Berfemmian armor—"

"You're going to complain about my armor?" She turned enough for him to glimpse cleavage. Even in the dusk of twilight, he saw that her skin was blotchy from the cold.

Angst smirked, and she smiled back, her eyes apologizing. A little.

"Ugh," Dallow grunted.

"What?" Angst asked.

"You two... Just...Never mind." Dallow shook his head. "If I may ask, since Angst is too afraid, there is something we've all been wondering."

"The sealed document from my mother?" she asked.

Angst winced. He'd been trying to ignore this. It was the first sliver in their divide. She'd lied about sneaking out, about being there for him. The entire time she'd been representing Unsel, and merely using them for transportation.

"Not the entire time," she said.

"Huh?" Tarness looked at Victoria, his thick eyebrows scrunched in confusion.

"Answering him, his thoughts," she said, jerking her head at Angst. "My mother and I had a falling out before I left. She gave me an ultimatum—either I go on adventures with Angst or I remain in Unsel as a princess. I chose Angst."

Angst looked at her, his eyes wide with surprise, but she stared at the ground.

"I found that parchment in my bags after almost drowning in the lake."

"You don't have to explain yourself, Your Majesty," Hector said.

"It's my choice," she answered, her voice filled with royalty. "And I will."

"But, I thought you were a seer. Why didn't you know it was in there?" Tarness asked.

"It's a thing, not a person," Dallow explained. "That's why she needs to be close, or even make contact in order to see our possible futures. Right?"

"Yes, Mr. Dallow," she said brightly. "That, and my abilities haven't been working one hundred percent, especially with any future that touches a foci."

"Can't you see your own future?" Tarness pressed.

"I know my future," she said worriedly. "But a lot of things could happen on the way. Honestly, I almost threw out the parchment. Using it meant I was there representing the crown instead of adventuring with friends, but Angst was so sick I decided to keep it in case. I guess I'm glad I did." She smiled at

Angst proudly before frowning at his expression. "What?"

"Your mother…" Angst grimaced.

"Careful," Hector whispered.

"You were doing exactly what you wanted, finally getting away from her, and out of that castle," he said through gritted teeth. This reaffirmed everything he hated about the queen. "And what does she do? She loosens the leash just enough, and then jerks it right back. I guarantee you, she'll still be pulling your strings from her grave—"

"Angst," Tarness and Dallow said at the same time.

The words had come out without thought. He'd meant them in Victoria's defense, but the timing couldn't have been worse. Victoria had gone pale. Her lip was quivering, and she gripped her chest as if she'd taken an arrow. She rode off along the sandy shore, the wings of her swifen stretching wide.

He looked at Hector.

"Fix this, Angst," Hector barked as if giving an order. "We'll set up camp."

"It's not that easy," Angst snapped. "We aren't all soldiers."

"You should be," Hector called out as Angst walked away.

* * * *

Angst drew power from Dulgirgraut to catch up, but it wasn't necessary. Victoria hadn't gone far, merely beyond sight of the others. She sat on a sandy hill, looking off into the ocean. Angst leaped from his slowing ram and clumsily flopped onto the sand. He fought mounds of the cold beach, struggling with every crawl before awkwardly resting beside her. There was no such thing as moving gracefully through sand in armor. She continued staring out, all color drained from her face.

"She can't fly," Victoria whispered. "Not without you or that sword."

"I think she can fly for you, Tori," he said. "When you really need her to."

She looked at him before collapsing into a heap of racking

tears and shattered heart. Angst drew his best friend close. He'd never felt so helpless, unable to bandage her pain with words or laughter or kindness. Ever-so-gently, Angst placed an arm on her shoulder. Victoria pulled him down to lie beside her in the sand, and buried herself in his chest.

The young princess, the young queen, sobbed helplessly, relentlessly in a way Angst had never seen. Patting her hair, he placed his cheek against her temple as tears dripped from his armor. He squeezed her tight, with every ounce of reassurance he could gather. Angst wished he could will love and understanding into the embrace, it didn't feel like a hug could be enough.

The sound of crunching sand made Angst lift his head. A gamlin, one of his sentinels, popped out of the ground inches from his feet. Its little face looked sad, and it rubbed its hands forlornly. Two more gamlin crawled out of the sand and stood at both sides of the first, looking remorseful.

Victoria pulled herself away from his chest slowly and looked at the creatures. "What..." she sputtered. "What are they doing?"

"Understanding," Angst said sadly. "Now that Earth is gone, they've lost their mother, too, I guess. My...the gamlin are intelligent, in their own way. They feel, they regret, and they mourn."

"She's really dead, Angst. Tyrell too. My only family." She looked up at him with doey eyes.

Angst wanted nothing more than to make it better. It felt as if a hand had gripped his heart and squeezed. "Not your only family."

She smiled at this, touching his cheek thoughtfully. Angst leaned in, longing to hold her close, closer, but there was something else. Tori tilted her head up, and her lips were slightly parted. His heart raced forward even as his mind reeled back. He needed her to know how much he loved her but knew it was wrong. They were so close, and a part of him wanted this, had always wanted this. They hovered only inches apart for moments, for an eternity, before she jerked her head back.

"What?" She glanced at the gamlin gripping her foot.

Another gamlin placed a hand on her shoulder and the third held Angst's arm. Victoria looked at him with reluctant eyes at a moment lost then opened her arms open wide. The three gamlin ran to her like toddlers. She carefully hugged them all, and Angst cuddled all four of them gently for a moment before letting go and purposely falling over to one side. Victoria giggled as she pushed the gamlin away, poking the tummy of the closest. They skittered back to their triangular point, crossing their arms.

Angst pushed himself up to his knees and looked into her eyes. She deserved more time; both to mourn and to come to terms with being queen. He knew she would get through this, though, and would do what he could to help. She was his best friend, and she deserved it.

"I can do this." Victoria sniffed.

"I know you can," Angst agreed. "I'm sorry," he said quietly. "For being so upset about the parchment."

"You have nothing to apologize for," she said. "You were right. I didn't tell you about it, and in spite of that, you still believed in me. I heard you tell Hector, felt you believe in me. That's how I was able to keep up the facade. Everything from negotiating with the king to whatever I was doing with Crloc. I was trying to be like you, for you, Angst."

Now his eyes were blurry with wet as he held Victoria once again.

"I know I can be a bitch, and I ignore you too much," she said quietly.

"And you're mean," he whispered.

She started shoving away until she saw him smirk.

"You *can* be a bitch, and I hate it when you ignore me because you know it hurts and you still do it," he said. "So, yes, you are mean. But I believe in you because you're amazing, and you're my best friend. You always will be."

"Just..." She swallowed hard. "Just shut up."

After another long hug, she looked up.

"Angst," she sounded concerned.

"What?" he asked.

"Look over your shoulder," she said.

He didn't need to. The warm glow of Dulgirgraut reflected in Victoria's wide eyes. He smiled.

"Are we in danger?" She frowned.

He cocked his head to the side and closed his eyes. Music. A deep, somber dirge. Distant but distinctly different from Chryslaenor.

"No, I think it's starting to come back." Angst nodded. "Maybe this is what I needed, to clear the air."

"You two should be alone," she suggested.

He stood and held out his hand. Victoria took it and pulled herself up. She brushed sand off herself and then him, finishing with a firm smack to his rear. Angst looked at her in surprise, which made her giggle.

"I'm sorry for...stuff," she said.

"Me too," Angst agreed as they walked along the beach. "All of it."

"Is everything okay?" she asked.

"Nothing has changed," Angst said. "Your Highness," he mocked.

Victoria shoved her shoulder into him, but didn't let go of his arm. "I need a drink," she muttered.

"Just one?"

"All of them."

11

After delivering Victoria to camp, Angst continued his walk along the shoreline, periodically staring out at the ocean. She'd suggested stripping off his armor and boots and walking barefoot in the sand. About how freeing it would feel, in spite of the cold. It was definitely cold. His teeth chattered slightly as the wake pulled and pushed, sloshing over his naked toes, which were now mostly numb. He'd left footprints behind him, but the icy ocean soon lapped at his trail, washing away his breadcrumbs. He'd never been this close to the ocean. The freezing water kept him alert, and the sand was…well, it was sort of fun.

Victoria was like that sand, ever-changing in the ebb and flow of tides he barely understood. Mere weeks ago, he'd awoken beside her naked body, leaving him absolutely torn between guilt and wonder. He was married and shouldn't have even been sleeping with her—never mind naked, never mind enjoying it—but he was so convinced his marriage was broken that he wondered if his princess was an answer. It felt like they'd resolved their issues and were friends again. Mostly. That almost-kiss still hung before him like an unanswered question, leaving him unsure once again.

After seeing the death of her mother and Tyrell, Victoria hadn't turned to him; she had turned away. Their unbreakable friendship—which had seemed on the verge of more than friendship—was pushed aside like it had never happened. The wariness he felt in her was like Heather's. It was as if they expected something else, or wanted more from him, no matter how much he gave. The only thing they had in common was him, and their reactions were identical. There had to be something missing. Something he said, or didn't say. Something he did, or didn't do. Or maybe it was just him.

Angst still felt broken. His friends had come all this way to help him bond with a foci again, to save him. And yes, Dulgirgraut made him complete and strong, like he could be the hero he'd always wanted to be. The one he was meant to be. But then why the emptiness? Why did it feel like something was still missing? Great deeds, heroic events, magical things were all part of his life, but was this it? Shouldn't he just be happy with the direction of his life? Looking up from his sandy toes, he took a deep breath and admired the shoreline. A reflection of moonlight on the beach caught his eye.

From this distance, he could barely make out a shape lying in the sand. Was it a large fish washed up on shore, or something more dangerous, waiting for a snack? He really wasn't in the mood to be dinner. It didn't move, and as he approached, the silhouette took shape. Was it a body? He sped up, cursing his numb feet which made it hard to run.

Angst rested Dulgirgraut on its tip and dropped to inspect the unmoving figure. A mess of light blue hair matted her face and was buried in the sand. A shadow of a memory niggled at him. Hadn't he seen blue hair when he was chasing Magic through Unsel? That felt like years ago, and he shook away the memory, focusing on the body before him. He gently pushed her hair back, carefully freeing it from its sandy blanket. Her skin was also a light, unexpected shade of blue. Her head was partially sunken into the sand, but the visible side of her face was stunning. She had high cheekbones, very full lips, and a smallish nose. He touched her face, which was cold as death, and ran his fingers down to thin cuts along her neck.

"Wait, those can't be cuts, there's no blood." He frowned. "What are you?"

He placed a hand on her shoulder and jumped back when an eye blinked. She weakly coughed wet sand from her mouth and rolled to her back, lifting her buried arm from the sand. An ugly mess of barbed metal and thin steel nails rose from her sandy bed; her arm was caught in a trap. The clutch was attached to a chain that stretched to a large stone outcrop. The barbs dug wincingly deep into her hand and arms. She didn't scream, but her face contorted in agony. She looked drained, too exhausted to pull away.

Angst reached for the trap. She shook her head vehemently in warning.

"It's okay. I'm amazing, I can do anything," he said, hoping humor would make it a little better.

She barely lifted her head. Even in this weak state, the blue woman was gorgeous, and he couldn't help but be dramatic. He snapped his fingers, and a bright blue aura surrounded his hands. Her large, dark eye became wider, and she sucked in her lips.

"I'm not going to hurt you," he promised.

Carefully, Angst touched the tip of a rusty spike. The metal melted away, falling into a heap of brown and copper sand. He stopped changing the trap when all that remained were barbs so he could pull the teeth out manually, figuring it would be better than leaving the nasty dust in her arm. The woman tried pushing away and winced as she fell back on her face. The cuts on her neck now opened and closed rapidly, desperately.

"What do you need?" Angst pleaded. "What can I do?"

There was a loud splash, and Angst looked down at a long fin flapping in the breaking waves. Fin? He hadn't bothered to inspect her body beyond her hair and face. He saw now that everything below her waist was a silvery shimmer of scale.

"You're a fish?" he said in amazement.

She stopped struggling, her head snapping up. Thick, dark blue eyebrows frowned over a dangerous glare. *Mermaid!* he heard loudly in his mind. *Can't breathe!* She grasped at the cuts on her neck. He was such an idiot! They weren't cuts, they were gills!

"You need water!" Angst dug his hands into the sand under her torso. He wrenched her from her sandy confine and rolled her over to reveal an amazingly muscular stomach and firm breasts. He shook the distraction from his head, looking up at the helpless fish-woman. She smiled weakly.

"Ocean?" he asked.

She nodded. Barely nodded.

With a deep breath, Angst lifted her from the sand. Her body was cold, and limp, and heavy. The mermaid's head lolled with every rushed step he took. Cold water soaked into his leather riding pants, sapping strength from his legs and stiffening each step. He wanted to stop, but when he looked down, her eyes were shut, her body hanging listlessly.

"No dying!" Angst yelled. An eye cracked open. "I'm not taking a freezing bath with a beautiful…woman, just to have her die in my arms!"

He adjusted her body awkwardly, shifting his arms and fingers so he wouldn't drop her while trying not to grope anything he shouldn't. How could she live in this water? It was beyond freezing, even colder than she was. His breath quickened and his heart raced. Everything below his waist was becoming numb and waterlogged. His legs struggled against the water as his feet sought sand. Unsure if she would live through submersion, he slowly lowered her into the water. Like a fish set loose from a hook, her tail flapped violently, freeing her from his hold and knocking him down. He gasped as the water engulfed him.

Angst kicked back against the sandy floor to keep his head above the waves. He spat and coughed, swimming backward toward shore as he struggled to find footing. When his butt finally touched the beach, Angst pushed himself upright. He sat, his teeth chattering, and shuddered violently. The mermaid was nowhere to be seen.

"You're welcome," he called out.

A hundred yards away, the silvery silhouette of a large fish with breasts flew out of the ocean only to dive back in. It was the flawless pirouette of a dancer freed from all restraint.

"I guess that counts as a thank you." He smiled to himself. "Wow, was she something."

Angst attempted to stand, his knees creaking from the cold, which had seeped into his bones. Submersed to his thighs, he turned toward the beach and took a labored step forward. It was so cold, his stiffness felt stiff. Something grabbed his ankle, pulling him back. It was gentle but firm, at first, then more violent, yanking him hard enough that he fell forward.

"Wait, I—" His face met water and sand as he was dragged out to sea.

Angst gasped for air, flailing his arms as he skimmed over the surface of the ocean. He stopped suddenly, and the woman swam around him twice as he attempted to tread water with his quickly cramping legs.

"Are you okay?" he asked around a mouthful of water. "Why am I out here?"

"You trapped me!" she said in his mind.

"What?" he said. "I freed you!"

She dove under water, and he struggled to shore, which seemed forever away. He had barely moved when she gripped his ankle. Again. He kicked and gasped desperately before being dragged beneath the waves.

12

Unsel

Maarja paced for several steps, which was all the space the hall provided for her long legs. The Nordruaut, who stood taller than the tallest man in Unsel, twice taller than Angst, fit this room like a toddler in last year's clothes. A white fur loincloth cinched by light leather ties, swayed with every movement. She straightened the white and soft gray fur that barely covered her chest and shoulders, leaving her reddish tanned midriff exposed. Her legs and arms were bare, save for leather arm and leg straps holding ceremonial stone daggers. Her short fur boots, which were meant to be worn outside, slapped the tile floor noisily. Wearing all of this indoors made her feel more confined than the smallness of the room. Her pacing only stopped on the rare occasion when the unnatural shaking seized the room beneath her feet.

Maarja didn't just pause in her march, she froze as if the very source of the quakes had held her legs to the floor. Her heart raced to break free, and she forced her breathing to remain calm before it was noticed. She'd faced monsters twice her size, killed a wild bookeen mount with her bare hands, and chased down herds of creatures in the hunt without breaking a sweat—but the quakes were unseen, out of her control, and filled her entire being with fear.

She looked at her small friend, Jintorich, who sat calmly on a squat wooden table. His tiny legs were crossed and his staff rested on them. The little man ignored the quakes, and something about that was a comfort. He was an anomaly she barely grasped. A warrior who would've fit in her pocket, brimming with bravery and, lately, advice. He had fought fiercely to protect Unsel from the Fulk'han incursion and seemed unalarmed by much of anything, in spite of his size. Maarja had never before seen a Meldusian, but had heard they were all petite in stature. She had yet to hear his story, of how the Vex'kvette had changed his people, but his appearance was striking.

Jintorich's plume of dark eyebrows slouched like his tall thin ears. Wispy brown hair flowed over his bulbous forehead like a waterfall. His protruding eyes were shut, and he breathed slowly, as if in deep sleep or deeper meditation. Occasionally, a heavy sigh would blow long eyebrow hair over his sizeable toes, which peeked out from under his thick, white robes—the apparent tickle would make him jerk to attention before falling back into his trance.

It was no surprise she was so fond of him. He battled like a tiny warrior but was patient in every way she wasn't. It was as if he were the most powerful person in the castle, hidden in the most unassuming package.

"I'm jealous of your reserve," she said.

"And I of your energy," he squeaked in his tiny voice. "You look ready to break through the wall."

"I've considered it," she confided, dropping to the floor and crossing her legs. "This room is too small."

"That's a matter of perspective," he said with a wink, his thin ears raising high over his head.

"Heh." Her chuckle wasn't really that polite. "I just hate being made to wait."

"Did you expect something different when you agreed to be Ambassador?" Jintorich asked.

"I expected..."

"Tarness," he finished.

She'd told him about the large black man, more than once. Tarness was always on her mind, and the distraction frustrated her to no end. He wasn't Nordruaut, merely an oversized human. She didn't even know how well he could hunt! But he'd looked at her like no other, and she chided herself for not taking him on the spot.

"Yes," she said, looking up, brushing fine platinum hair from her face. "That's the reason I agreed to come."

"But not the reason you were asked?" Jintorich stood.

She looked into his little black eyes. "Jarle, my skadii, is worried about civil war or worse. He fears Eastern Nordruaut would attack the smaller nations."

"So you come to enlist the help of Unsel?" he asked, his eyebrows lifting in surprise.

"Of Angst," she admitted. "And his weapon. Jarle believes there could be another weapon of power, and worries that Eastern Nordruaut would march if there was a wielder."

"I always thought the Nordruaut were hunters, not warmongers." Jintorich scratched his jutting chin with a thick fingernail.

"There is a story, but this is not the time to tell it," she said with regret. "We used to be warriors, thousands of years ago. A great leader taught us that war only leads to destruction and death. That war was nothing more than longing for things we already possessed. We gave up the march of war for the glory of the hunt. Twenty years ago, something happened, and there was a split of East and West. There's been no civil war because both sides are evenly matched."

"If they have a wielder of foci," Jintorich continued for her. "Jarle hopes that Angst will be on his side to keep the balance, to avoid war."

"Yes." Maarja bit her lip and stood again to pace. She was done with this conversation. "Aren't you also here to see Angst?"

"Indeed," Jintorich stated. "And his foci. My people need to understand—"

"My people need him first," she snapped, almost in a panic. The words had come before she thought, and she instinctively covered her mouth, but did not apologize.

"There is no concern, my friend," Jintorich stated with a winsome smile. "I am very patient."

Before he could explain further, the door opened.

Vars entered the room with an oily smile that made Maarja want to start the hunt now. Despite his advanced years, she could tell he would be a formidable opponent for a minute. Maybe two. Tall, for a human, with shoulders strong enough to carry the thick old steel armor covered in gold leaf. His piercing eyes studied the room like a veteran before a sneer of disgust took over his entire face. He showed no fear or concern at her size, and she reassessed—it might take three whole minutes to break him. Maybe.

"My sincere apologies, Ambassadors," he said with the barest of nods. "The queen was called away on other duties."

"Queen?" Maarja said in surprise. "She was crowned? Why were we not invited?"

Vars's eyes grew and his gray cheeks seemed to suck inward. "Of course, you are correct," he said through a set jaw. "She has yet to be crowned. It is a title of courtesy."

"How long must we wait?" Maarja asked.

"There is much preparation for Queen Isabelle's funeral." Vars sighed impatiently.

"Any word on Angst?" Jintorich asked as he stood. "Or his companions?"

"Just that they live," Vars acknowledged with a chill in his voice.

"Then, by Her Majesty's command," Jintorich bowed, "we will continue to patiently wait."

"We will wait," Maarja agreed with less conviction.

Vars looked from the small man to the enormous woman and raised a curious eyebrow before nodding once and departing.

"They don't know what to do with us," Jintorich said, staring at the door. "But they won't ask us to leave."

"I want to leave," she admitted. "I feel like I should return to my people."

"We are where we need to be, for now." He sat down and placed his staff in his lap.

"Don't you worry about your people?" she asked.

"I have no concern. We are one. One of many," he said with finality. "I would like to know more about Angst and his foci. Would you tell me that story?"

Maarja smiled. With a grateful sigh, she removed several furs to reveal tight leather undergarments. She'd been dying to share this story, having practiced it many times in her head. She raised her hands and held out her fingers.

"We heard them through the woods a hundred leagues off, like they were a legion of soldiers," she began in a whisper. "We pushed through the trees to take them off guard, and you wouldn't believe their faces. You could taste their fear..."

* * * *

Wilfred the Short had somehow miscalculated. He drummed his thick fingers on a pile of dry parchment as he pondered. He'd been sitting right by Angst the night his friend had lifted that giant sword, and immediately knew the man was meant for something more than filing papers. In spite of being a wielder, Angst had trained and befriended many soldiers. He was close friends with Isabelle's daughter, and was, maybe, smart enough to understand his potential.

At Victoria's prompting, Wilfred had advised the queen to send Angst on a quest. He'd known it would be dangerous but also realized that if Angst was successful, they would both advance. Angst would finally become the hero he longed to be, and Wilfred would be recognized, once again, as a prominent advisor.

He coughed, and wondered if he wasn't allergic to the paper dust in the filing room. Instead of being rewarded for his exceptional counsel, the queen had punished him with Angst's job. It was such a waste. Wilfred was still well-connected. His network reached throughout the castle like a spider web that stretched far beyond these walls. All nations knew his name despite never having met him. His goal had always been intelligence for the greater good. He knew how to get it, and how to make sense of it. He breathed in bureaucracy and exhaled knowledge, but down here he only exhaled boredom. Where once he'd said, 'Poor Angst,' he now said 'Poor Wilfred,' and wondered if he would be found decades later in a pile of parchment and dust.

How could he have let this happen? The princess herself had encouraged him. But noise and rumor had it she'd also asked the queen to send him here. Even after months of bitterly being wedged between the cellar and the real world, he had a hard time believing Victoria was evil. But, why else would she hide him away for so long? Did he deserve this punishment?

The door creaked loudly as it rushed open, letting in such bright light that he winced and held up a hand against its brash entrance. The candle nearest the door went out, and several pieces of parchment flew off a nearby table, rocking in the air until they landed on the dusty floor. Hours of sorting slowly drifted to the ground.

A figure entered the room, and he could barely greet it with a grunt.

"Please, only by appointment." He waved his hand dismissively. "Or make your request with the clerk and your document will be available in seventy-two hours, hopefully."

The figure continued its approach, dragging a stool directly across from him and plopping onto it. Alloria was dressed in a teal corset and black leggings. Her face was painted to match her attire. A single strand of honey-brown hair curled over her eye, and the rest of her hair was hidden by an old crown. While her clothing was slightly mismatched, the queen regent stunned, and Wilfred gasped at her beauty and importance.

He stood quickly from his own stool, papers on his lap falling to the ground, and knelt then realized he was behind a table. She chuckled as he knocked over laws and declarations to make his way around and kneel properly before her.

"Your Majesty," he said with his head lowered, his thin, un-kempt brown hair tickling his forehead.

"Wilfred, isn't it?" she asked.

"Yes, Your Highness." He couldn't help but look up.

Her full lips broadened to a smile that melted every ounce of bitterness in his heart. This was his moment.

"You're a friend of Angst." She twirled her free lock of hair. "He's spoken well of you."

"He has?" Wilfred asked in surprise. He'd assumed Angst was upset and had the princess relocate him as punishment.

"Indeed." She smiled, urging him to rise. "He said you're one of the smartest, most competent men in Unsel."

"He did?" Wilfred asked. He stood as tall as possible. "Well, yes. Yes, I am."

"Now more than ever, Unsel needs you." She leaned forward, her cleavage pressing up and together. "I need you."

The room shook for a second as the ground quaked. The princess yelped and lurched forward. Wilfred caught her by the armpits, holding her upright but at arm's length.

She pulled back and brushed dust from her bodice. "Thank you," she said sincerely. "It's coming, and we need you now."

Wilfred frowned and nodded, otherwise ignoring the presentation before him. "Your Majesty, I will always serve Unsel, however you need me."

"Then it's time to come out of the basement." Her winning smile broadened from ear to ear.

Wilfred ran fingers through his wispy hair, sighed with relief, and followed her glory out of his prison, never once looking back.

13

The mermaid pulled Angst down deeper, until the last bit of moonlight faded from his vision. Air filled his cheeks and his chest throbbed while his muscles refused to move. He might've been scared, but he was also getting angry. Angst grunted at the effort of lifting his glowing arms upward. Reaching out with his mind, he created an orb-shaped air shield directly overhead, large enough to encompass him and his new companion. He then forced the shield into the ocean, the effort driving the remaining air from his lungs. The remaining bubbles left his mouth and crept around the outside of the air shield as it enveloped him. He grabbed the hand on his foot and jerked her into the orb. Still weak from being trapped, she reached for the gills on her neck as she lay helplessly on the curved floor, her tail flapping listlessly. The cold completely forgotten, he took in desperate gulps of air. Angst stared at her, squinting to watch her movements in the pale light emanating from his arms.

"I just saved your life!" Angst croaked, pointing in the direction he thought they came from. "This is a crappy way to thank me!"

She frowned.

He wanted to pace, but there was nowhere to go. "Usually I get a hug or a thank you." He was breathing faster and becoming lightheaded. "Hugs are good." He rested his hands on his knees. "But you, you drag me out to the ocean?" He fought to catch his breath and took a wobbly step forward. "What were you going to do? Kill me and eat me?"

She cowered, covering her face with her arm.

"Stop that. I'm not going to hurt you," he promised weakly.

"Pirate!" He heard her voice in his mind. *"That is what you all say."*

"Look, I'm no pirate, miss." Was 'miss' the right title? He hated this; he was supposed to be a hero and she made him feel like a villain. "I'm going to set you free again, and then I'm going to try to swim back to shore, if you'll let me." He began to shiver.

While it was hard for Angst to clearly see the mermaid, she stared at him for the longest time, the anger slowly disappearing from her face. His legs went numb, and he dropped to his knees. In spite of his exhaustion, he really wanted to know what she looked like. The dim glow from his hands only teased with the silhouette of her figure. He forced himself to make eye contact. She didn't seem to care that she was naked, which made him smile like a twelve-year-old. She frowned at him in confusion, and continued to study him as if reading his mind.

Angst looked around, his neck stiffening. He had to find a way to warm himself, and he had to get back, but the bubble was so dark, he couldn't see the beach. Could the *mermaid* be trusted? She had just tried to kill him, but she had also been trapped. He hoped those wide eyes were filled with curiosity, and not crazy. "Um, do you know which way I'm supposed to go?"

The mermaid pursed her lips as though holding back a laugh. *"I shall bring you there,"* she offered.

"You're not going to drown me?" he asked. "Or eat me or something?"

"Not yet." She playfully licked her lips with a snakish tongue. *"Let us out of this thing and I shall see you to shore."*

"But I'll be cold," he whined teasingly.

"I can read you," she said slyly. *"Look at me and you will not be cold."*

"Ha!" Angst laughed. He took a deep breath and let go of the bubble, leaving them immersed in water. They both watched the bubble rise over them before popping.

"You did that?" she asked.

He couldn't speak, so he merely nodded. It was awkward trying to wink underwater.

The mermaid came close enough to Angst that he could make eye contact. She hesitated and, for a brief moment, he felt a connection, not magical but personal, as if she were someone he should have in his life. She smiled, and nodded, and moved to hold him close. His body relaxed, his muscles unlocked. Had she warmed him or was he just used to the water now? Gripping his arms, she swam faster than he could've imagined. Water rushed around his head, making his ears flap against the current.

When he could finally feel rocks and sand underfoot, she stopped. He expected her to let go and swim away as fast as she could, which made his heart sink a little.

"Carry me to shore," she said with a smile.

With an embarrassing grunt, he hefted the mermaid to a nearby stone jutting out several feet from the sandy shore—the very stone she'd been shackled to. She wrapped her arms around his neck, her face was close to his. Her firm breasts were squished against his drenched tunic. In spite of their wet bodies and the cold air, it was nice. He placed her on the rock as gently as he could, and she slowly let him go.

Angst took several steps back until he could see her in full. He drew in a deep breath but stopped mid-sigh to gawk. Until now, he'd only seen her in sand and water. He covered his open mouth, but couldn't tear his eyes away from her exotic beauty. Her torso appeared human from breast to waist, which rode low, very low, to her shimmery silver tail. Delicate scales began below her stomach like pants that covered too little. He inched around her as she squeezed water from her blue hair, which streamed onto her very pale blue shoulders in curls, partially covering her chest. An inch of fin jutted from her spine and the back of her thin, muscular arms.

There was a distant, low hum of music from Dulgirgraut, and

Angst flicked a glance over his shoulder to see a burgundy glow. "Now?" Angst waved it away dismissively. "Of all times, you want to start talking now? How about shush it!" The music continued, but was quiet enough to be drowned out by the waves licking at the long-forgotten numbness of his feet.

She shifted her body to face him, and lifting a hand from her rocky throne, beckoned him closer. He walked slowly, still straining to make out her face with the bright moon shining behind her. The glow from Dulgirgraut hinted at large black eyes and very full lips. The mermaid looked dangerous, and wild, and intoxicating.

She smiled at his reaction before looking down at her body with a touch of concern, as though worried about her appearance.

"Maybe we should start over," he said, offering his hand. "Hi, I'm Angst."

She took his hand in both of hers and held it near her chest. He smiled stupidly and his heart fluttering in his chest.

"What are you?" she asked. *"Are you pirate?"*

"No, definitely not," he said. "I'm, uh, I'm a human."

She tilted her head to one side and frowned. *"Is that what you do? You hooman?"*

"Well, no. Of course you've only seen the bad hoo, er, humans." Angst rolled his eyes at how incredibly smooth he wasn't. There were days he longed for Dallow's book smarts. "I'm not a bad human, really. I'm, well, I'm a hero." He arched his back and stuck out his chest proudly, though he couldn't help noticing that his stomach stuck out too.

"Hero?" she asked.

"Yeah," he replied. "I try to save people."

"Are you the one come to save us, An-gst?"

"I really hope so," he answered dumbly.

At this, she smiled and reached for his hand. Hers was surprisingly warm, but her grip was weak. Dark blood dribbled from her arms. He wanted to heal her. He'd seen Rose do it, and Dallow, but he couldn't do it without help. Angst reluctantly pulled away and walked to Dulgirgraut.

"Do not leave me." She sounded worried.

He returned with the giant sword, which still glowed softly. She looked concerned, and wiggled on the rock as if considering a quick exit. He took her injured arm as gently as he could. She tried jerking it away but seemed unable.

"Please trust me," he said with all the charm he could muster before closing his eyes. "I'm a hero, remember?"

How did they do this? She was far too pretty to leave damaged. There was a trickle of information, no more than a tiny drop of condensation on a parched tongue. Was it Dulgirgraut? He thought he felt a connection between them, and a tingling sensation made the flesh of his arm itch. Angst tried drawing in a little more. The itch became hot, and his pulse soared. He could do this! He could heal her. Without hesitation, he pulled the wounds into himself, and immediately wished he hadn't. The rush of pain made him cry out. The steel jaws had chipped bone, driving splinters into muscle. Gritting his teeth, he willed their bones into place, urged their muscles to knit, and their skin to reform whole. Finally, the intense pain became heat once again, and then a numbing tingle in their arms.

The moment passed, and the mermaid's high-pitched voice sighed in his mind as he opened his eyes. The wound on her arm was gone, and she sat comfortably upright with renewed vigor. He smiled proudly. He'd healed someone. Her eyes filled with gratitude, she pulled him in for an embrace. Her heart beat in his own chest, an irregular gallop, a new band that couldn't find the beat. Angst gazed into her large black eyes.

"You are the one," she said hopefully. *"You can save us, An-gst."*

"Save you from what?" he asked. "What's wrong?"

"We are trapped and dying. All of us. I am dying, An-gst." She leaned closer to him.

He started to pull away, but she drew him closer, her lips an inch from his. Her breath smelled of the salty ocean. A pencil-thin forked tongue flicked around his mouth. His breath caught;

he didn't know what to do. He leaned in, or she did, and their lips met as she thanked him. Hers were warm, and her thin tongue darted into his mouth. He froze, not knowing if he should pull away because this was wrong, or stay because…hot, naked mermaid.

"Thank you for finding me, An-gst. You can save us." Her thoughts were a whisper. *"You will save me."* She sat upright and glanced over her shoulder, down the long beach.

"Who are you?" His head was spinning. When was the last time anyone had kissed him like that other than his wife?

"I am Moyra. Find me." She kissed him once more, licking his lip seductively before launching into the air. Moyra's silvery tail shone in the moonlight and another tall fin jutted from her neck and back. She dove far into the distant ocean.

Her head popped out of the water. Even at this distance, he could feel her looking at him, through him, and more than anything, he wanted to help. She smiled at him, her fuller-than-full lips grinning. The smile was all for him, not distracted by cute boys or diluted by a bitter wife look. He lost himself in that smile for a moment before she dipped her head into the water and was gone.

"Um, Angst?" Hector said. "Your sword is glowing. I take it that's a good sign?"

He jerked around to see Hector on the other side of the rock. He looked down instinctively.

"So are your cheeks," Hector observed quizzically.

"Oh, yeah, of course." Angst rolled his eyes. A sudden chill came over him now that she was gone. "Dulgirgraut, being stupid," he said dismissively.

"Why do you sound nervous?" Hector walked around the rock. "And why are you soaking wet?"

Angst looked out at the ocean. There was no sign of Moyra, and he wondered if he would ever see her again. "It's nothing. So, why are you here?"

"Dinner is ready." Hector's voice was filled with concern. "I wanted to see how things were going. To see if you were all right."

"Oh, just fine." Angst glanced at Hector before looking off.

"Why do you keep staring at the ocean?" his friend asked. "You look like you just saw a mermaid."

"I just…well, I—" Angst sighed and his shoulders dropped.

"Oh no," Hector said.

14

Back at the camp, Angst had stripped to nothing but a blanket, shivering violently before the fire. Even his bones were cold. And the sand! Every time he shifted, another layer spilled off. There was so much of the stuff, he was convinced the sand had actually mated in the folds of his skin.

Victoria placed a hand on Angst's flushed cheek and gasped, pulling it back as if he were tainted with every disease. "A mermaid?" Tori's eyes widened, and she crossed her arms. "I thought they were just stories."

"They are," Dallow said, scratching beneath his kerchief. "Or were."

"Nope," Angst said, trying not to look at the ocean, or Victoria. "She was definitely real."

"Really? A mermaid," Tori said in disgust, hugging herself tighter while tugging on a long strand of hair. "Aren't they dangerous?"

"Yes, if the stories are true. Very." Hector's bushy eyebrows furrowed as he studied Angst. "Are you certain all your parts are still there?"

"Yes," he said sardonically. He turned to Tori and, as heroically as he could, tried to sell the situation. "She needed help."

"Right," Tori said, dripping skepticism. "A creature that isn't supposed to exist, and is known for eating men, needed help."

"She was trapped. What was I supposed to do?" Angst said in

106

frustration.

"What did she look like?" Dallow asked, far more excited than the others. "Did she have gills?"

"Yeah!" Angst said with a broad grin, his focus completely on Dallow. "She was gorgeous. Full figure, firm breasts, blue and silver scales, with large dark eyes, and a fin along her spine."

"That's amazing!" Dallow leaned forward, his eye sockets glowing. "Like the pictures in my books. If it's all true, you need to be careful. They really do eat men."

"I didn't get that impression." Angst looked off. "She was actually affectionate."

"What?" Victoria placed her hand on his before he could stop her. "You kissed her?"

"Another one?" Tarness grunted. He was drawing in the sand with a burned stick.

Hector shook his head as he sat down beside Dallow, handing him a stick with cooked meat something on the end.

"She kissed me." Angst realized he'd been staring at the ocean again, and looked at the fire with a sigh.

"I've heard that one before," Victoria said with a *hmph*, releasing his hand. She tugged on her hair. "What is it with you?"

"Exactly!" Hector agreed.

"Do you have to make friends with everything that has boobs?" she asked.

"Well...yeah!" Angst said, trying to be funny.

"I don't believe you kissed an ugly fish!" She cringed.

"She's not a fish! And she kissed me..." He felt baited. "Is that what this is really about? That I kissed another girl?"

"The issue isn't that you let another girl...thing kiss you." Victoria huffed.

"No?" He huddled into a shivering ball; the fire wasn't warm enough to battle the frost coming from Victoria.

"The issue is you don't have a pair! You run from your destiny, not to it. You keep getting lost in the moment, because now is easier than what you may have to become later." She was pounding on his chest, her fists thumping loudly. "You're willing to sacrifice everything for those you love, and even those you don't, but maybe it's time for less sacrifice and more doing. It's time for you to become who you were meant to be and stop running away from your potential like a little boy."

"Wow," Dallow said.

"Wow," Tarness agreed.

"Exactly why she's going to be a great queen," Hector said proudly.

"Wait, so was she ugly?" Victoria asked.

Hector sighed heavily, shaking his head.

"Do you really want to know?" Angst held out his hand to Tori.

"Of course she wasn't," Tarness said, throwing his stick into the fire. "It's Angst."

"The question is, what does she want?" Hector sounded worried.

"She said something about saving her." Angst shrugged. "I don't know what from."

"We should get some sleep," Hector urged. "We have a day's ride ahead."

"I'm going to set up my tent!" Victoria stomped off.

Which was when Angst noticed there were only four tents.

* * * *

Despite Angst's desire to race toward their destination, they rode snail's-pace slow. He could feel time wasted with every step, as if the sand underfoot were an hourglass holding them back. But Hector advised, and Tori agreed, that they should approach with caution.

"We aren't exactly invited guests," Hector reminded him every time Angst whined about their pace.

Angst spent the day trying to sneak looks at the ocean without getting caught by Tori. By mid-afternoon, he'd counted twelve icy glares and one turned-up nose. It was like a game, and he was pretty sure he was losing. Especially since he saw nothing but gray and waves—his new friend was apparently keeping her distance.

"We should walk the rest of the way," Hector said, dismounting his panther swifen molded from dark sand. "They're wary of magic being used openly. It's very 'don't ask, don't tell.'"

Angst patted his ram, which snorted loudly before disappearing. His gear dropped to the ground. He watched the others detach their equipment before dismissing their swifen.

"I always forget to do it like that," Tarness remarked with a smirk, his dark mood from the other night mostly abated.

Angst hefted his tote on his back, pushing Dulgirgraut to the side so they wouldn't bump. He took several steps to grab Victoria's bag.

"I can carry my own," she snapped.

"I know." He smiled, throwing her bag over his other shoulder, trying not to look like an overburdened mule with both bags and Dulgirgraut all leashed to his back. "Stop being angry at me."

"No," she said curtly. The ends of the hair nearest her mouth were frayed and disheveled from fidgeting.

"How do you know this place?" Tarness asked Hector, effortlessly schlepping three full bags of supplies and gear on one broad shoulder.

"I spent several years helping negotiate the import and export of anything black market," Hector said. "Mostly goods, some people."

Tarness nodded at this. Dallow gaped in surprise.

"Negotiate? You make it sound official." Victoria *tsk*ed. "How did you not get arrested?"

"Well, your mom was probably the biggest importer of contraband in Unsel," Hector said lightly.

"What?" Victoria screeched in an Isabelle-like squawk.

"It's good for the economy, and safer when the crown is in control." Hector placed both hands on his hips. "It's something I always admired about the queen. She knew it was going to happen anyway and took the lead. She minimized crime, cornered some of the markets, and was able to put an invisible tax on illegal goods. When it's time, I'll tell you how she did it."

Victoria's eyes went saucer-wide and her face blanched. It must've been bad enough talking about her mother in the past tense, but to find out that she was hip deep in something illegal?

Tori reeled, and Angst gripped her arm. "Too much," he warned Hector.

Hector lifted both hands in surrender, rolling his eyes.

"Look, we all handle grief in our own way." Angst stared his old friend.

He looked at Tori, who seemed on the verge of breaking. Tears streamed down her cheeks as she attempted to keep her composure. Angst stared at Hector, dropping the bags he held.

"I'll get them," Tarness offered.

"Thanks, Tarness," Angst said. "I'll meet you guys there."

"No." Victoria picked up her bag before Tarness could. "Your friend is an ass," she said to Angst, sniffing loudly.

"Often," Angst agreed.

"Just being honest," Hector said defensively.

"Wrap that present in some tact next time," she said sharply. "It'll be easier to accept."

Hector ignored her and made eye contact with Angst, nodding once before taking the lead. Angst and Tori stayed behind as their friends walked away. She set her pack down and grabbed a kerchief to blow her nose. She wiped her eyes and sniffed deeply in the most un-princess-like fashion. He picked up her bag and waited.

"How long does this take?" she asked in frustration.

"What's that?" Angst asked.

"Grieving." Her wide eyes and puffy cheeks made her seem lost and worried.

"Oh, I'm sure it takes many," he said.

"Many what?" she asked.

"Many days and many casks of ale and port." He smiled.

"Ale and port sound really, really good," she agreed, retrieving her satchel. "Ale and mead and port and a bath and a warm bed."

"That sounds perfect," Angst said. "You still look worried. Is there something else?"

She took a deep breath. "I'm afraid something's going to happen, something terrible."

Her hand shook, and he held it with both of his. "What do you think it is?"

"I saw something, once. One of the paths..." She stopped, her expression instantly changing to one of wonder. She pulled her hand back and patted his arm. "Look!"

Far ahead, far beyond their friends, the ground sparkled as if someone had taken a cup full of starlight and tipped it over the beach. He couldn't understand where the stars had come from since it was still dusk. Angst and Victoria looked at each other and smiled. Hand in hand, they rushed toward the others.

"Dallow, what is it?" Victoria called out.

"I believe it's a geode," Dallow answered. "A geode massive enough to hold a city."

"From here it looks like stars!" Victoria said excitedly.

"There's a pirate city in those stars," Hector said with a knowing smile. "A pretty good hiding place, especially at night."

"Pirates?" Victoria said.

Angst couldn't tell if it was a question or comment. They caught up with their friends. Hector held up a warning hand, and Tarness set down his three satchels.

"Yes, pirates," said an angry voice.

Two men and one woman stood in the shadows, barely seen except for the glint from their weapons.

The woman who'd spoken pointed her cutlass at them. "Put your weapons down."

15

Unsel

"She said to gather a team of magic-wielders who could become soldiers!" Rook stormed along a path between tables and a wall at The Wizard's Revenge. "You were there!"

Janda nodded stiffly, red curls bobbing along her pale cheeks. She held up two fingers to signal to Graloon that they would need more ale. "It doesn't make any sense," she said. "She either lied to us, or something changed."

Rook ignored the heads turning to follow him as though they were watching a joust. He walked past the angry and worried faces of patrons who remained silent; no words were really needed. They'd been through this before, while he'd just taken freedom for granted. Still, they listened, clinging to his words, hoping to grasp something positive from his rant.

"It was a blatant lie right to my face," he said, jerking a thumb toward himself. Blood rushed to his head, pounding with every angry word, as if he'd just finished a battle. "How do you go from, 'Let's put together an army of wielders' to 'Magic is illegal' in a matter of days?"

"I don't know, Butter." She shook her head. "But I'm sure we can figure this out."

Rook grabbed a mug of ale out of the air, ignoring the second that floated by to land gently before Janda. She sipped foam off the top while Rook gulped his down. When finished, he let go of the mug and watched in surprise as it fell to the floor. It shattered, small bits of glass skidding under tables. He grunted as he knelt to pick up the pieces.

"No worries, son," said Graloon in his gruff voice. He patted the soldier comfortingly.

"I'm sorry, Graloon. I thought that, you know, that thing that happens with the mugs," Rook twirled a finger in the air, "would carry it back."

"Some magic happens on its own, but most requires effort and concentration, like anything else in life." Graloon said, his sagging cheeks lifting with a friendly smile. "This isn't the first mug broken in my bar, and it better not be the last."

The glassy remains of the mug gathered together in a pile and floated to a nearby bin, handily dropping into it. A fresh mug of frothy mead hovered before Rook, and he accepted it delicately.

"Thanks," Rook said with a tight smile. It was such an efficient way of doing things, but, in spite of his time spent with wielders, it still made him skittish.

"So, just how illegal is magic now?" Graloon asked, tightening the greasy old apron that covered most of his vast belly.

"This ale landing in my hand is enough to see us both in irons. So...very." Rook grunted. "I'm not sure how they'll enforce it. It's like five men trying to catch a giant lochabar shark with a net. There may be more men, but the shark has more power, and now it has lunch."

"Except these folks aren't trained soldiers," Graloon said, nodding at the onlookers.

"They defended Unsel against those steel-beaked birds," Rook said defensively, and several nodded in agreement.

"They did, but it was still Angst who took them out," Graloon said. "Their magic has been partly illegal for so long, only a few feel ready to fight."

"But I thought they wanted to defend Unsel," Rook said in frustration.

Janda daintily took the empty mug from his hand before it

ended up in pieces on the floor. Graloon nodded to her appreciatively.

"Of course they do... Well, they did, for Unsel, and maybe Queen Isabelle—she seemed to be coming around." Graloon shook his head. "But not for this new queen."

"Then for who?" Janda asked.

"She's not queen yet," Rook interrupted Janda.

"What?" Graloon asked, looking as if he'd been smacked.

"Alloria's not the queen. She may be leader, even second in line, but she isn't queen," Rook said. "Princess Victoria is still in line to be queen of Unsel."

The people at nearby tables nodded, and Graloon smiled then slapped the table as if Rook had announced a battle won. "Then there's hope."

"How do you figure?" Rook asked.

"Victoria and Angst are close, and it doesn't seem to bother her at all that he can wield." Graloon patted Rook on the shoulder roughly. "There's hope."

"If she makes it back. Those holes are only weeks away, and they're already planning the queen's funeral," Rook said worriedly.

"Don't borrow trouble," Graloon said dismissively. "Angst seems to have a way of—"

There was a noisy pounding at the entrance. Graloon took a step forward, but Rook held his shoulder as the pounding became a steady boom, growing louder by the second.

"Everyone down!" Rook stepped in front of Janda and hovered over her, his armored back facing the door.

It smashed inward, landing hard with a crash. Chips of wood flew toward them but stopped in mid-air before striking anyone and fell to the ground. Eight soldiers with swords at the ready rushed around a battering ram to spread out along the back wall. Vars entered the room with a look of disgust on his face. He rolled open a scroll and cleared his throat.

"By order of her Royal Majesty, Queen Alloria, The Wizard's Revenge is to be shut down immediately," Vars said. He glared at Rook. "Patrons are to leave, and Graloon is under arrest for the support and wielding of magics."

"What is this?" Graloon blurted out. "What right do you have, does she have, to order this? Look around, there's no magic here!"

Vars studied the room calmly to see that no hands were glowing, nothing floated in the air, and the bar appeared clean of magics. His thin lips pinched into a smile and his eyes slitted. "Bring in the rest."

The door-ram had been pulled back and twenty more soldiers shuffled into the room. Graloon closed his eyes in defeat as The Wizard's Revenge expanded to accommodate the sudden rush of people.

"Arrest him, and anyone else who works here." Vars pointed. "Kill anyone who fights back."

Rook stormed to Vars and stood nose-to-nose, his fists clenched. Nearby soldiers looked at each other and shrugged, unsure what to do with their comrade.

"You're making a mistake, Vars!" Rook shouted. "We need these people to defend against what's coming!"

"These are the queen's orders!" Vars roared. "You need to stand down!"

"She's not the queen," Rook said. "My queen is Victoria!"

Vars took a step back, swinging fast and wide, his heavily gauntleted fist rushing toward Rook's face.

* * * *

Azaktrha

Rose felt like she'd been hiding for days, or was it nights? Time seemed mashed together in this dark city that received only the barest tease of daylight. It was almost enough to give her hope. During those brief moments of light, she'd glimpsed the enormity of the city. She was surrounded by varying sizes of rectangular pyramids with steep staircases, archways taller than ancient graymaul trees, and expansive walkways made for heavy traffic. The layout almost reminded her of Gressmore Ruins, but that didn't make sense. Those ruins were just half-buried marble pillars and broken buildings. This place was alive with its glowing shell-covered walls and smelly fish-men. But still, something about both cities nagged at her thoughts.

Something tugged at her sleeve, and she rolled her eyes. "What do you want, creeper?" she said sharply, warning him with a finger before he could reply. "Don't you dare talk in my mind!"

Creeper shook his head and pointed around the corner. She banged the back of her head against the building in frustration before braving a peek. Twenty or more fish-men approached cautiously, spread out like a gang. Rose and her companion had found safety in alleys and side streets. Hideaways where they could catch their breath or take the briefest of naps. A good hiding place didn't last long, the fish-men were always on the hunt. She could've kicked herself for leaving that pile of weapons in the middle of the road after her dinner. It was only a matter of time before they would have to defend themselves, or she would have to feast.

"Your friends are relentless!" she hissed. "I'm not sure I could absorb that many, and I don't want to leave a trail. We need to keep moving!"

Rose rushed down the alley as quietly as she could. Creeper was pulling at her arm with his long, moist fingers, encouraging her to go back toward the main road.

Rose jerked her arm out of his hand. "Quit touching me!" she barely whispered. "We're not going that way, we'd run right into them! Don't be stupid!"

Her mouth felt dry and her panting grew loud as she ran faster. Was there nowhere to hide? The little beast kept tugging at her arm. Rose was half-tempted to absorb enough of Creeper's life to make him fall asleep, again. It was so dark, and he was so distracting, that she almost ran into the dead-end.

"Dark Vivek curse this place!" Rose said aloud. "Why didn't you say something?"

It was hard to tell, but she was sure he was frowning. She didn't wait to figure it out and ran back toward the street. There were no doors or side alleys, forcing them to brave the open. The horde of fish-men were only fifty yards away. Creeper hopped up and down as she contemplated how hungry she was. Not hungry enough.

"Run!" she cried, leaping into the street and running away from the creatures.

There was no battle cry or screams of "Get her!" which would've encouraged her to run faster. Instead, she was chased by a gaggle of creepy mutes who wanted to eat her hands. The only sound coming from behind her was the slapping of webbed feet and clinking of weapons as the fish-men tried to gallop on all fours with full hands. She hated running, and already felt her lungs burning.

"I'm getting hungry," she grunted between gulps of air.

Creeper covered his head protectively as he ran beside her, trying his best to keep up on two legs. They ran, and ran, and sweat beaded her brow. The smelly air was heavy, crushing, as they rushed into shadows. All she could see was darkness ahead. Her heart raced as black lightning bit and caressed her arms.

"Wait," Creeper said in her mind. *"Stop!"*

"I said to stay out of my head!" she roared as she smashed into a solid something.

Chryslaenor thunked loudly, and Rose screamed in pain as she careened off an invisible wall, falling back and tripping over the great blade. She dropped the foci and rolled to her back. Once again, everything hurt. She had to get up; they were coming. She pushed herself over and winced, her wrist either broken or sprained, and she couldn't open one of her eyes. Orange blood dripped freely from her nose.

"I'm really ready to go home." She struggled to her hands and knees.

The rattle of weapons and slapping of feet had stopped, the chase apparently over. She took a deep breath, drawing in energy for the coming battle. Rose looked up to see twenty of the fish-men pointing at her and Creeper. That wasn't good. She looked to her left and saw even more fish-men.

"I hate all of you," she said, spitting orange blood. All heads turned to her right. She followed their gazes, and her eyebrows rose. "Really?"

He was tall, and muscular, and mostly naked, his dark skin glistening in the dim light. He had tight, curly hair, and a strong, heroic jaw. Rose felt hers drop as the most beautiful man she'd ever seen twirled a bladed staff with daggers at both end. He stared into her eyes and grimaced. His gaze flitted from her to the fish-men waiting to attack. He leaped toward her, his staff ready to strike.

"This is a good way to die," she mused, mesmerized.

16

Fulk'han

It was the worst insult Guldrich could imagine: being led from the war room by two gray men as if he were a thief. And only two men? Both would've made easy additions to the kill marks on his arms, but they marched beside him with hands on their hilts as if fast enough to wield before he dispatched them. He would not, of course. It made no sense to kill them now. Where would he run to? His job was to fulfill Takarn-Ivan's last wishes—to expand the Fulk'han Empire—and he had failed.

The fools wanted to throw more bodies at Unsel, as if this were a normal war. Unsel had prepared and was more dangerous than the emperor imagined. They not only had an army, but a militia of wielders, and a champion. The Fulk'han army was formidable, especially now, but there were no wielders that he knew of. Their only hope was to find a champion powerful enough to be worthy of Takarn-Ivan.

When they reached the remains of the Takarn, both men knelt. Guldrich sighed and lowered his head briefly, hoping his irreverence would go unnoticed. Something tickled his calf, and he turned his head to see the purple woman from the war room. She winked as her tail crept up his leg to his back. He shuddered, unable to ignore her untimely attentions. She wrapped herself around him and bit his ear even as his envoy stood and watched in confusion.

"Now is not the time, mistress," one of the soldiers said, obviously uncomfortable with her display of affection.

His heart beat with desire, but a soldier's caution made him wary. He turned to face his captors. "In respect to my service, give me this one moment," he said in a low voice.

The soldiers looked at each other. One shrugged, the other nodded, and they turned away to face the enormous glowing tree husk. The purple woman purred lustfully and kissed him full on the mouth. He was drawn in by her passion and energy, by the feel of her body undulating against his. As if she were climbing up a cliff, she pushed herself up on his broad shoulders. She lifted her fist and threw a black ball toward the two men. It bounced off the ground before hovering in the air before them. Colors swirled into a whirling mass that sucked in all light, turning until they became a tall, dark oval that hung vertically in the air.

"What?" a soldier stuttered. "What is this?"

The woman launched off Guldrich's shoulders. She landed on one, kicking his back and driving him into the oval. His screams cut off as he was lost to the darkness. The second guard lifted his sword high when she landed on all fours before him like a panther. She pounced, grabbing his forearms and flipping over his head, tossing him into the darkness.

Quiet. Stunning quiet was all that remained after the brief tussle. Guldrich stared in shock, jumping with a start when the oval crackled as though it were a bonfire. Was he free or would he be next? He locked his legs in place when she stood and faced him. She approached slowly, seductively, drawing him in with every movement.

"You are free," she said, circling him, her tail finding its way everywhere.

"To what end?" Guldrich turned enough to keep her in sight, not trusting the purple woman behind him.

"Good question." She smiled. "To flee? To retreat?"

"No," he grunted, his hand clenching into a fist.

Her tail ran along his forearm until it relaxed.

"You were in there. You saw." He breathed deeply to keep his anger at a simmer. "The idiots want to go to war without wielders or a champion. Instead, they would kill me and destroy the empire that could be. Better had the Vex'kvette left us farmers."

"Then do something about it." She gripped his boney chest armor and pulled him close, his back now to the dark portal.

"Who are you?" he whispered. "What do you want of me?"

She looked up into his eyes as she inched forward. He stepped back. "I am Felicia, and you are right," she said. "Without a champion, we are nothing."

"And where do we find one of those?" he asked.

She nodded over his shoulder at the portal, mere inches away.

"The champion is in there?" he asked.

"He's certainly not here," she said slyly. "You have a choice, Guldrich. Stay and be killed. Run in fear and see Fulk'han defeated. Or…" She nodded toward the portal once again.

She was not like any other Fulk'han woman he had met, and seemed much more than any woman he had bedded. Quick, strong, and wise. He felt drawn to her and was hungry for more.

"I'll find you a champion," he stated. "I'll find a champion for Takarn-Ivan and for Fulk'han."

Her full lips broadened to a smile that became a kiss. She pulled away and took his hand, placing a ruby ring on his finger. He looked down at it quizzically, but quickly forgot it as she pressed her mouth to his.

"Come back with my champion," she demanded, "or die trying."

He did, indeed, like this one, and couldn't help the smile that spread across his thin gray lips. Guldrich leaned in for one last kiss, barely managing a peck before she pushed him into the darkness.

* * * *

Nordruaut

Feemi lay on the cushioned pallet, covered in warm furs, waiting for yet another lonely night to pass. She had promised herself to Niihlu, leaving Jarle and traveling East. Niihlu had offered her the world, but when he won the right to be the Nordruaut champion, he was rewarded with a curse that affected them both. The foci, Ghorfjend, coated his body with ice that fell from his arms with every movement. Since wielding the war axe, Niihlu would barely speak to her, and she wondered if the ice had penetrated his heart. He now had power, and fame, but she was left with an empty pallet.

"I swear I will bed you soon," he had said, his long face filled with worry, and frost coating every word like a cloud. "I just...I just need to understand this first."

That bedding had never happened. He ignored her, and it was slow to sink in that she'd made a mistake. She had wanted so much, and been left with nothing but rumors. Terrible rumors of his cheating, and deaths. Maybe Jarle had been right about being covetous, that her life should be about the hunt and not about wanting something she didn't need. Now that Jarle was here, would the old man take her back?

Drapes to her entryway flew aside as someone entered the room. He was grunting heavily and looked around as though lost. He appeared short through her sleepy eyes.

"Niihlu?" she asked, sitting up and holding the fur bedding over her naked chest. "Have you finally come for me?"

"What?" The man's head jerked about to focus on her voice. He took a step forward, and his foot clunked loudly against the pallet.

"Are you drunk?" She reached to a bedside table, uncapping the jar of sun beetles.

A dim light filled the room. She turned to face Niihlu with a broad smile.

"Did you summon me here, wielder?" the man demanded.

He was dark gray with leathery protrusions that looked like

turtle shell. His eyes were silver slits behind a diamond-shaped helm carved from bone. Similar bones jutted from his sides, enveloping his chest like armor. The creature was horrific, and she looked around the room for a weapon to kill him.

"In here!" he whispered.

A second gray man rushed into the room. He appeared identical to the first in every way. She spied her longbow and dagger directly behind the intruders and hopped up to a crouch, throwing the blankets aside. The two gray men gawked at her nudity, one nudging the other with an elbow.

Men are the same in any package.

Would she even require her dagger to kill the smaller man?

A third gray man, larger than the others, pushed past the curtain. This one wasn't wearing a helmet, carried no weapon, and his arm was covered in orderly scars and fresh cuts.

"Guldrich!" one of the smaller gray men called out.

"Later," the large one snapped. "We've been tricked! Now we have to kill our way out!"

They all stared at her hungrily.

"Niihlu!" Feemi yelled.

17

Angst dropped his bag and wielded Dulgirgraut. The pirates stepped back, mouths agape as he hefted the enormous red glowing blade high into the air. With a dramatic grunt, he drove the foci two feet into the beach, making the ground shake in the process. He walked around it with a mischievous grin.

"Now what?" he asked.

"Uh..." The woman faced the others. "Why are his eyes glowing?"

The three pirates weren't dressed for a formal. Their leader was a short, dark-skinned woman so thin her cinched tan pantaloons would've fallen off with a wrong wiggle. She wore a cropped leather jacket that would barely keep someone warm in the spring. Her hair was a grandiose unkempt black mass that appeared more dangerous than her chipped scimitar. The second woman, who had yet to speak, was mousy, as if underfed, or overworked, or both. She shivered beneath layers of patched linen reeking of sweaty socks. Most of her light-brown hair was forced under a greasy kerchief. Everything about their companion was oily, from his hair to his trousers. His dark eyes flitted between the giant sword, drinking in Victoria, and finding a quick escape. He was the first to notice their predicament.

"I'm stuck," he exclaimed, his voice filled with panic.

"I am, too," said the dark-skinned woman. She bent her knees, rocking from side to side, attempting to wiggle out of the trap.

Victoria turned her back to their assailants and placed her hands on her hips, frowning at Angst. Her red cape and blond hair spun about dramatically. "You didn't know they were coming?" she asked in surprise. "Again?"

"Actually, he did know," Hector said in Angst's defense. "That's the reason you both hung back, and the rest of us went ahead."

"One of the reasons." Angst winked at her. "The gamlin warned me...and they didn't eat anyone!"

Three gamlin popped out of the ground to surround the pirates, pawing at the beach and licking their lips hungrily. The pirate leader poked at a gamlin with her sword. It looked back at Angst with a discernible frown, rubbing its little hands together anxiously.

"No," Angst said warningly.

The gamlin grabbed the sword from her hand and dove into the sand, dragging it with him. When he popped back up seconds later, it was gone.

"We really didn't need the gamlin to know the pirates were coming," Hector said. "You'd think with all this water nearby, they wouldn't smell so ripe."

"We can hear you," the woman called out, her lips tight and eyes wild.

"Ugh, I can smell them too." Victoria crinkled her nose in disgust. "Are all pirates stinky?"

"How can we get a full night's sleep with that?" Dallow agreed, turning up his nose. "Maybe we don't have to stay in town."

"We can always stay in tents." Tarness grinned. "About a mile down the beach."

"We're standing right here!" the first pirate said in despair, now tugging futilely on her leg.

Angst smiled at the banter, hoping the pirates would get the impression that they were no threat. He didn't want to harm them if they decided to attack. So far, so good. The pirates were worried, their leader looked ready to pass out.

Victoria's eyes flitted from the pirates to the twinkling stars of the massive geode. Angst could only assume she was trying to figure out where to get one. He shook his head.

"It's so shiny!" she said in answer to his thoughts. "I really want one."

"It's too big," Tarness proclaimed.

"It's a giant rock," Dallow said with a wry smile. "There is no reason Angst couldn't carry it to Unsel."

Victoria squeed loud enough to make the pirates cover their ears. "Please?" She pulled on Angst's arm.

"Thanks," he said to Dallow.

"My pleasure," Dallow said, grinning ear to ear.

"Who are you people?" the dark-skinned woman asked.

Hector placed his hands behind his back and ambled over to them. "We're here to see Jarblech. Why don't you three lead the way?"

* * * *

The pirate town was a patchwork of wood buildings, a mix of single story shacks and unevenly-stacked dwellings several stories high. It was as if entire buildings had been stolen from neighboring towns and crammed into the geode as needed. Torches burned along their path, teasing with their warmth. Directly over the geode, Angst saw the masts of several ships that must've been stashed away in a cove behind the town. The pirates led them to an unmarked building, a spectacle of busy noise and bright lights.

"What's your name?" Angst asked their leader.

"Tamara," she said quietly. Her thin lips flashed a smile, but her eyes still burned hot.

"Tamara the pirate." He let the words flow off his tongue. "I like that. So, Tamara the pirate, why the hate?"

"You're either Melkier soldiers," she looked him up and down judgmentally, "or you led them here."

"Do I look like a soldier?" Angst smiled broadly. "Do I wear their black armor?"

"Not *their* black armor," she huffed. "But they can't be far behind. You don't exactly look like you could sneak away from them." She nodded, either at his belly or the big sword.

"I'm about as sneaky as that hair," Angst said, teasing a bit defensively.

"Angst," Victoria warned.

Tamara stopped and turned to face him, her nostrils flaring as if he'd insulted her greatest achievement.

"Don't worry, Tamara," he said darkly. "Melkier soldiers won't be bothering you for a long time."

She frowned as she looked them over. "Come on, sneaky," she said, leading them into the building.

The old bar tried to be seedy. The floors were aged but clean, only a little sticky from the ale spilled that night. The greasy bar food smelled good enough to make Tarness wipe his chin—it wasn't burnt like Angst would've expected from a bar run by pirates. Netting hung from rafters like birthday decorations, holding old starfish, mollusks, and a harpoon. Cracked tables were placed thoughtfully to maximize usage of the available space, each filled with wiry, muscular pirates playing cards. The bar defied itself, rough around the edges yet still polished and welcoming. And there was something else that drew Angst in, something he really liked about this place but couldn't put a finger on.

An old bard woman in the corner played a gentle jest with the ensemble of instruments that made up her kendagar. Victoria looked at Angst with eyes that wanted to get lost in dancing and tabletops. Angst winked at the prospect, hoping it would happen for every reason, right and wrong. Dallow tripped and caught himself on Hector's shoulder.

"It seems to only work outside." He frowned and jerked the memndus stone from his temple in frustration. "For now."

Hector merely nodded, scanning the room until his eyes locked onto five pirates engrossed in a card game at a corner table. A broad shouldered pirate with black, oily hair stood behind the head of the table with crossed arms. Several of the gamblers were listing, barely conscious, and with few remaining coins before them. The more-sober opponents glared warily at a sturdy woman with a wide chin. She had a big nose, a grimace that at one time could've been a smile, and a tall heap of coins. She laid her cards on the table. One pirate stood, spat on the floor, and stomped out of the bar. Another's head fell to the table with a loud thud either from losing or booze. As the winner gathered her winnings, her bodyguard tapped her shoulder and pointed at Hector.

The handsome woman's eyes went misty as she pushed up from the table. Shorter than Angst, and wide as Tarness, she had a round face and large dark eyes, but her years and weight rested heavily on her. A do-rag failed to restrain gray curls that fought for freedom. Angst couldn't see even a hint of beauty hidden behind weatherworn wrinkles and gray age other than maybe those eyes—black pools that rivaled Rose's. She walked straight to Hector and, without warning, struck him in the mouth.

Before Angst could reach for Dulgirgraut, Hector gripped the back of her neck as if he were picking up a kitten and mashed his lips to hers. Her mouth sucked his in, creating a vortex of discomfort in the room. Angst looked at Tori, who was focusing intently on the ground, blushing brightly. Dallow sighed deeply while Tarness stared on in frustration.

After a full meal of the painfully awkward moment, the two wrenched their lips apart. She raised a hand to strike him again, but Hector held her wrist roughly and smirked. "I deserved one," he warned.

"That's your opinion," she said in a scratchy voice, pulling her hand free and dragging him in for another kiss.

"You've got to be kidding me," Angst said, rolling his eyes.

"Now you know how we feel," Tarness chided.

"What?" Victoria asked, spinning to face him.

"We don't do that," Angst said defensively.

"Only because you're chicken," Tarness teased.

Angst and Tori frowned at him but were interrupted before either could reply.

"You're as beautiful as I remember." Hector sounded sincere.

"You've always been a bad liar," she said with a wary grin. "Interesting crew. You're here for reasons. You going to tell me some of them?"

"Let's sit," Hector suggested, pulling away from their embrace.

She nodded at the muscular pirate, who waved off the table. Almost all the players scrambled away, leaving a softly snoring woman behind. The tall pirate lifted the chair as if shaking crumbs out of a dishrag, and the body collapsed to the floor in a passed-out heap. The pirate brushed off the chair and smiled at Victoria. She daintily stepped over the fallen drunk and sat with a smile. Everyone followed suit.

Angst looked over his shoulder to check out the room. Few had taken notice of their entrance, even ignoring Dulgirgraut. He tried making eye contact or stealing a smile, but no one would glance in his direction. Something nagged at him, and it made him antsy, but couldn't help the smile on his face. Maybe it was the anticipation of a fun night? He gave up trying to figure it out and turned around to see his friends sitting quietly. A pretty redheaded barkeep, who was dressed very conservatively for a pirate bar, set a round of mead at their table.

Hector raised his mug for a toast with his old companion. "To more profitable times." After taking a long draw, he looked around the table.

"Angst, Tori, Dallow, and Tarness, this is Jarblech." Hector nodded at everyone in turn.

She studied each of them, her eyes drinking in Victoria, Angst, and Dulgirgraut until they'd had their fill.

"How long have you owned this place?" Hector asked.

"I took it over a year ago when the former owner went missing," she said.

"On purpose?" Hector's eyebrow raised.

"I can't say," she said warningly, placing both hands on the table.

"You have rooms?" he asked.

Jarblech waved the barkeep off and nodded once in confirmation. She dug a stubby finger under her do-rag and scratched for too long. Hector didn't seem to notice, but Victoria squinted and goose bumps speckled her arms.

"You're not here for rooms," she said, after apparently digging a hole in her skull.

"We need passage," Hector said.

"I didn't assume you were here for luvin'," she said gruffly.

"Don't assume." Hector winked.

"That's reason enough to take you in," she teased. "Almost."

"I—" Angst began.

Hector held out a hand to stop him from speaking.

"That's quite the spatula you've got there." She nodded at the sword over his shoulder. "And a lot of magics."

Hector peered at Angst as if it was his fault the sword wasn't hidden better. Angst rolled his eyes and shook his head.

"Not hard to figure out. Too heavy for most to heft, and he's a little guy," she continued, ignoring Angst's indignation. "I sense danger. Where are you bringing the princess?"

"How—?" Victoria questioned before Hector cut her off too.

"I've done business with your mother," she said. "A total bitch, and very shrewd."

Tori was now scratching her arms. Angst was surprised she hadn't drawn blood.

"Where to, love?" Jarblech asked Hector. "Waters aren't safe these days. For a hefty price, I can see you up the coast."

"Are you still good?" Hector asked.

"Nobody better," she boasted, picking something out of her front teeth with her tongue. "We *are* talking on the water, right?"

"Probably," Hector flirted.

Angst really hoped he didn't sound like this when he spoke to women. What could Hector possibly see in her?

"You haven't answered my question." She grunted. "Where?"

After a long pause, Hector finally said, "There's a place off the coast of Angoria. It's not on the map, but—"

"Nope!"

"Not so fast, it's not like—"

"Nope!"

"We've got money, if that's the prob—"

"Nope!"

"But there's—"

"Nope!"

It went on like this for minutes. Very long minutes.

"Everyone could die," Angst said, ignoring Hector's interrupting hand.

"Pardon?"

"Everyone on Ehrde could die," Angst said.

"That doesn't affect me," she said, crossing her arms.

"Really?" Angst asked. "You aren't a part of everyone?"

"How is it that everyone could die?" She eyed the sword. "That thing really is big. Why is it glowing?"

"It is?" Angst asked. In the back of his mind, he could almost, barely, hear a song. He looked at Victoria and smiled. "It does that, sometimes. Look, it's complicated. Do you really want to know?"

"No."

"Will you take us?"

"No."

"Why not?" Angst leaned forward. "Are you afraid?"

"Don't make me kill you." Jarblech reached to her side.

As Angst stood, he heard every pirate behind him come to their feet.

"That island, it's death," Jarblech warned. "You know who lives between here and there? She doesn't let anyone near that place."

"So you are afraid?" Angst prodded.

He could feel it coming and could've stopped it but knew where the dagger was headed. It landed with a thud at the edge of the table directly in front of Angst.

"I didn't ask if you were afraid of me," Angst snapped, urging the dagger to rise from the table and float to her. "Who is *she*?"

"The lady of the sea." Jarblech waved her hands wildly. "No one survives a trip to Angoria these days. She'll crush the life out of any boat that tries. It's not as easy as showing up with a giant magic sword and swinging it about."

"You won't take us?" Hector asked.

"My ship wouldn't be safe. It'd be destroyed like all others," she said. "I'm sorry but not even my baby could bring you, and I've got the biggest, fastest ship in the harbor."

"What ship is safe? How can we get there?"

"You'd need a boat made out of steel to get there and back, and there is no such thing," she spat. "Ain't enough luvin' for that trip."

Angst and Hector made eye contact before Hector continued. "So you'd take us with a metal ship?"

"Yeah, sure, whatever," she said dismissively. "You can all sit down now," she yelled to the pirates.

"I can't move," a woman called out from behind Angst.

"My legs are stuck," another woman said in a husky voice.

"That's why your bar makes me so happy!" Angst shouted. He spun about to look, grinning from ear to ear. "Your pirates are all women!"

18

Unsel

Maarja ignored the rude stares from people who scurried out from under her long gait. Every person was hunched over and bundled in heavy layers of winter clothing—as if this were an actual winter. They gawked openly at her height, exposed skin, or both, depending on whether eyes lingered or strayed. She wanted to swat them away like flies, but had to remember she was a guest in Unsel, and they weren't really flies.

Maarja and Jintorich stopped at an unkempt street that most seemed to avoid, even walking on the road in favor of the walkway. A horse and carriage made an arc, inching closer to the "safe" side as if circumventing a hole in the ground. The cursed street was a dark path of cold, broken cobblestone that curved out of view several blocks in. It was empty and quiet. They looked at each other, but Jintorich merely shrugged. She nodded, and they made their way past boarded shops and "Keep Out" signs.

"Are you certain this is the way?" Maarja asked. "This entire area of town looks abandoned."

"It's hard to get much from the castle staff, but it seems Angst has some friends," Jintorich said, huffing out clouds of air as his legs shuffled quickly to keep up. "They said he frequented a bar in this area."

"Let me ask next time," she said with a wicked smile. "For some reason I make them nervous."

"It was odd," he said in his high voice. "Some at the castle really did appear to want to help, but they seemed reluctant."

"Maybe they were under orders," she said.

"Probably." He didn't sound convinced.

As they went around another bend, Maarja felt the tiniest tug on her white fur boots. She slowed at Jintorich's beckoning, following him around the curved road. Dozens of Unsel soldiers stood in front of a stone building that seemed misplaced. Neat and tidy, it was squeezed tight between abandoned shops with broken windows and shoddy wooden doors. A sign overhead read "Wizard's Revenge." The entry was missing a door, which rested on its side against the jamb. They could hear shouting as soldiers lined up to enter, weapons ready for battle.

"Let me sneak ahead and scout..."

Maarja ignored Jintorich and took three lumbering steps toward the remaining line of soldiers. Every day spent in Unsel was more frustrating. Princess Alloria avoided them, Vars was rude and condescending, people seemed unwilling to help, and she had little patience for more waiting. Her people needed Angst, and she needed answers. The guards lifted swords and shields defensively at her approach, and stepped back as a group.

"What's going on here?" she said, placing her fists on her hips.

Her voice must've been louder than they were used to, because one soldier in the front dropped his sword. A tiny man—they were all tiny—stepped forward as threateningly as he could.

"Leave this place, monster," he commanded, the quaver in his voice almost under control. "This is Unsel business."

Before he had time to breathe, Maarja picked the fly up by his head and threw him down the street. The man screamed until he crashed into the second story of an old building and fell into a broken heap on the cobblestone. She grabbed another and grimaced at him as the rest scattered.

"This is a poor place to hunt," she scoffed before tossing him away. She knelt, forcing her head and shoulder through the bar entrance. The room expanded so quickly that soldiers inside jumped, several tripping over their own feet as they sought the retreating walls.

* * * *

Vars jerked his head about, interrupting his swing as Maarja entered through the doorway, the room growing to accommodate her size. Rook dodged the punch, slugging the older man in his armored stomach before wielding his sword.

"What are you doing here, Nordruaut?" Vars coughed, pushing away from Rook.

"We seek friends of Angst," she stated. "You've been little help."

"You were to wait for the queen!" Spittle flecked his chin with every word as he fought to remain upright.

"We're friends of Angst," Graloon said heartily.

She lowered her gaze, looking darkly at Vars, who swallowed hard and wiped his chin.

"I do not answer to your *princess*," she said in a quiet, dangerous voice. "And you will show me the respect due an ambassador, or I will leave for home and return with two more Nordruaut. More than enough to decimate an army of small men, such as yourself."

"This business is none of yours. Leave now," Vars commanded.

"This is not a place you want to be, Vars," Rook said, jerking his thumb toward the wielders. "You don't want to upset them."

Vars and Rook turned their heads to see fire covering Janda's hands, and her eyes burned a fierce red. The nearest guards shuffled nervously, holding up shields, sweat already dripping freely.

"Magics are illegal." Vars's shout was weak and his eyes wide with madness. "The queen—"

Men and women stood behind Janda, their faces stern and determined. Hands, arms, and eyes shone brightly—a rainbow of light behind her. Sounds of power filled the room, static electricity bit at the air, ocean waves sloshed, and fire crackled. Rook shivered at the raw power behind him, but couldn't control the winning smile that spread across his lips.

"As you can see," Graloon said gruffly, "she's not *our* queen."

Soldiers had already retreated to the Nordruaut, who wouldn't let any exit. She grabbed the nearest one and shoved him out, squeezing him between herself and the doorframe. A yelp was followed by several pops before he went silent. She reached for another, eyes filled with anticipation, but waited for Rook's signal.

Vars's eyes flashed angrily at the soldiers' retreat. Rook threw down his sword, grabbed Vars's breastplate with both hands, and shoved him against the wall. A look of hate and disdain covered Vars's face, followed quickly by bitter despair.

"You fool," Rook spat. "Don't you see? Unsel will be destroyed without them! Is that what you want?"

"You don't know what you're in or how deep it goes," Vars snarled. "Out! Everyone out!" he barked at the remaining soldiers.

Maarja made her way completely into the room, stretching to her full height. Graloon winced as the room grew larger still. Rook let go, and Vars brushed off his golden leaf-embroidered plate armor as though wiping off filth. He tried staring Rook down, but their eyes merely dueled.

"You just don't get it, do you?" Rook asked.

"This isn't over," Vars bit off every word as he backed toward the door.

"You keep saying that," Rook replied. "I'm ready when you are."

Vars backed out of the room, glaring at Rook with crazy eyes. Soldiers along the walls reluctantly followed, some angry, but most flashed the wielders apologetic looks or just stared at the ground guiltily. As the last few exited, they called out, "Hey," or, "What's this?" as Jintorich pushed against armored knees to make his way into the room. He shook his head in frustration, slamming his staff down hard. It flashed white and struck the wooden floor noisily. His beady eyes sought Maarja, who merely shrugged.

"Tall people," Jintorich scoffed in his squeaky voice.

"Me?" she asked, her eyebrows rising with his temper.

"Don't make me come up there," he said.

"Fine, I shouldn't have run ahead." She smirked, holding up both hands defensively.

Jintorich nodded curtly and hopped up onto a table beside her. Graloon approached them, wincing as he pushed against his temple with the palm of his hand. He looked up at Maarja, who remained standing in the now insanely tall Wizard's Revenge.

"Miss," he said politely, beckoning her toward the floor. "Would you mind having a seat? I feel like my head is going to split."

She sought Jintorich, who shrugged. She looked around, careful not to crush any chairs or people before sitting and crossing her legs. Graloon sighed with relief as the room immediately shrank.

"So much better," he said gratefully. "I'm Graloon. May I get you anything?"

"Ale." She nodded.

"Yes," Jintorich agreed. "If you please."

Rook and Janda approached, holding their hands up in greeting. He was still hot from confrontation, and took several deep, calming breaths.

"Maarja, Jintorich, thank you!" He smiled and shook hands with Jintorich as best he could—the Meldusian's hand was incredibly small, almost like a child's. He frowned when Maarja reluctantly shook his hand and felt like a child himself. "Your timing couldn't have been any better."

"I'm certain it's nothing they couldn't have taken care of." She nodded toward the other wielders in the room.

"Maybe," he replied. "But fortunately we didn't have to."

She nodded gruffly and said nothing more, staring at him as if waiting for something.

He turned to the Meldusian. "You're looking for Angst?" Rook asked.

"His friends, yes," Jintorich squeaked. "We both have need of his counsel. Do you know when he will return?"

"No. Hopefully soon," Rook said.

"What was all this?" Jintorich asked. "Why were you being arrested?"

"Because we wield magic," Janda said, looking over the other guests, who were just sitting. "Most of the people here do."

"Alloria has made magic entirely illegal, and apparently all wielders are now outlaws." Rook sighed. "I can't imagine I'm in any better standing."

Janda rubbed his shoulder consolingly.

"It makes no sense," he growled. "How can they make all wielders illegal, but still be waiting for Angst?"

"None of this makes sense," Graloon said as a trail of mugs floated behind him. "The important thing is, how are we going to keep everyone safe?"

A mug the size of Jintorich landed at his feet, and he smiled broadly. The same size mug, no larger than Maarja's thumb, floated to her hand. She frowned and drank it like a shot before eyeing Jintorich's ale. He got up and stood in front of the mug defensively, which made her laugh.

"Whelp." Graloon sat hard on a wooden bench and rubbed his back. "Now what?"

"We need to defend against the soldiers and the monsters," Rook said, smashing a fist on the table. "We need a militia."

Patrons nearby nodded or shook their heads.

"Do we have time for that? Or money?" Graloon asked. "That requires training, and armor—for wielders, I'd assume armor like Angst's."

"Butter." Janda placed a hand on his fist. "We need to get everyone out before we begin to worry about that. Vars could send his soldiers door to door. They could start arresting people tonight, or even worse, killing them."

"You're right," Rook agreed reluctantly. "Safety first then

war."

Maarja grinned wickedly at this, nodding at Jintorich in anticipation. Jintorich patted her leg and pointed to a large cask floating beside her. Her eyes lit up as she took it in hand and removed the cork, drinking deeply. Ale flowed down her chin, wetting her chest and soaking into her fur covering.

"We can go to Angst and Heather's," Janda suggested. "Everyone stays away from there because of Scar."

"Great idea!" Rook said, kissing her on the cheek.

"But what about the beast?" Graloon asked. "Isn't he out of control?"

"Maybe we can get the blacksmiths to make a giant collar?" Rook asked. "We'll figure something out."

"Still, that's a lot of people," Graloon said. "There must be fifty or so with all the families."

"Some of the wielders can make temporary huts," Janda said. "Others can hunt for food. Everyone can pitch in somehow."

"We need to do this quickly," Rook said, loud enough for everyone to hear. "Janda and I will give you directions, but you have to gather your families tonight. Spread the word. Tell the other wielders they have to leave."

"Wait," Janda said with a frown. "We need to tell Heather, and Jaden."

"They're at the castle," Rook said. "We can't warn them. Any of us would be killed on arrival."

"Angst won't be happy about leaving her behind," Graloon said.

"Why would this decision upset Angst?" Jintorich asked.

"Heather is Angst's wife," Rook explained. "He wouldn't want her in danger."

"We are still welcome at the castle," Maarja said, momentarily lowering her cask. "We can give her this message."

"It could be dangerous," Rook said. "I guarantee that Vars is reporting your interference."

Maarja stood to her full height again, making Graloon wince and squeak like Jintorich. She downed the remainder of her drink and wiped froth from her chin. "Good, I welcome this danger." She nodded, throwing the cask to the ground. It shattered like porcelain, leaving a heap of wood and iron bands. "Coming, my friend?"

"Good luck to you all." Jintorich waved at them. He hopped off the table and scrambled after her.

Maarja knelt to face Rook. "Good hunt," she said with a smile before squeezing out the doorway.

The room shakily returned to normal size, as if struggling to shrink. Sweat dripped from Graloon's brow, and he looked exhausted.

"You okay?" Rook asked.

"I feel like I just gave birth." He grunted. "Next time let's meet with her outside."

19

Azakthra

Rose gawked in awe at the man. He landed with the grace of a swan, barely touching the ground before launching back into the air. His twin-bladed staff spun about twice before reaching out as if an extension of his arm. He drove it deep into the heart of a surprised fish-man. Jerking it out as he turned, he then sliced the necks of two assailants at either side. He rolled toward her, the blades held out horizontally. She gawked at the dark man standing before her. She must've been dreaming. His barrel chest heaved with every breath, sweat dripping from his curly light-brown hair. The side of his mouth raised in a smirk at her expression. She wanted to caress his square jaw and lose herself in his dark eyes. Rose sighed, completely forgetting the silent horde of shocked creatures.

"Fight!" he commanded, leaping backward as if diving into the ocean, flipping over to land on his feet behind a fish-man he stabbed through the back.

"R-right," she stuttered, her breath catching.

Rose felt a tug at her torn sleeve. Creeper pointed at the invisible wall she'd slammed into. A splotch of her now-orange blood painted the wall—the stain looked remarkably like her face. Higher up, Chryslaenor had left behind a crack the length of her finger and almost too hard to see. She was relieved the beautiful

141

man hadn't seen her crash into it. Or at least hoped he hadn't.

"Not now, Creeper!" Rose snapped, spinning around. The gorgeous man had already killed eight of the little monsters. "I'm hungry!"

A gaggle of the fish-men were hopping toward her, shaking their old, banged up weapons. She lifted Chryslaenor overhead. Black lightning stung her thin, pale arms, crackling loudly as it arced toward her assailants, reaching out like fingers. As a group they skidded to a halt, those in front retreating while the ones behind tripped over them, creating a tangled heap of arms and legs. Creeper hid behind his forearms while the attackers levitated several feet over the ground, completely helpless.

She sucked in their life, ravenously eating her fill while healing her new injuries. Two brave, or foolish, little monsters leaped from her side only to be caught in the black lightning. Within seconds, dusty remains dropped into piles on the rough ground. They were delicious, all of them, and despite feeling satiated, she wanted more. Her hero was bleeding from his arms and face. He was covered in creatures like bees on honey, unable to leap to freedom.

Carefully, so carefully, she reached out with the lightning, plucking them off one at a time, cautious not to include him in her meal. It was tempting; she could feel his health, his life, and badly wanted to taste that, absorb it into herself. Her arms shook from fighting the temptation as his attackers became lifeless husks.

He tripped back to freedom. Now it was his turn to gawk in awe of her power. His eyes didn't mirror her passion, and disappointment made her stomach drop. His was the look of calculation, of surprise and consideration. He didn't smile at her, or drink her in with his gaze. The beautiful man merely stared on with wide eyes as if bewildered. Then he saw Creeper standing behind her and ran toward them with his staff pointed at her companion's face.

"Not him!" she said taking a hand off Chryslaenor and holding it out to stop the man. "He's with me."

His eyes narrowed, but he stopped. Creeper clung onto her leg as if that would protect him. She wielded the foci once again, pointing it at the beasts surrounding them. They halted, looking down at the piles of their dead comrades and backing away from the giant blade of death.

"I think they're going to retreat," Rose said, hoping he understood.

The man ignored her, once again diving into the fray, grunting as he swung the staff in a wide arc. A fish-man's arm dropped to the ground, followed by the leg of another, then a hand, and a body, before he finally buried his blade in a head. The attackers were frightened now, and their actions became frantic, desperate.

"Stop! They're done!" she pleaded. "I can't absorb any more!"

He kept fighting as they clawed and bit at his body. She forced the lightning out, hefting those attacking him into the air and absorbing just enough to kill them. The rest of the monsters ran, scattering like marbles. She dropped Chryslaenor and fell to her knees. She'd taken in too much, and felt like vomiting. The residual power was so sickeningly sweet, as if she'd bathed in molasses, and she just wanted to lie down and hold herself.

He lay there, moaning in pain, dark blood pooling around him. Rose crawled to her hero and placed a hand on his arm. He tried jerking it away, his eyes wide with fear, but he was too injured. Before healing him, she planted a kiss on his lips. It was barely returned, as if she were a relative, but that was enough. She expunged the darkness, healing him to his original, beautiful self.

"Thank you," he said, abruptly standing and picking up his staff.

She waited for his hand to help her up, but it never came. Maybe he hadn't liked the kiss? She was more nervous now than before the attack.

"Thank *you*," she said with a swoon in her voice that made her blush. "Who are you?"

He was a head taller than her, which she loved. He looked down with an unnatural, reserved smile on his face. Maybe he was just from somewhere else. Maybe she'd just misinterpreted their ways.

"I am ANduaut," he said in his tenor voice. "And you are?"

"Hi," she said, taking his hand and shaking it. "I'm Rose."

She felt a tug at her sleeve once more. She sighed. "Oh, and this is Creeper."

ANduaut nodded dismissively. "What is this place?"

"I was hoping you could tell me," she said.

"I really don't know," he said. "I don't understand how I got here, but I hate it. It's cold and smells of dead fish."

"Probably my fault. I've killed a few of them," she joked.

"As have I." He sneered. Or was it a smile? He was so hard to read.

"Do you know how we can get out?" she asked, crossing her arms.

"No, but maybe we can explore and find an escape."

"Together?" She smiled, her heart racing.

"Of course," he said flatly.

* * * *

Nordruaut

The gray men were much larger and more powerful than humans, two of them easily eight feet tall, the biggest almost nine. They glared at Jarle, their beady eyes flickering behind broken masks coated in dark blood. The creatures had been forced to their bone-covered knees, where they waited for death or escape.

He inspected their armor: thick protrusions that gripped their skin like skeletal fingers. It appeared to grow out of their ribs and legs. A rough, turtle-shell-skin protected their backs and arms. It was as if the Fulk'han had been bred for combat. And in spite of their stoic demeanor, there was a sense of unflinching pride in the arch of their spines, their squared shoulders, their thrust-forward chins.

The invaders had fought fiercely, and wide cracks splintered their armor. Bodies littered the corridor; two Nordruaut men had already been gutted by the time they'd arrived. Niihlu had shoved Jarle aside, splaying the first gray man open with his foci. His opponent had split in half, freezing solid before either side struck the ground. Jarle stared on in awe and fear as the two remaining grays backed into Feemi's room. Niihlu tore down the wall with one swing as Rasaol arrived, shouting that he wanted prisoners.

Feemi. Jarle shook his head sadly. It had been long minutes since Niihlu had entered her room. Jarle took a step forward, and Rasaol placed a hand on his shoulder.

"I wouldn't," Rasaol warned. "Leave him be."

"She was one of mine," Jarle said grimly.

He stepped over rubble, entering through the widened doorway. The room was cold, as if he were outside and without furs. Niihlu sat on his knees, holding Feemi's hand against his chest. The great axe leaned against the wall at an angle so it fit in the room. Frost covered his body, and ice dripped from his elbows, shattering as it landed on the floor. Niihlu's pale face and gray eyes were contorted by pain and guilt.

"What have they done to you?" Jarle whispered.

Niihlu hunched over Feemi's body, unmoving.

"This was not your fault, Niihlu," Jarle said. He wanted to place a hand on the younger man's head, but thought better of it.

"Yes, yes, it was," Niihlu choked out the words.

His young ward sat back, exposing the dead Nordruaut woman. The hand he held and the attached arm were frozen solid. Wounds on her neck and chest protruded grotesquely—red meat covered by patches of white ice. It was as if Niihlu had tried bandaging her with chunks of iceberg.

"How... What happened, son?" Jarle asked.

"These things, these weapons can heal. It told me so," the distraught man explained. He squeezed her hand desperately, and bits of frozen finger dropped to the floor. "She was alive. I tried, truly tried to listen to Ghorfjend. The weapon failed me, failed her. Her wounds froze shut... She died so fast. I am cursed."

"Those wounds, Niihlu," Jarle said softly. "They were too much, even for magic. Even for that." He pointed to the foci.

"Perhaps." Niihlu nodded. His head remained bowed for long moments before he spoke. "Thank you for being here. You were always good to me, Jarle. To us."

"I tried," he said.

"I loved her."

"Then let's go find out why they killed her." Jarle's anger came out in a barely-contained growl.

Niihlu's distraught eyes became dangerous as he stood and slowly walked to the giant axe, hefting it like a stick. Jarle followed him to the corridor, and both gray men turned at their approach.

"Let me go, animal," the scarred gray snapped. "I will not be held prisoner by your likes."

"Why did you kill her?" Jarle asked.

"She was there," the smaller gray spat. "That's reason enough."

Niihlu touched the man's armor with the tip of Ghorfjend. The gray man screamed as ice covered his chest, reaching out to his arms and legs until he was silent.

Niihlu faced the larger of the three Fulk'han. "Who are you?"

"I am Guldrich of Fulk'han," the man said proudly.

"How did you get in here?" Niihlu asked, frosty air leaving his lips with every word.

"I don't know," the gray said, staring at his companion.

Niihlu touched the dead gray man with his axe and gave a tiny push. The corpse crumbled to shards that he kicked down the corridor.

"I told you," the gray man said defensively. "I don't know how we arrived, but she attacked us!"

Rasaol backhanded the gray man with enough strength that chips of bone flew. The gray did not fall, but held his ground, looking squarely into Rasaol's eyes. Dark blood dripped from his chin, framing the man's teeth as he smiled.

"Do you see, Jarle?" the king asked. "How powerful they've become?"

"Everything I've seen here is far more dangerous than I anticipated." Jarle frowned, fighting a shiver of concern. Nordruaut did not shiver.

Ghorfjend flared brightly, as if it were on fire. White flames dripped to the floor, hissing on contact. Jarle finally saw fear in the eyes of the remaining gray men.

"Speak truth now. You have only moments." Frost coated Jarle's lips as if he stood at the northern tip of Ehrde. "Why are you here?"

"You are like him, the one that killed Takarn. The Angst," the gray man spluttered at Niihlu.

"I'm nothing like Angst," Niihlu said in a crisp voice. "He would let you live. Tell me how you arrived here!"

"I do not know how I got here," he replied through gritted teeth. "I have no desire to be here, and after I escape, the only reason I would come to this wretched place again is to destroy all of you!"

"Lies," Rasaol said. "Lies and deceit. They spy on us, they invade us, kill our people, and all that remains is lies. Kill him!"

"No!" Jarle shouted, holding up a hand as Niihlu lifted the axe.

"What is this?" Rasaol asked, his jaw tightening.

"This is not our way," Jarle said. "We are not murderers!"

"This is not murder, it's justice!" Rasaol's eyes were wide with fury.

"We don't murder prisoners." Jarle kept his voice calm. "Our laws dictate that all disputes, even one so grievous, must be resolved by challenge. Niihlu, do you wish to fight this Fulk'han?"

Rasaol looked at Niihlu's confused gaze then back at Jarle, shaking his head. He burst out laughing and patted Jarle on the shoulder. "We will see justice met with your old ways."

Jarle nodded, but Niihlu shook with a fury.

"This is nonsense." Niihlu pointed the axe at the Fulk'han. "He killed Feemi and lies about sneaking in. If I kill him now or later, what difference does it make?"

"Murder is their way, not ours, Niihlu," Jarle said sincerely, gripping his companion's shoulder. He jerked back his hand, barely able to bend his fingers from the burning cold. "What have they done to you, son?"

"He chose to be our champion." Rasaol stared at the beastly gray man crouching on the floor. "And of all times, we need one now."

20

Angst let go, releasing their bones so they could move again. Some of the pirates smiled at him, some looked wary, and one winked. Tori smacked him on the arm, but he was mostly oblivious. He smiled at each and every one of them before sitting back down.

"They aren't all women," Jarblech said grumpily. "Though sometimes I wish they were."

"That's new," Hector said. "What happened?"

"It's those felking mermaids!" She spat on the floor and banged her fist on the table, making Tori jump. "The stupid men just jump in after them and are gone. Eaten by those monsters."

"Huh." Angst felt his friends' eyes on him. "You don't say."

"Over half our men are gone. We can't even let them near the water unsupervised!" She was shaking, her fists balled up in anger. "All we can do is trap those bitches on the shore and hope that scares away the others."

"Are they really *all* bad?" Angst asked in disbelief. Moyra *had* tried to kill him, but surely it was more like self-defense? She had almost died in a trap. He had a hard time believing she was a killer.

"The worst sort of monsters you can imagine." One of Jarblech's eyes was wide and crazy, and her nose twitched nervously.

"They sound just awful," Victoria agreed, peering pointedly

at Angst.

"We keep the men in at night, under guard. That's why you don't see them in here," she said. "They can't seem to help themselves."

"So we've noticed." Tarness smirked.

"Can we start with the drinking now?" Angst asked.

"Will any of your mates mind if my friends here have a little party?" Hector pointed at Angst and Victoria. "They've been cooped up and need to let loose a bit."

Angst looked to Tori, whose eyes were as big as his. He couldn't believe Hector was encouraging them to drink. How much had that kiss with Jarblech affected his friend? He closed his mouth but gawked openly at Hector.

"Yeah, of course." Jarblech smirked. "This place could use a some livening up." She rubbed each of her fingers as if counting the money.

Hector leaned over to Angst and Victoria and whispered, "You've got plenty of gold, Your Highness? Enough to buy rounds for everyone?"

"More than enough," she said with a nod.

He looked at Angst. "Drink them under the table."

"Really?" Angst couldn't control the ear-to-ear grin.

"I don't want a single one of them able to get up in the morning. Got it?"

"Trust me, I can do this!" He patted Hector on the shoulder.

"I'm going to go change!" Victoria said in excitement.

"If you've got something strong," Angst called out, "the first round is on me!"

"You come with me." Jarblech pulled Hector by the wrist and led him to nearby stairs. "I have some new things to show you."

Tamara brushed by Angst and Tarness, staring at the floor on her way toward the exit.

"Aren't you staying?" Angst asked, grabbing her arm.

She jerked it out of his hand and moved in until her face was inches from his. "Are you going to force me to stay, wielder?"

"Of course not," he said calmly. "Look, I'm sorry if we

scared you. Keeping you from moving was safer than hurting you in a fight."

"I wasn't scared," she muttered, pulling away and looking back at the ground.

"Bad choice of words," Tarness said, his eyes drinking her in. "What if we apologize?"

"No," she said.

"And buy you drinks?" Angst offered.

"No," she said. "I should probably go."

"But it's time for a party!" Victoria said from behind Angst and Tarness.

Angst smiled. He felt like he'd just opened the present he'd always wanted. Victoria was wearing the white, silky dress from the last inn they'd danced at. It was eye-poppingly low cut, showing most of her pale cleavage. High slits displayed legs up to here with every step. Her eyes met his, and she smiled fondly at the attention.

"I need a drink," Angst said.

"Yup," Tarness quickly agreed, his eyes lingering on Tori. "Me too."

"What about you, Tamara?" Victoria asked. "What can we do to get you to stay?"

Without warning, Tamara stepped forward and kissed Tori squarely on the mouth. To Angst's surprise, the princess didn't pull back right away. When she finally did, Tamara was smiling as if all had been forgiven.

"I'm going to go clean up," Tamara said to Tori before spinning on her heel and rushing out of the pub.

"I need a drink," Angst repeated.

"Yup," Tarness quickly agreed, his eyes wide. "Me too."

"Jealous?" Tori said, looking slyly at Angst.

"Of course I am!" His eyes mischievous slits. "I'd love to make out with a pirate!"

"We all know you're too chicken." Tarness winked.

* * * *

151

The ground shook relentlessly. Or maybe it was his stomach. Angst winced at the bright light before clenching his eyelids together. Maybe if he tried hard enough, he could force himself to sleep. Even in this dream state, a powerful hangover was bearing down, and he wanted more than anything to remain comatose through the worst of it.

"Just open your eyes, you big baby," Victoria called out. She sounded frustrated, another reason to go back to sleep.

"No, I'm sleeping." The odd floating sensation of his dreams wasn't uncomfortable. Maybe if he just ignored everything else...

"I'm cold," Tori stated. "How do I stop being naked again?"

"I'm pretty sure I don't remember," Angst muttered, unable to keep one of his eyes from opening.

His blurry friend was crossing her arms in front of her chest. She wore white furs in the Nordruaut style. A long feather stuck out of her hair, and woolen gloves covered her hands. She was definitely not naked, but there was no backing out now, and he reluctantly opened his other eye. Even asleep, he could feel his temples throb from the alcohol. His nose was stuffy and his throat scratchy. "What was that stuff we drank? It was spicy, and salty, and tasted like raisins."

"Don't remind me." She burped and grimaced, and a blue cape suddenly appeared, draping over her shoulders and back. "Ugh, I can't concentrate."

"You know, if this was my dream," Angst said in his gravelly voice, "I could probably will you to be *completely* naked."

"Sure, go ahead." She was mostly ignoring him now and looking around.

"You're fun," Angst said dryly.

"I was fun last night," she pointed out.

"Too fun. You really got me drunk," he said. "You got everyone drunk. I'm not sure a single pirate made it up to their rooms. Did I?"

"Yup," she said. "Right between Tamara and me."

"What?" His stomach wrenched and his eyes widened as he

grappled a wave of panic. "Are you...are *we* wearing clothes...?"

"You'll have to wait and see," she said with a little tease in her voice.

"Wait, why are we sleeping together again? I thought you needed time to yourself?" Angst pressed his palms against his temples to relieve the building pressure. "And why get me so drunk? I'm pretty sure a little drunk would've been great."

"You needed the break," she said. "I was trying to help."

Even through the thick haze of booze, he wasn't convinced. "And?"

"Well..." She stopped looking around and made eye contact. "I still want to see Unsel, and my mom."

Angst raised an eyebrow and opened his mouth to speak.

"I know, I know...but I'm having a hard time letting go," she said. "I was hoping if you were relaxed, not completely in control, we wouldn't come back here."

"Here?" he asked in surprise.

The ground shook once more and was suddenly covered in shadow. Angst tore his eyes away from his beautiful friend and looked up. Boulders flew toward them, wrapped in fire or ice. Monstrous elements hurled missles from their mountain perches. The elements were giants, far larger than the avatars he'd met and fiercer than Angst could fathom. Suddenly, they stopped their attacks, and the field was clear.

"We need to go," Victoria prodded, jerking on his arm. "Can't you concentrate? Focus on Unsel?"

"I'm focusing on not throwing up." He swallowed hard. "Does that count?"

"Angst, look over there," said a child's voice. "See? Coming at us!"

He swayed as he focused intently on the girl, wishing desperately that he could fall over and hug the ground. A girl, no older than twelve, floated toward them. She seemed familiar, a little. Cute pug nose with a tiny mole, long blue dress, mane of light brown hair...

"Aerella!" He smiled in spite of himself. "You were soooo cute when you were young!"

"Did you have to get him this drunk, Your Majesty?" Aerella asked, crossing her arms and peering down her nose like an angry parent. She turned to Angst. "I'm surprised you were even able to make it here."

Aerella placed a glowing hand on Angst's forehead, wiping away his confusion and dehydration like cleaning a chalkboard.

"Hey!" Angst said with a broad grin as the hands squeezing his stomach let go. He stretched as her touch released the pain in his forehead and tension in his shoulders. It felt as if he'd eaten a full, greasy breakfast, drunk a gallon of water, and slept away the rest of the morning.

"Angst!" Victoria tried catching his attention. "Take me to Unsel! I need to know!"

"You need to finish this first," Aerella said firmly. "It's the most important thing you can do. Now look around!"

There was a loud crash, a noisy embrace of steel and death that rang throughout the valley. Armies in leather and chain armor had poured in like water released from a dam. It was a chaotic mess of Berfemmian, Nordruaut, Fulk'han, and wielders.

"Why are they even here?" Angst asked, watching hundreds of soldiers from various nations collide as they met. "They're no match for the elements!"

"Angst!" Victoria stomped her foot.

"They're not here to fight the elements." Aerella pointed at an approaching dark cloud.

Victoria struck his arm, and he grabbed her hand before she could do it again. She struggled against his grip, yelling, but he couldn't hear her. Behind Fire, a flock of birds darkened the sky...except they were much too large to be birds.

"Dragons," Angst whispered.

From the corner of his eye, he could see Aerella point to where Air had stood. Giant cavastil covered the eastern horizon, their metal beaks glistening in the sunlight. Their screams filled the air like a thousand fingernails on chalkboard.

"No!" Tori yelled. "You've got to take me home, please!"

"Stop it!" Aerella argued. "He has to see it through to the end."

"I need to see Unsel!" Victoria demanded, grabbing at Aerella's arm. "I'm the princess! I may be the queen! It's important!"

"It isn't. You don't even—"

"Shut up!" Victoria turned to Angst. Her hands were shaking and tears streamed down her cheeks. "Wake up," she begged "I can't hear anymore."

He looked from Aerella's shocked expression to Victoria's panic-ridden face. "But—" Before he could say anything, she pulled him into a kiss and the dream was gone.

21

"Angst." Tarness's deep voice boomed in his head. His friend was gently tapping his temple.

His eyes jerked open, and he took in a deep, surprised breath. The sudden shock of leaving the dream was almost as unexpected as finding he wasn't alone. He was spooning Victoria closely, tightly, as if holding on for dear life. His chin dug into her bare shoulder, and waves of blond curls covered his face. He lifted his head to see that not only was she topless, so was he. He sighed inwardly and tried pulling away, only to find he was Tamara's little spoon. She rolled onto her back, giving Angst and Tarness an eyeful of her thin, dark torso. Angst frowned when he saw scars under her breast and along her arm.

"Give me a couple minutes," Angst said. How on Ehrde could he unsandwich himself without passing out from embarrassment? "Five tops."

"It's dusk," Tarness said, his voice thick melancholy. "We need to get outside and do this thing before they can get themselves together."

Angst knew Tarness was upset, or jealous. He wanted to say something, but the door shut behind his friend before the words came out. His chest tightened as he thought about explaining this newest predicament to Hector. Now more than ever, Angst didn't need to be judged. At least, not without being able to explain how he'd ended up being the middle of the sandwich. He didn't even remember being drunk. He did recall a dream… Had Aerella been there again? How had he woken so suddenly? It was drifting away. At least he wasn't hungover. That was nice.

As he carefully pushed himself up with one arm and spider-crawled over his friend, Victoria rolled to her front. Tori seemed deep in sleep, and peacefully at rest, the smell of alcohol permeating the air. He leaned in to kiss her forehead and noticed that her eyes were puffy and damp. Had she been crying?

A gentle rap at the door hastened his departure. Angst inched it open and whispered, "Let me get into armor, if I can find it."

* * * *

Dallow and Tarness led Angst out of the geode as dawn's sunbeams fought their way through angry clouds. Only the edge of the town was visible behind him, with the rest deep in geode shadows. He stumbled and returned his focus to their destination.

"You okay?" Tarness grumbled. "Have a little bit of a headache this morning?"

"Nope," Angst replied smugly. "I feel pretty good."

"How is that possible?" Dallow placed long fingers on Angst's forehead. "I'm surprised you could even get up."

"I'm surprised he's not dead," Tarness quipped.

"He's not clammy and he is walking in a straight line." Dallow pulled his hand away. "Were you drinking water?"

"Nope," Angst said. "Something about the dream."

"What I saw was one of my dreams," Tarness said, "not yours."

"No, not that. Can we talk about that later?" Angst said, shaking his head. "It was a foci-dream. Aerella was there. Did she heal me?"

"Wait, what?" Dallow came to a full stop.

"I agree. That's huge news, Angst," Tarness said sincerely. "A cure for hangovers?"

"I know, right?" Angst said excitedly. "I was hoping Dallow

could help me figure it out."

"Sure," Dallow said, shaking his head. "But that's not the important part. She healed you in the dream? What else happened?"

"Oh, right," Angst said, frowning in concentration. "I can't remember, I think we saw more of the battle—"

"I don't think we've got time for this, Angst," Tarness interrupted. "We need to finish this before the town wakes up."

"Agreed." Angst peered over his shoulder to see Dulgirgraut glowing. "Looks like we're ready."

"Doesn't that mean we are in danger?" Dallow's brow furrowed behind his blue kerchief.

"Still figuring this one out," Angst said hopefully, pointing over his shoulder with a thumb. "But I think that means it's ready. I hope."

Tarness looked at Dallow as if their friend still had eyes, and Dallow shrugged. He was getting better at seeing with the memndus stone, which made Angst smile.

"Are you sure this won't make it too heavy?" Angst asked.

"Positive." Dallow's eyes glowed white. "Floatation isn't about weight, it's about density and how much fluid is displaced by the boat."

They stopped at the edge of the docks behind the geode, fifty yards from Jarblech's docked schooner. The ship was large enough that Angst wondered if their plan was truly necessary. He gauged the vessel, trying to better understand the shape. It was thinner than the other ships but just as long. Even unmoving, it looked fast, with three masts reaching high up to the sky, and black sails ready to drop.

"Use air to hold it in place so you can see what needs to be done." Dallow lifted both hands as if holding up a model of the ship.

"Are you powerful enough to do that?" Tarness questioned.

Angst turned around to face his friend. Behind him, the ship moaned and creaked with the strain of being hefted out of the water, like giant's feet crossing an old wooden floor. Water fell from the hull in sheets, showering the harbor noisily. Angst smiled at his friends' open mouths, his eyebrows raising cockily over his burgundy glowing eyes.

"Show off," Dallow chided.

"That was loud," Tarness warned. "They'll be coming soon."

"Keep everyone clear until I'm done." Angst turned and brought his hands together, and a light blue hue surrounded them.

The ship hovered twenty feet over the water. Angst moved one hand around, as though inspecting an apple, and the ship followed, spinning slowly so he could view all sides. This was as sneaky as a herd of whales doing back flips, and he could already hear distant yells from the pirates in the geode.

"The tricky part will be pulling enough from the ground," he said, frowning. "It's down there, but it's *way* down there."

Hector ran toward them with a pirate scimitar in both hands. He wore his leather riding breeches and a loose night shirt that was open wide, showing a chest full of curly gray hair. He shuffled to a stop and knelt to tie his boots. "They won't be far behind," he said through gasping breaths. In spite of his worried tone, his eyes smiled and his lips curled into a mischievous grin. "She's a light sleeper and—"

"Hector?" Jarblech shrieked from town. She stopped at the edge of the geode, staring at her ship as it hovered over the docks, spinning about slowly as if hanging by a string. "Sound the bells!"

A loud, tinny clanging echoed from the hollow stone. Jarblech marched toward them, and Angst could feel her anger, even at this distance. Pirates in various stages of dress converged behind her, sunshine glinting off the steel of their swords and daggers. A dozen became two and then a horde as the entire town came toward them.

"Can you hold them all off?" Angst asked.

"We'll do our best," Hector promised, "but hurry."

"Not sure this is a job to hurry," Angst said, letting his mind wander deep into the earth.

"What in the Dark Vivek are you doing to my felking boat?" Jarblech shouted, cursing loudly from the portyard. The pirates looked hungover, still drunk, or just angry.

"He said hurry, right?" Tarness said.

"She reminds me of Rose," Dallow said. "Such pretty words."

"What does felk mean?" Tarness asked.

"I think it means sex?" Dallow answered.

"How is that a curse?"

Dallow merely shrugged.

"If you two are done." Angst said. "I need to concentrate." He reached far into the ground below with his mind. Minutes passed slowly as he sought veins of metal.

Jarblech and her not-so-merry band of pirates arrived, hot and ready to fight. She raised a thick cudgel and advanced on Angst. Tarness stepped between them, shaking his head.

"I wouldn't hit Angst right now," Hector warned as he stood next to Tarness. He let go of a cutlass and raised a hand in surrender. "He'll drop your ship."

Angst grunted. The metal he found was like cobwebs—small veins of steel strung together. A larger piece would've been so much easier to coax to the surface. Even with the power of Dulgirgraut, this took a lot of concentration.

"This is why I hate magics," Jarblech snapped. "I'll gut the lot of you if my ship isn't, well, just... Put it down. Now!"

"Just wait," Angst said through gritted teeth.

"I don't need to just wait!" Jarblech gripped Hector's shield and eyed him threateningly. "I said now, or I'm going to— What in the felk?"

A silvery geyser shot from the water like a volcano. All pirates took a step back, gasping loudly, watching in awe as a mass of metal latched onto the exterior of her ship, splattering against the hull like paint thrown on a wall. Angst moved his hands as if molding clay into pottery, spinning the ship as it was encompassed in a metal cocoon.

"That's my ship!" Jarblech shouted. "Bring the girl."

Two pirates dragged a kicking Victoria through the crowd.

She wore an oversized shirt, and her bare legs flailed about. Both men bore bruises and seemed upset.

Angst stopped and turned, watching them cower from the glow of his angry gaze. He wielded Dulgirgraut and pointed the giant blade at Jarblech.

"Look at what he's doing!" Hector warned. "Hurt her, and he will destroy all of you!"

Jarblech looked from Angst to Victoria, obviously torn.

"Please," Angst said. "Trust me."

With a nod, Victoria was released. She ran to Angst. "Finish it," she grumbled.

Angst faced the schooner once again. His anger made it easier to draw more metal from the ground to completely wrap the ship. Smoothing the steel against the exterior, he forced metal into every crevice and splinter of wood. Once the ship was wrapped, Angst willed the metal to bore and twist into the sides, anchoring the new steel casing to the wooden hull. The pirates gasped in awe, looking from the ship to Jarblech. She lowered her cudgel, her mouth agape. Hector held up the shield but looked at Tarness and Dallow. Tarness shook his head and Dallow's eyes glowed white behind the kerchief as he cataloged everything. Within minutes, the ship had been transformed from pirate freighter to a warship unlike any in Ehrde.

The last of the steel spluttered from the geyser and froze into place as he stopped pulling. Sweat dripped from his brow as Angst lowered the boat slowly, worried that it might sink. He was relieved that it floated just as before. Taking a deep breath, he turned around, pleased with himself, only to find fury in Jarblech's eyes. Her cheeks were red and her fists shook.

"What have you done?" she asked. "She was so beautiful!"

Angst studied her, looking at the angry spikes decorating her leather wristbands and collar. He snapped his fingers. Enormous metal spikes popped into place along the bow of the ship and below the deck railing. Angst smiled widely, showing all his teeth.

Jarblech's leaned her head to one side as she studied her boat and a small grin crept up her cheek. "That's a little better."

"Would this make you feel safe enough to bring us to Angoria?" Hector asked, placing a calming hand on her shoulder.

Her eyes assessed them, calculating everything. "I'm not even going to tell you what this will cost."

"Please?" Angst asked.

"Full inspection, make sure that thing can still float!" Jarblech commanded. "Someone get me some rum! A lot of rum!"

Angst smiled to himself as he stared at the ship. He felt a little hope that things might be coming together. Beside the docked ship, a steel sculpture rose from the water, flat blades of curved metal that twisted ten feet into the air. The remnants of his geyser. It was sort of, accidentally, art—and he was as proud of his oops as he was of the refinished ship. From the corner of his eye, he could see the burgundy glow of Dulgirgraut and shook his head.

"What?" he asked the sword. "We worked together, we did a great job. What do you guys think?"

There was no answer. Actually, there was no noise at all. When Angst turned, nobody was moving. As if frozen in ice, his friends and the town of pirates were all eerily still.

He frowned and cocked his head to one side. "Guys?" he asked. "Tori?"

Wind gushed from all directions. His hair flapped from side to side as he spun about, holding Dulgirgraut high to shield from attack. Angst continued turning, looking for the source, stopping when a dark, angry tornado appeared between the pirates and the geode. Information—he needed to know what this was and how to stop it. Dulgirgraut shared nothing as several smaller tornados reached out from the larger one, making the shape of an enormous figure. It was tall, three times the size of any man. The wind slowed to a breeze and the creature solidified enough to form a face that smiled broadly. It looked over the pirates as if they didn't exist and stared straight at him.

"You must be Angst," Air said.

22

"You've heard the saying, 'the air was still?'" Air asked as he approached, floating through the pirates like a wispy ghost. "Yeah, that's me."

Angst sought out his friends, his eyes glowing so brightly they created beams in the dust kicked up by the element. He inched closer, wary of every sound and movement, his giant sword aimed at Air's abdomen.

Air looked at it with annoyed respect. He delicately touched it as if preparing to gently push it aside then jerked his hand back as the blade sparked on contact.

"Let them go." Angst coughed, having a hard time catching his breath. Was Air making it hard to breathe? His head throbbed and he felt dizzy from a small battle in his lungs. He reached out to Dulgirgraut with his mind, seeking help, but heard only a dull song in return.

"We need to talk," Air said sincerely.

"Fine, once you release them," Angst wheezed.

His friends gasped and clutched their chests. They dropped to their knees in the sand. He still fought for his breath; it was barely enough to keep from passing out.

"Everyone okay?" he asked.

"Yes," Hector replied.

"The pirates aren't moving." Tarness was already up on one knee, eyeing Tamara in her stillness and Victoria gasping for

163

breath. Angst recognized the anger building in his face.

"I think they will be fine," Dallow advised. "I'm unaffected, but it was an odd experience. I could watch, but I couldn't move. I didn't even realize I was breathing."

"I took care of that for you," Air said. "See, no harm done. Now, can we speak before she comes and ruins our meeting?"

"You mean Water?" Angst asked.

"Who else?" Air confirmed. The top of his torso remained mostly still while his tornadic legs wandered like spinning tops. "She's planning to kill you. She means to make it hurt."

"Am I on a list?" Angst asked in despair, lowering his sword several inches.

"We've taken notice, all of us," he said. "Well, those of us remaining."

"Don't you elements have a war-thing going on?" Angst asked. "Can't you finish your own battle without involving me and mine?"

"It's not that simple," Air said. "You've got another one of those things, and you declared yourself the element of humans, remember?" He sounded very serious and golden lightning sparked within his large, dark eye sockets.

"I was a little upset," Angst explained. He grimaced. "Actually, I still am."

"And you killed Water's lover," Air said heavily.

"Her lover?" Angst asked, perplexed.

"Well, just as we utilize human hosts, we sometimes take human companions," he replied smugly.

"You're kidding!" Angst rolled his eyes. "That's the most ridiculous thing I've ever heard."

"Angst," Victoria pleaded.

"So," Angst said in disbelief. "She thinks I killed Mr. Water?"

Tarness coughed back a chuckle, while Dallow sucked in his lips.

"Sometimes," Hector said flatly, "I think you should let me negotiate and save your heroics for beating up big things."

"Supposedly when you were chasing Magic across Ehrde," Air continued, ignoring his friends. "Think back, Angst. Water said she was there when you did it. She would've had blue hair."

Angst strained for the memories; so much had happened, it felt like decades ago. The chase was just a blur, a fading nightmare he was happy to let go. He set Dulgirgraut on its tip to hover and wait.

"Speak your thoughts aloud, if you please." Air made a beckoning movement with his hands.

Angst took a deep breath and sighed, and the air leaving his mouth became an image of dusty ground that formed into the base of Ivan's arena. He stepped back and the view expanded with every breath. He peered up at Air warningly, unsure of this new trick.

"Amazing," Dallow said. His forehead scrunched as he pressed the memndus stone close to his temple.

"Just a trick, so we can all see," Air said, gently pulling with both windy hands as if dragging the memories out with a rope. "Please, tell us."

Victoria walked to him and held his hand then closed her eyes and concentrated.

Air tilted his head to one side at the exchange. "Ah, so the element Human has taken a companion too."

Angst glared at him then squeezed his eyes shut in concentration.

"I'll help you find the memory, Angst," she said, placing a second hand on top of his. "How did you defeat Ivan?"

"He was a giant, much larger than a Nordruaut, more like a small mountain. His body was made of purple tubes and a white mask hovered in front of his face," Angst said. "I used a stone platform to lift me up so I could face him, and then leaped off, cutting into him with Chryslaenor. I did it over and over again until he split apart."

When Angst opened his eyes, Victoria's were wide, her face pale. She swallowed hard at the horrific vision forming in the air before them. The monstrous body of Takarn-Ivan was splayed like thick strips of purple beef. Angst was a mess of Ivan's blood and his own, his jaw set and his eyes glowing blue. The creature reached up into the sky, its arms and fingers stretching into forever until it formed a twisted tree that split open to reveal darkness. Freed from the confines of Ivan's body, a black beam of light rushed away from that tree, leaving a path of death. The vision momentarily paused, awaiting Angst's storytelling.

"That must've been scary," she said, gulping loudly as if fighting bile.

"Yes, but what Magic planned next was worse." He couldn't control the catch in his throat. "After it escaped Ivan's body and became the beam of darkness, it threatened to possess someone I love and went straight to Unsel."

"It was going to attack Heather?" Victoria asked.

"Or you," he said. "It left Fulk'han so fast I could barely keep up. It tore through towns and houses and animals and trees." Angst clenched his fists. "Magic didn't care who or what it killed, it was just filled with hate."

The vision resumed—cloudy, as if viewed through the memndus—showing a distant image of Ehrde moving in slow motion as Angst, on his sturdy ram swifen, chased Magic through forests and villages.

"Do you remember a woman with blue hair?" Air coaxed, studying the unfolding story.

"You do," Victoria encouraged.

"Yes, I do now," Angst said, and the vision sped by quickly as minutes became seconds then slowed. "She had hair like the mermaid."

The dark beam of power made a sharp turn and headed directly toward a small farm. Angst tried to move around it, but the beam was too fast. It raced through a yard in front of a village, killing an old man who was standing near a beautiful woman with blue hair. The image stopped, and Air took a step forward, kneeling to inspect her. Angst was out of breath from remembering, or from the spell that put the memory on display. Dizziness made it hard to focus on the image of the blue-haired woman.

"That would be Water," Air said.

"She's cute," Angst said.

"Really?" Victoria backhanded him in the chest.

"The rest of the story you all know." Angst took a step back, trying to wave the vision away like campfire smoke.

"I want to see," Air said. "Please continue."

Angst glanced at his friends, who were in various stages of recovery, and the pirates, still frozen. Dulgirgraut was within arm's reach. His lungs now ached from the spell, and he wasn't sure how much more he could endure before passing out.

"How about no?" Angst replied, letting go of Victoria and reaching for his sword.

Air continued pulling, and Angst coughed as his lungs emptied. He gasped for breath, clutching at his throat. With every gasp, more of the story was drawn from him. The image slowed momentarily to show Water screaming Angst's name before a speedy race to Unsel. In a blur, they watched the metallic-beaked cavastil birds smash into the ground—which made Air wince—the destruction of the castle and finally trapping of Magic as Angst skidded to a stop at Victoria's feet. Air waved a hand, dismissing the image. Angst dropped to a knee, sucking in deep gulps of oxygen.

"I'm not sure if we should be partners, if I should kill you, or just run," Air said, tapping a dusty, spinning finger against his chin thoughtfully.

"I'd suggest running," Angst said through his now dry and scratchy throat.

"You hold such amazing power, such potential." Air ignored Angst's remark. "I don't remember any Al'eyrn before you wielding so much."

"What do you want?" Angst asked.

"Enemy of my enemy..." Air sighed. "We both have the same problems. We need to be rid of the others. Fire, Magic, Water. You can't do it without me. It will take two."

"Why do you have to fight? Can't you all just work together and leave us alone?"

"From the mouths of babes," Air said thoughtfully. "Maybe someday, but not this time."

"You should reconsider, before it's too late." Angst defied his exhaustion and stood, placing a hand on the hilt of Dulgirgraut. "Fire is already damaged, Magic can't be in great shape, and I can handle Water."

Air's laughter sounded like thunder. "You speak as large as your sword, young human. Even you are no match for Water or her wrath. Together we could win, maybe, but alone?"

"I'm not alone," Angst said proudly. "Maybe we just need to start with you." He wielded Dulgirgraut and pointed it at Air.

Hector leaped forward with a scimitar in both hands while Dallow summoned an enormous fireball that grew as it approached the element.

Air grimaced. "Enough." He reached up with a windy hand and pulled down.

A funnel formed over the element, reaching up so high it sucked in clouds. Everyone gasped at the sudden change in pressure as a gale shot out from Air in every direction. Trees were uprooted and thrown into the ocean like discarded weeds. Angst instinctively created an air shield, earning him an admonishing tone from Dulgirgraut for trying to fight air with air, but no further assistance. His shield shattered as quickly as he built it.

Tarness inched forward in his fury, and Angst couldn't help but be impressed by his raw power. Angst locked his legs to the ground, anchoring his bones to the earth below. He reached out to do the same for his friends but couldn't feel them. In that brief instance of concentration, they were gone. His cheeks pulled back and his ears burned as he looked around to find that everyone was missing. He forced one leg forward then another. The wind and sand bit into his skin, flaying off layers, but he kept advancing.

"What did you do with them?"

"I said, enough," Air yelled.

"Where are they?" Angst coughed, his voice but a whisper in the storm. He gripped his neck, desperate to breathe.

"You aren't ready even for me, much less her," Air said in disappointment. "You're not a threat. You're a waste of time."

He dropped to his knees, the stars of faint flashing in his eyes.

"I hope you can swim as well as your friends." Air backhanded Angst.

Angst soared high into the sky, leaving Dulgirgraut behind in the sand. He landed hard in the ocean amongst a dozen screaming people as everything went black.

23

Unsel

Heather sighed deeply. What on Ehrde had she done to deserve this? It wasn't just about giving up an hour every day to advise, which really meant listening and nodding. There was something she hated, absolutely hated, about being here. It could simply be that it felt like spring with the fountain and the flowers, in spite of the icy, blustering winter outside. Maybe it was the exclusive nature, a feeling that she didn't belong—not that she wanted to. But more likely, it was Angst. The maiden's courtyard was his place to secretly meet with Victoria, and the very thought made her cringe. She didn't hate the princess, something she reminded herself daily. She didn't hate Angst, which she also reminded herself daily. But together?

"Is everything okay, Heather?" Alloria asked, her tone walking a fine line between courtesy and impatience.

Heather took that as her cue to grasp her baby belly and adjust her hips, resting her weight on the other cheek. In her most uncomfortably pregnant voice, she replied, "Yes, Your Majesty. The baby is just restless."

"Ooh!" Alloria grinned, hopping over to place a hand on Heather's shifting mass.

She never asked if it was okay to grope and rub Heather's stomach as if making a wish. Heather forced her wince to the other eye, hoping it would appear to be a full smile. Fortunately, the sudden movement woke her package, and an elbow, or a foot, made a brief appearance as it stretched her insides enough to create a visible bump.

"I don't... I just..." Alloria jerked her hand back as if bitten. "I'd never get used to that."

"Have you not spent much time around pregnant women, Your Highness?" she asked.

"No, I had too many moms." She sighed. "None who stayed around long enough to make babies, I guess."

Is this the true Alloria peeking out?

It was almost genuinely sad. Alloria looked at the ground as if the words had slipped out and landed in a pile at her feet. These weeks as queen regent had already aged her, which made Heather smile cattily. Alloria was dressing slightly more conservatively, or maybe that was just around Heather. The most noticeable change was that the big, obnoxious hair that cried out to men for a romp in the hay was now tucked away under an old fashioned crown. For the life of her, Heather couldn't understand how all that hair could be confined in such a small space.

"I just meant being that size." Alloria frowned in concern, motioning over Heather's entire girth. "It must be uncomfortable."

"More than you know," Heather replied dryly. What she wouldn't have given to wield her own giant sword right now.

"What was I discussing?" she said quickly. "Oh, yes, Angst."

The young princess droned on in an airy voice that made it hard for Heather to pay attention. She was standing, waving her hands excitedly as she laid out how she would protect the city, and the castle. Hoping that she wouldn't have to evacuate. The entirety of her plan required Angst arriving in time.

"What was that?" Heather asked. "You said Angst?"

"Yes." Alloria frowned again. "Your husband needs to hurry. I need my champion!"

"As do I." Heather sighed, once again smiling through a wince.

Was this really what Angst wanted? Young princesses fawning over him to save the kingdom while he rode off to adventure? She sighed. Of course it was. The thought made her happy, and grumpy. She wanted Angst to feel good about himself, to fulfill the destiny he always whined about—it was important to him, so it was important to her—but how did she fit into this glorious future of dragon slaying and maiden saving? Because, fortunately, she was neither a dragon nor a helpless maiden. It was one of the issues that caused such strife between them. That unfulfilled longing to be somewhere else, to be needed by others, but not to—

"You shouldn't be in here!" Alloria shrilled, placing her hands on her hips.

Heather snapped out of her princess-avoidance-trance to see Vars marching into the room. He wore a doublet and leggings, appearing much less threatening without the old plate armor. His face was wrinkled with anxiety, but his eyes flashed anger. He lifted a fist, which made Heather yelp in concern. Alloria didn't flinch, as if she knew he wouldn't swing. Vars's fist shook with rage before he cupped the side of his head where an ear was missing. Heather started to turn away but couldn't tear her eyes from the sight. Hadn't he had an ear the last time she saw him? Now it was just a hole, as though he'd been born without it.

"I'm sorry, what was that?" he growled as he approached them. "I can't hear you!"

"You obviously didn't need it, since you don't bother to listen!" Alloria declared, straightening out her crown and crossing her arms. "You went to arrest the wielders, without my permission—"

"You made magic illegal," he argued. "I was following through on your decree."

"But did I issue warrants? Did I command those arrests?" she continued. "And not only did you fail to follow my orders, you also failed to arrest a single one of them."

Heather's stomach churned and her blood boiled. When had magic become illegal? Why was she stuck here when her friends were in danger? She was getting upset but couldn't tell if her tumultuous emotions were feeding their argument. They were getting angrier by the second, but not unnaturally so. She tried controlling her breathing to calm everyone down, but the shouting continued.

"Magic is illegal?" Heather asked. "What about me? What about Angst?"

"Yes, what about her?" Vars yelled. "Why hasn't she been arrested?"

"Nobody is getting arrested!" Alloria said firmly. "Is that clear?"

"The only thing clear is that space between your ears!" Vars said with a grimace.

Alloria made a high-pitched gasp before pointing to the door. "At least I still have mine!" She turned to Heather, her face mostly bright and cheery. "I promise, nobody will be arrested, dear. You and Angst will be fine." Alloria spun sharply and reached up as if to grab Vars's ear. "Oops, I guess I can't do that now." She held the back of his arm instead, which he jerked out of her hand. "We'll finish this in my study!"

Heather frowned as the three practically glowing red ears left the room and wondered who would break down and cry first. How could they possibly be the team to save Unsel? It was as if someone had deliberately put chaos in charge just to wreak havoc. That craziness had to be hunger talking, and she winced at Alloria's remark earlier about getting big. Bitch. Maybe she should thank Vars for cutting their meeting short.

Before she had the chance to rock herself upright, Jaden's sad face popped through the door and looked around. She sighed. Somehow Jaden had become loyal to Angst, so much so that Rook had easily convinced him to stay by her side. He was cute, with his firm jaw, dark-rooted blond hair, and sharp blue eyes, and incredibly adept at wielding magic, but self-absorbed to the point of self-worship. Jaden and Victoria were obviously attracted to each other, and Heather really wanted them to be happy, run away together, and not come back.

He searched the room, careful not to be caught where only women were supposed to be allowed, before striding in proudly. Jaden and Alloria were the two lone survivors of Cliffview's collapse into the ocean, and with Victoria gone, he seemed more lost than ever.

"Come in, dear," she said politely. "Alloria and Vars argued their way out already, and she had cleared the room for quite some time."

"I figured as much from the shouting." Jaden's grin was tight. "Still best of friends, those two?"

"I'm sure they'll figure it out," she said dryly. "Once one of them is dead."

He smiled at this and then looked guilty as he asked, "Anything?"

"No." She sighed. "You?"

"Still nothing. I was able to communicate with Victoria through stone a week ago, and suddenly I can't." He grunted. "How does magic just stop working?"

Still upset he hadn't told her about their chats sooner, Heather could only shrug. How could they not have told anyone about the spell allowing them to communicate through stone? He could've passed messages to Angst. Or, even better, she could've learned the spell herself, just to tell Angst how much she loved him. She felt like someone had dropped her heart on the floor. Caught up in her melancholy, Jaden sat on the cracked marble floor, crossed his legs, and set his chin in his hands for a good pout. Heather rolled her eyes. Why did she have an ability that required her to be the hopeful one?

"I'm sure they're fine," she said, brushing away her unkempt brown, curly hair nervously. "Scar lived, which means Angst is alive, and you know he'll keep the princess safe."

"True," Jaden said. "But look at what Scar's become! The poor dog can't control all the power Angst's taking on."

It was too much. Her guard instantly shattered as a dam of tears broke free. Heather couldn't control the sobs, and so, neither could Jaden.

174

"I'm sorry," he said between tears.

"Are we interrupting?" a squeaky voice said from the door.

Heather looked up to see the Meldusian and Nordruaut ambassadors enter the courtyard. The clacker of the small man's feet echoed throughout the room as he tried keeping up with his enormous companion's steps. She'd knelt to enter, but seemed very pleased to stand upright, until she looked around.

"This room is useless," she grunted, stretching her broad arms.

Heather tried not to gawk at the pair, but what else could she do? The Meldusian was so tiny, so ugly he was almost cute. The Nordruaut was so...naked. Angst must've loved that. Heather sighed and shook her head.

"I am Jintorich, and my friend is Maarja." He bowed then held out a small kerchief, handing it to Heather. "Are you Angst's wife?"

"Oh, thank you." Heather took the kerchief, which was almost half the size of Jintorich, and patted her eyes. "Yes, I'm Heather. This is our friend, Jaden."

They both nodded at Jaden, who stood, wiping his eyes in embarrassment.

"Do you know Angst?" Heather asked.

"I met your husband," Maarja said with a nod. "You must be a very patient woman."

"I already like you," Heather replied.

Jaden reached out to shake hands, but Maarja just looked at it as if wondering why it didn't hold mead. Jintorich took several fingers and shook them politely before hopping up onto Heather's bench. He inspected her stomach and leaned his tall ear close.

"Manners," Maarja snapped.

"Oh, yes," Jintorich peeped apologetically. "I used to be a physician, so I just assume. May I?"

"Um. Sure, okay," Heather said, looking at Jaden uncertainly.

Jaden shrugged helpfully.

Jintorich's cheek rested gently on her stomach then his ear

curled around her belly like a finger grasping her waist. Her heart stuttered in surprise, but before she could shove his head away, it popped up.

"Healthy," he said. "Quite healthy, as are you."

"Thank you." Heather beamed broadly enough that everyone in the room smiled.

"Have you heard from them?" Maarja asked. "Have you heard from Angst or Tarness?"

"No," Heather said. "I have reason to believe he's alive though."

"Please share." Jintorich sat on the bench, crossing his legs and placing his staff on his lap.

The Meldusian looked at her with a kind smile and waited patiently. The Nordruaut seemed less patient, but Maarja's questions mirrored Heather's concern for Angst.

"Why not?" Heather began, "Angst and his friends found a giant monster dog that had apparently come from the Vex'kvette. After defeating it, the monster changed into a puppy that was dying. Angst healed it with Chryslaenor, and now they share this bond. Everything that happens to Angst affects Scar. The puppy's alive, but completely out of control."

"I remember his dog," Maarja said. "Where is it now?"

"Scar?" Heather asked. "He's at our home. Why?"

"Vars tried arresting the wielders at the Wizard's Revenge," Jintorich explained.

"What?" Jaden said sharply.

"We helped them scare him away," Jintorich continued. "And now the wielders are planning to gather to seek refuge on your land."

"No!" Heather started rocking to stand. "No! Scar is confused, he doesn't understand. He'll hurt all of them, or worse!"

"Rook and Janda were hoping that would keep Unsel soldiers away," Jintorich said.

"Janda should know how dangerous Scar is." Heather stood shakily. "We have to warn them."

"You can't go there, Heather," Jaden said. "It's not safe."

"It's safe here?" Heather asked. "Alloria says she won't arrest me, but I don't trust Vars."

"You're safer here than with Scar acting like he is," Jaden said firmly. "They won't harm you as long as they need your husband."

"You could go, Jaden," she said. "You're fast enough on your swifen to get there first."

"No, I couldn't," Jaden said, though he beamed at the compliment. "I need to keep you safe, for Angst."

"We will keep her safe," Maarja promised. "No harm will come to her."

"Yes, we are both warriors." Jintorich stood, his staff flashing white as it struck the stone bench.

"No, really, if anything happened to you..." Jaden said. "I just wouldn't want Angst to be upset."

Heather gathered her emotional reserve. She thought of her baby and how excited she was to hold it. She thought of Angst coming home, and how hopeful she was that he was safe. She thought of her friends, and worried at the danger they faced at her home. She took that excitement, that hope, that worry, and with all her focus, gently held Jaden's hand and said, "Please."

As if jolted by lightning while being slapped across the face, Jaden took a shocked step back, holding up his hands. He was breathing rapidly, and she worried she'd pushed too much.

"*Yes!* Yes, you're absolutely right!" He began to summon his swifen. "I'll go now!"

"You should probably do that outside, dear," Heather said with a gentle smile.

"But wait, what will we eat?" he asked. "Where will everyone sleep?"

Heather needed to keep this momentum going, not only to help everyone arriving, but to give her a break from Jaden. "You could build temporary housing from stone. Angst says there's plenty. You can wield stone, can't you?"

"Yes, someone taught me once." He looked confused.

"And there's gold in a cellar under the house," she said.

"Enough to feed an army."

"I don't know." He hesitated.

"Go!" she commanded.

"Going!" He spun about to face Maarja and Jintorich. "And you will keep her safe?"

Both of them nodded, their eyebrows raised high in surprise. He sprinted out of the room, a man on a mission.

Heather returned to the bench, letting her shoulders slouch with a long sigh. "Thank you," she finally said.

"Whatever for?" Jintorich asked.

"Jaden means well, trying to keep me safe," Heather said. "But he's been smothering me. I've been trying to get rid of him for days."

Jintorich smiled and nodded. "Would you tell us more about Angst, and his foci?"

"Of course," Heather said, happy to talk about her husband. She reached out a hand for Maarja to come closer.

"I think I'm fine over here," Maarja said with a wary smile.

24

Angst woke to cold, and to something pressed firmly against his mouth. He felt like he was floating and opened his eyes to a blurry darkness. He was underwater and immediately tried twisting out of an embrace so tight it could've crushed the life from him. His arms and legs were too weak to break free, and the sheer panic of being fully submerged made it impossible to wield magic.

He had to calm down, and tried focusing on what had happened. The element had thrown him so high that landing in the ocean had felt like hitting solid ground. Water cocooned him as he sank, filling his mouth and nose. That should've been it. So, why was he alive?

Angst stopped fighting because he was still breathing, and whatever was pressed against his mouth was soft and nice. The embrace became less of a grapple and more of a hug. He took a deep breath and tasted something funny. Almost…fishy. Something moist flicked playfully at his tongue, like a teenager on a first date. He jerked his tongue back and it was gone.

The strong arms pulled him up. Hesitant beams of light snuck through ocean waves as they approached the surface, making it bright enough to see Moyra's large, dark eyes. Stopping an arm's length from the water's edge, the mermaid looked at him as she breathed for both of them.

"I am glad you are alive, An-gst." Her voice echoed in his

mind. "I worried you would drown."

His breathing quickened. Had his friends been thrown into the ocean too? Were they drowning right now? He had to find them!

"You are safe. Your friends are safe. I promise."

He glanced upward.

"We need to swim farther out," she warned. *"If the pirates see me, they will kill me."*

Angst pulled his head away to nod, hoping she understood. He was completely helpless in his heavy armor and far too exhausted to wield himself to safety. Why was he so exhausted? What had Air done?

They swam fast, and she kept her lips pressed to his, pushing air into his lungs when he wouldn't draw it in voluntarily. It was unnatural, and Angst struggled to breathe normally. He gulped in air and tasted something else. Not fish. It tasted like…iron. He pushed away, flailing in panic. Moyra slowed, bringing them above the surface. Her lips freed his, and he breathed in as much fresh air as he could through the choppy waters. She frowned at him with her blue eyebrows and pouted with her overly full lips, even while her tongue licked the outside of his mouth.

"What?" Her voice sounded worried in his mind. *"What is wrong?"*

He licked his lips, cautiously. Her thin, forked tongue met his, and she smiled as if it was playtime. Now that he was thinking about it, all he could taste was iron. He must've gotten cut. That had to be it—this was his own blood. The tension in his shoulders melted.

"I tasted blood and thought you'd eaten someo…er, one of us," he said awkwardly. "A human."

Her frown returned as she tilted her head to one side. *"I did."*

"What?" he shouted then looked around in case someone was nearby, listening. Much quieter, he said, "What?"

"I ate hooman." Her face was twisted between confidence and confusion.

Blood had been in his mouth, human blood, and it wasn't his. Her tongue continued licking his lips as though it had a mind of its own. He buried his face in the ocean as his stomach emptied. It wasn't enough. He wanted to cry, or scream. His heart raced. He had to remain calm, Moyra was the only one who could return him to shallow waters. He pulled up, gasping for air, and his stomach lurched, giving him only seconds to shove his face under the water again. It was embarrassing to throw up in front of her. He struggled to calm the panic in his gut as he pulled his head out of the water and looked into her eyes.

He gripped her shoulders firmly. "We are not food. I'm not food." He frowned. "Do you look at me and think food?"

"Not you." She sucked in her lips and looked away. *"But they are not you!"*

"They are me! You can't eat us," he admonished, shaking her. "None of us! Do we eat you because you're part fish?"

Her dark eyes were now downcast and her pouty lips trembled. She shivered, and her buoyancy waned, sinking them inches deeper. It was like she'd never been scolded, but she had to know or they couldn't be friends. Couldn't be anything.

"I am not a dumb fish!" she thought loud enough to make him wince. She sounded hurt.

"I'm sorry," Angst apologized. "It was an example, a bad one. I don't think you're a fish."

"You think I am a dumb fish."

"No, I promise I don't." He struggled to find the words. He needed her. There was no way he could swim to shore on his own. "I think you're a person."

Moyra looked up from the water, her eyes filled with the contemplation of saving him or letting him sink. What could he do? Not only did he need her, he liked her. But she had also just eaten a human… He was so conflicted. Without her, he would die, and that probably had to take precedence. For now, at least.

"I like you, Moyra. I think you're fun." He smiled. "I want to be friends."

She immediately smiled and pursed her lips for a kiss, her long, forked tongue dancing playfully.

"Nope," he said, pulling away.

"Chi-cken," she replied, her eyes thinning.

"Oh, you know what that means?" he teased.

"Water chi-cken are stupid bottom dwellers that run away from everything," she explained. *"You are chi-cken."*

"Yes, I guess I am," he said. "Sometimes."

"I am sorry...for the man." She looked down.

"Please tell me he was dead," Angst pleaded, clinging to his last vestige of hope. "When you ate him?"

She stared into his eyes, and her darker-than-dark gaze seemed honest, or at least naïve to the subtleties of human deception.

"Please." He really wanted this to be true.

"His legs and arms were gone, he was bleeding deliciously." She spoke quickly, her eyes wide and a smile on her face. *"His heart was so slow."*

"Almost dead?" Angst asked.

"So very almost dead, An-gst," she promised. *"His breath was blood, his eyes were lost. I could not help myself. I am...I am sorry."*

"I believe you," he said.

"I will try to do as you ask," she said reluctantly. *"But I still do not understand."*

"Would you have eaten one of your own?"

"Oh no," she said, her nose scrunching in disgust. *"We cannot."*

"Why?" he asked.

"That is wrong," she said, her lips curling in disgust.

"Then you can't eat one of mine," he stressed. "If we're going to be friends."

"Oh." She thought on this for a while before committing. *"Okay."*

"Promise?"

She drew him closer, though he wouldn't have thought it possible. Her eyes seemed relieved. She planted her warm lips on his, and he had no choice but to meet them.

Moyra pulled away and smiled. *"I am not chi-cken."*

"So I've noticed." He couldn't help the sigh. His head, free from one crisis, immediately jumped into another. "We need to get back! My friends—"

"Are safe." She smiled.

"How do you know?" He asked.

"You talk to me in pictures, not words." She pointed at her head. *"I saw your friends and saved them."*

"So you can read my mind too?" The water suddenly felt colder. Or was that his blood?

"You mostly think of these." She looked down while wiggling her torso, making her breasts threaten to bounce out of the ocean.

"Great," he said, forcing eye contact. "Actually, it is great. Thank you for saving them. I should get back, they'll be worried."

"Go ahead and swim," she teased.

"I don't think I can," he pleaded. "I'm exhausted. More than I should be."

"Maybe you need to eat." She feigned sincerity. *"I know where you could find some fresh hooman."*

Her body shook as she laughed, her bare breasts now jiggling out of the water. She noticed him trying not to stare and, for some reason, laughed harder. *"I will see you to shore, silly hooman,"* she said. *"So you can eat some trees and walking things."*

This really set her off, and he felt suddenly lost in her world. It was great that she had a sense of humor, but the joke baffled him. He watched her body shudder and heard her laughter in his mind. How many times in his life had he lost himself like that, to something silly that nobody else got? That trigger that was solely his own, that kept prompting more, uncontrollable giggles. It was so human, and that realization made him feel closer to her.

"Are you okay now?" he asked. "Are we?"

She sucked in her lips, as if fighting off one last bout, before nodding with mock sincerity. She pressed her mouth to his and kissed him. He knew he should stop, and guilt swelled in his chest, but it was so easy to get caught up in her. When she pulled away, he couldn't help but grin.

"Yes, chi-cken." She smirked. *"We are fine."* Moyra smiled, nodded once, and swam fast enough to make his ears flap.

* * * *

Angst crawled toward shore, shock from the cold water making him dig into the sand with stiff fingers and drag himself along more dramatically than he'd wanted. Moyra had rushed him to waist-deep water behind a small reef. She'd been reluctant to let him go so far from shore, but he'd promised he could make it, fearful that the pirates would attack her on sight. The trek was farther than he'd thought, though, and he was now sick with exhaustion. Hector and Tarness ran into the water, gripping him under his arms and pulling him to shore.

He rested on all fours to catch his breath. Tori was kissing his cheeks, crying desperately. Hector was yelling something while Dallow asked a hundred questions.

"Are we all okay?" he spluttered. "Are we all here?"

"All of us are here, Angst," Hector said softly. "But not all of the pirates. Several men are missing."

"I saw her," Tori said after composing herself. "I think your mermaid saved me."

"Me too," Dallow agreed. "I couldn't see, but no human can move in water like that."

"And me," Tarness said, his voice heavy. "She was something."

"I don't understand," Jarblech said. He hadn't seen her approach. "Two men are still missing, but most were saved by mermaids."

"Just one," Angst said, feeling hopeful that they would see her in a better light. "Maybe they aren't all as bad as you thought."

"Tell that to the ones still missing," she replied gruffly.

"Moyra saved everyone who could be saved," Angst snapped.

"Moyra?" Jarblech said, placing both hands on her hips. She

eyed Hector, who shook his head, and then returned her dark gaze to Angst. "So, she's yours?"

"Mine?" Angst struggled to stand on his own. "It's not like she's a pet."

"You're right." She got in his face. "You can't tame a shark."

"Is that why nobody tamed you?" Angst shouted.

Hector grabbed her wrist and squeezed, and a long curved dagger dropped to the sand. "Save that for me," he said with a wink.

"Funny." Her thin eyes opened a little, and she yanked her arm free of his grip. "Look at what that attack did to my ships! Falcon's the only one left!"

"Because of Angst," Hector said, crossing his arms, his bushy eyebrows raised high.

"Yeah," she said reluctantly, staring intently at a pebble in the sand.

"Angst?" Hector asked with a nudge.

His friend was right. They needed her, and her ship. Angst sighed deeply and looked around. The shipyard was flotsam and kindling save for one steel ship. The town, however, was in much better shape.

"Well," Angst said half-heartedly. He wasn't in the mood to be nice. "I guess it could've been worse."

It was too much, and Jarblech's hands shot out, reaching for Angst's neck. She stopped when they heard screaming and both turned to see pirates sprinting toward them. There was a gentle tremor as the geode leaned forward. It swayed like a drunken sailor unsure of which direction to fall. Jarblech screamed something incomprehensible. As if in slow motion, the enormous, hollow stone collapsed over the town, covering it in a dome. The entire pirate city was gone, hidden beneath the monstrous rock like a turtle.

"Worse?" Jarblech screamed. She spat, pointing at the missing town. "You come here and bring nothing but destruction and death! It's not safe around you lot! There's no way I'm taking you to Angoria! I won't do it!" She wrapped her hands around his throat, squeezing tight.

"That's enough." Angst pulled them off. He stomped toward the dome, pushing his way through the pirates until he reached Dulgirgraut. Those nearest moved away, giving Angst several feet of space. "It's not safe around me? It's not safe anywhere. There are dragons to the East, monsters swimming in the ocean, and giant creatures who claim to be living elements!"

He was pacing now, his pathway growing with his anger as pirates stepped away. Victoria raised her hand to point at him, but Hector held it down, and nodded to shush her.

"We can either sit idly by, waiting to die, or we can take the battle to them!" He swung Dulgirgraut like it was an extension of his arm, pointing at the geode. Pirates leaped out of the way. "I'm taking your boat, whether you come with or not!"

"It's not safe," Jarblech muttered. "We'll all die."

"You aren't safer with anyone else!" he shouted.

Angst spun about, both hands meeting on the hilt of Dulgirgraut. A burgundy glow surrounded the blade, and he took a deep breath. The ground shook as the geode tilted upward. It was heavy, but he let his fury flow through the blade and used that power like a lever. His arms shook from the strain, and he focused, ignoring the gasps and cries around him. The geode reared back with a noisy crunch, slowly returning to its place. It settled to once again half-hide the town, which was mostly undamaged. Angst anchored the rock, melding it into the ground, letting it sink deeper into the earth so it wouldn't fall again. The tip of Dulgirgraut fell to the ground, the red glow surrounding it faded. His heart was racing and he felt the chill of cold sweat in the gentle breeze. He faced Jarblech, whose mouth was wide open.

She closed it, sucking in her lips. "She's my boat," she said quietly. "I'll be steering her to Angoria."

25

Unsel

Rook should've been tired, having departed at the break of dawn, but was instead anxious to the point of jittery. Their plan was a mix of bad, rushed ideas tossed into a bucket with hope and happenstance. They faced so many unknowns, from Unsel behind to Scar ahead, that patience did not come naturally and the half-day ride to Angst and Heather's felt like an obstacle. He'd spent most of his time contemplating what-ifs until Janda nudged him into courtesy, reminding him to converse with their eight wards. An older family with a teen boy and girl, an even older man, and Janda's niece, nephew, and brother-in-law. Her sister, Nikkola, and the other ten wielders who'd defended Unsel from the cavastil bird attack had split up to guard each group. It probably wasn't necessary, but he believed a mass exodus of people would bring unwanted attention.

Rook hadn't taken into consideration how slow it would be to ride with families. Not everyone could summon swifen, like Janda's red glass lioness. That was something he felt all wielders should know. The efficiency and speed of twenty wielders on swifen was exciting and could be an asset to his militia, or even Unsel, if things ever got straightened out. He hoped Angst would see Victoria back safely, and soon. Not just to save the day, but to repair the mess of laws Alloria and Vars seemed to toss at Unsel like darts.

They reached the narrow, multi-colored stone pathway, which meant they were only fifteen miles away. The ground rumbled, making the old man look around, and the younger children whine nervously.

"I'm surprised we can feel the sinkholes all the way out here," Janda said, frowning in concern.

There was a loud crash followed by a string of creative profanity. The mom covered her daughter's ears while her son giggled. She glared at Rook as though he were the one cursing. He frowned and pulled ahead.

"I don't think it's the sinkholes. Wait here with them," Rook commanded. "I'll ride ahead to check."

Rook went only a hundred yards before he stopped and dismounted. To the side of the path, he could make out what looked like a big mushroom. A single gray stone dome peeked over the hill. Squeezing through the tree line, Rook wielded his sword and approached the mushroom cautiously. It was massive, taller than a mounted man and wider than a cabin. He slowed as he crested the hill, staring in awe at a dozen giant mushroom caps scattered around the hillside, each spread roughly a hundred yards apart. They looked like enormous bubbles resting on water's surface. All of them had two holes large enough to enter, both in the front and on top. He could hear Jaden cursing nearby and hurried.

The young man was sitting, wiping blood from his nose and lip. He looked gaunt, with disheveled hair and dark circles under his eyes. Facial hair made a patchy shadow beneath his chin, and Rook winced at the smell.

"You okay?" Rook asked, sheathing his sword.

"Rook?" Jaden said, attempting to push himself up. He plopped back down and reached out a hand. "Yeah, just exhausted."

"What is all this?" Rook asked, looking around in awe.

"Chatlen," Jaden explained. "Temporary housing for all the refugee wielders."

"Temporary?" Rook said in astonishment.

"Yeah, I figured that stone would be easy for Angst to get rid of," he said, "and sturdy enough to keep everyone safe."

"Safe? From what?" Rook asked.

"Scar." Jaden shook his head. "I rode straight to the house last night and found him sitting there. A cute puppy, and then bam!" he shouted, making Rook jump. "Big as a house. Bigger! Three tails, six eyes, covered in steel daggers, and angry! But, fortunately, preoccupied with bubbles that come from the ground. And those bubbles...I barely escaped. They grabbed up bugs and squirrels, and all of it floated toward him."

"I've heard the story." Rook frowned. "That's how Angst found him. They thought it was caused by the Vex'kvette."

"It was close. That beast is a danger," Jaden said, his eyes wide. "He runs free, but I think these are sturdy enough to fend him off. Or hopefully he'll ignore them."

"Hopefully?" Rook asked.

Jaden merely shrugged, and Rook nodded in agreement. What else could they do?

"I didn't know you could wield stone," Rook said. He was amazed at everything Jaden had accomplished.

"Not well. Not nearly as well as Angst," he said. "I'm better with spells, which are a combination of elements."

Rook nodded politely, pretending to understand. "You made a small town. I think that counts as doing well. But the name, chatlen?"

"That's what the buildings are called," Jaden said. "I was thinking we could call this place Jadenville."

"Or Rookshire," Rook said with a broad smile.

Jaden winced, leaning back until Rook heard a pop. "Want to see inside?"

Rook was impressed. In spite of the young man's exhaustion, Jaden was obviously proud of his creations. He helped Jaden up and followed him through the arched doorway. It was like entering a round cave with perfectly smooth walls and floor. Along the base of the walls were four rectangles, each of them six feet long with an ankle-high stone frame. The hole he'd seen in the roof formed a convex cylinder, like a hollow birdbath that hung upside down. Below the cylinder was a waist-tall stone bucket roughly three feet across. The bucket had a two-foot lip all around it.

"Is that a fire pit?" Rook pointed at the bucket. "And a chimney?"

"For cooking, and warmth," Jaden said, nodding proudly. He patted the lip. "And a table to eat on."

"And those?" Rook asked in bewilderment, pointing at the rectangles.

"For bedding," Jaden explained. "They can be filled with a mattress, or straw or—"

Rook grabbed his shoulders and pulled him in for an unexpected hug. "You, my friend, have just made this whole thing possible. We may even survive. How did you know to do all of this?"

"The chatlen?" he asked, his eyes oddly distant. "I'm really not sure. I've seen them before, but I can't remember where."

"Not just the buildings," Rook said. "How did you know we were coming?"

"Maarja and Jintorich told Heather what happened at the Wizard's Revenge." His face became dark. "Then Heather *encouraged* me to do all of this. I feel a little used."

"Remind me not to make her angry," Rook stated. "But we may need to use you some more."

"I assumed." Jaden looked tired. "How many?"

Rook counted on his fingers. "Maybe five?"

"That's it?"

"Alloria sent out a proclamation late last night stating that nobody would be arrested," Rook explained.

"And people believed her?" Jaden asked.

Rook shrugged.

"I can handle five, I'm sure," Jaden said with a sigh. He looked at Rook for a long moment. "And?"

"And a big one. A really big one," Rook said then explained

to Jaden's weary expression. "We can't all meet out in the snow."

* * * *

Jadenville...or Rookshire

Twenty wielders had made it safely, alone or with their families. Each had chosen their temporary housing, and settled in quickly with more compliments than complaints. For some, their new living quarters were nicer than what they had in Unsel. In the center of the stone town, Jaden had erected a building sizeable enough for everyone to meet in. It was almost identical to the smaller mushrooms, except for stone chairs scattered around the larger fire pit. The lip around the pit was only inches off the ground, and wide enough for Rook to stand on—allowing him to pace in a circle and address everyone. The wielders had met there after tucking in their children, wives, or husbands. They were tired and anxious and waited with the patience of a child sitting in front of unopened presents.

"Is this all of us?" Rook asked.

"There may be more coming tomorrow," Nikkola answered. "But no firm commitments."

"We should send someone back to town to check on them," Andec said. "A non-wielder."

"My husband would do that," an older woman answered. "Maybe he'll get arrested, and I'll finally be rid of him."

Several chuckled, and Rook nodded at her gratefully. Her humor chiseled at the edge they all felt, and he saw a few shoulders drop like his did.

"Jaden there built all of this," he said, before noticing that the young man was sound asleep. "Be sure to thank him when he's not passed out."

Several more chuckles and a few smiles appeared but were soon clouded by apprehension.

"I know you're worried. So am I. There's a lot we need to do," Rook said. "We need food, bedding, firewood, and soldiers."

"Soldiers?" several shouted while others mumbled.

"If Alloria changes her mind once again and sends soldiers of Unsel, we need to be prepared," he said, holding out his hands to calm them.

"But that requires armor, which means money," a sharp-nosed man said.

"So does the food." The woman sitting next to him rubbed her hands fretfully. "And, well, everything else."

"We're all going to have to work together," Janda interrupted. "Each of us have abilities. We need to explain what we can do and see if it can help the rest."

"What about him?" the sharp-nosed man asked, pointing at Rook. "What does he do?"

"He stands there and looks cute," Nikkola shouted.

More laughter, mostly from women, painted Rook's cheeks bright red. Janda shot her sister a warning look that was returned with a mocking tongue.

"I have more leadership experience than anyone here," Rook explained, trying to change the subject. "But if you want the job...?"

The man kept staring but said nothing.

"Good." Rook nodded. "Until then, shut up."

"What about the stuff we can't make?" a young woman from the other side of the fire asked. "Armor requires a blacksmith, and steel. We can hunt, but we need more than meat to survive. All of that costs gold."

Rook looked around the room to see blank stares. Even Janda shrugged. "I take it none of you can make gold?"

He hadn't expected so much laughter.

"If I could, I'd have invited you all to stay at my castle." An old man guffawed.

"Gold," Jaden said, waking with a start. "Heather said there's plenty of gold in the cellar. More than plenty."

Wood in the fireplace settled as the room shook. It didn't last long enough to be sinkhole tremors, or briefly enough to be

Jaden's dome building. As the rumbling became louder and more frequent, it sounded like a galloping horse. Most wielders in the room stood and many arms and hands glowed with different colors as they gathered their powers. The thumping stopped nearby. All was silent until Scar howled in anguish. An enormous snout shoved into the entrance, huffing embers and ash toward the far wall, making wielders scramble to the sides of the room or stamp out burning sticks. The snorting stopped and the young pup yelped several times.

"What in the…?" someone said.

Scar barked so loudly that some screamed. He rammed into the dome again and again.

Rook saw pale faces filled with fear, but at least everyone would be okay. "That would be Angst's dog," Rook said. "It's my understanding he changes erratically, between monster and puppy."

There was another yip from a puppy and the cooing sound of a small girl. Rook recognized Janda's niece as she entered with the black lab pup in her arms. Everyone rushed away from the entrance, shuffling to each side of Rook. Janda and Nikkola inched forward with warning hands.

"Kala, honey," Nikkola said in a wavering voice. She took baby steps with her hands held out. "Please put the puppy down."

"No," Janda whispered sharply. "Please take the puppy outside."

The twelve-year-old girl petted the lab puppy calmly. Its fine black coat neatly matched her long black hair. As the women approached, the girl frowned and the dog's eyes flashed red.

"Stop." He hopped off the shelf around the fire pit.

Both women peered at him with defensive, angry eyes. He waved them back and walked to Kala, kneeling and holding out a hand to Scar.

"Scar isn't feeling very well," Rook said gently. "Your mum is worried he could hurt you."

"He won't," Kala said confidently. She looked down at the

pup, who nuzzled himself into her armpit. "Scar is just a lit-tle...off. He just needs the right kind of attention."

Rook attempted to pet Scar, but the pup grumbled, his eyes glowing red. Kala's eyes flashed red, and Rook jerked his hand back. "What else does Scar need?"

She frowned, her eyes still glowing a dark shade of red as she continued petting Scar. Finally, she smiled. "Scar wants Angst to come home."

"Oh," Rook said, forcing his voice to be calm. "I'm sure that will be soon."

"And Scar wants him to...to..." She screwed up her face in concentration. "Get it back?"

26

Nordruaut

"This is nonsense," Rasaol said in a harsh whisper. "We should have just killed him."

They stood in the great hall staring at their captive. Guldrich was asleep on the floor, chained to a wall and balled up like an animal. He snored every few breaths, his ears twitching nervously.

"We aren't at war," Jarle replied firmly. He wiped the stress from his face like drawing off rain water. "The law dictates that disputes are resolved by a challenge. And so it will be done."

"You don't need to tell me this," Rasaol snapped. "But we should be at war. We will be soon."

Jarle studied his peer and noticed a wildness in his eyes, as if the pupils were too small and falling away. Rasaol regained his composure quickly, but the shock of that irrational glare made it hard not to see the old king as mad. Rasaol put on a smile and took a breath not quite deep enough to cleanse madness.

"You act as though we are under constant attack," Jarle accused. "Has this happened before?"

"Not like this." Rasaol tugged at his beard. "We've found the creatures' bodies several times, frozen, or barely alive. Last week, there were five huddled behind the hall, caught dead in the ice."

"I've not heard of such a thing," Jarle said in disbelief. "Were they attacking? Were they spying?"

"From what I could see, they were only dying." Rasaol sniffed. "They weren't even wearing furs or leathers to stay warm."

"What?" Jarle crossed his muscular arms. "How did they even get here? We are days away from the Fulk'han border."

Rasaol shook his head.

Jarle stared at the man for any sign of knowledge, but Rasaol only peered at the fire.

"Whatever the magics that changed the Fulk'han also brings them here," Rasaol said with conviction. "That is why we need to prepare for war, before that nation of zealots invade."

"And you chose Niihlu to champion us?" Jarle asked.

"He wanted it," Rasaol admitted. "More than anyone."

"Exactly why he was the wrong choice!" Jarle turned on Rasaol angrily, making the king step back. "I saw the hunger in his eyes throughout our travels. He tried to take one of those weapons from travelers during our hunt. He lost to the challenge."

"The hunger?" Rasaol asked.

"Greed, my king," Jarle said with bitter disappointment. "His desire for property, for something that wasn't his…it was offensive."

"Aren't you taking the old way of doing things a bit far?" Rasaol scoffed, waving his hand. "There is nothing wrong with wanting something. There is nothing wrong with fighting for what you want!"

"You have forgotten," Jarle said in surprise. "We live with nature, with the land and animals around us. We don't go to war with other peoples of Ehrde. Do you forget what happened when all Nordruaut was hungry with greed? What it cost?"

"Of course I remember," Rasaol said, nodding with his head while his eyes told a different story. "The young see things differently."

"Which is why we need to teach them," Jarle said with measured patience. "They need to see we still believe this."

"When we are at war, Jarle?" Rasaol asked. "Now is not the time for lessons about how small we are in the life of Ehrde. It's time to protect our own. They mean to kill us, and we have no choice but to attack them first."

"But we are small," Jarle replied. "We are a mere piece of Ehrde. The stories teach us that we are symbiotic with every-thing—"

"Your Majesty." A young Nordruaut male jogged into the room, interrupting Rasaol's yawn. He eyed Jarle warily, hesitant to speak in front of the other man.

"What?" Rasaol said, looking cautiously at Jarle from the corner of his eyes. "Another attack?"

"Another woman," the young man said in a deep voice. "Niihlu."

"That fool," Rasaol said, sighing deeply and closing his eyes.

"What is it?" Jarle asked.

"When he tries to have sex with women, they die," Rasaol said in a heavy voice. His wild eyes were now exhausted and old.

"What?" Jarle snapped. "Then why would he even try? That's murder!"

"Bring us to him," Rasaol commanded. "Now!"

* * * *

Guldrich opened an eye and watched them leave the room. The tension between the two men had been delicious, and he would have loved to needle them into battle. Nordruaut, the eastern half, seemed to be looking over the edge and peering at war from a distance. How hard would it be to nudge them clos-er? His mind raced. There was so little time. He was no match for the Nordruaut with the axe. The challenge tomorrow wouldn't be about killing their champion, it would be about pushing them closer to that ledge.

* * * *

She lay there, a rigid husk where only an hour earlier she had been warm and breathing. Her torso was like an icy lake whose thin center had collapsed into dark waters. Frozen shoulders and arms reached out but the forearms had been torn from her body. Her face was like a beautiful statue, and she stared eerily at the ceiling with a finely chiseled gasp of surprise. Jarle knelt beside her body and held his hand over her eyes before realizing they would not shut. He stood quickly and reared about with an angry finger pointed at Niihlu.

Frosty air hovered about Niihlu's bitter glare as he stared at the woman's body, completely ignoring Jarle's threatening posture.

"What were you thinking?" Rasaol asked before Jarle could speak.

"I thought I could control it," Niihlu said, every word crackling like splintered ice.

"You forced her to do this?" Jarle asked. Furious, he shoved the man's shoulder, jerking back his hand at the sting of cold.

"Never," Niihlu spat. "She came to me…"

"This is four, Niihlu," Rasaol said. "Four Nordruaut dead because you thought you had control. Why?"

"I'm so cold," Niihlu said.

Jarle had seen that same despair in the younger man's eyes when Feemi had been killed. He could only imagine every death hollowing the younger man out, coring Niihlu until he was an empty shell.

"Yet you still did this?" Jarle asked, pointing at the dead woman. "You knew this could happen!"

"I thought I could control it," Niihlu said again, looking at Rasaol.

"You heard him," Rasaol said in an unconvincing voice. "It was an accident."

"Was Feemi the fourth *accident*, or the fifth?" Jarle snapped.

With an angry roar, Niihlu struck out. The palm of his hand

landed on Jarle's chest with such force that Jarle flew back against the wall. An icy cloud filled the air in his wake.

"Niihlu!" Rasaol shouted, staring down the young man.

Niihlu stormed out of the room as Rasaol approached Jarle. He knelt, waving away the frost hanging in the air. Jarle coughed and accepted Rasaol's hand as he stood.

"How is it you live?" Rasaol asked in surprise. "I never thought our western brothers to be so sturdy."

"I don't know." Jarle looked at his chest, brushing away frozen bits of leather to show he was otherwise unharmed. "I've been struck much harder."

"Maybe he was holding back," Rasaol said.

"You heard him! He doesn't have that kind of control," Jarle said sharply. "That's no champion, my king. Whatever you have created is broken."

27

"What did you do to Falcon?" Jarblech demanded from the deck. "What did you do to my ship?"

Her voice was the dying scream of a dragon, and loud enough to drag Angst out of his hammock and upstairs without further prodding. She stormed along the railing, slamming the wood planks with every step as though stomping on beetles—making sailors rush from underfoot to avoid being trampled. Jarblech's curses seared the sleep from Angst's eyes and was more effective at waking him than a freezing cold bath. Awake but groggy, he was barely fast enough to jump back from her accusing finger as she spun to face him.

"I almost killed my pilot for not following commands," she spit out and wiped her mouth. "What in the felk do I do with you?"

"I'm kinda sleepy," Angst said, stifling a yawn. "A hug would be nice."

"No jokes on deck." She grimaced, fighting back the barest of smirks.

"Wouldn't even consider it, cap'n." He gave into the yawn, arching his back and wincing. After three nights, he was convinced the hammock was purposefully twisting his spine until the top half would permanently face the wrong direction.

"Landies." She rolled her eyes then shouted at her pirates. "Find that wind or you'll be swimming back to port!"

She grabbed his tunic with both hands and pulled him toward her foot, which he tripped over to land roughly on his chest. "Hey!" he said, but before he could complain more, she rammed her hands between his shoulders. The weight of the blow forced all the air from his lungs. He winced as his back popped at every joint from below his shoulder to the base of his skull. He blinked slowly, dizzy from the sudden rush of air to his lungs and blood to his brain. Angst rolled over and sat upright, wide-eyed and feeling brought back to life.

Angst rotated his shoulder, which cracked noisily. He breathed deeply and smiled. "That…that was fantastic!" he said. "Thank you!"

"Yeah, yeah," she said dismissively, helping him to his feet. "Now, before I kill you, what's wrong with her?"

He looked around. Sails were heaved-ho and held wind, the boat didn't list, and they moved forward, albeit slowly. He didn't see the problem. Jarblech snapped her finger and pumped her right fist into the air as if cheering at a jousting match. The pilot, Tamara, spun the wheel as far starboard as it would go. The ship continued moving forward when it should've turned. Hesitantly, it followed Tamara's change in course, but so slowly it was like the ship had a bad hangover. Jarblech looked at Angst, her eyes desperate for help. She cocked her head to one side without stating the obvious.

"Oh," he said. "That," Angst said, raising his eyebrows. He held out his hands. A gentle blue glow surrounded them, making nearby pirates stare nervously at each other and inch away. He searched the ship for holes or dents, or possibly an anchor or something dragging them down. All appeared to be well—the steel was just as solid as when he'd formed it.

"She, um, your ship isn't damaged," he said, leaning from side to side. His back felt amazing. "I guess I don't understand. What's going on?"

"Quit that," she snapped, and he stopped leaning. "She's sluggish, moving like an old lady. An old lady who weighs about two tons."

"Well, I'm sure the steel armor has added some weight," Angst suggested. "Dallow could explain better, but that would be my guess."

"Some weight?" she said sharply. "She's carried plenty of cargo without dragging us down like this! We're barely moving! It'd be faster to walk."

"I could always drop the steel," Angst suggested.

"Do that and I'm turning us about," she grumbled.

"Not very quickly," he teased, and then became overly serious under her glare, mocking her dark gaze.

"Can't you give her a push?" she asked. "Throw some wind at my sails?"

"Uh, well," he said hesitantly, "I don't do wind."

"You lifted her up and dressed her in steel," she reminded him. "And you can't give her a push?"

"I suppose I can," Angst said with a frown. "But I don't think I could do it all day."

She peered at him as though preparing to undo her fix to his back.

"Fine. I'll try." Angst lifted his glowing hands. He was unsure where to grab it...her. So, the way he would try to move any heavy object, he got behind the ship with an air shield and pushed.

The ship abruptly rocked to one side, making most on deck fall to their knees.

"Sorry," Angst said. He tilted his head the other direction and the ship followed, too much.

Jarblech's smacked him across his face, and he immediately stopped. The ship returned to an upright position, but the pirates waited cautiously, remaining on their hands and knees.

"Are you trying to sink her?" she roared.

"Hit me again and I might," Angst said, wiggling his jaw.

"You've got to be gentle," she stressed.

"You first," Angst grumbled.

"What's going on?" Tarness came on deck.

"Is someone trying to sink the ship?" Hector said from behind him.

Victoria tripped up the stairs, ran to the nearest railing, and yacked loudly over the side. She stopped long enough to shoot Angst a look of pure death before vomiting in the ocean once more. Angst bared his teeth in an open-mouthed grimace. This was going to take a lot of apologies, and he wondered if it wasn't a good time to go home.

"Jarblech says the ship is sluggish and wanted me to give it a push." The captain's eyes became dangerous. "That's worse than Heather's wife-look. Oh, fine. I'm supposed to give *her* a push."

Jarblech nodded once with appreciation. "Now try again!"

With a sigh, Angst pushed, slowly at first, and then with greater force. The boat jerked, listed, and began turning. Like a chorus, the pirates cursed him. One screamed as she fell from the lookout, swinging from the ropes. Victoria was tossed over—all he could see was her hands holding onto the railing.

"Angst!" Tori screamed.

"No, no, no!" Jarblech yelled. Her fists were balled up and ready to strike.

"I can fix this," Angst said, but the boat continued spinning around in a circle like a top.

This wasn't going to end well, so he let go of the ship when it was almost going in the right direction. Tarness pulled Victoria back on deck. Vomit coated her hair and shoulder. She did not look pleased as she knelt by the railing and shakily wiped it off.

"Try holding onto her sides," Tarness advised.

"What about pushing the sails?" Hector asked.

"He'll bust the masts," she snarled. "You don't belong on a ship, wielder."

"Angst, I think I'm going to be sick again," Victoria cried.

Now they were all yelling a confusing mixture of suggestions and scoldings. Angst's hands stopped glowing, and he lowered them. He shoved through his consultants and walked to the barracks entrance.

"Where do you think you're going?" Jarblech called after him.

"Back to bed," Angst replied.

"You need to figure this out," the captain called after him. "I don't want to be stuck out here, it's dangerous!"

Angst waved her off as he walked down the stairs into the hold.

"A bit moody, that one," she said.

"You don't even know." Hector shook his head.

* * * *

Angst returned to the deck after several hours of almost-sleep in the hammock. It was sunny and cool but not cold. They were slowly heading south, and it was becoming mild. Dark clouds formed in the far distance, menacing and beautiful. He took a draw of musty water from a metal cup. It was disgusting, and he could barely gulp it down. He'd been told not to waste water so drank the rest quickly to minimize the damage to his taste buds.

In spite of his concerns, he wasn't greeted by an angry crew or a knife to the gut. Everything seemed back to normal, save a few worried looks and bitter glances. The pirates mostly avoided him, which was ideal. Victoria, on the other hand, seemed to be in a state of almost-dead by the railing, and he wondered if she'd been there throughout his early morning nap. He was cautiously approaching when he felt a tap on the back of his armor.

"No armor, Mr. Angst," Jarblech said behind him.

"I thought we were in constant danger," Angst argued.

"We are," Jarblech said dismissively. "Which is why you need to be armor-less."

"You know," he put on his most charming smile, "most beautiful women take me out to dinner before asking me to get undressed."

"You'll be dinner at the bottom of the ocean if you don't take it off," she said dryly.

"I hate not having my armor on," Angst grumbled. "It'll be hard to get to when it's hidden away in some barrel."

"Well, I hate your giant sword glowing red and hovering over the bow like a beacon for every ship-eating monster," Jarblech retorted. "It's like a sign pointing right at an all-you-can-eat-buffet."

"Dulgirgraut has been like that since we left," Angst explained. "I'm not one to argue."

"So you say," Jarblech said. "I'll live with it, and you live with the armor in the floating barrels. You get knocked overboard with that armor on, and you'll drown."

Angst glanced over the edge of the ship to be splashed in the face by sea water. He wondered what, or who, could've done that. "I'm pretty sure I'd survive, somehow," he said with a smirk, wiping drops off his face and shaking his hand dry. "But if removing my armor makes you happy, I can manage, for now."

"Done," Jarblech said, spitting into her open hand and holding it out.

He reluctantly shook in agreement, wincing as he pulled away from the sticky mess. Jarblech smiled as if she'd won something. Angst nodded, grimacing as he gripped the railing with a spit-covered palm, skidding it along the wood to clean off as much as he could. Jarblech slapped him roughly on the shoulder as she made her way up to the steering wheel. Angst watched in amazement. No matter how much the ship rocked, Jarblech walked across the deck as though she were on solid ground.

Victoria was leaning over the edge and dry heaving. He slid over a few steps and placed a caring hand on her shoulder. She glanced up long enough to convey, emphatically, that it was his fault. Her cheeks appeared sunken and there were dark circles under her large eyes. He wanted to hold her until it ended, but barely even dared the thought in her current condition.

"Hector says this will pass," Angst said in his softest voice.

"Dallow is mixing something," Tori rasped. "And then I'll sleep."

"Assuming you can even swallow it," Angst said.

Her cheeks puffed out at the word swallow, and she was once again over the railing.

"Sorry," Angst said, trying to hold her hair back.

"Do you enjoy watching me vomit?" she finally asked, spitting out bile and waving him off.

He stepped away helplessly, at a complete loss for what to do.

"Figure out how to get us there faster, and get me off this boat!" Her voice was scratchy, and she seemed short of breath. "Go! Take your armor off and get to it!"

* * * *

"Are you even listening?" Jarblech asked, her temper building with every word.

"Yes," Angst lied. "Of course I was…am."

"Dallow gave up hours ago," she said sharply. "It was impressive how much he knew, and how stupid you are."

"It's always impressive how much Dallow knows," Angst said with raised eyebrows, ignoring the slight.

"Hector said it would take a woman," she said. "That you wouldn't listen to anyone else."

He nodded attentively from his perch on the stairs leading up to the top deck, staring off at the distant storm clouds. Something nagged in the back of his mind; the clouds looked unnatural. They were bigger than he was used to seeing, and spun like a top. Maybe it was just the way storms formed in the ocean. He sought Dulgirgraut for information, who offered nothing, merely hovering and glowing like a giant, useless candle. He was tempted to leave it on the ship for decoration. It flashed once, making nearby pirates jump, but there was no answer, not even a song.

"Then what did I say?" she prodded, digging under her do-rag with a finger.

"It was about moving the boat in waves," Angst said dismissively. "Ouch!"

She'd smacked the back of his head, again.

"You know, that really doesn't help me remember," he grunted. "Even my mother didn't smack me like that."

"She should have," Jarblech groused. "That poor woman."

Her head covering was now on the ground, its removal releasing such a tangled mass of gray, oily curls that Angst feared they were alive. He stood quickly and scrambled back as she lowered her head and proceeded to scratch. The gentle wind raked through her coils of hair, rocking them like wind chimes. Angst tried looking away, but was mesmerized by the sheen and movement, as if each follicle of hair fought to escape, seeking freedom from its tyrannical owner. He reached out to poke a particularly threatening appendage, wondering if it would recoil or eat his fingernail.

"What?" she asked, glancing up at his finger.

"I, uh…" he hedged. "Nothing, nothing at all."

"Go on," she prodded.

"Do you wash it?" he asked.

"Wash it? Of course not!" She seemed offended at the suggestion. "Natural oils keep your hair healthy. You don't see any bald spots on this head!"

"Well, that much is true," he agreed and then chuckled. "Certainly not like Hector."

"I wasn't talking about Hector," she said with a raised eyebrow.

"I don't have any bald spots!" Angst retorted, instinctively reaching up to his full head of peppered gray hair.

"No, of course not," she mocked. "We aren't getting anywhere, are we?"

"I'm pretty sure I could still spin the boat in circles," he said, still testing the thickness of the hair on his crown, undecided if he could feel hair or skin. He was sure it was hair.

Shaking her head, Jarblech led him to the helm. Tamara stood at the wheel, staring off at the distant sea. Her back was arched proudly. She wore silk pantaloons tucked into black knee-high boots. Her linen pirate shirt was open well below her small breasts, held tight by the blue sash around her waist. Her black skin glistened from sweat or sea, and she looked satisfied, as though she truly enjoyed what she was doing. Angst really liked this. It felt like she'd found her thing. So few in the world did what they loved or loved what they did, and he envied the younger woman.

"You're familiar with Tamara," she said wryly. "She's better at the helm than anyone."

"So I've noticed," he said, winking at the young woman.

Tamara's thin lips smiled as broadly as Jarblech's growing frown.

"Think you can teach this one enough to keep us afloat?" Jarblech asked Tamara.

"Yes, Captain," Tamara replied crisply, her face sincere and her shoulders back.

"Can you pay attention to her long enough to learn something?" she asked Angst, poking him in the chest firmly.

"If you promise to put your hair away," he taunted. "It's more frightening than that storm."

"Ha!" she said, tossing her hair in his direction like a dog shaking out water. "My hair is glorious, and that little storm is nothing, landie. Now learn fast so you can push my schooner through that wittle stowm safely and I can get you off it...her...ugh!" She grabbed her kerchief and marched away.

"I think she's planning to kill me in my sleep," Angst said, crossing his arms.

"Are you kidding?" Tamara leaned against the wheel. "I think she's really taken to you!"

* * * *

"No, no, no!" Jarblech roared, fighting her way up steps with her stubby legs.

"Oh, what now?" Angst frowned. "It's only been fifteen minutes."

"How can she possibly teach you anything when she's giggling like that?" Spittle from Jarblech's lips flecked onto Angst's chest. She turned to Tamara with an intense glare. "Pirates don't giggle!"

"Yes, Captain!" Tamara said, standing to attention while fighting back a smile.

Jarblech grimaced at both of them before spinning on her heel. The helmswoman giggled before Jarblech had even taken a step. The pirate captain spun about to see the young woman stepping away from Angst, gripping her side as if poked.

"She's an excellent instructor," Angst said, quickly pulling his arms behind his back. "I'm sure I'll understand how to boat in no time."

"How...to...boat?" Jarblech said in disbelief, carefully articulating the words. "We don't have time for this...this nonsense."

"That's stern and aft and port and starboard," he said hastily, pointing in each direction. "And those are masts. See? Learning."

Jarblech shook her head and Tamara was losing a battle with laughter. He crossed his hands in opposite directions. "I mean port and starboard are the other directions."

Jarblech peered back and forth between them, both smirking like children getting away with something. "I'm calling in reinforcements."

"But, he's learning, Captain!" Tamara said defensively.

"Henrecht won't put up with any of this nonsense," she snapped.

Tamara frowned as the tallest woman Angst had ever seen south of Nordruaut approached. Was she the bodyguard that had stood behind Jarblech during the poker match? Her attire was similar to Tamara's, but her pants and leggings were different shades of purple. Angst could make out broad shoulders and strong muscles beneath her pirate garb. A dark bandana wrapped around her short red hair neatly, and an enormous scimitar hung from her waist. Neither her mouth nor her eyes smiled as she took position behind Tamara with crossed arms. Angst smirked and raised an eyebrow, but Henrecht stared on coolly.

"Finally," Jarblech said with a sigh. "The moment he becomes distracted, break him in half."

"Yes, Captain." Henrecht nodded curtly, her voice husky and

sincere.

Jarblech looked at each of them and nodded as if finally accomplishing something. She approached the stairs but jerked to a stop when Henrecht giggled. The captain's head hung low as she slowly walked away in defeat.

* * * *

"Captain!" Tamara called out as Falcon jutted forward.

"What's this?" Jarblech asked, holding up a finger to check the wind.

"It's not natural, Captain," Tamara said, letting go of the wheel and hugging herself. "Look at the sails!"

The flax cloth of the sail billowed in the wrong direction as the ship picked up speed.

"Drop them!" Jarblech yelled. "Bring in the sails, now!"

Pirates around the ship scrambled to lower sail as Hector, Tarness, and Dallow made their way back up to the deck.

"We're moving!" Hector said before frowning at her angry demeanor. "Hey, what's wrong?"

"Where is he?" Jarblech demanded. "I want him on deck now!"

"He wasn't below," Tarness said, his thick eyebrows frowning. "I can't imagine he fell in."

"He should," she said. "Moving at this speed without warning. He could've snapped a mast."

"Dallow, anything?" Hector asked.

"Nothing I can see on deck, or floating in the water," Dallow called out, one hand pressed firmly to his temple. "Just a large fish or dolphin really near the port side, it's hard to make out."

"Dolphin?" Tamara questioned. "This time of year?"

"Shush, everyone." Hector raised a hand. "This way."

He led them down the stairs to the left side of the ship. Water sloshed noisily against the ship. Sniffing the air for direction, he faced port, inching forward. The splashing became louder and water reached the deck as the ship continued to speed up. Hector broached the railing and leaned over, Tarness and Jarblech practically perched on each shoulder. He paused, worried at what he might find until they heard Angst laugh.

"What in the...?" Jarblech's jaw dropped.

Angst rested in a makeshift hammock that hovered inches over the ocean. A beautiful blue-haired mermaid clung to his arm, smiling and nodding, her great fin splashing in the wake. She glanced up in shock, her eyes wide and lips pursed. She kissed Angst on the cheek then fell away into the dark ocean. Angst was still laughing as they dragged him back up on deck, wiping tears from his eyes.

"I don't remember the last time I laughed like that," he said, catching his breath. "She is hilarious."

"What is it with you?" Jarblech began inspecting him, rubbing at the spot where Moyra had kissed him. "I don't see blood."

"What? Of course not." Angst calmed himself. "She's a friend."

"She's a monster," Jarblech snapped. "Those things kill pirates."

"And pirates kill them, right?" Angst said, his voice becoming darker.

"You would choose one of them over one of mine?" Jarblech thumbed her chest.

"No," he said firmly. "I would choose everyone."

Hector placed a calming hand on Angst's shoulder, which Angst jerked away.

"You can thank her later," Angst said.

"Thank her for what?" Jarblech asked.

Angst walked to the middle of the ship and held out both hands. His eyes glowed red and a bright blue hue hovered about his arms as the ship raced forward even faster.

"Which way, Captain?" he asked.

"She...she taught you this?" Jarblech was stunned. "How?"

"She knows the water better than anyone." Angst nodded with a broad smile. "I guess you owe her your thanks."

"I hate owing," she said, spitting on the deck. "Pilot, call out directions for the landie."

"Left, landie," Tamara shouted. "About five degrees."

"Yes, ma'am," Angst said brightly as the boat gently shifted direction.

Jarblech peered over the railing. She shook her head at the distant form of a blue woman with a long tail diving in and out of their wake.

"What is it?" Hector asked quietly.

"Angst should be dead," she whispered gruffly. "Mermaids don't make humans friends. Ever. Humans, especially men, are food."

"Angst has a way with women." Hector rubbed a thumb along his scar.

"I've noticed," she said. "But this is different. *They* are different, Hector. They aren't human. Something about this isn't right."

"I'll add it to the list," Hector said with a frown.

28

Unsel

Wilfred sank lower into his chair, surprised to find he longed to be back in the basement cursing his life as a paper shuffler. He had come to the war room expecting to see the long wood table filled with generals and advisors. Instead, the war in this room was between two people. At one end of the table sat Alloria, looking emotionally and physically deflated. Her cheeks were sunken, the sparkle in her eyes had dimmed, and he couldn't help but notice that her breasts appeared smaller. Maybe it was her ultra-conservative pale green dress that fit snug from waist to neck. More than likely, it was the heavy cost of leadership during trying times.

At the other end of the table, Vars hunched over, appearing, for once, as old as he was. He wore a simple gray tunic and leggings, and his slouching shoulders no longer seemed strong enough to hold his armor up. His hands shook, and he refused to make eye contact with either of them. Wilfred sat in the middle. Judge. Referee. Negotiator.

In spite of their haggard appearance and tired demeanor, every word brimmed with vitriol and bitterness. What should've been a brainstorming session to save Unsel felt more like divorce proceedings. At first, he'd compared their fight to two cats battling over territory, but after the longest hour of his life, he'd decided that neither had the finesse of a cat. This was more like two ducks bobbing in a lake for the same piece of bread.

"Stop, please," Wilfred said, wondering if his head would still be attached after the interruption.

They did, undoubtedly more out of shock than respect, looking up from the table in surprised wonder.

"No disrespect intended," he continued. "But why am I here?"

"I couldn't agree more," Vars said in a gravelly voice.

"See?" Alloria said, crossing her arms. "He's the reason we can't get anything accomplished."

"Your Majesty, Captain Guard," he nodded at each in turn, "we have one week to implement some sort of defense, or evacuate the city. I would highly recommend doing both. Vars, you need to gather every general and get them on board with a plan to defend this city. Your Majesty, bring in the rest of Isabelle's advisors to coordinate an evacuation."

"All she thinks about is her coronation," Vars snapped.

"And he won't obey a single order," she said, setting both palms on the table and leaning forward.

"You don't take any of my advice. You should be drawing from my experience," Vars replied. "That's why we were paired."

Wilfred tilted his head in confusion at this, giving Alloria a questioning look that she ignored. "Stop," he said again. He sighed deeply and did his best to sit upright. "Have any preparations been made, at all, to evacuate the city?"

"There's no need to evacuate," Alloria stated. "We'll mount a defense to keep Unsel safe."

"This we can agree on." Vars nodded curtly. "I'll have enough soldiers here within the week to handle anything that comes at us."

"Okay," Wilfred said, drawing out the word. "Have you worked out the magic problem?"

"The problem's been eliminated," Vars said, his lip curling into a sneer. "The wielders have left Unsel."

"That very well could be the problem." Wilfred shook his head. "The gargoyle creatures can't be harmed by anything but magic."

"We don't know that for a fact," Vars disagreed.

"But the hundred soldiers that died from the last attack," Wilfred said, "it's my understanding they couldn't even defend themselves."

"There simply weren't enough," Vars stated. "With more soldiers—"

"We'll have a bigger pile of dead bodies," Alloria interjected. "Which is exactly why we need Angst."

Vars's jaw set and his cheeks reddened. Wilfred's turned about to see if she really meant what she'd said. Her arms were crossed, and her gaze unflinching. Apparently Angst was her white knight.

"Are you aware of what happened at Melkier?" Wilfred asked. "Angst was last spotted fighting dragons in Melkier right before most of the city was destroyed by a giant fireball. Even if he did survive, there's no telling where he is now."

"I believe in him," Alloria said quietly.

Wilfred looked at the queen regent and had to remember how young she was. Whatever relationship Angst had with this young woman had provided her with an unrealistic hope that would need to be handled delicately. Added to that, the hate seething from Vars at the very mention of Angst's name made this conversation a treacherous walk on a thin rope over a raging fire.

"I believe in Angst too, Your Majesty," Wilfred said, ignoring Vars's scoff. "With all that's happening in Ehrde, it's more than possible he'll come flying in to save the day. But, it's our job to plan for all possibilities, not just the ones we want to happen."

Both Queen Regent and Captain Guard nodded slowly, reluctantly, and Wilfred smiled at the baby step. There was still time to save the people of Unsel; there had to be.

"What would you advise?" Vars said stoically.

"We announce Her Majesty's coronation in thirty days,"

Wilfred began. He held out a hand to quiet her protest. "There isn't time to properly plan and execute this otherwise, Your Highness. In addition, telling the people of Unsel that we're scheduling this in thirty days gives them time to mourn their queen but also says that we expect to survive this crisis."

They both nodded again. Alloria looked as if someone had stolen her puppy, but she said nothing.

"What else?" Vars encouraged.

"I agree that you need to gather your armies, but we also need to plan an evacuation," Wilfred continued. "A war zone is no place for women and children."

Vars's lips were as thin as his narrow eyes, but he nodded curtly. Alloria also nodded in agreement, and, for the first time in a week, Wilfred had the tiniest hope that all could be well.

"Then that's it," Vars said, pushing himself up from the table. "We have work to do."

"There is one more thing," Wilfred said. "We need help from the magic wielders to defend the city."

"Absolutely not!" Vars slammed a fist on the table. "The first wielder to step foot back in Unsel will be shot dead."

"No, they will not," Alloria countered. "Magic will remain illegal, but I will not order any of their deaths, and neither will you. This was made very clear to both of us."

"It was not made clear to me," Vars disagreed.

"Maybe you aren't hearing too well these days," Alloria said cattily.

Vars's eyes widened as he shouted his pithy retort. The queen regent immediately retaliated with an insult. Wilfred sank into his chair once again, resting his hands on his rotund belly, and groaned. That thread, that tiny thread that held it all together unraveled, and he wondered if it would be possible to rein them in one more time. More than ever, he longed for the basement, and found himself hoping that Angst would return and save him, too.

29

"Is this you?" Hector asked, swallowing hard and paling fast.

They were being tossed about like dice in a cup, bracing themselves as best they could in the smallish cabin as the waves had their way with the ship. Angst couldn't lock everyone's bones to the wooden floor, so they'd created a chain with Tarness as the anchor. Unfortunately, he was hard to hold onto, his strong, dark arms slick with sweat.

"I was told to take a break when we reached the edge of the storm." Angst held a hand up defensively. "She didn't want me *messing up her ship even more*," he said, mocking Jarblech's voice.

"That woman is insane," Hector snapped. "Ships just aren't supposed to move like this!"

"Are we even upright?" Tarness asked.

"For now," Dallow answered.

"I feel wonderful," Tori said with a smile.

"We told her to hurry," Angst stated, feeling exceptionally calm in spite of the madness surrounding them. "That we need to get there at all costs."

"I hate that phrase, especially when you use it near Dulgirgraut," Hector said, his pale face green as he swallowed hard. "Isn't that the phrase that cursed Gressmore?"

"When Dulgirgraut starts working right," Angst sniped, "then I'll be careful how I use it."

"You two need to quit," Dallow snapped. "This isn't the time."

Angst smirked at Hector. The man's piercing gray eyes were stoic, but the corner of his thin lips lifted slightly. Victoria held onto Angst's arm with both of hers, now overly calm thanks to Dallow's tonic, which had settled her sickness. The door to their quarters crashed open, and the wild-haired captain shoved her head through. The bandana was long gone and half her mass of oily gray curls was matted down from the storm.

"What have you done now?" Jarblech roared, pointing a finger at Angst. Even with wind-burned cheeks and sun-ripened skin, she seemed pale.

"Why does everyone think this is me?" Angst asked nobody. "This is the storm, right?"

"Like none I've sailed," Jarblech proclaimed.

"I tried to warn you," Angst said, nodding toward the door. "Show us."

They awkwardly tripped over each other as they followed Jarblech down the wet hall and up slick stairs to the deck. It was dark as pitch, but frequent flashes of lightning revealed glimpses of the nightmare they faced. They breached the deck only to stop in awe. Like fingers from the sky, a dozen darkened waterspouts reached down from heavy clouds that appeared low enough to touch. The waterspouts gouged into a raging ocean where no man should've set sail. An onslaught of lightning thrashed the water, and whirlpools seemed to eat the spouts like a drunkard drawing straight from the keg. The storm was madness, like an orchestra warming up with every instrument playing a different tune. It would've torn a wooden boat to pieces.

"I'm going back to the cabin," Dallow announced.

"You okay?" Angst asked.

"No," Dallow said sadly. "I can't see a thing. I'm completely useless."

"You aren't useless," Tarness said.

"Stay on deck, we're going to need you," Angst commanded. "Tarness, hold onto him."

"What do we do? Can I plow right through the center?" Jarblech asked, an adventurous madness in her eyes. "Or is this…something else?"

"This isn't just a storm," Hector said. "I have a bad feeling about this."

"I think you're right," Jarblech grumbled and then yelled, "Tamara! Hard to starboard, turn us around."

There was a loud wrenching sound as the boat shuddered in an attempt to turn.

"We're still moving toward it," Tarness yelled.

"We're caught in the tow," Jarblech shouted.

"It's pulling us in!" Tori cried fretfully.

"There's nothing I can do about it," Jarblech said. "But they're not going to get me without a fight."

"There are alternatives to fighting," Dallow said, placing a hand on Jarblech's shoulder.

"Get us out of here," Hector said to Angst. "Can you back us up?"

Angst used the water to propel the ship, as Moyra had taught him. He didn't know where they were, so urged them back. The sails were down, and he felt no drag from the wind, but it was as if the very water was deciding their course.

"Why aren't we moving?" Tarness asked. "Is it the storm?"

"This is something else," Angst said, shaking his head.

The ship groaned as if the metal hull was being torn asunder. Once again, Falcon listed.

"Is that you?" Jarblech held a threatening fist up by her chin.

"No, Captain," Angst said, looking around in confusion. He reached out, felt the hull being pressed inward, and roughed it back into shape.

"Something struck the right side," Tamara cried out.

"No, it's crushing us from all sides." Angst grunted. "I'm fighting it."

Pirates shouted in fear as lightning flashed to show two bodies lifted into the air by large tentacles.

"What…what is that?" Victoria stuttered.

"Never in Ehrde..." Jarblech's voice trailed off.

From nowhere, Hector wielded two wicked blades—long steel sticks with wide sharp ends. "Take Dallow," he said to Jarblech. He faced Tarness. "Hands!" Hector yelled to Tarness as he jumped towards the man.

Tarness held his hands together, creating a small platform that Hector landed on. Tarness lifted while Hector leaped into the air. They watched in a flash of lightning as the man sprang high at a tentacle, cleaving into it and freeing the captive pirate.

"So hawt," Jarblech said, patting Dallow's hand.

Dallow shook his head.

Tarness ran forward with sword and shield, roaring at the creature, the storm, and the madness. A tentacle struck his back with a loud slap. He spun about and sliced the end off with a grunt. There were screams followed by a noisy splash from aft. They turned to see a lone pirate peering over the edge.

She turned to face them and pointed, her voice shaky. "It took Hilde and Becka! Just gone, into the water!"

"What took them?" Angst yelled. "Was it more tentacles?"

"No," she said, staring up at the clouds. "It swooped in so fast. Those things, there!" She pointed to the sky.

"Now what are we dealing with?" Jarblech asked.

"I can see blurred figures circling in the clouds. It doesn't seem to be a formation but..." Angst targeted shadowy monsters through the flashing haze with a finger. Jarblech's head weaved and bobbed as she watched it paint a line to the predators. "There. Gargoyles!"

A frightening thud was soon followed by several more as three giant green gargoyle creatures landed on deck.

"Felk," Angst said.

"Get off my ship!" Jarblech roared, stomping forward with her arms held out, appearing ready to tear the creatures apart with her bare hands.

Angst wondered for a moment if she could actually do it, but Dallow held her back.

"Get everyone below," Dallow yelled. Jarblech flashed him a

glare that would've killed a normal man. "You too. They can only be killed by magic."

"How can I get them below?" Jarblech bellowed. "They can't hear me!"

"I've got this," Tori said, wielding her two thin swords and running into the fray.

"Tori, no!" Angst shouted. He watched helplessly as she jumped, leaping off a tentacle and diving over a gargoyle, who barely missed scooping her up. She was gone, but within moments, pirates were running toward the hold to trip down the stairs.

"Wow," Jarblech said. "She's amazing!"

"I know," Angst said in a worried tone. "Dallow, when they get down, can you shield them?"

"Yes!" he said proudly. "That, I can do."

"You too," Angst said to Jarblech, pointing below deck.

"What about you?" she asked.

"I'm getting my sword," he said.

Dulgirgraut hovered over the hull, glowing like a dark red beacon in the storm. Angst stumbled through flaying wind and rain to grasp a mast. The foci felt so close. He pushed forward as the boat leaned, throwing him headfirst into the next mast. He saw shadowy stars until Tarness's strong grip pulled him up. His friend wordlessly held out a bracing arm that Angst hazily gripped onto for as long as he could. When he let go, he tripped forward uncontrollably into Hector's arms. His head throbbed, and he felt like vomiting. A flash of lightning showed the hungry delight of battle in Hector's eyes as his friend rolled back, pulling Angst with him before throwing him forward. Angst continued rolling to his knees and crawled the rest of the way to reach the foci. Leaning against the base, he inched upright to standing and gripped the hilt.

"A little help," he pleaded weakly with the sword.

Tarness backed up to him, and a body flew through the air toward them. Angst thought it was Hector, but Victoria shocked him by landing lithely nearby with a water-logged splat.

To everyone's surprise, Tamara slid to their feet and clasped onto Angst's leg. "Everyone should be below, including the two pulled over—they were thrown back on deck."

"What are you doing here?" Victoria said, her voice panicked. "You should be below."

"Safer with you than down in that coffin." She pulled herself up to stand then wrapped a dark, muscular arm around Tori's waist. "What now?"

"Angst's got this," Tarness said confidently.

"Isn't that like saying *what could go wrong now*?" Tori questioned.

"Yup." Angst grimaced. His palms were sweaty. How would Dulgirgraut perform? How would he wield magic?

"You'll do fine," Tori said encouragingly. "I promise."

There was a flash of red in his mind and the unfamiliar song of this new foci. He felt calm as strength and power filled his body.

"Okay," Angst said with a deep breath.

He swung at a landing gargoyle, slicing it in half. He lifted Dulgirgraut high and struck at the top half with the flat of the blade, making it splatter. Cold green goop slopped onto their faces as the bottom half fell into a puddle.

"One down, a hundred to go," Tarness said.

"Duck!" Victoria yelled.

Five of the creatures pounced to dogpile them. Angst hefted Dulgirgraut to shield them from the blow, but nothing happened. They peeked over the edge of the large blade to see what had saved them. Cavastil birds tore through their gargoyle attackers, showering the deck of the ship with green ooze. Lightning flashed to show tentacles flapping around the ship, aimlessly grabbing gargoyles and cavastil birds, ripping them to pieces or dragging them underwater.

"What do we do?" Tarness asked.

"Kill everything," Angst said through gritted teeth, his head finally clear.

He blurred forward, slicing through birds, tentacles, and gargoyles. He worked a tight circle around his friends, doing his best to protect them. Lifting a hand, he scooped up two gargoyles in an air shield and shot them off beyond the clouds. Tarness smashed a gargoyle overboard with his shield while Tori fenced with one of the bird's metal beaks. Hector rolled to a bird and shoved it into a gargoyle, both crashing into a hairy tentacle that dragged them into the ocean.

"Angst, there are too many," Victoria shouted over the battle.

"We can do this!" Angst believed it was the right moment. He could feel the sword fill his body with strength, he could hear the whisper of the song.

"No, we can't," she said. "Something's coming. Someone."

The ship listed, and Victoria screamed. The boat was being tossed around once again, and in the distance, Water. She stood a mile tall. A stormy ocean that walked and moved like a woman. Gargoyles poured out of her gigantic watery arms, darkening the sky with their great numbers. The shadowy figure of water peered at the ship, and Angst felt her looking straight at him. She lurched forward, her mouth opening wide, screaming as she dove into the ocean.

"That's not good," Tarness said.

30

Nordruaut

A steady thumping echoed slowly within the great hall Owenqua, as though it had a beating heart. The beat was slow, at first, as the challengers prepared for battle. No words were spoken, but none were needed—their eyes told all. Squinting eyes spoke of their confusion about the need for this fight. Analyzed the fighters, and their king. Wide eyes gawked at the formidable gray man, a creature new to Ehrde, who did not seem so very natural with his turtle-shell skin and bony armored protrusions. Some eyes rolled as they looked back and forth between Guldrich and their champion, Niihlu, having already decided the outcome. Others wanted for battle, a thirst for death that would not succumb to tradition. Guldrich's eyes were filled with purpose, while Niihlu's hungered. Jarle tried connecting with each gaze to understand what drove the thoughts behind them. The Nordruaut people were changing, and there was more at stake here than just a fight.

The great hall was as bare as those attending. Tables and chairs had been removed; the only things remaining were animal skins and furs hanging on the walls. A few burning logs in the center fireplace kept the room from freezing. Nothing here could be repurposed as a weapon, no obstruction remained that could be hidden behind, save the fireplace. Those attending and those challenging shivered from anticipation or cold. The hall was just shy of numb, brisk enough to keep everyone alert. This fight would be raw and open .

The single row of Nordruaut men and women standing in a circle around the walls thumped their long spears and stomped their feet faster and faster until King Rasaol held up one hand. The beating slowed. He stepped forward, out of the circle, and all eyes were now focused on him.

"A challenge met is justice served," he said solemnly, raising a fist high into the air. "A prisoner of war will always be executed, as spoken by our laws. I have been reminded that war has not yet been declared. It has always been our way that disagreements within, or without Nordruaut are instead decided here. This Fulk'han," he said, disdain dripping from his words, "Guldrich, has infiltrated our lands and killed our people. He claims this was trickery. Our champion," his voice lifted in pride, "Niihlu, will defend Nordruaut honor. Let the story be told that the winner is just." He bowed his head and stepped back into the circle of watchers, like any other Nordruaut attending this precursor to a funeral.

Guldrich crouched, vicious claws protruding from open hands as he took cautious steps around his prey. Niihlu remained still, frost hovering about his body and sheets of sloshy ice falling from his forearms where they crossed in front of his thick chest. His nose raised high, and he looked down at the creature through the frosty clouds leaving his nostrils. Both men were barely covered in loincloths, their only protection from curious eyes that drank in their tense-as-cable muscular bodies.

"Go," Rasaol said, lowering his arm.

Even before Rasaol's hand met his waist, Guldrich sprang with the desperate hunger of a panther fighting to feed its young. His claws shredded Niihlu's pectorals with four deep gashes that would've brought any mere mortal within inches of death. The beating of Owenqua's heart sped up as the grotesque cuts splayed skin and muscle. Guldrich's nails snapped free before he disengaged. Onlookers gasped when the gaps in Niihlu's chest quickly filled with icy red scars. He stared on with stoic confidence.

Guldrich rolled to his knees and spun, claws sprouting anew for another attack. He grinned viciously, his eyes keen on battle. "You shatter my claws as you shatter the women you sex," he accused. "I'm nothing more than a soldier, but you are a murderer of the helpless."

Niihlu frowned and took a step back, his young eyes filled with surprise. He crossed his forearms to protect his face as though forgetting his great power as the Fulk'han leaped forward. Guldrich sank his claws deep into the Nordruaut's chest before pushing off with his legs, flipping back to crouch for the next attack. Eight holes in Niihlu's chest immediately bulged with ice, and the audience looked at each other with concern.

"You chose this murderer of women, this weak, pathetic man to be your hero because he was strongest or because he wanted it more than anyone else?" Guldrich taunted. "Nordruaut aren't supposed to want or desire, but you put the greediest man on display!"

Niihlu's face contorted as he gave in to fury. He roared in anger as he launched at the Fulk'han, and his hand shot toward the gray man's throat. Guldrich leaped aside gracefully as Niihlu's clutched the throat of an old man against the wall, freezing it and killing him instantly.

Jarle glared at the king, who lifted his hand as if considering how he could end the fight. Rasaol met his gaze, and Jarle shook his head no. The circle could not be broken, and the fight would not be stopped; that was the law. But the Fulk'han was right. How could he know so much? Had he been awake during their conversation? Had others talked while they were away?

"Your indecision is why you fail!" Guldrich shouted, staring at Rasaol, who lowered his hand. "Are you hunters or conquerors? Peaceful nature-lovers, or war-thirsty empire builders? You must choose—the old way, or the new!"

Guldrich circled the fireplace, giving himself more time to taunt. His three clawed toes clicked noisily between the irregular beating of spears and stomping of feet. Niihlu was shaking with rage, and ice fell from his arms like a waterfall, splattering those nearby as he shuffled around to follow.

"Embrace the old ways, Niihlu," Guldrich growled. "You don't deserve what you've been given."

"You will die like your Takarn, coward," Niihlu threatened.

Guldrich roared, leaping through the grate, his claws breaking with angry snaps as he tore through Niihlu's forehead. Niihlu swung wildly, smashing the gray man's ribs and throwing him to the floor. Guldrich's bone armor cracked, his rib casing splayed as he grunted. He landed on a shoulder, which popped loudly. He shakily pushed himself up into a pensive crouch.

Water flowed like blood over Niihlu's forehead, crystalizing and blinding the young man. He clawed helplessly at the mess of ice forming over his eyes, only creating a larger mask. Crying out in frustration, he swung wildly at the air. The heartbeat in Owenqua became a murmur. An unsteady beat. An arrhythmia that threatened to burst as the onlookers' eyes questioned everything unfolding before them.

"You are all blind to your future. So stuck in ways that keep you from saving yourself. You make for easy pickings." Guldrich leaped forward, his claws pointed at Niihlu's throat. "You will die, but I will not!"

Niihlu lowered his hands. Fighting blind, he reached out and grabbed Guldrich's forearm. From elbow to finger, the Fulk'han's arm froze solid. Niihlu smashed his palm into his opponent's chest. Guldrich screamed in pain as his forearm snapped free, and he flew through the doors of Owenqua, which tore open like paper, leaving a trail of splinters and twisted metal in the snow.

"It's over," Rasaol announced, his shoulders dropped and his voice filled with relief. He strode to the door.

Jarle followed Rasaol with hasty steps. He spared a look back to see if Niihlu was following for the kill. The champion was still fighting the ice covering his eyes while roughly shaking off helping hands. There were more questions than victory, and more than ever, Jarle wanted to tell calming stories and remind the attending Nordruaut why they should not choose this path.

"No," Rasaol shouted.

Jarle's attention tore away from the crowd as he walked into the freezing cold Nordruaut morning. His king stood barefoot and almost naked in the knee-high snow, gawking at the imprint left by Guldrich's body. It trailed off into the early morning darkness, a shuffling through the snow that was already too far away to be heard.

"He was right," Jarle said sadly.

"That he wouldn't die?" Rasaol snapped.

"No," Jarle replied solemnly. "He was right about all of it."

31

"She's here!" Angst called out. "Water!"

"What?" Jarblech barked from the doorway. "What are you talking about, wielder? Who?"

"The lady of the sea," Victoria shouted.

The ship stopped. In spite of the storm and the wind and the enormous waves, the ship held still as if stuck on a reef. The waves settled, no longer pushed or pulled by winds. Between intervals of ear-shaking thunder came the sound of splashing. It wasn't a wave striking the shoreline, or a bucket being emptied, it was as if a moon had landed in the ocean. A tidal wave grew from the water, rising hundreds of feet into the night sky, once again taking the shape of a woman. She was every drowning nightmare, every storm he'd wanted to hide from as a child, and as stunningly beautiful as any great force of nature.

"*Angst!*" the watery creature roared, her voice filled with spite.

Rain splattered the deck, the intensity increasing with every breath.

"I guess I'm not the only one," Jarblech muttered in disbelief.

"Nope," he choked, pulling free from Tori's grip on his shoulders.

"Be careful," she said.

They all stopped, turning to her in disbelief. She shrugged, her face wrought with worry.

"Sure." Angst tried winking through the shower before turning back to face Water with his foci. He muttered to Dulgirgraut from the corner of his mouth, "Now would be a good time to tell me what you know." He opened his mind, his heart, his everything to feel...nothing. Power, raw power flowed from the sword, and his eyes glowed so brightly he could see their red reflection in the pouring rain, but the giant sword did not divulge a single drip of knowledge. "You suck," he said admonishingly.

"I've waited too long for this," Water roared. "You thoughtlessly killed mine. Now I kill you and yours!"

"What?" Angst asked.

"You bear the responsibility!" She raised two fists over the ship. "And everyone you care about will pay the price!"

"But that doesn't mean everyone here should die," he pleaded.

"Yes," she said, spreading her fingers wide. "Yes, it does."

Tamara cried out as she rose into the air. Tori held on until Angst pulled her back so she wouldn't be taken as well. He looked for the tentacle or gargoyle that held Tamara aloft, but found none.

"Please, Angst," Victoria cried, her face already filled with grief. "Don't let it happen."

Tamara hovered there, writhing and fighting as her arms were forced outward and her fingers spread. Her panicked eyes sought Angst's. "Help me. It hurts!"

"What do I do?" he begged Dulgirgraut. The sword didn't reply. "Tarness, throw me at her!" Angst commanded.

"It's too late," Victoria said, looking away.

What he saw made his chin quiver. Water drained from Tamara's hands and feet. Her face and torso deflated and her skin tightened to her skeleton. She cried out in pain, begging to be saved. Angst stood ready to do something, anything, but Tori was right. The screams stopped and the tattered remains of their friend's clothes dropped into the ocean. Tori choked back tears, and a coldness overtook Angst. The wind picked up, and gusts of water flowed through his thinning hair. Rain fell in sheets, and the ocean poured over the sides to flush them out. His joints ached from cold as he raised Dulgirgraut.

She reared back, laughing at his vain attempt. "And you think that trifle can destroy me?"

"You wouldn't be the first," he said, setting a foot back to brace himself.

Her face was wild with anger.

"Wrong answer," Hector said.

"It's not over." Tori wrapped her arms around Angst's chest.

Water threw the ocean at them, a constant hammering that flayed and burned.

With all his might, he wielded air, erecting a shield against the attack. "It won't last long," Angst gasped. "Fireball. All of us."

"What do you mean, all of us?" Tarness asked in despair.

"I think he meant to say some of us," Hector agreed.

"Whoever can," Angst pleaded. "Now!"

It wasn't the planet or star that Fire had thrown at them, but it was large enough to light the sky and dry the deck. A ball of fire the size of the castle at Unsel tore into Water. She screamed, her body hissing as it lost cohesion to the mass of flames. The storms stopped, the monsters stopped, even the tentacles were gone.

"Was that it?" Tarness asked. "Did we do it?"

They all looked to Tori for confirmation. Her face was contorted in fear. She shook her head, her arms still wrapped around Angst.

Water rose from the ocean in all her fury. Sheets of rain showered them as waves threatened to roll the ship, forcing Angst to concentrate on keeping her steady. The monsters were still gone, but they weren't needed. There was such a deluge of water, it was almost impossible to breathe. Angst threw another fireball at the creature, and another, a non-stop barrage of flames that tore through her. She wasn't happy, and replied with drowning water that became colder with every passing second.

"She is trying to freeze us," Dallow called out.

Angst reached deep into the sea, deep into the ground beneath, and pulled up everything he could. Water moved back as he forced dirt and steel and sand at the element. It wasn't an organized attack from an experienced wielder, but the desperate attempt of a man trying to save his friends, and it felt like throwing sand in a bully's eyes. Water swiped desperately at his attack until she stopped moving, solidifying to ice. Thin sandy towers reached out of the ocean like long fingers, strands of sludge and stone that deflected off her hardened body.

Exhaustion overtook Angst, and the fingers of earth retreated into the sea. Her icy figure once again became fluid, and she grew in fury, even more enormous than before. Water reveled in his defeat, rearing back for a laugh that sounded like thundering waterfalls.

"I'm sorry," he said.

"Shut it," Victoria snapped and pointed upward. "It's not over. Look."

The clouds had formed eyes and a nose, dark shadows in the storm that could be seen with every lightning strike. Below the eyes, a cloudy mouth opened to scream out wind. A body took shape beneath the clouds. Shoulders extended to arms and hands, which reached out with fingers like tornadoes. Even before Angst could brace for the end, a man-shaped tornado the size of Water stepped between her and the ship. Rushing air from the funnel ripped into Water, and the rain suddenly stopped as Air stripped away layers and layers of storm. Lightning thrashed at her from the sky above. Water threw her head back, her mouth open wide in a scream until she finally dove to ocean safety. A tornado rushed toward them. Angst sought knowledge from Dulgirgraut, desperate to know how to defend against Water and Air, but the sword remained silent. The tornado slowed as it met their ship.

"We can't do this alone, Angst. It will take two," the wind whispered in his ear, and all was still.

* * * *

232

Without warning, the sun appeared—a beautiful beacon of hope and light that made everyone hide behind arms and squinting eyelids. The nightmare was over as quickly as it had begun. The captain touched every shoulder, looked every member of the crew in the eye, and said their names aloud. Angst stayed nearby, keeping a watchful eye on the horizon for retribution. Dulgirgraut hovered over the bow once more, glowing gently as if nothing had happened.

"Four women are missing, including Tamara," Jarblech said, her voice unsure and her face haggard.

"Tamara's dead." Angst couldn't stop shaking. "The Lady of the Sea took her, and…" He bowed his head.

"It happens." Jarblech's voice caught as she placed a hand on Angst's shoulder. "The ocean is a cruel mistress."

"I tried," he said. "We all did."

"I know," Jarblech said, patting him. He was surprised that she wasn't angry, or throwing him overboard. "Tamara was a fine pilot, and a friend. We will celebrate her life with a feast as soon as we find the others. Can your friends help?"

"We'll do our best," Hector said. "Dallow, can you check the surrounding area from above?"

"Already on it," the tall man said, his eyes glowing brightly behind the blue kerchief.

"Everyone else take a spot and see what you can find," Hector commanded.

"I'm searching below deck to make sure they aren't still hiding." Jarblech covered her face with a hand and left them.

Angst hurried portside toward the front of the ship. His heart hurt to beat as though wrapped in a thick layer of guilt. Had he not dragged these people out here, Tamara wouldn't have died. All he could hope for now was to find the others. He reached out to feel for the mineral in bones, but the sea was alive with creatures of all sizes and it was too hard to distinguish. The brightness of the sun and the choppiness of the ocean made it hard to see. The waves created shadows, and his eyes played tricks on him. Was that something bobbing far out or just the water? He squinted, holding his breath and leaning forward. The waves rocked and the sun hid behind a cloud long enough to make out a hand reaching up.

"Overboard!" he shouted, kicking off his shoes.

She was easily a hundred and fifty yards or more away, and waving frantically at Angst.

"A woman," Angst shouted over his shoulder. "Overboard!" He placed one foot on the railing. "I won't lose another one!"

His friends came running to him as he took a deep breath and launched into the air.

"Angst, no," Victoria said. "That's her, that's—"

32

"Found 'em!" Jarblech dragged a stocky woman up on deck by her ear, and two women followed, looking sheepish as they held hands. The captain's hair was a lopsided mass of gray and black, matted down on one side and reaching for freedom on the other. "This one was getting drunk. These two, well, they thought everyone was going to die."

"Angst," Victoria called, her hand cupped around her mouth. She was pale and leaned over, wincing.

"What'd he do now?" Jarblech asked with a gruff sigh. She let go of the ear, glowering like a disappointed parent, and pointed at a spot for the three to sit like children in trouble.

"He dove in to save one of your pirates," Tarness said, a smirk on his lips. "But Tori thinks it was the mermaid."

"I tried to stop him," she said, her eyes filled with worry. She swallowed hard. "He said he saw a woman."

"Damn mermaids, they're all over the place here," Jarblech complained bitterly. "Didn't I mention that?"

"No," Tarness and Hector said in unison.

"It was her, or one of them," Dallow said with a sigh, his hand on the memndus stone against his temple. "And they just went underwater."

"Is he safe?" Victoria asked, gripping her stomach as if there were anything left to empty.

"No," Jarblech spat. "She'll probably drown him, or eat him,

235

or mate with him then eat him." She stopped when Hector held up a hand in warning. "What do you want to do? Head over there?"

They all looked at Victoria, who stared off in the distance. She closed her eyes in concentration, and after a long moment shook her head in disdain. She turned to Jarblech. "You mentioned a feast for Tamara? This will probably take a while."

* * * *

They floated feet below the ocean's cover, with Moyra's arms wrapped around his neck. The water moved, but they didn't, and the feeling of weightlessness overcame him. He looked into her eyes and saw...something so compelling. An endless hunger that drew him in. Could he possibly give enough? Would that all-consuming hunger devour him? He should've been afraid, should've been fighting to free himself before he was consumed, but in those large, dark eyes, dark as the deep ocean, he also found acceptance. She believed in him, or wanted to, and it was every bit the encouragement he needed.

Their lips pressed firmly together as they breathed the same air. It wasn't a kiss...or not just a kiss. Angst needed every breath she gave him, and he tasted her in the air they shared. He knew it was wrong, and felt like a moth, but she burned so brightly.

Angst pulled his head back, Moyra still holding him as close as clothes. His belly was tucked in under her firm breasts, which heaved against his chest. He was grateful for their barriers—his clothes, her scales—as though this made it a little okay.

She held her mouth to his, and it wasn't air, not yet. Her lips were closed and his were open. He was already longing to breathe, but she teased, her thin tongue dancing along his lips. As his eyes widened in panic, her mouth opened to remind him that she was air and life. He drew in deeply as her tongue flicked across his, dizzy from the lack of oxygen and rushing blood from passion he knew was wrong. Guilt was overpowered by the need to survive, and that, somehow, had to make his transgressions forgivable.

Moyra had told him she saw his thoughts as pictures—now he wondered if she could translate their meaning. Rather than overthink it, he spoke in his mind like he had with Tori.

"Am I dead?" he thought. *"I hate dying."*

"You are safe with me, An-gst," she said in his mind. *"Not dead, but I was so worried when the monsters attacked."*

"I'm glad I'm not dead," he thought in relief. *"I don't think I would taste very good."*

"I think you taste wonderful," she teased, taking full advantage of his need to breathe.

Her face was becoming harder to see. The light was fading as they sank lower into the ocean. His heart raced, and he kicked frantically as panic overtook him. Her grip moved to his shoulders, forcing him down. He tried pulling away, but her arms were incredibly strong. He thought she shook her head, but it was almost impossible to see. They stopped moving, and she allowed him to breathe, which he did in desperate gulps.

"Do you trust me, An-gst?"

"I want to." He breathed her in slowly, steadily. The fear became distress, and his heart slowed to a jog. As he calmed, he could hear the distant song of Dulgirgraut. It was sincere, soothing, and his eyes began to glow so he could see her face more clearly. She waited with all the patience he would've expected from a butterfly, squinting, her face taut, and her tail jerking from side to side. What was he so afraid of? Certainly not Moyra—she could've killed him without this adventure—the fear was his own and he buried it as much as he could. Dulgirgraut stopped singing and the glow from his eyes faded so she became a beautiful silhouette on a dark foggy night.

"Yes," he finally confirmed. *"Where are you taking me?"*

"I need to show you something," she pleaded. *"So you can save us."*

"Here? Now?" Angst thought. *"I don't understand."*

"Trust," she requested, placing a hand on his chest. *"Breathe*

out all your air then take in all that you can."

He did, sucking in until his lungs verged on bursting. Grabbing his hand, she pulled him into a deep dive. Angst mostly ignored his fear, which nested in his stomach and roiled with noisy anxiety. They shot through the water like an arrow, deeper and darker until the only sign of movement was his rolling cheeks. He swallowed hard, wiggling his jaw until his ears popped. How far had they gone? How could she show him if he couldn't see? Moyra slowed and held him close, helping him through gasps. She gripped the back of his head, forcing their mouths together when he instinctively jerked back. Finally, he breathed normally enough that she eased her hold, finishing with a kiss.

"I could really get used to that," he teased, trying to take his mind off the numbing cold and darkness.

"You are cute, for a hooman," she thought. *"Take another breath. Squeeze when you need me."*

"Are we almost there?" he asked.

"No." She said nothing else.

Angst breathed through her lips, adjusting her hold so they grasped each other's wrists. They continued their decent into darkness, stopping when Angst's lungs burned and his vision filled with stars. Their passage seemed to take a long time, in spite of her speed. He worried for his friends and could only imagine their panic.

* * * *

"These sweet potatoes are excellent," Tarness said gratefully.

"It's the cinnamon," Jarblech said with a proud smile. "Makes them taste like pie."

Tarness nodded with a full mouth, swallowing it down with some watery mead. He was every cook's favorite customer, except at buffets. He smiled broadly at his friends; they knew this was his second favorite thing to do and that seemed to warm the room.

"I agree, your chef is excellent," Hector said raising a goblet.

"Tamara."

They all repeated his toast before drinking deeply.

"The food smells delicious," Victoria said, hugging herself as she entered the small room. Dallow followed her closely.

"You're okay to eat?" Hector asked in relief.

"Good enough to fight, good enough to eat," she said sullenly. "Dallow fixed me up again."

"Glad to be of service," Dallow said simply, putting away his memndus stone and feeling his way to a seat.

Victoria sat, her head lowered. She sighed deeply.

"We celebrate her life, Your Highness," Jarblech said. "She lived and died a pirate's adventure. That's how she wanted it."

"I'd love to know more," Victoria said with a nod before grabbing a plate. She created a pile of food that challenged Tarness's.

"What about Angst?" Jarblech asked. "Aren't you worried about the mermaid?"

"You said they are pretty?" Dallow asked.

"Stunning," Jarblech said in confusion.

"If it's the one we saw," Tarness said, "she really is gorgeous."

Victoria rolled her eyes, but couldn't speak her mind around the sweet cake in her mouth.

"I don't mean to alarm anyone, but nobody ever survives a mermaid abduction," Jarblech said. "Ever."

"He'll be fine," Victoria said dismissively. "Please, tell us about Tamara's adventures."

* * * *

It warmed from a numbing cold to fall lake water. Their descent was met with dim lights, small dots below that looked like stars in the sky. A brighter one in the distance could've been the moon.

"I like your thoughts," she thought, slowing but not stopping. *"Sometimes they are pretty."*

"So are you," he flirted.

As their lips met, Angst almost broke the connection with a smile. His mind spun. How incredible was this? He was swimming toward stars at the bottom of the ocean with a beautiful mermaid. Moyra pulled away with a curious frown, and licked him teasingly as she brought him toward the lights. The distant moon grew as they approached, but was hard to make out at this speed. His ears flapped; she swam so much faster than he could even run. Angst strained to see against the rushing water and the light filling his eyes. They were close to the bottom now: a sandy landscape scattered with colorful rock and towering coral. Hard-shelled monsters with too many legs scuttled out of sight while a school of pan-shaped fish with wings lazily passed overhead. He recognized nothing. It was an entirely new world, so different from his own, and so amazingly beautiful that he didn't have the words. She gripped his hand tightly, apparently loving the appreciation in his thoughts.

Thick plants rose from the ocean floor, a dim ball of light the size of his head resting atop each. They were bunched together in groups, slowly swaying back and forth in the ocean tide.

"What are those?" Angst thought, reaching out to touch one.

She pulled his hand back. *"Our children,"* Moyra said sadly. *"They remain unhatched after many, many years."*

They swam until they arrived at a bevy of ten round glowing eggs.

"These are my babies. Or could be," she said quietly. *"You can touch one, but gently."*

With that same level of baby-caution he would've brought to holding his own newborn, Angst placed a hand on the glowing egg. It was warm, and flashed brightly at his touch. He jerked his hand back and shot her an excited smile. She nodded, and he placed his hand on another. It moved! Her babies were alive.

"It's... They're beautiful," he thought.

"Thank you," she replied demurely, kissing his cheek.

"When will they, um..." He didn't know if 'hatch' was the right word.

"They will not," she said, her smile thinning. *"I wait."*

"How long have you waited?"

"Longer than you, An-gst," she said. He assumed she meant longer than he'd been alive.

"Why don't they, um, you know, hatch?" he asked carefully. He floated on his own, holding out his arms, as if that helped him do anything.

"They need a father," she said, staring at her nest.

"Wow. I..." He didn't know what to say. He wanted to help, he really wanted to help, but not like that. *"I-I don't think I can do that. I'm not sure how that would work, and...I'm married."*

She laughed so hard that precious air left her mouth in giant globules. She swam around and around him in apparent glee as she reveled in his thoughts. He looked around for something to hide behind, and wondered if he could make it to the surface on his own. When she finally noticed he was desperate for air, she stopped.

"Oh, silly hooman," she said in his mind. *"No, we cannot mate."*

He was embarrassed and relieved at the same time. He may not know everything expected of a hero, but he certainly knew what Heather expected.

"Let us go," she said, still giggling. *"I am not done sharing with you. You will soon understand."*

Angst actually felt the warmth of a blush in spite of the numbing cold water. She rested a hand on his cheek as if letting him know it was okay before pulling him quickly along to the brighter ball of light in the distance.

33

They leaned back on their hands, sitting on the deck of the ship with their legs shoved between slats of railing. Tori's belly was full of good food and better rum, a gentle buzz tickling her nose. The air was still, warm enough, and the lapping water against the hull of the boat was hypnotic. An almost full moon danced with the waves, creating a thousand more stars than were in the sky. The panic was gone, the tugs on her heart were in Unsel and far, far below them, and for this one, brief moment she reveled in this well-deserved respite.

Hector and Tarness rocked their legs like kids and smoked cigars like old men. Dallow's legs were crossed, his eyes glowing brightly behind the kerchief as he puffed thoughtfully on his pipe. It was a perfect moment as they buried the chaos faced only hours before in quiet. Tori reached over and plucked the cigar from Tarness's fingers, taking a long drag without coughing once. They all looked at her in surprise when she returned it, shrugged, and settled back to enjoy the stars.

"How much time do you think we've got?" Hector said, his bushy eyebrows frowning.

"Do you always have to ruin a moment?" Tarness chided, looking at his cigar before puffing. He followed up with a hearty draw of rum.

"My cigar is almost out," Hector said lazily, and looked squarely at the princess. "I wasn't sure if I should get some sleep or sharpen my sword."

The vision in her mind was murky, a net that dragged through the sands of possibility. Angst could've been dead, but she was mostly sure he wasn't. She saw hazy lights hidden by a large shadow that gave her goose bumps. He could kill the mermaid bitch, or save her, or fondle her. That last image was probably the right one, and she grimaced. Angst was her champion, and she shouldn't have had to share. She grabbed Tarness's rum, despite his frown, and gulped a burning mouthful. She handed it back, not empty, and he nodded. From the corner of her eye, she saw Dulgirgraut flash brightly. She peered at it as if it were the enemy. Had it actually flashed? Was it taunting her while splintering her visions more than usual?

"Two hours, best guessh," she failed at not slurring. Tori wanted them to stay up and wait with her, in case he needed her...them.

Hector nodded once, but she thought he eyed her suspiciously.

"Probably with a team of monsters in tow." Tarness smiled wickedly.

Dulgirgraut flashed again, and Tori envisioned a shadow that made her hairs stand on end. It was enormous, cold, and almost impossible to fathom.

"Just one," Tori said, raising several fingers.

"Hmph, he's getting soft." Tarness grunted, drinking the rest of the rum like a shot. "Time for water." He wrestled his legs from between the slats before standing and making his way to the cabins below.

"Are you certain?" Dallow asked, looking at her with white eyes shining through the kerchief. "About the one monster?"

"Nevvverr," she said, fighting to get out the words. Her head was dizzy, and more than anything she wanted to cozy up with Angst for a solid night's sleep. Wow, she hadn't had that much to drink, but her tongue was acting like it. "Best guess." Hadn't she just said that?

"Good enough for me." Hector nodded, rolling back neatly

over his shoulder to stand. He followed Tarness. "Be right back."

"You okay, Princess?" Dallow asked. He pulled his legs from between the railings and inched closer.

"Um," was all she said. "I feel good. A little too good."

"Could be the cure for your sea sickness," he said, placing long fingers on her forehead. "It may not mix well with alcohol."

Long moments passed as she gathered her bearings. She still hurt inside from Tamara's passing, but Dallow's cure and the rum were blissfully numbing. The world spun a bit much, and she hadn't been this drunk since sleeping with Angst, which made her smirk drunkenly. She lifted her head with a start; it was resting on Dallow's shoulder. He leaned toward her, so she could find a comfortable nook, but was otherwise respectful.

"Is Angst acting different?" Victoria mumbled, forcing her mouth around the words. "Ever since that fish bitch..."

"He's just excited to have a new toy," Hector explained, sitting back down, and Dallow slugged him in the arm.

"Oh?" she said with a raised eyebrow. "Am I the old toy?"

"Of course not, Your Majesty," Hector said carefully. "It's just...it's just Angst. He meets someone new and becomes fascinated."

"We all get tired of hearing about them," Tarness said, sitting beside her. "I do, anyway."

"He went on about you for ages," Dallow agreed. "Still does."

"It's good, in a way," Hector explained. "Every time he makes a new friend, he suddenly wants to become the hero we all need, or at least that's what he thinks."

"Oh," Tori said quietly. "He still does? Goes on about me?"

"Yes," they all replied with various degrees of sighs.

And this made her smile.

* * * *

After several minutes of swimming, the nests were far behind them, and the only light came from the half-circle blob in the distance. They swam low between columns of coral, slowly, carefully. She was darting to and fro, avoiding rocky edges, but curiously chose not to swim above them. Her eyes flicked about nervously and his heart began to race. Moyra said, or thought, nothing, but he could sense her tension. Again, he heard a muffled song from Dulgirgraut, and the red hue from his eyes was strong enough to make out her curvy scales.

"Dim your light!" Moyra said loudly, making him wince.

"Wait, what is that?" he said in awe.

Like a storm cloud blocking the sun, an enormous figure hid the light they swam toward. It must've been insanely large, or incredibly close, because the light was like a moon on the horizon. Angst couldn't distinguish the outline of its body. It was round or oval, and bumpy, and...how big could it be? Moyra jerked him behind a coral pillar, and positioned their backs to the creature.

"Please, An-gst," she pleaded. *"Your light eyes."*

He'd never even considered how to dim his blatant advertisement that he was a wielder—it was his ego glowing as much as a tool to frighten away the foolish. That creature probably wasn't foolish, and Angst hastily shut his eyes. He tried looking at the inside of his eyelids, focusing until they went dark. Angst opened them and began to peek around the rock, but she pulled his mouth to hers. Moyra's lips were more passion than air, and her blue hair floated in the water, framing their faces. He breathed, but barely, and after a long moment, she withdrew, looking relieved.

"I was worried you would alert the beast and had to distract you." Her reason was solid, but her smirk made it flimsy.

Angst smiled at this and tried to wink, a flirtation lost in the ocean or in translation. He frowned and jerked his head in the direction of the thing. *"What is that?"* he asked again.

"Curse-bringer, unforgiving beast, stealer of children, millennial hatred, anti-good, monster of all, everything I hate about myself," she went on and on, a rush of thoughts and emotions

that made little sense in his mind. *"We have no name. There is no name. It is nameless, that beast of monster. He is the oldest living creature in Ehrde, and not even your great weapon could stop him from killing us."*

"Maybe," he grumbled. *"What's he doing here?"*

"He traps my people." She pointed then spoke so quickly it was hard to understand. *"All of them in that city is why I have no babies and am all alone but for you and me."*

He held her hand, squeezed it to calm her, and leaned in for another breath. Sharp bursts of air blasted into his lungs, making him cough. Whatever that thing was, it scared her, a lot. He let go of her hand and pulled her into a calming hug that did nothing. His sense of her was expanding quickly. It was exciting and frightening, as if they were letting down barriers, becoming closer in ways he couldn't with any other.

"City?" he asked in surprise, then remembered the spell he'd cast with Dallow, how it had shown a memndus stone next to a mage city in the middle of the ocean.

"Long ago, too many of your years, the monster cursed them to that city," she said, refusing to meet his eyes in spite of his desire and will.

"Take me there," he said firmly. Rose had to be there; he needed a closer look. He had to see what sort of trouble she was in, to see if there was a way to get to her.

"Too much danger," she pleaded quickly, her voice high-pitched. *"It will see us."*

"You brought me here," he said. *"Now let me hero."*

She stared at him, her large eyes pinched with worry. *"I will try."* Moyra sounded concerned.

She breathed into him once more before swiftly pulling him toward the light. They swam along the ocean floor, diving in and out of rock formations at a breakneck pace. Angst caught glimpses of the city and the shadow of something beyond the light every time they cleared the rocks.

When they finally stopped, he fought his natural reaction to gasp, releasing several bubbles from his open mouth. From a half mile away, he could make out a dome. It was like an enormous bubble had risen from the bottom of the sea, and stuck halfway. Inside the dome was a city with grand buildings that looked triangular, their tips almost reaching the top of the dome. It had to be the mage city, but how did it get down here? Water thundered in the distance, a constant low thrumming that reverberated in his chest.

"What's that sound?" he asked.

"A hole in the ocean," she said hurriedly.

"Oh," was all he could think to reply.

He pointed to urge her toward the dome. Her cheeks sucked in with worry, but she rushed them forward without argument. They hugged the ocean floor closer than she'd ever held him, leaving a sandy storm in their wake. They reached the edge, and he rested his hand on the dome. It was like glass, like an air shield. It would take a team of Dallows to understand this spell, or curse. He cupped his hands and peered through them as if sneaking a look through a dirty window. Everything was blurry, but he made out three figures: two with their backs against the barrier, and a third smaller something hopping up and down. Rose had to be in there.

Angst's heart lifted, and he was so incredibly grateful she'd shown this to him. What a gift. How many people had ever seen this sight? It was possible he was the first. Moyra instantly reacted to his happiness by pressing her lips to his, not breathing this time, merely kissing. Her tongue flicked gently in his mouth once again and instinctively his reached out. He let himself give in to her desire. His hands were on her hips, and Moyra's entire body shivered with hunger and passion. She leaned in aggressively and several sharp teeth caught his bottom lip. It hurt for only a second, but his mouth began to bleed.

Moyra instantly pushed away, her face creased with panic. Angst tried pulling her back, to no avail. He held out his hand to stop her from worrying, to let her know it was okay. In a flash, she swam away, and he looked around desperately. How would he breathe? His chest was already tightening. There wasn't enough air to create a shield or bubble, and his lungs ached. Sea salt burned his wounded lip, and he dared not open his mouth even to lick it clean for fear of letting the air out. A cloud of blood hovered around his face. His chest heaved, filling his cheeks as he tried to rebreathe his own air. She was nowhere to be seen. He cried out with his thoughts, but Moyra didn't reply. How far away had she swum already? Angst had never felt so desperate, so alone. There was nothing else to do, so he opened his mouth and screamed aloud.

"Moyra, help!"

"I cannot." She sounded distant in his mind. *"It is the blood. So hungry!"*

34

Azaktrha

Rose tugged at her hair, sifting through the fine red strands over and over again. Her chest and throat ached from sobbing, but for the first time since being dragged from Unsel, she felt some relief. Suddenly, she wasn't alone. The handsome stranger rested beside her with his legs crossed as they leaned back against the barrier. ANduaut listened attentively, silently, as she told her story. She'd spoken hesitantly at first, telling him how the princess had stabbed her, how she'd been drawn to Chryslaenor, and that it had killed the guards—which was when the tears began. She couldn't imagine the story translated well through her wracking sobs—it didn't even make sense to her! She explained that the sword had abducted her, made her sleep outside, and forced her to draw in the health of helpless victims. She'd been kidnapped and forced to ride on the back of a monster before jumping to her death. And then she didn't even get to die.

It was a nightmare to relive, but as she purged the memories, muscles unknotted in her shoulders and face. Her tension was washed away by a heady feeling, like the start of a drinking binge. Still, she couldn't help being disappointed that he didn't place a calming hand on her thigh or pull her to his chest for a hug. He was so quiet she would've wondered if he were still alive, except that he stared at Creeper warily. Creeper affectionately moved closer as the story worsened, and she almost started petting him like a cat before coming to her senses and shoving him off her lap.

"That sounds awful," ANduaut finally said, though his wide eyes clearly said, 'how crazy is this woman?'

"Where are you from?" she said, hoping to take the focus off her, and learn more about the handsome stranger. "How did you get here?"

"I am of the Vex'steppe tribes," he stated, watching her face closely.

Rose pushed herself away from the barrier, scrambling to stand.

He grabbed her wrist, his grip like a vise. "I won't hurt you, Rose," he said firmly.

"But, the tribes are dangerous," she stuttered.

"Yes, we are," he said with a disarming smirk that made her stop struggling. "But not to friends."

She winced at that word, but it was better than being called enemy. Or lunch. Her entire life she'd heard that the Vex'steppe was filled with tribes of barbaric killers who slaughtered on sight and ate their foes. They were almost as dangerous as the Berfemmian, a thought which made her shudder. He released her, frowning at the bruises on her arm under his grip. Her skin was orange and blotchy and healed almost instantly as he stared with wide eyes. The healing reminded her of the hunger that always skirted around the edges of her thoughts. It was growing like an insatiable glutton. Her hand shook as she reached out to him, but she balled it into a fist and forced it back to her lap, unwilling to give up control. This man was delicious in so many ways she struggled between absorbing his health or stripping naked and hoping for the best.

"I've been brought here against my will, just like you," he said, warily eyeing her hand. "This place is foreign and cold. I don't even know where we are. Do you?"

"Not really," she stated. "Like I said, I jumped into a large hole in the middle of the ocean."

ANduaut's face scrunched in confusion, as if he didn't understand her at all. He was cute but seemed slow to grasp what she'd said; it was like talking to a plant.

"So this is what?" He rapped a knuckle on the dark wall over his shoulder.

Creeper hopped up and down, pointing behind them.

"Yes, we see it," Rose said, wishing her *friend* would find somewhere else to be at that moment.

Creeper patted her leg with his webbed fingers and pointed at the wall. He squinted his eyes and covered his head for protection before saying, *"Angst,"* in her mind.

"Get out of my head!" she screamed. "You shouldn't even know who Angst is! Stay out!" She kicked at debris on the ground.

Creeper scurried out through a doorway, his thin green arms flailing over his head in panic.

Her nostrils flared as she spun around to look at the barrier and saw nothing. She shook her head at the foolish thought that Angst could actually be in the ocean behind that wall.

ANduaut was looking at her like she'd gone crazy. She sat back down beside him.

"What?" she snapped. "You couldn't hear the little creep?"

ANduaut shook his head.

"He can talk in my head, but I told him not to." She tapped her forehead with a finger. "And apparently he's been reading my thoughts, too."

He shook his head again, like he didn't understand or didn't care. "I asked, what is this wall we lean on?"

"It's a barrier that keeps the ocean out."

"What?" ANduaut rolled forward and leaped away.

Laughter overtook her like a spring storm. It went on for minutes, uncontrollable and embarrassing, until her face hurt. She could barely see him through new tears, but he looked upset. She held up an apologetic hand that was mostly useless as she fought through waves of dying chuckles to regain control.

"You look like you got stung by a wasp," she said, doing her best to fight another wave. "What was that? What are you so afraid of?"

"I can't swim." ANduaut's eyes were still wide as they shot between her and the barrier.

This made her laugh harder, which felt so much better than the crying.

"If...if this barrier broke," she gasped for breath, "do you think jumping away would help? That anyone could swim to safety with an entire ocean over us?"

"No," he said dumbly, apparently irritated by her laughter. His eyes were dark, and he looked hurt.

She regained her composure, but wished Angst was with her instead—she could've teased *him* about this for days.

"I'm sorry I laughed," she said as sincerely as she could. "It's just...I've been through so much."

The disdain left his face, and he nodded. "I understand."

"What do we do now?" She sighed. "We've got to be here for a reason."

"We should find shelter, in case more creatures come back," he said, offering her a hand up. "Would you like to explore this place with me?"

"Yeah," she said in a breathy voice, taking his hand in hers and not letting go.

* * * *

Unsel

At the behest of a soldier guarding the entrance to the Queen's Hall, Jintorich and Maarja entered the makeshift throne room. Jintorich could tell that the guards' awkward stares were making Maarja uneasy—*uneasy* meaning that the soldiers were lucky to be breathing. His new friend's patience waned quickly as the city unraveled around them, both bureaucratically, and physically. Cracks appeared in the walls and foundation as the quakes from the sinkholes approaching the castle increased in size and frequency. Every fifteen minutes they shook the resolve of each soldier and citizen in Unsel. Queen Isabelle may have signed over her crown upon death, but she was unable to imbue Princess Alloria with the respect and leadership qualities that Unsel required.

Two soldiers guarded a foot in front of the queen regent's throne while Vars stood to her right and a short, chubby man to her left. Jintorich was unable to hold back a squeak of surprise at the sight of Alloria, making brief eye contact with an equally stunned Maarja. Weary wasn't a strong enough word to describe the young woman. She was the second-to-last breath of the terminally ill. A starving animal unable to escape quicksand. The first pawn sacrificed on the chess board. Her hair was thin and wispy, her breasts all but deflated and held tight in an ash-gray bodice that was as plain as a peasant's. Her skin was taut and sallow, and the mischievous sparkle in her eyes appeared to have been stolen from her, held hostage beyond arm's reach.

Alloria rested in an exhausted recline as if stricken by a wasting disease. Pity for the young woman stirred in him. The stress from leadership was taking its toll. Vars faced away in disgust, looking formidable in his full gold-leaf-embroidered armor. The man seethed with anger, ignoring their approach to stare at the back of the room. He, too, did not appear healthy, but hid much in pomp. The short man placed a hand on Alloria's back to urge her up, but she shrugged him off. He looked from Alloria to Vars and sighed deeply before approaching.

"Thank you for your patience, ambassadors," he said with a polite nod. "I am Wilfred, advisor to Queen Regent Alloria."

He held out a hand to shake with both ambassadors, doing a respectable job of making it seem only slightly awkward when his hand was three times the size of Jintorich's, and three times smaller than Maarja's.

"The queen regent apologizes for the delay," he stated in a worried voice.

They nodded in unison.

"The Captain Guard also regrets the altercation at the Wizard's Revenge."

Vars sniffed, but made no attempt to agree.

Wilfred continued. "We would respectfully—"

"Why are you even here?" Alloria said, her tone a deep pool of exhaustion and disrespect.

Wilfred sighed and closed his eyes as if summoning his reserves of strength.

"We are waiting for Angst, Your Highness," Jintorich said stiffly.

"You and everyone else," Alloria said with a shake of her head. "If my champion still lives, he will be making the entrance of his life."

"Your champ—" Maarja began to ask.

"We will remain patient," Jintorich interrupted, holding up a hand. "The safety of Unsel is his first responsibility."

"Which is why I agreed to see you." Alloria finally pushed herself upright. "Unsel doesn't feel safe with either of you here. Especially her." She pointed at Maarja.

"Your Highness," Wilfred said in surprise, his face even paler than before. "This is not what we discussed."

Maarja raised a thick, blond eyebrow and smiled. She crossed her arms, staring down the nervous guards. The soldiers seemed to start shaking even before the earthquake hit, both looking away in time for her to hide her own fears.

"We will defend ourselves when threatened," Jintorich said firmly. "Your guards should not have attacked. Do ambassadors no longer retain autonomy in Unsel?"

"You involved yourself in internal affairs," she said, now sitting up on her own.

In spite of her apparent exhaustion, she was still spry enough to counter. Coming from a woman who had only moments ago seemed near death, it made him wonder how much of what they saw was actually true. Was Alloria really close to defeat, or had she made a calculated retreat into waiting?

"After you continuously ignored us," Jintorich said, blowing a tuft of eyebrow hair from his face, "we sought help on our own. You have done nothing but treat us with disrespect."

"We are in the middle of a crisis," she snapped, miraculously standing. "We have lost a queen, and could soon lose a kingdom."

"You had wielders here who could have saved you," he interjected.

"They were the first to evacuate," she replied.

"They were practically chased away," Jintorich said, pointing at a window. "But the people who are helpless have not been evacuated."

"You don't understand the plan," she said.

"Do you, Your Highness?" he asked.

Maarja and the guards watched the argument as if viewing a duel, their heads darting back and forth while they held their breath in anticipation. He drilled arguments into Alloria like a badger sinking its teeth, not relenting until she finally went limp. She collapsed into the high-backed chair, her arm falling over her forehead. Without waiting for her attendees to even take note, Jintorich bounded forward. He moved quickly under the guards' crossed pikes, which failed to bar his path, and hopped up onto her throne. The soldiers turned to pull him off, but Maarja rested a warning hand on the shoulder of each man. They both winced as she squeezed, forcing them to remain still. Vars did nothing other than watch, a hint of hope in his eyes.

"I don't think you should..." Wilfred began, casting around the room with a look for help that was reluctant at best and fearful at worst. He spoke more firmly. "Ambassador, please. That is our future queen!"

"Who seems to be very ill, Advisor Wilfred," Jintorich said, placing his small, white staff on the seat beside her. "I'm a physician. Let me try to help."

"I don't wish to be enemies, Meldusian," Alloria said weakly.

"An argument does not make us enemies, Your Majesty," Jintorich said with a smile. "My family enjoys a hearty discussion before every meal. But considering your condition, I should have been gentler."

He rested stubby-fingered hands on her forehead, and took two of her fingers in his grasp. Jintorich jerked back in surprise, letting go and holding both hands up. His plume of eyebrows frowned around his dark eyes, and his ears stood upright. "I...I don't understand," he stuttered. He placed fingers on her wrist and shook his head.

She had tears in her eyes as he pulled away, and for the first time he saw genuine worry, and sadness. "As you can see, Ambassador," she said quietly. "There is no help for me."

"I...I'm sorry," he said. "I don't know where to even begin. How are you even here?"

"My champion keeps me safe and alive without even knowing it," Alloria said, peering over her shoulder at Vars. "Far safer than you!"

"No!" Vars said in shock. "That's why you gave *him* the ring?"

Alloria's eyes were thin and calculating, her smile smug as she looked at the tiny ambassador. She reached to pick up his staff as if to hand it back to him. It flashed with light, making everyone in the room cover their eyes. She shook as she lifted it. At first the staff seemed to be a great burden, as if she were picking up a weapon too big and heavy for her wasting frame, but then the shaking became unnatural. Her lips pulled back as she bared her teeth in a grimace.

"Your Majesty?" Wilfred asked in concern.

"What is this?" she screamed, her eyes wide with madness. "What is this talking in my head? What is *Albrostihl*?"

"No!" Jintorich shouted, grabbing the staff and jerking it from her hand. He leaped back, holding the staff covetously as he moved out of arm's reach. "You shouldn't know its name. You shouldn't even be able to lift it!"

A wildness had overtaken her as though released from a cage. She screamed and reached up with both hands, pushing against her temples as if keeping her brain in. Her eyes protruded, and her mouth hung open in a silent scream.

"You have no heartbeat, you have no warmth, and you were

able to lift Albrostihl," Jintorich said, his voice filled with more wonder than fear.

She looked at him, still holding her head, her eyes now resigned and begging for sanity.

"What are you?" he questioned.

It was too much for the young woman, and with a pain-filled scream, she ran from the hall.

"This did not go well at all," Jintorich said, shaking his head as he returned to Maarja's side. With an incredible leap, he landed on her shoulder and perched there, holding out his staff defensively.

The soldiers seemed at a complete loss for what to do. Wilfred frowned in confusion. All eyes turned to Vars.

"It seems we should've had this meeting a long time ago. Thank you, Meldusian," Vars said darkly. He pointed at the guards with two fingers and urged them to follow. "With the bitch gone, we're going to do this my way. You two, with me. We're saving Unsel."

Vars and the soldiers rushed out of the hall, leaving Jintorich, Maarja, Wilfred, and an empty throne.

"So," Maarja asked Wilfred. "Now that you're ruling Unsel, what is your plan?"

35

Angst gripped his throat. He felt life passing quickly, and he was bombarded by memories, and regret. He wasn't the one who'd borne the cost of becoming a hero. Heather had put up with so much, had supported so much. Despite their differences and struggles, he loved her and didn't want to leave her alone. Cool water entered his nostrils as his lungs tried drawing in. He wouldn't leave her alone. It couldn't end this way. They were pregnant and not only was he a hero, he was going to be a father. He beat on the dome, working his way down to the edge, desperate to locate an entrance. Reefs and coral had grown around the dome, it had been there that long. He kicked in frustration, his pants catching on the rocky shoal. His head rolled back in frustration, and large bubbles of air escaped his mouth.

"It is so hard. I want to... I cannot help myself," he heard in his mind. She appeared before him, squeezing between Angst and the dome, licking her lips hungrily. Her mouth was open wide, revealing rows and rows of teeth, as if ready to take a bite.

"Don't do this," he thought weakly. *"Do you really want me to die?"*

His heart tried pounding free from his chest, his lungs ached to the point of failure. He was too exhausted, too frightened to save himself with magic. His arms began to list. Moyra grimaced as she pressed her mouth against his. Angst gasped for air through her while she gripped his shirt and held him close. There was no playful kiss or silly banter, Moyra's gaze was piercing and dangerous.

"I cannot," she cried out in his mind, pulling her mouth away.

He drew in a gulp of water and coughed. He dared not breathe in more, but his throat itched and tickled at the same time. She saw his desperation and gave him air.

"You are not food, you are not food," he heard over and over. *"I cannot love you. You are not food. I promised."*

His mind was dizzy with confusion. Her words filled with the instinct to feed, and—did she say love? Moyra grasped at his back and hair, her eyes torn between hunger and hunter. Full consciousness returned, and he wanted nothing more than to swim to the surface.

She bared her rows and rows of thin, horrific teeth then flicked her tongue wildly against his torn lip, lapping up the blood. He swallowed hard, thinking about how much of his face those teeth could take with them. His stomach wrenched with disgust. Moyra withdrew slowly, reluctantly then she tugged at his shoulder. He didn't budge, his leg still caught in the coral.

"Now," she thought, her voice high-pitched. *"We have to get you out of here now."*

There was a loud thud, and Angst looked up to a vision of creature that was too enormous to fathom. It dwarfed Fire, and Ivan, and moved at a measured pace. Tentacles reached toward them. Moyra jerked his jaw open, forcing air into his mouth before tearing off, slapping at tentacles. Dozens shot at her.

The burst of air did the opposite of what she'd intended. He coughed twice and covered his mouth, pinching his nose. Water tickled his throat and lungs. He tried to cough inward, clamping his mouth shut, but it wasn't working.

Seconds passed. Hours, days, and years passed. The creature followed her slowly until she was far from sight. His lungs ached and he was becoming dizzy when she returned. She nervously forced air into him. She licked his blood as he coughed through her mouth. He was embarrassed at his reaction, but she didn't seem to care. Moyra rolled upside down, and slugged the reef that held his leg. Rock exploded, stinging his hands and face. Without hesitation, she breathed for him again, but he caught the scared look in her eye.

He could hear her distant thoughts. *"Love, not food. Need hero. Need An-gst. Love, not food."* She drew away slowly, her eyes now awash with guilt. Moyra grabbed his arms, and they swam.

Dulgirgraut sang in his mind but told him nothing, making his heart race furiously as they approached the rock towers. He heard a crunching sound from above and sensed an enormous rock falling toward them. He raised his glowing hand and slowly pushed the boulder aside, fighting the water every inch. The creature had returned. The beast reached out long tentacles with coarse hairs, seeking methodically, as though it had all the time in the world. He looked at Moyra, who stared at them in panic. She pulled him along, diving under an enormous outcrop of reef.

"Air!" Angst thought, shaking her arms.

Her head jerked to face him, and she leaned in to give him quick breaths. It was long enough for the creature to reach him, to reach them. Hairs dug painfully into his leg and her fin, ripping out chunks of meat. Her eyes rolled back as cloudy blood from his wound drifted to her nostrils. Angst found footing, jerked away from her grasp, and kicked off the rocks.

"No!" she screamed, making him wince.

The blue glow around his arms bubbled with air, and for that moment, he felt no need to breathe. A song, two songs, a rush of music and power filled his mind and body. His leg throbbed with pain as blood spilled from his wound. He felt violated. Fury overtook him, and Angst began pulling earth from below the ocean floor.

"You want tentacles," he shouted in a stream of bubbles. "Try these!"

A hundred arms of sand and mud and rock shot upward, wrapping around the great beast and dragging it to a halt. Without thinking, without knowing if it would work, he summoned the biggest fireball he could. Power from the foci flowed through his body, deep into his chest. He let it grow until it was too much to contain then set it free. The heat was unbearable, burning hairs on his arms and destroying everything in its path. It dissipated quickly, but not before ripping a hole in the beast. Thousands of tentacles splayed under the shock of the impact. He waited for a second. For two. Moyra coiled around him, giving him breath he wasn't sure he needed.

Angst watched hopefully as the monster remained still. He waited for painfully long moments. How many would pass before they were safe? They should've fled, but he had to know. Had he actually killed that monstrosity? He looked at Moyra, who had the barest of smiles. An ounce of tension left his shoulders before her eyes became wide with fear.

"No," Angst said, awash with panic as he faced the monster.

The nearest appendage wiggled, soon followed by others. A green glop of murky ooze filled in the hole created by his fireball. He screamed a curse as the monster healed.

"Get us out of here," he thought.

Moyra grabbed him under both armpits and swam faster than Angst would've thought possible. He watched their wake. The beast was already following them and speeding up as if angered, tentacles darting from it like arrows. She swam in and out of the rock maze, barely keeping ahead of the creature, dodging every attack it threw at them. Angst couldn't make out a shape other than the reaching tentacles and that it was the largest living thing he'd ever seen. Angst held out his hands, throwing boulders in its path. It slowed enough for Moyra to help him breathe.

"I do not know where to take you. Where will you be safe?" she asked desperately as she licked the blood streaming from his mouth, leering covetously at his bloody leg. He sensed her restraint, and could only assume he was nothing more to her than a short, chubby sandwich.

"I'm not food," he forced into her head. "Did you say you love me?"

"Where is safe?" she pleaded.

"Sword," he said, looking up, thinking of Dulgirgraut on the bow of the ship.

She nodded, giving him a quick burst of air, but withdrew slowly, each gift of air seeming more of a struggle. Moyra turned so he could wrap his arms around her waist as if they were sharing a horse. She swam upward, spinning about, darting in and out to avoid tentacles. His ears popped again and again. He felt weak and sick and cold; nothing about his body was right as they ascended. Dulgirgraut rang in his mind—a beacon, a song that kept him alive, but only this side of almost. His entire body was glowing uncontrollably, which made him shiver with fear. It had never happened before. They quickly approached the dark shadow of a ship and, with a last burst of speed, shot from the water to land on deck.

He rolled and tumbled with her in his arms. Dazed but alive, he gratefully gasped in air the less fun way.

"Mermaid!" pirates yelled, surrounding them.

Curved swords and angry daggers rang out around them, and she buried her face in his chest. There were more yells as the crew advanced on them. Angst held her with the desperation of a child who'd found a lost cat.

"You've got to be kidding me!" Hector shook his head.

"That's her? The mermaid?" Dallow said in delight.

"Wow," Tarness said, his eyes wide.

"Whore," Victoria admonished drunkenly.

Angst somehow pushed himself to sitting, the all-too-naked mermaid resting in his lap, her face hidden in his shoulder. Her blue hair was disheveled, exposing her breasts. Shaky blades inched closer as pirates gathered their courage.

"I will kill every single one of you," Angst warned, his body still glowing. His leg was mending, and the pounding in his lungs and chest had abated.

"Put those things down before he turns them to dust," Jarblech commanded, marching up to them both. "Why hasn't she eaten you yet? Too small a catch?"

"Probably," Angst wheezed. He couldn't stand, and Tarness

lifted both of them. Angst held her as tightly as he could. "Thanks," he said to his friend, who merely nodded.

Moyra looked up into his eyes, but her gaze kept flitting to his lip and leg.

"You wanted to eat me, didn't you?" he whispered.

"Ashamed," she thought guiltily, her voice very quiet.

"Why didn't you?" he asked.

"I am sorry," she pleaded, her voice filled with panic.

"Don't be," he said with a smile. "Why didn't you?"

"Love," she thought weakly.

"Love," he said firmly.

"Does this conversation seem a little one sided?" Tarness asked.

"You can't hear her?" Angst asked. "She's talking in my mind."

"Oh?" Victoria said curtly. "I can hear both of you."

"Please save them," Moyra thought to him. *"You have to save my people."*

"I'll save you," he promised. "I'll save you all."

The ship rocked as though it were a toy sailboat being picked up by a toddler. The mermaid's head jerked from side to side.

"It is here!" Moyra yelled loudly enough to make Angst and Tori wince. She leaned in, gripping the back of his neck and kissing him. Victoria grunted out loud. *"Love."*

Angst reluctantly pulled away. "Tarness, bring us to port, please."

Tarness carried them to the edge.

"Get away," he pleaded in his mind. *"Far away."*

Angst sighed in relief as she dove from his arms back into the ocean. He watched, sadness and longing filling his heart, until she was gone. The ship rocked a second time, violently enough that Tarness gripped the rail.

"Incoming!" Angst yelled. He pointed at his sword. "That! Now!"

Tarness tripped his way to Dulgirgraut and gently set Angst down on shaky legs, careful to let him grab the hilt. Angst couldn't tell if he held himself aloft or if the hilt had glued to his hand.

"Incoming?" Jarblech asked. "Did we strike an iceberg?"

There was a scream, and Angst watched in horrified disbelief as tentacles plucked a pirate from the deck and tore her into pieces.

* * * *

"What did you do?" Hector grabbed Angst's arm and spun him about.

"She needed help," Angst snapped.

"Of course she did." Hector rolled his eyes. "We can't save everyone!"

"That's our job," Angst said firmly.

There was a thunk as the creature smashed the ship's metal exterior, rocking it violently.

"You're going to owe me a boat for helping your girlfriend," Jarblech bellowed.

"Which girlfriend?" Angst smirked despite his dizzy head and weak legs.

Victoria smacked him upside the head, and Jarblech nodded in approval. "The other one," the pirate said in a low, threatening tone.

"I know where we need to go now!" Angst barked. "We don't have time for this!"

"What do we do, Angst?" Tarness asked.

A largish tentacle smashed toward Tarness. Angst leaped into the air, swinging Dulgirgraut in a wide vertical arc, slicing the end off before hairy feelers could dig into his friend.

"That!" Angst said, watching the appendage undulate and inch toward the railing as though it were crawling away. It slipped over the side of the ship. "Cut off every single one while I hold this ship together."

"Spread out. Everyone take a point," Hector ordered. "Jarblech, in the cabin with your pirates! You can't defend yourself with daggers."

"We aren't going into a coffin," she proclaimed. "Give me something I can use, now!"

From behind his back, Hector pulled a Lochabar axe. "If you can use it, this is large enough to give you some distance."

"I can use it," she said, taking it from him. It was two feet taller than her, and she looked up at the tip. "I think I can use it." She headed aft, followed by several pirate women with swords.

A thin tentacle smacked Tarness's shield with a thud, thick hairs boring into the metal. He struggled, hacking at the appendage until it freed itself. Three more darted over the edge of the ship after the first made contact. Tarness grunted as he sliced at them, chopping at them like the roots of a tree.

"Dallow?" Tarness called out.

His friend reached to his temple and pressed the memndus shard closer. "How big is this thing, Angst? I see a shadow, a silhouette of the creature, under the ship. But it's everywhere!"

"Best guess, Dallow?" Hector asked in his gravelly voice, chopping at a limb with an angry-looking axe. Thick green blood sloshed onto the deck. "How big?"

"Maybe a quarter mile, a half-mile in length. It's like a small island. A really hungry small island."

"That's not possible," Tori said in panic. She gripped Dallow's shoulder and dragged him to the wheel. "Help get us out of here."

Dallow tripped over his own feet as his concentration was broken, but remained standing. He dodged angry tentacles expertly, having the distinct advantage of seeing the entire attack from above. He braced his feet and pulled Jarblech close, just in time to avoid the hairy appendage slapping onto the deck.

"I hate you, Angst," Victoria screamed. "Now duck!"

Angst's head jerked back when he heard her.

"I said duck!" she pleaded as another pirate was lifted into the air.

Five angry tentacles engulfed the woman's body, and she screamed in anguish as hairy spikes bored into her skin and pulled, splitting her into pieces. Blood and gore splashed onto

Victoria and the two remaining pirates. Angst stepped toward his friend, but Hector held his shoulder.

"She'll be fine," he said. "Watch."

Victoria shuddered before gripping the arms of the other two women. "Do as I say," she cried out in fury, "or you will die. Do you understand?"

The women nodded, and moments later, they all leaped back together as a tentacle slapped the deck. Both women thanked her before chopping off the end. Together, they dodged another striking out in unison. Victoria directed them like a furious choir, her anger sobering with every word and curse as they fought.

With the suddenness of a lightning strike in broad daylight, the attack stopped. The silence was deafening and everyone looked around for an answer.

"We need to get out of here!" Angst shouted. "I'm pushing her forward!"

The ship began to turn sharply starboard, leaning enough to make Angst bend a knee to stay level. He almost fell as they jerked to a sudden stop. There was a loud wrenching sound of metal and wood. Angst held the sword up, his eyes glowing bright red. He tried forcing the ship to keep moving, and it gave a horrific metallic cry as it bent. He sensed his metal cocoon surrounding the ship pull apart as sharp hair from the creature's many arms sank into his protection. He couldn't stop it. Dulgirgraut provided no answer, yet still glowed burgundy, imbuing him with power. He heard the song but didn't understand. He could feel the metal hull split apart like a peeled banana.

A sudden gust of wind blew at his damp hair.

"Can't you use that wind to get us out of here?" he yelled before realizing the sails were down.

From behind, he heard a yelp that sounded like Tori, followed by several more.

The ship was being torn out from under him. Metal bent and wood cracked as it sank into the ocean. No matter how much magic he drew from the foci, his best efforts were no match for the raw power of the creature.

"What are you?" he screamed.

He watched Tarness being lifted into the air.

"No!" Angst pleaded. The ship began to list. Angst looked around in desperation to find everyone gone. He was the only one left. His exhaustion overtook him; a mind-numbing pain wracked his body as he dropped to his knees. "Tori! Hector!" he yelled. "What have I done?" He finally collapsed as a horrific crunching destroyed the remains of the ship.

"Moyra," he whispered. "I'm sorry."

36

Angoria

Cool wind woke him to sore muscles that immediately pined for attention, roiling like the very ocean, boiling like lava. His arm felt heavy, and Angst was surprised to find Dulgirgraut hanging from it, his hand permanently cramped around the hilt. Just like the sword, his legs dangled, but at least they were warm and dry. Dry? Hadn't he just leaped out of the ocean with Moyra?

Strong hands shifted under his sore armpits, and he looked up to see chainmail reflecting in the waning moon, and colorful, incandescent wings. He could make out the sincere face of a beautiful young woman he already wanted to know. Forcing his eyes away Angst sought his friends. All was lost in a haze of fog. How could there be fog? Were they in clouds? He caught the occasional glimpse of leg or distant lights that seemed like beacons in the dusk.

"Hi?" he asked.

She didn't reply.

"Thank you," he said hopefully.

Still nothing. Neither entreaties, threats, nor charm seemed to interest his keeper, and he wondered what sort of appetizer he might become.

"You're awake," Jarblech said. "You owe me a boat!"

"Felk," Angst said.

"Watch your mouth," Victoria said.

"Are we all here?" Angst called out, and his friends shouted back.

"Shush," his captor, his savior said.

"You talk," he replied encouragingly, but she said nothing else.

The sun peeked over the horizon, burning his eyes after so much darkness. Angst looked down and then immediately stopped looking down. The last time he'd been this high, he'd ridden a dragon, and that had ended up in a mess. Averting his eyes from the ocean, he looked around to find his friends being carried helplessly by gorgeous women in various coverings of chain and plate. They looked like the stories he'd heard of the Berfemmian, but the wings of light were unexpected. Beautiful feathers of every color spread out over their shoulders. He could see through them, but they had to be solid enough to fly. It was incredible.

The women with luminous wings came closer, and as a group, they dove to the ground. His stomach lurched, and Tori screamed as they descended, but he felt helpless. How could he risk an attack when he couldn't save all his friends at once? The ground came at him quickly as he was unceremoniously dropped onto a sandy beach. Angst tried rolling over to his feet only to end up flat on his back, the sword making it too awkward to continue the motion.

Hector landed behind him, hardly making a sound as he hit the sand. Tarness crashed with a noisy thud while the others scrambled to stand. They were a motley crew of his friends and the remaining pirates.

"What happened?" Angst pushed himself up. "I wasn't done! I wanted to fight that thing, to save her—"

"Stand down, Angst, this isn't the time," Hector warned.

"What are you talking about? Who pulled us from the battle? I want answers." Angst's gaze followed Hector's pointing finger. "I want...oh..."

Angst watched in open-mouthed amazement at the dozen women landing in front of them. They glided like geese over a lake before landing. Brightly colored wings flapped gently as each one gained solid footing. Feathers of warm reds, bright golds, and fiery oranges shimmered brightly. They folded, tucking away behind them, and then disappeared entirely. He set Dulgirgraut between his shoulders and stared in awe.

Angst recognized the face of the tall, gorgeous brunette who'd flown him to safety. Her slitted eyes appeared wary, or angry. When she saw Angst gawking, she unsuccessfully masked a smile. The young woman was all legs, long and tanned, and her thighs were completely naked. She wore the shortest black shorts Angst had ever seen, with sides armored in silver scales. Her long legs were partly covered by shiny black boots that drew his eye almost as much as the shorts. The woman wore a contraption similar to Victoria's chain bra, but hers was adorned with more metallic scale. Her stomach was firm, as if she'd just finished a round of a thousand sit-ups. Dark auburn hair teased her shoulders, framing a beautiful face with large, dark eyes, full lips, and a strong jaw.

Having completely forgotten that his friends were behind him, Angst drew in a breath of 'finally,' as if he'd waited for this moment his entire life, and prepared to speak when another young woman strode over to the tall one. She, too, was fit, though a head shorter than his savior. Her skin was very tan, almost olive in tone. Her brown hair was pulled to the sides in pigtails. She had a beautiful round face and light green eyes that shone with alertness. The shorter one's armor was different yet. One leg was mostly protected by plate while the other was left bare. A plate armor corset, unfortunately covering her chest, stopped well above her midriff, which was a perfect sculpture of abdominal muscles and smooth tanned skin. More plate covered her shoulders and one arm all the way to her fingers, though the opposite arm was bare. The women were so attractive, Angst almost found them hard to look at. Almost.

"It's good to be home, Faeoris," the shorter one said.

The taller woman leaned over and kissed her full on her lips. It was not the friendly peck of a friend, but the passionate kiss of lovers. Angst's sword dropped from his back, and after the kiss ended, he turned around to look at Tarness.

"I know." Tarness shook his head in disbelief.

A silly grin crept across Angst's mouth as he faced the women.

"Um, shouldn't we warn him who they are?" Victoria said.

"Shh," Hector whispered, moving his hands to shush her. "Don't ruin it for me."

Angst didn't understand, and really didn't care. He took a few steps forward and put his hands on his hips, sticking his chest out proudly.

"Hi, I'm Angst," he said with less conviction than intended. He leaned over, fumbling awkwardly with the giant sword and returning it to his back.

"I've never understood, how does skimpy armor even work?" Dallow questioned.

Faeoris nodded, and the shorter woman walked to Angst, one foot in front of the other, her hips swaying like a pendulum. Angst started to speak again, but found the words weren't leaving his mouth as all thought turned to fantasy. When she was a mere five feet away, her sultry smile became fierce. Before Angst could think, she leaped, spinning in the air, and the side of her foot met Angst's temple squarely. Angst flipped over once to land in an unmoving sprawl.

"Like that," Hector said, laughing so hard he could barely hold up his hands. "We surrender."

"Is he okay?" Tori asked.

"I hope so." Hector lowered a hand to wipe tears from his eyes. "Because I never plan to let this one go."

* * * *

An ache in his cheek woke Angst. The entire side of his head fluctuated between numbness and throbbing. A quick glimpse of

271

bright light made him squeeze his eyes shut again while testing his jaw. Sharp pains shot from the joint, but it reluctantly opened. He reached to rub it, making chains clank loudly behind him.

Angst was wide awake now and pulled at both hands to discover they were both restrained. Someone had used chains? He could will himself free in seconds. Angst wiggled and frowned. Was he on a mattress?

"You're finally awake!" a young woman said excitedly. "Now we can get started!"

"Started?" Angst asked in surprise.

He turned his head to find the tall, gorgeous Berfemmian walking toward him seductively. She was thin, and young, and so lovely Angst was completely bewildered that she would bother to move seductively at all. She now wore a scale skirt that somehow covered even less than her shorts—completely exposing the sides of her long, long legs. She reached behind her neck and her loosely hanging chainmail top fell to the floor with a metallic clink. Her breasts were surprisingly large for her thin frame, smaller than Victoria's, but still, there they were—firm and ready.

Angst's first reaction was to smile, his second was to look down at his third reaction. A sheet puddled over his hips, hiding his nakedness. Couldn't she have at least pulled it up over his belly? He sighed before returning to gawking at the young woman.

"Am I dead?" Angst asked.

"What?" she said, slowing her prowl. "Of course you're not dead. Not yet. Why do you think you're dead? Are you in pain?"

"This is just how I pictured it after I died," he said, making her smirk. "Except there are three or four of you, and the sheet covers my belly."

She frowned again. "If you're not in pain, I expect you to perform. It looks like you're ready."

"If by perform, you mean sing, you really don't want that," he said. "I love to sing, but it makes people wince."

She huffed in frustration. "Not sing, foolish human. We are going to mate!"

"Then I *am* dead!" He rolled his head back and laughed. "I'm sure that's a valid excuse."

She raised a long, long leg to straddle him and sat down. Angst thought about dead cats and how Tarness smelled after a fight and eating his wife's roast duck. Nothing worked. She made a grinding motion while leaning forward, with her very full lips poised to kiss.

"Wait. Before we, um, mate…" Angst interrupted.

She sat up, her muscular legs squeezing too tight, and he swallowed a wince of pain.

"Why the chains?" he asked. "I can't imagine you have a hard time finding a boyfriend."

"What's a boyfriend?" she asked.

"Well, it's usually the first step—"

"You talk too much." She sat up, her breasts bouncing hypnotically. Her frown was not seductive. "We've tried mating with other races. They typically don't survive," she said, as though this news was as normal as eating. "The chains keep you from pushing me away."

At a loss for words, he stared at her in disbelief. As amazing as this could be, she was going to sex him to death.

"How could you possibly kill me with sex?" Angst asked.

"It's not like I'm human," she said.

She began to grind again. It was nice, really nice. This couldn't possibly kill him. Right? And anyway, wasn't it his responsibility to make peaceful accord with another nation? Then he remembered Moyra's teeth.

"Why are you doing this?" he asked. "Usually, for me, there are a lot of dinners and begging involved."

"You have to give me your seed," she said, her voice very determined. "It's that time. I need to make babies."

"What?" Angst exclaimed, partially sitting up until he pulled against the chains. "You're just going to go ahead and have your way with me for the sake of making babies? Why me?"

"Well, you look...sturdy," she said in a not-flattering tone. "And I chose you because you're their leader."

"Not the answer I was looking for," Angst said. The chains around his hands and feet fell away like sand, and before she could respond, Angst rolled to one side, throwing her to the floor. "I'm not in the mood tonight, honey."

He stood, awkwardly wrapping himself in the sheets. He could feel cold air around his midriff and rear and knew he wasn't doing it right. A flush warmed his cheeks...the ones on his face.

The young woman flipped back, landing on her feet, and crouched, looking ready to spring forward and return Angst to oblivion. She yelled a horrific war cry and shifted to snap a kick at his face. It remained in place, as did her other. She gawked at Angst's glowing hands.

He raised an eyebrow and smirked.

She roared in frustration.

"A little upsetting, is it, not getting it when you really want it? Now you know what it's like to be married," he said dryly. "Pants?"

She ignored him, instead pulling at her reluctant feet.

"Tell me where my pants are or you have to see me naked," he said.

"Under the bed," she snapped.

Angst knelt and reached under the bed.

"Gross," she complained. "You're so hairy."

"Hey, this wasn't my idea." He grunted as he dragged his pants and tunic from their hiding place. His cheeks were on fire, he was dying from embarrassment, and this was no longer re-motely sexy.

He shimmied into his pants while trying to remain covered by the sheet. When he was mostly dressed, he looked back at Fae-oris. She stared at the ground like a wild animal locked in a cage. Angst felt bad, but couldn't risk freeing her. Something about her, a sadness almost hidden, made him wonder if there were more to this than sex and mating. Women never, ever came to him for sex. Heather, yes, but the rest of them, his friends, wanted something else. Advice mostly, sometimes a buddy to hang out with, but sex? No. He hated his life.

"Are my friends okay?" he asked.

"You were going to be first since you are the leader," she said with a sigh. "The other men are…ready to go."

Angst picked up her chain top from the floor and stared at it like it was a puzzle. She swiped for it but missed. Angst looked her over one more time and sighed. She really was perfect.

"You're beautiful," he said, reluctantly handing it back to her. "You're Faeoris, right?"

"Yes," she said, wiggling into her shimmery top. "How did you know?"

"Your friend," he said. "The one who had her way with my jaw. She said your name."

"She is my *essent*," she said, looking down in frustration at her unmoving legs.

Her what? Maybe he'd misheard her. Rather than embarrassing himself by asking, he ignored it. "Thank you for saving us, Faeoris. I owe you." He looked back at the bed. "Just not this."

"Why?" she pleaded. "It's time. We need the sex to make babies!"

"I'm married." He sighed.

"What is this *married*?" she asked, crossing her arms.

"I can only have one mate," he replied.

"That's stupid," she spat. "Why only one?"

"Good question," he replied, but the joke was lost on her. "I need to see my friends. Where are they?"

"I won't tell you!" She stared at the wall, refusing to make eye contact.

"Fine," Angst said, frustrated. "I'll go find them."

"You won't be able to stop all of us," she warned.

"Actually, yes, I will," Angst said calmly. "I could do this to them right now if needed." He pointed at her stuck legs.

"You have that much power?" Faeoris asked in amazement. "You would have made good babies."

"I hope so," Angst said distantly.

She nodded, her lower lip very pouty and her eyes glossy. "Just go! Take your friends and leave us alone."

Angst returned to the bed and sat. For some reason, he felt like he'd done something wrong. She seemed to be falling apart. Tears streamed from her face. Faeoris would wipe them away then cross her arms before having to wipe them away again. He sighed. Why did they always have to cry?

"If I let you go, do you promise not to kill me?" he asked. "Or hit me? Or kick me in the face?"

She nodded reluctantly. Angst waved a hand and the bonds that held her to the ground disappeared. She lifted both legs, rubbing each in turn.

"You let me free," she said in surprise. "You trust me?"

"You tried to have sex with me. We aren't exactly enemies." Angst smiled. "And you saved my friends. I owe you this much."

She approached carefully, and Angst's heart raced. He hoped he wouldn't have to defend himself against such a beautiful creature. She sat next to him and placed her hands in her lap.

"So, what was this about, Faeoris?" he asked calmly. "I can't imagine you have a thing for short, old, chubby men."

"No," she said quickly and then her voice became apologetic. "I'm sorry, it's not that—"

"It's okay, I'm used to it." He laughed. "Go on."

"We fly to Vex'steppe every winter to mate with the tribes," she said. "We stay there for the winter. When the babies are born, we leave the boys for them to raise and bring the girls back home. For the first time, they turned us away!"

How could they make babies in that short a time? It probably wasn't the moment to ask, so he would have to assume it was because, as she'd said, they weren't human.

"I'm sorry, Faeoris," he said. "But you can't kill me or my friends to make babies."

"What do you expect us to do? This is ripping me apart! We need to mate or my people will die. We need to reproduce!"

"Why not fly back and have it out with them?"

"The wings only work for the one trip."

"How do you know?"

"Because that's how it's always been."

He gently took her hand. "Dallow could explain this better, but your wings have to come from a spell. They have to be some sort of magic," Angst said. "Magic comes when you need it. It always has for me. You just need to figure out how."

Faeoris was overtaken by wracking sobs, and Angst pulled her in for a hug. She seemed reluctant at first, as though she'd never been held, but finally gave in. His shirt become wet with tears as he patted her fine brown hair. Angst fought back a bitter chuckle. He apparently had a knack for kicking women out of his bed and making them cry. It had been different with Nicadilia, who was fake and distasteful. This time, he felt genuinely upset on Faeoris's behalf.

"My mother...died...before...leaving...and...I tried..." Sobs punctuated her words, and she couldn't catch her breath. "I failed at leading my people."

Angst pulled Faeoris down to lie next to him. She followed, her head still on his chest, and her feet dangling over the end of the bed. When her breathing slowed, he finally asked, "Tell me about your people, Faeoris. Tell me what happened. Tell me about your mom."

"My mother was incredible," she whispered. "And I miss her so very much."

37

Jadenville

"Do you want to tell me what that was about?" Rook whispered sharply.

Rook and Jaden sat at a stone table across from Janda and her sister, Nikkola. At first glance, he would never have guessed they were related. Janda had a mass of fiery red curls, while Nikkola's shoulder-length hair was blacker than black. Nikkola was much curvier than Janda, carrying extra weight in her breasts and hips that seemed to encourage a little flaunting and sass. She was as quick to tease as Janda was to attack. It wasn't until that teasing and interaction started that he could tell they were obviously siblings. It was that look of history and family that passed between them in a glance, the look they shared right now.

"She's always been good with animals," Nikkola said with some apology in her tone. "Did we bring back any ale?"

Even before Rook could turn his head, four frothy mugs landed on their table. They all sighed deeply, toasted Graloon, and took long draws. Their favorite barkeep and savior had wisely suggested making their headquarters the new, temporary location of the Wizard's Revenge. It hadn't taken much encouragement for Jaden to deliver.

"You made a bar already?" Nikkola asked.

"How could I argue when he asked?" Jaden lifted his mug to the barkeep, who smiled and nodded before getting busy organizing. "I know how important bars can be in a social environment and—"

"Thanks." Rook cut him off. "You did good."

Jaden seemed focused on his drink, frowning at being interrupted.

"You were saying about Kala?" Rook encouraged the sisters to continue.

"My niece is good with animals," Janda said. "Actually, she's already adept at wielding magic."

"Great," Rook said, throwing up his free hand. "Now we have children who can wield. I thought you had to be older, or something."

"What would you know about it?" Nikkola snapped. "Magic has to be hidden, especially the children who can wield. Which is hard because they need so much attention so they don't destroy anything."

"I'm sorry, you're right. I don't know," Rook said, trying to hide the worry in his voice. "So, this is common, with kids?"

"Drapes," Nikkola said under her breath before taking a sip.

Janda's eyes went wide. "You said you wouldn't tell!"

Nikkola grinned mischievously. Rook raised his eyebrows and waited.

"Well, when I was about Kala's age, I may or may not have set the drapes on fire," Janda said, her face flushing brightly.

"Mom and Dad were so upset," Nikkola ribbed.

"You started it," she said defensively. "You were always picking fights."

Rook held up a hand to interrupt, and both women started laughing.

"That's just what Dad would've done," Nikkola said between chuckles.

Rook smiled before drinking deeply. There was so much about Janda he didn't know, especially about her family. That word was at the bottom of the list in his bachelor vocabulary.

Could he possibly have time in his life for family and soldiering? Certainly not now, but it was possible that one day this would all end, and he could step away from being a soldier. He kept drinking.

"You okay there, Dad?" Jaden asked.

"Of course," Rook said, resisting the urge to knock the younger man out. "So, that's it. She's good with animals to the point that they talk in her head."

"That was new," Nikkola admitted. "But she kind of copies things."

"Things?" Jaden frowned.

"Mom!" Kala called out as she entered the room.

Janda's niece was a skinny thing, one of those cute as a button kids with bowed knees, large eyes, and a smile that wouldn't stop. Her hair was as black as her mother's, and long, below her shoulders. Her skin was slightly darker, almost olive, taking after her father. She was so loving and polite that people were always happy to see her, until they saw Scar. It broke Rook's heart that the lab pup had gotten caught up in this mess. Scar was the perpetual puppy; his tail wagged at everything. He appeared normal, except for the red scar that looked mostly healed from stomach to back. It was a rough reminder of the giant, metal-covered, red-eyed beast he could become. He hadn't left Kala's side since she found him, and hadn't changed once. It was amazing, and frightening, and nobody knew what to do.

"Hi, honey." Nikkola hugged her daughter before brushing hair from her face.

"Am I in trouble?" she asked.

"I just wanted to make sure you're okay," she replied.

"Scar promised he won't change," Kala said, already sounding bored.

"Of course," Nikkola said in an unconvincing tone. She was fidgeting, seemingly unsure of what to do with her hands. "What have you two been doing?"

"Scar showed me where Mr. Angst keeps all the metals. It's so pretty!" she said.

"Oh?" Rook asked. "I'd like to see too."

"Uh huh," Kala said without missing a beat. "And I've been practicing!" She was very proud and thrust her chest out.

"What have you been practicing," Rook asked. "Cartwheels? Summersaults?"

She looked rather sheepish, her hands behind her back and her eyes on her feet.

"Were you practicing magic?" Nikkola prodded.

Kala nodded mutely.

"We've talked about this," she admonished. "But it's okay here with the other wielders."

"So, I can show you?" Her eyes brightened and her fists balled up with all the excitement and energy of youth.

"Of course you can, honey," Nikkola said encouragingly.

Kala stepped back and frowned in concentration. She muttered some words in Acratic and waved her arms around.

"You're kidding me," Jaden said in astonishment a few moments later.

The creature that appeared was mostly a miniature horse. It had six legs and pink fuzzy antlers that matched its pink and yellow zebra stripes. Its very large dark eyes were creepy, but cute in a way that would've surely warranted an extra hug from the young girl, except that the swifen was covered in blue flames. Kala clapped excitedly and Scar yipped as she lovingly wrapped her arms around its neck, the flames blowing out of the way like smoke dispersed by wind.

"I...I haven't seen that one before," Jaden said, scratching his head.

"I thought it would look cool," she said. "I like animals."

"Right," he replied. "How did you do that?"

"I saw you teaching everyone how to make theirs," she said proudly. "It hurt to pull out my hair, but isn't she pretty!"

Everyone nodded in disbelief.

"Can I ride her some more?" she asked.

"Some more?" Nikkola asked.

"I'm sorry," Kala said, obviously realizing she'd let the truth slip out in her excitement. "I'll be careful."

Nikkola looked from her daughter, to Scar, to the swifen, and then back to Scar. She took a deep breath and smiled cautiously. "Promise only to ride the path to Angst's."

Kala squealed and kissed her mom's cheek. "Thank you!"

"Keep Scar close," her mom said. "And be in before dark!"

"I will!" the little girl lied like a twelve-year-old. She led the lab and the horse-thing through the entrance. "Come on!"

"You were saying," Jaden said, his eyes wide with shock. "About copying things?"

"I've seen her do that before," Nikkola said. "She started a fire in the fireplace after watching Janda."

"And she apparently watched me teach the other wielders how to summon their swifen," Jaden said, shaking his head.

"Wait," Rook said. "How is this even possible? I thought she was just good with animals."

"She's good at a lot of things," Nikkola said proudly. "What's wrong with that?"

"Angst can magic stone, Janda can magic fire," he said very quickly, the worry in his voice apparent. "She can do all of it?"

"According to Angst, we can all do all of it," Janda explained. "We can all summon swifen, right?"

"Yes," he agreed reluctantly, crossing his arms.

"The swifen aren't fire, or earth. They're spells that combine several elements," Janda said. "Angst says we can wield all the elements, we just don't know how."

"I can wield stone, but not as well as Angst," Jaden said. "We tend to be adept at things, but can be taught all of it."

"But, she's so young," Rook said, rubbing his fingers through his hair.

"You once told me you got in your first fight at eleven," Janda said. "And you beat up two boys twice your size."

"That's because they were jackasses," Rook said proudly. "And I've always been an proficient fighter. My dad taught me young."

"Exactly," Jaden said. "And it seems that young Kala is very adept."

"Is she going to be okay?" Rook asked. "I mean, spending that time with Scar."

Everything Nikkola was hiding wrenched up her face. Guilt and worry wrinkled her forehead and cheeks, and she looked ready to cry. Janda shot him a look as she placed a consoling hand on her sister's shoulder. He felt bad, but needed to know.

"I worry about her all the time," Nikkola said brokenly. "But it keeps everyone safe, so what else do we do?"

Rook watched Graloon as the man organized his new bar. Bottles and flagons floated around his head, and Rook wondered when this room would start growing and shrinking to accommodate patrons like the Wizard's Revenge.

"I have an idea," Rook said.

38

Angoria

Angst took a deep breath of fresh air and felt it soak into every pore of his body. Something about this place warmed his heart. The comfortable temperatures—cool, but far from cold—were a welcome change after camping in early winter weather. He sat with his friends and the Berfemmian at a long marble table that rested on a patio. The patio was a cliff-side peninsula hovering over a stunning ocean view. Tall, ivy-covered pillars stood behind him at the entrance, connected to a two-foot-high marble railing that framed the dining area protectively. He'd pulled Victoria away from that two thousand foot drop, reminding that he was fine with heights, but hated his friends near heights. Tori had merely rolled her eyes and threatened to walk the railing like a balance beam if he didn't behave.

Hector, Dallow, and Victoria sat beside him at the stone table, directly facing eight of the most beautiful half-naked women Angst had ever seen. It was one of those moments he could only hope he appeared more smooth than he felt. He feared that his every glance would become a wide-eyed stare, and every smile would end with a drooly open mouth. But between giggles on the other side of the table, and his quickly bruising arm nearest Tori, he couldn't have been doing too badly.

They feasted on honeyed breads, and wine, and cakes, and

sweet fruits, and tangy meats. It was so much better than camp-ing rations that Angst got up to give Faeoris a grateful hug. She smiled around a mouthful of breakfast, and nearby Berfemmian nodded approvingly.

He returned to his seat and met eyes with Marisha, the petite warrior who'd greeted him with her foot. He liked her eyes bet-ter. They were a light shade of green, bright and sharp. The young woman's olive skin and round face gave her such an exot-ic look, he could've almost ignored the jolt to his ribs from Victoria's elbow. He glanced up to see Faeoris staring down at him so fiercely that, between the two reactions, he thought it best not to look at Marisha any longer.

Not only were they beautiful, the Berfemmian were fun. Fae-oris had made the rounds after their long evening of talking and napping. Thankfully, the warriors seemed more eager to accept Angst and his friends. He would've loved to stay, if it weren't for the minor inconveniences of Heather, her pregnancy, Rose facing death, and the imminent destruction of Unsel.

After a breakfast of small talk and Hector stories, Angst be-came antsy. Dulgirgraut was still on the beach, and he hated being this far away from his foci, despite their poor relationship. He also felt like they were wasting time. He already felt a tie with Faeoris and wanted to know more about her people, but Rose needed them. He left breakfast to walk along the railing, which was barely tall enough to keep someone from toppling over the cliff edge and served more as a reminder than a safety measure. The sandy beach looked so distant from this height, he couldn't help but think of Faeoris's story.

Her mother had died from a fall as she was preparing to lead the Berfemmian migration. Every year, they flew to Vex'steppe and mated with the tribes. It would've been Faeoris's first flight, but after leaping over the cliff, they'd been stopped in mid-air by an old man, who'd demanded their submission. Angst shook his head. Even after such a short time with these people, he could tell they would choose death before servitude. And she had. De-spite losing her mother, Faeoris had done what she could to succeed, but everything seemed to be working against her—even the Vex'steppe tribes, who'd turned them away. He admired her, a lot.

And what of the tall old man? Who could he be? Another host representing an element, or a new foe altogether? He suspected there was something much bigger happening. Maybe that was what Aerella had been trying to tell them through the dream he could barely remember. He could only see glimpses of the great battle, in a field, with giants and monsters and men…but not enough to make sense of the dream's purpose.

Angst stepped back from his thoughts, letting them soak in while watching everyone. Tori awkwardly straightened her acquired Berfemmian armor top, obviously feeling out of place. Hector argued with Marisha about something, embellishing his words with hands and arms. Dallow's hands were pressed together, tapping his chin thoughtfully with his fingers as he took everything in, and Tarness was missing, probably having more fun than the rest of them. His gaze ended on Faeoris, who noticed immediately and smiled. She wasn't offended by his leering, nor did she mock him. It made him happy that it was okay to be himself.

"You don't understand, Marisha," Hector growled. "We need to get to that city."

"You can drown, or you can get eaten by the monster," she said firmly. "The choice is yours."

"Why can't you fly us there?" Hector asked. "You flew us off the boat."

"Because I don't have wings! You were just lucky," she replied. "We were on our way back from Vex'steppe and saw the attack. It's only because of Faeoris that we saved you. I would've let you all die." Her eyes were fierce and her disposition bitchy. "Now that we're back on the island, the wings are gone until next time. Don't think you'll get another—"

"Stop that," Angst interrupted, and everyone looked at him as he stood. He stared directly at Marisha. "You wouldn't have let us die."

To his surprise, both Marisha and Hector shot him looks so cold, he felt slapped by a spray of ice.

He could understand Marisha's response, but Hector's? He couldn't imagine what else he'd interrupted, but ignored the glares. "Well?" he pressed.

Her eyes softened, and she avoided his gaze.

"And what do you mean you don't have wings?" Angst asked irritably.

Faeoris walked to him and stood as awkwardly close as Victoria used to. "I told you, they only appear when it's time to mate, my friend." The very word, friend, sounded forced and awkward coming from her.

Angst smiled, and blushed, but didn't step away. He felt close to her after their long night, but wouldn't dare show fear or submission to any Berfemmian, especially Faeoris. From the corner of his eye, Angst saw Victoria cringe at the exchange. He wasn't trying to hurt her feelings, but couldn't show weakness. He could only hope that Tori would sense his intentions with Faeoris. This was going to get complicated.

"I don't think that's completely right, Faeoris" he said, as gently as he could.

Faeoris frowned as her expression darkened. She tensed, every Berfemmian around the table tensed, the entire island suddenly tensed and went quiet. Angst couldn't even hear birds in the distance. Obviously, it wasn't going to be easy opposing his new *friend*—it seemed nobody wanted to argue with her.

"From my experience, magic happens when you need it, when you will it." Angst placed his hands on Faeoris's muscular shoulders. They were taut and ready, but she didn't pull away.

Dallow flashed him an eyeless gaze as if he already knew what Angst was planning. Victoria jerked her head no.

"I can't make my wings appear," Marisha snapped as she stood, glancing over her shoulders. "Look."

Angst winked at Faeoris and walked around the table to face Marisha. He tried to restrain his awe. Did they all have to be gorgeous? The young woman remained still, peering at Angst.

He adjusted his jaw cautiously, remembering their last encounter.

"No kicking," he whispered.

One of her cheeks lifted in a cautious smile. Angst placed a glowing hand on the stone table. A shape oozed out of the stone, and Victoria coughed in disapproval—perhaps she expected it to form a rose. Within seconds, Angst had created a stone dagger. The handle had fine indentations as though wrapped in string made from marble. It was half the length of Marisha's arm, and she took the blade, holding it out to inspect it thoroughly. She flipped it in the air, deftly catching the handle. It spun in the palm of her hand before she licked the blade once then nodded her acceptance, tucking it into her belt next to the others.

"I willed this," he said, looking around. "And you can will your wings."

"It's never been done." Faeoris seemed upset. Her arms were crossed and her eyes flashed between Angst and Marisha, who frowned at her, apparently surprised by the cold reaction.

Angst returned to his new friend and gave her his best smile. "How important am I to you?"

"We...we are friends," Faeoris answered, looking around as if embarrassed.

"So you trust me?" Angst asked.

Faeoris paused, looking at him. Angst held both hands out, palms up, as though seeking acceptance. She looked worried, almost upset.

"Angst, no," Victoria said. "It might not work."

"What are you going to do now?" Hector asked in a worried tone.

"Do you trust me?" Angst asked firmly. It was a lot to ask after only one night, but he had a feeling.

Faeoris squared her shoulders. She looked at Marisha nervously before making eye contact with Angst. She placed her hands on his. "I trust you, Angst."

"Then don't let me die," Angst said.

"No!" Victoria yelled as she stood.

Angst sprinted to the edge and leaped over the stone railing, diving headfirst to the sandy shore. The ground came faster than he'd expected. He tried to roll in mid-air, wanting to hold his hand up, hoping she would be there, but it was never that easy. Instead, he flailed, his hands and legs flopping helplessly as the ground rushed up to meet him. There was no time for his magic. He thought of Heather being pregnant, and felt so bad that he—

His knee, hip, and spine strained as he jerked to a stop. An unnatural pop in his body made him squeak. Angst looked overhead. The sandy shore was just beyond arm's reach. He looked toward his feet at Faeoris's panicked face. She held his ankle in a grip so firm his foot was already numb. Beautiful wings of light—gold and pink and orange and yellow—stretched out over her shoulders as if she were held aloft by a rainbow. Her eyes were fury, and glassy, as tears dripped down her cheeks. He knew he would have a lot of apologizing to do.

They spun around as they hovered, and to his surprise, Faeoris wasn't alone. Every Berfemmian that had been sitting at the table was now floating in mid-air, wings of light flapping gently. They'd all jumped over the edge to save him, or her. He'd done the right thing. When he couldn't hold back his smug smile, she let go. Angst landed on the unforgiving sand, his head jerking to one side and his shoulder screaming in pain.

He rolled over and sprawled out, smiling at his victory through gritted teeth. His neck and shoulder would hurt until Dallow taught him to heal himself, but this would last forever. The other Berfemmian flew up and away, leaving Faeoris behind. She seemed torn between following her friends, helping Angst return to the patio, or picking him up and dropping him again.

"I believe in you, too," Angst said as he got to his feet, rubbing his sore neck and wondering how he would rub his sore everything else.

He couldn't make out her expression as she flew off, but he remembered the angry tears and knew this wouldn't be easily forgiven. Angst looked at the long path ahead that led to a tall, wide flight of stone steps. He walked over to Dulgirgraut, half-buried in the sand, left there since he'd been knocked out by Marisha the night before. Angst picked up the foci and cried out in pain as he set it on the familiar spot, hovering over his back. He rolled his shoulder several times, frustrated it wasn't feeling better already.

"At least now they know," he said to Dulgirgraut, not really expecting a reply.

39

After such a quick fall, it didn't seem right that the walk up would take so long. There must've been thousands of stairs. Thousands. They were short, wide things just tall enough to make it awkward to take two at a time. Angst decided that progress was best made by taking two steps, and then one, and then two. After every thirtyish stairs he would stop and look around to make sure nobody saw him sit. He had convinced himself the stairway had to end soon when a large, dark man lumbered down toward him.

"I came to make sure you're okay," Tarness huffed. "You're about halfway there."

"Ugh," Angst grunted, giving the enormous black man a brotherly slap on his shoulder.

"That was dumb, Angst," Tarness admonished. "You could've died."

"But I didn't," he said.

"You upset everyone," his friend continued.

"I've got to be good at something," Angst said with a grin.

"Hector is talking them down now," Tarness said.

"Oh good." Angst couldn't hold back the sarcasm. "And you?"

"I'm doing fine!" Tarness lied.

He appeared satiated. There was a twinkle in both eyes that told Angst his night had been busy, but there was something else. His friend was burying emotions under the thick brows that always made him appear angry. Angst knew better. Tarness was hiding something.

They began walking up the stairs, slowly. Tarness said nothing, and Angst could've easily ignored the tension, but didn't want to. He related to Tarness more than any other, and didn't want their friendship to be lost in this adventure. He could only imagine what was wrong. His friend had taken a personal offense to every woman attracted to Angst.

"You're upset about the mermaid," Angst began. "And Tori, and—"

"I was," he said with a smirk. "Being Angst sounds fun, sometimes. There are a lot of beautiful women in your life."

"You probably had as many last night," Angst said.

"No," Tarness replied, shaking his head. "Just three."

"Three?" Angst asked in surprise, remembering that Faeoris had warned she would sex him to death. "Just three?"

His friend merely shrugged.

They paused between steps, squatting to stretch their knees and calves. Bones popped and ground beneath their strained muscles, making them both laugh. They continued at a slower pace, trying to keep up with their breathing.

"It is fun," Angst said. "But usually, it ends in hurt. My hurt. I can't tell you how many I've lost. One day, Rose will move on and I won't see her anymore. I'll lose Moyra because of who I am. I can't even imagine how tough it will be to lose Tori. I lose all of them. I tell myself I've added something to their lives, that I've helped them along, made them smile and feel loved. And I get memories. Great memories, but they're ghosts of what was. I miss them, every single one, and on my bad days, on the worst days, it hurts far more than you could imagine."

Tarness looked up and smirked. "But all that sex?"

"Ha!" Angst said. "I've been married twenty years. I don't get sex." He winked.

"Not even with the mermaid?" Tarness asked, sounding happier. He placed an arm around Angst, making him wince as it met his shoulder.

"I wish," Angst said amorously.

"But that night, with Victoria and Tamara...?" Tarness sighed.

"I don't even remember how I got to bed. That's not something I wanted to happen," Angst said, running his hand through thinning hair. It felt sticky from saltwater and longer than he liked. "I need to talk to Tori about that night, it's not right. I feel like I crossed the line when I only wanted to jump on it. I was so embarrassed when you opened the door, I don't even like thinking about it. You've got to believe me."

"And Moyra?" Tarness prodded.

"I..." He didn't know what to say. He wanted to be honest with his friend, but his feelings for the mermaid were far stronger than he wanted to admit, even to himself. "I'm sure she's not for me."

"Why not you?" he said. "She's obviously interested."

"Probably because I'm so *very* handsome and charming."

"Don't forget young." Tarness laughed. "There's something I've been wanting to ask about your mermaid girlfriend."

"She's not my girlfriend," Angst snapped, more harshly than he meant to.

Tarness smirked. "How do you, um, where do you... When you do stuff...?"

"I don't do anything." Angst sighed in frustration. He couldn't tell if Tarness was teasing or trawling. "Not with her or anyone! Not to mention, I couldn't...she has about a billion teeth."

"Really?" Tarness said, his eyes wide in terror.

"Rows of teeth." He drew his fingers along his own while squinting his eyes.

"Rows? Like a shark?"

"Rows." Angst nodded. "And she really does eat men. They all do."

"Gross," Tarness said with a shudder.

"I know," Angst agreed. "I threw up in front of her. I was really embarrassed, but it's disgusting."

"And that's it?" Tarness asked in disbelief.

"We barely talk. Well, I talk." He knew he wasn't making any sense and his cheeks warmed as he floundered for words.

"How do you not talk?" Tarness placed his chin on a hand, ready for story time.

"I talk to her…we talk to each other…in our minds." Angst winced. "It's complicated."

Tarness raised an eyebrow, and Angst shrugged.

"Now she reads your mind too?" Tarness's second eyebrow joined the first. "I'm beginning to think we can all read your mind."

"She doesn't read my mind." Angst frowned and said quietly, "At least I hope not."

"What about breathing underwater?" he asked. "You were down there a long time."

Now his ears burned hot and he'd run out of sighs. He stared at his large friend, who was barely able to hold in his broad grin.

"You've got a mess, Angst," Tarness said. "Are you okay?"

"Yeeeaah." Angst let the word draw out long. "Actually, no, I don't have a clue. Dulgirgraut and I can't seem to work together right. Victoria is always upset at me, and then I wake up naked next to her. The mermaid is confusing. I don't even know what she really wants. And now, I'm sure, Faeoris is angry."

"It sounds like torture," Tarness said, rolling his eyes.

"Hey, it's not all fun and girls," Angst said with a smirk. "Everyone wants something different from me, and I can't do it all."

"Don't worry about what we want. You need to just be Angst." Tarness smiled broadly. "You'll figure Dulgirgraut out. You're smart, Angst, really smart. So, it'll happen. You're right about Tori—she will move on. Enjoy this time with her, because it won't last. And the mermaid? I'm sorry, but that won't last either. It sounds like she's using you for something."

"Using me?" Angst asked.

"I've been used all my life," Tarness said firmly. "She's using you. That's why I came to meet you, so I could tell you that without the others hearing."

His friend spoke true every fear that was in his mind. Angst walked slower to gather his thoughts. He was going to lose them both, somehow. These moments, these precious moments were so fleeting, they were already gone. This weighed so heavily on his heart, it hurt too much to cry.

"Your mermaid saved me," Tarness said. "She's pretty naked."

"Pretty when she's naked?" Angst asked with a full smile. He looked around as if someone were watching then spoke under his breath, "Did you see those breasts?"

"And that mouth," Tarness said, giving his eyebrows another workout.

They walked, arms around each other's shoulders, comparing notes as they made their way up the stairs.

* * * *

Angst's knee clicked noisily with every step, grinding from wear as they reached the top. A thick humidity hung between his tunic and chest, coating him in slick sweat. He suddenly missed the coolness of winter. The stone courtyard at the top of the stairs was empty, but Tarness wouldn't sit. Sweat flopped from his forehead like he'd just dunked his head in the ocean, and Angst wondered how his friend had gotten down the stairs so fast. After glancing around, he set Dulgirgraut on its tip and collapsed. He really hoped they'd be left alone for a while—his heart was beating hard. Angst lifted with his shoulders and twisted; his back popped, and he sighed.

"I don't see any of the Berfemmian, Tarness," he said between husky breaths. "I think we're safe to rest."

With a loud *fwump* and a deep sigh of relief, Tarness landed next to him on the stairs.

Angst patted his knee and nodded knowingly. "I just want to sit here and be old," Angst said.

"Can't you ever find ugly people to spend time with?" Tarness asked. "Maybe someone we don't have to be so impressive around?"

"No way." Angst chuckled. "I wouldn't want you to call me chicken."

"Ha!" Tarness gasped.

"There you are!" Faeoris shouted from the courtyard.

"Back to being young," Angst muttered.

"Let me know how that works for you." Tarness leaned back with a wide grin.

Angst was lifted high into the air by the back of his tunic as Faeoris tossed him twenty feet away.

"Never do that again!" she roared.

Angst stood, dusting himself off and rubbing an elbow that was now leaking blood. "I don't plan to!"

She leaped to him gracefully and attempted to pick him up under his shoulders. He remained in place, this time prepared and anchored to the ground. She pulled back in frustration, wiped his sweat from her hands with a disgusted scowl, and tried shoving him.

He grunted with pain, but didn't budge. "What are you doing?" he snapped.

"You could've been killed!" Her tone was frantic.

"Yeah!" he shouted. "Just now, when you threw me!"

"You said we were friends!" Her arms were crossed as if she were squeezed between walls of emotion. "Why would you do that?"

"I had to show you what you're capable of!" he shouted. "I knew you'd be there for me."

She obviously didn't know how to answer. Her eyes roamed his face as she apparently tried to find some fault in his reasoning. He was exhausted, and upset, but he also felt an electricity, an energy from their argument, or from wielding magic. He was too tired to fight it, and he let his senses reach out to feel the sword, the minerals around him, the air, the magic that connected everything.

"You think you already know me that well," she said.

"Sometimes," he said cockily. "Yeah."

"Do you know this?" She leaped into the air and spun, and her foot flew toward his face just as Marisha's had.

Angst felt it, all of it. The movement of the air, her bones rising high and twisting around. What was this? He leaned back. Her heel swung inches from his nose but didn't make contact. He didn't understand why they were fighting, but he didn't care. He was almost giddy, unable to hold back his grin. She roared in frustration, swinging at him with incredible speed. He dodged every blow, and started giggling. Was he just enjoying her irritation? She smiled through gritted teeth and took two steps back. He couldn't help but take her in; she was absolutely stunning. Sweat glistened from her bare cleavage and heaving midriff, her leg muscles were taut and ready. Her beauty was such an unfair advantage, and she used it. Faeoris jumped high and kicked out with both legs. He dropped before she connected, rolling over his back to one knee. She laughed aloud as she landed. This was like foreplay, except this time he wasn't tied to a bed. Angst leaped to tackle her. She rolled back, and meant to keep rolling until Angst anchored her bones to the ground so he would end up on top. He kissed her on the cheek, which made her scream a battle cry, shoving him with such force he flew into the air.

* * * *

"I don't see how this helps," Victoria whispered from behind a nearby bush.

"That's because you're jealous," Hector explained. "Angst thinks he knows everything, but he's not prepared for this." He held out a hand.

Victoria looked at him in surprise and then accepted the hand. She smiled. "You really think this will work?"

"It obviously can't come from me," he said. "But it needs to come from someone."

"I hate this." She shook her head. "It should be me out there."

"And that thinking is part of the reason he hasn't been able to focus," Hector said, without looking at her. "My future queen needs this to happen."

"Meh," she said under her breath.

* * * *

Faeoris covered her mouth, her eyes wide with concern. Wings of light appeared in a bright flash between her shoulders as she flew toward Angst to catch him. She hovered, and waited, but he didn't fall. He stood on an invisible shield of air and looked down at her.

"Air," he shouted in explanation. "Catch!" He launched off the platform and landed in her arms. He kissed her on the cheek again, which made her smirk. "I'm starting to enjoy this."

"All I get is this wrestling?" she said with raised eyebrows as they lowered slowly to the courtyard.

"It's all I have to offer," he said.

"That's not enough." Faeoris frowned. Her chest and face were flushed, and she was breathing heavily. It was both intoxicating, and frightening.

"I'm sorry...I can't," he said, worried he'd pushed her too far.

"I know. You said that," she replied. "I need to calm down."

"What can I do to help?" Angst asked. "I can leave. Sometimes my very presence drives women to screaming fits."

"I believe you," she said dryly as they landed. "But we can't have sex, and wrestling with you just makes me angrier. You probably don't know sealtian."

"Of course I do," Angst said. "Some."

"Some?" she said in surprise. "I thought you knew everything." Her words were thick with sarcasm.

"Most," Angst lied. "I'm pretty sure all of them."

"Will you," she asked. "With me?"

Angst kissed her on the cheek once more, making her frown, before he hurried to Dulgirgraut. Ignoring the bright burgundy glow that already surrounded the blade, he hefted it and scrambled back to her. Crouching, he held it horizontal to the ground. He looked at her, and she stood at the ready with a staff.

* * * *

"I don't get it?" Victoria asked.

"She had to break him down," Hector explained in a gruff whisper. "Get the fight out of him so he could relax and do the sealtian."

"What are sealtian?" Tarness whispered, now crouching with them.

"They're a pattern of movements used to find balance with your chosen weapon," Tori said in a monotone, as if repeating it verbatim. "What? How do you think Tyrell taught me?"

"I'm surprised you aren't a fan," Hector taunted, his gray eyes mischievous. "They're like dancing."

"I hate this," Victoria whispered.

"This has nothing to do with you." Hector smiled, mostly ignoring the princess. "He needs this almost as much as he needs you."

"He needs me?" she asked hopefully.

"Shush," he replied.

"I think he needs her, too," Tarness whispered.

Victoria slugged him in the arm. Hector shot them both a chilling gaze.

"Sorry, dad," Tarness mocked.

* * * *

Angst focused, lifting the sword vertically over his head with both hands. The red light surrounding the foci now covered his forearms. His mind was emptied, exhausted, but his body still burned with energy from their wrestling. He took a deep breath and concentrated, feeling her movements next to him. Angst sensed her arms move, lowering the staff. He lowered his sword so it was horizontal to the ground. They moved together, mirror images performing the same dance, bending like reeds, crouching like tigers, stretching like swans ready to take flight. Instinctively, they continued to the fourth sealtian, and then the fifth, flowing into each one as naturally as water.

* * * *

"I never taught him those!" Hector said excitedly. "He would get so impatient and frustrated that we couldn't get past the first few."

"Awesome," Victoria said dryly.

"It really is!" Hector said proudly.

"How many are there?" Tarness asked, stretching a leg.

"Thirty," Hector replied. "Each one takes a minute, so be patient."

* * * *

The sweat was cleansing, and the ocean breeze that rolled over his bare arms exhilarating. His connection with Faeoris was different than any other he'd experienced. It was as if her body guided his own. He'd lost track of time, and didn't care. He felt complete, accomplished. This wasn't the success from a battle barely won, or getting away with something he shouldn't have; this was something more permanent. Angst didn't know when the music from Dulgirgraut had started accompanying his sealtian, when it had begun to flow in the rhythm of his movements, or when it stopped being just music. The sword's glow grew in him, and out from him. The music became information, and power. He squeezed the tears from his eyes, and let it happen.

* * * *

"What's this?" Hector said, standing. "I've never seen that one before."

"Maybe there are more sealtian," Tarness suggested.

"But I would know," he said pleadingly.

"Sucks, doesn't it?" Victoria rapped on his leg with the back of her knuckle.

* * * *

When Angst finally finished, his legs were together, his back straight, and Dulgirgraut held high above his head. His mouth dry from the hour long workout, he lowered the great blade, resting it on its tip. The connection, the bond between them was now tangible. Information didn't flow, but was there for the taking, and the foci had settled into his mind cozily, like a swaddled child. He looked at Faeoris with brightly glowing eyes and saw that her face was tracked with tears. She leaped into his arms and gave him a rib-bruising hug.

"Those last two sealtian," she said in a voice hoarse with emotion. "I thought they were lost forever. You did that!"

"We did it together," he said, tired and proud

"I couldn't have done it without you," she said. "You took lead ten movements ago."

"I didn't even know those last thirty existed," Hector said, leaving his hiding place.

Tarness and Victoria followed him, Tori's expression apprehensive. She frowned, focusing on Angst's face as though straining to read him.

"Did it work?" Tarness asked.

"Yeah," Angst said, smiling at Faeoris. "It really did." He was surprised by the Berfemmian's knowing look. "Wait, you knew?"

"See?" She pushed him roughly. "You don't know everything."

He looked at Hector, who grinned sheepishly.

"Fine, you were right," Angst acknowledged to Hector, gratefully placing a hand on his old mentor's shoulder.

"It wouldn't hurt my feelings if you said that again." Hector grinned from ear to ear.

Angst pulled him close and whispered in his ear.

Hector barked out a laugh. "I guess that will have to do." He chuckled.

40

Azaktrha

ANduaut and Rose stood by the barrier that kept the ocean out and them in. Creeper was curled up into a ball, covering his eyes with webbed fingers as if crying. The top of his head and his knees were pressed firmly against the clear wall, and his other hand reached high. Something moved beyond the barrier, opposite his hand. It was gone before she could make it out, and her gaze returned to the pathetic figure of her companion.

He *was* pathetic, and part of her wanted to laugh, but she also felt a smattering of guilt. She'd been pretty harsh to the little fish-man, and she supposed she should show some gratitude. He'd tried to warn her of danger multiple times. Rose knelt beside him and placed a hand on his shivering arm. She could feel his life, tantalizingly delicious to her touch. Creeper jerked his hand away, refusing to roll over and face her.

"Are you okay?" she asked.

He merely shrugged in response.

"I may have been a little mean," she said quietly. "But sometimes you just…"

She let that thought trail off. Experience was teaching her that people didn't always appreciate being told what they were doing wrong, especially when they were upset. They should've.

"Come on, Creeper," she said. "You need to help us find a

way out. You want to leave, don't you?"

He shrugged again.

She sought ANduaut for help, but he was gone. Why would he leave her now? *Typical man.*

"I wish you could speak," she said forlornly. "These one-way conversations are exhausting."

Creeper turned to face her, his face contorted with apparent frustration. He tapped near the blue oval on his forehead then pointed at her.

"Oh, that," she said. "It's just that there seems to be so much going on in my head right now, I hate introducing something else. Hearing you in my mind freaks me out."

His large eyes became sad, and he rolled over to sit up with his back against the barrier. He sighed deeply. He was a pouty little thing, and inspiring him out of his malaise already seemed more work than it should've been. But, she sat on the ground, crossing her legs. Could she really trust him? After all these days, he hadn't done anything to harm her, and he only wanted to communicate. She shuddered at the thought of lowering any barriers, afraid to let anyone learn the depth of her hunger, but maybe it was just talking. Maybe just this once.

"Why did you say Angst?" she asked. She tapped her forehead when he was reticent to reply. "Go on."

"I saw him beyond the curse," he said in her mind. *"Your Angst was out there."*

"He's not my Angst," she said, articulating the name to correct Creeper. Her heart skipped several beats as she reminded herself to be realistic and not hopeful. "How do you know it was Angst?"

"You speak to me in pictures. I see what you say in my mind," he tried explaining. *"I recognized him."*

"My words are pictures? How is that even possible?" She scowled. "Do you see how much I want to beat you senseless for being in my mind?"

His mouth dropped open, revealing rows of teeth, and he covered his face, scrambling to push away from her.

CHAPTER FORTY

She grabbed his wrist. "It's okay. Stop," she urged. "I won't hurt you. I guess maybe this mind-talking thing does work."

He peeked out from his fingers and saw that it was safe.

"But, how could Angst be all the way down here? Aren't we at the bottom of the ocean?" she asked in disbelief. "How could he breathe? Was he using magic?"

"He was with a mermaid," Creeper said.

"Of course he was," she said, feeling the tiniest trace of hope.

"She could have kept him alive," Creeper went on. *"Breathed for him."*

"Gross," Rose said, dismissing the thought. Her mind was now racing, and she fought back tears. She'd almost lost hope. Was it really possible? Could Dallow, Angst, and the others be here to save her? Angst. He had so much power with the foci. That power could feed her, fill her... She shook her head, struggling to block off the thoughts that kept sneaking in. She looked out beyond the barrier and saw nothing but darkness.

"Gendel," he said, interrupting her thoughts.

"What's that?" she asked.

"My name is not Creeper," he said, sounding annoyed. *"My name is Gendel."*

"I...I'll remember that, Gendel," Rose said, taken aback. She'd never considered that he had a name, which made her feel a little guilty.

"I was not always like this," he went on, looking down at his body in disgust. *"I was not always a Creeper, as you call me. I was something else, bigger and stronger than this thing you see."*

"Uh huh," she said, her attention still partly on her friends. "So how did this happen to you?"

"I led my people to this city, to explore the ruins," he said. *"We were attacked by that creature."*

"I know that creature," she said. "I hate it, whatever it is. Someone should kill it."

"It is the oldest living creature on Ehrde, and it cannot be stopped," he said with a sigh. *"We tried to fight it, but after kill-*

ing so many, the monster trapped the rest of us in here. We have been here ever since."

"When did this happen?" she asked.

"Long ago. Long, long before you," he said, and she assumed he meant before she was born.

"So why do your people keep attacking me?" she asked. She held out her thin arm and wiggled her fingers. "Why did that little bastard eat my hand?"

Creeper rolled back over, covering his head and shaking violently. His webbed ears folded painfully under his clenched fists.

"I'm not going to hurt you," she said, hoping she wouldn't have to. "I promise, Gendel."

"They have not been attacking you," he muttered, still facing away. *"They have been trying to attack me."*

"I...but...oh," she said, her anger growing as everything came into place. He'd been with her since the beginning, or they thought she'd been with him. Every time they showed up, she'd fought them off. He *had* been using her to protect himself. She took deep breaths, reminding herself that she'd promised not to harm him. Rose was pretty sure that harming included maiming and killing.

"I have been alone for so long," he pleaded. *"I have been alone, without my friends, in a body that does not even feel like mine. You would not understand."*

Gendel's words squeezed the anger out of her heart like juice from a plum. She'd only just regained control of her body, and it was still changing. The sword didn't force her to go anywhere, but now her blood was orange, and her hunger for eating life was growing exponentially.

"I understand, all too well," she said with a grimace. "What you did isn't right, but I really do understand."

"I am sorry," he offered, reaching out with a hand.

She nodded curtly, not fully accepting his apology. "So why are they after you?"

"They blame me for all of it. For leading them to the city, and getting trapped by the curse," he said. *"And after so many*

*years, they are almost like animals. All they remember is re-
venge."*

"Cree...Gendel," she corrected herself. "You want out of here
as badly as we do. Do you know a way?"

"Maybe," he said. *"But I cannot by myself."*

"Why didn't you say so?" she shouted, pushing herself back
up to stand.

Gendel sighed and tapped his head as a reminder.

"You really need to grow a pair," she admonished. *"Let's go,
like, now!"*

He smiled, showing rows of teeth. She shivered, but said
nothing. He had at least earned the right to smile, even if it was
horrifying. Gendel ran down a walkway, his feet slapping the
pavement noisily.

"Come on!" He waved her to follow.

* * * *

Nordruaut

Short puffs of frosty air left his mouth as Guldrich grunted,
grappling with all his might. The sweat dripping from his brow
fell off in tiny balls of ice. His good arm was blotchy from the
freezing temperatures and blustering wind. Even the furs that
now covered him were barely enough to shield from the raw
cold.

There was a sloppy, wet sound and his hand dripped with
warm liquid. He wrenched his claws out, only breaking one this
time, and the Nordruaut dropped to the ground. The body
twitched in its final struggle for life. He rolled the giant over and
jerked the knife wedged between his ribs free. After wiping fur
and blood off the fine blade he'd won from another kill, he returned it to its sheath. The Nordruaut made fine weapons, but
who in their right mind wore armor made from animal skins and
fur?

He took tall steps over knee-high snow to find a clean patch,
free from blood and battle, and used the snow to scrub

Nordruaut off his hand and arm. Guldrich stretched his right arm, which had been removed below the elbow. Fresh, exposed muscles now covered the bones that had already grown back. He'd had no idea his own healing would be so powerful, and wondered how many pieces he would have to be diced into before finally dying. The arm was grotesque and useless as anything but a stick, but there it was.

Would he have to replace the kill marks he'd carved into the gray skin or would they grow back too? Guldrich laughed uncontrollably as he reviewed the three bloody kills sprawled about the snow bank. Why hadn't these fools killed him when they'd had the chance? They had different rules for times of war than they did for times of peace? It made no sense. They were amongst the most feared creatures in Unsel, and he'd just killed three with one arm. These *giants* were far weaker than he'd thought, and Fulk'han needed to know.

But who would he tell? He'd already marked the useless emperor and his cabinet on his list of soon-to-be dead, quickly followed by the magic-wielding bitch who'd sent him to this frozen death. The chill bit at his partially-formed arm, which tingled with a painful numbness, as though it had fallen asleep and couldn't be woken. One good thing about that silly fur armor—it was warm.

Guldrich made his way back to the dead Nordruauts and tugged fur off them until he found usable pieces. He searched their still-warm bodies for food, but they carried more bladders of mead or ale than anything substantial, as if hunting him had only been supposed to last a day. The killing was a distraction, and he needed to focus on making the long trek back to Fulk'han. He had no clue how far away home was, and laughed to himself again at the realization that he barely understood why he was here.

That wild bitch, that stranger, had magicked him hundreds of miles north into enemy territory. She'd said he would find a champion. They needed a champion or there would be no Fulk'han empire. Instead, he'd found nothing but a Nordruaut child with an axe that froze his arm off. He should cut her arm off to see how she liked healing through it. This thought quickly passed as he pocketed dry jerky and frozen bread. A snack to the giant, it was enough for two meals.

"South," he grunted to the bodies. "Tell your friends I'm headed south, and I'm leaving a trail of corpses behind until they give up their hunt."

41

Angoria

The next morning, Angst and his friends stood before Faeoris. They waited on the dais where she and Angst had performed the sealtian, where Angst had finally made the bond with Dulgir-graut work. He'd been right about one thing: this foci communicated very differently than Chryslaenor. There was no excited flood of information like a young teenager brimming with stories. This was more like a wise old politician who told you what you needed, but only when you needed it. The sword had strengths that he would need time to research and under-stand. It seemed especially adept at healing, and imbued Angst with even more knowledge, but not enough to replace Dallow's eyes.

Victoria coughed impatiently, and to no avail. Faeoris looked up into the clear sky, her eyes trailing three Berfemmian darting beneath clouds, diving at each other like hawks fighting over territory. Dallow's head bobbed and weaved as they flew until he winced. Angst jerked his gaze upward at a distant crashing sound, and one of the bodies fell like rain. Faeoris scoffed, her wings appeared, and she launched into the air, reaching the downed Berfemmian before she ended up becoming a puddle. Faeoris returned to the platform, unceremoniously dumping the unconscious warrior to the hard ground before continuing her watch.

"You have provided us with a new tool," she said gratefully to Angst.

"I'm not sure falling to your death is a good thing," he said warily.

"Don't you see?" she asked excitedly. "Aerial combat!"

"Great," Hector said dryly, rubbing the back of his neck.

"That isn't all," Victoria said, raising a finger. "You also now have freedom."

"I...we..." Faeoris stuttered as though she'd missed this, and when she spoke again, her tone was defensive. "We have left Angoria. We do every year."

"Only to mate," Angst said. "Now you can visit me whenever you want."

Faeoris smiled, while Hector and Victoria sighed deeply.

"Was it wise to tell them?" Hector whispered.

"She isn't stupid, just distracted," Victoria replied in a hushed tone. "She would've figured it out, and it benefits us to point it out now."

"It does benefit you," Faeoris said, peering cautiously at Hector.

"My apologies." Hector bowed politely. "Your hearing is as good as mine."

"Probably better," Faeoris said sternly.

They continued waiting politely.

"These formalities are killing me, and taking forever," Angst said, stepping forward and placing a hand on hers. "I need to get into that hole."

"You said we couldn't," Faeoris replied, her brow furrowed.

"What?" Victoria gasped.

Angst's breath caught in his chest; he was at a total loss for words. Had she really made a joke that crass? Wasn't that his job?

Faeoris burst out laughing, pointing at Angst with a long finger. "Your face," she said between gasps. The Berfemmian looked at each of his friends. "I don't suppose he's often without words."

"I may just like her after all," Victoria said with a broad grin aimed directly at Angst. "She's much better than the mermaid."

His ears and cheeks warmed at his friends' laughter, and he could feel all eyes on him. Faeoris's face had darkened, and she looked ready to pose a question when there was another crash high above. A colorful plume of light wings spread behind her as she launched upward. She returned with two limp Berfemmian, one in each arm, and dropped them beside the third.

"Are they dead?" Tarness asked.

"No," Faeoris grunted. "But it would serve them right."

"Why not practice lower to the ground, maybe by the beach?" Hector asked, his nose twitching anxiously. "A few bruises would probably teach them faster than dying."

"True." She nodded. "But not the beach. Too close to the ocean."

"You can't swim?" Angst taunted.

"I can do anything," she replied with a raised eyebrow. "If a Berfemmian were to become unconscious and land in the ocean, they would be eaten by the monsters."

"You mean that green monster thing that destroyed our ship?" Angst asked.

"I speak of the mermaids," she said. "That creature doesn't come near the beach. He stays by that hole."

"Not all mermaids are monsters," Angst muttered.

"Yes, yes, they are," Faeoris said firmly. "They are the illusion of humans who lure men and women into their trap before devouring them."

"They sound terrible," Victoria chided.

"They're like the pretty feasting plants that eat small bugs," she continued. "Or the butterflies of Cayman Expanse, beautiful until they swarm and spew toxic acid over your entire—"

"Okay, we get it. Some of them are bad," Angst said.

"Not some, Angst," Faeoris emphasized. "All of them. They used to be a greater threat, thousands of years ago, and then something happened."

"What?" Dallow asked excitedly.

"Nobody knows," she said. "It was as if they were cursed. Half of them disappeared, the rest went into hiding. They're still a danger, but one that can be avoided."

"A lot can change over time," Angst tried to explain. "You originally treated us like enemies, too. Now we're friends."

"True," she said thoughtfully.

"Speaking of being friends, we need your help," he pleaded. "The hole, the one in the ocean. Can you take us there?"

"That place is death. I will not take you to your death," she said. "I would not be a good friend."

"We have another friend down there," he continued.

"Your friend is dead," she said coldly. "That hole has no bottom. None who enters ever returns. We send the criminals there to die."

"It's not bottomless," Angst replied. "It's a city."

There was a collective round of surprise and disbelief, and he barely suppressed a grin. Having knowledge that nobody else had was kind of fun. This must've been what Dallow felt like. His friend's eyes immediately flashed white beneath the kerchief.

"How do you know this?" Faeoris asked.

"My friend, *the mermaid*," he let this rest in the air, "brought me to the bottom of the ocean. She showed me an enormous city covered by a dome. There were people in the city, alive and moving. The city itself is beautiful."

"A mage city?" Dallow asked hopefully. "I thought the Memndus stones showed us one close to Angoria, but it was hard to tell."

"That's what I thought," Angst said. "But what other type of city could possibly survive being completely submerged?"

"Rose has to be there," Dallow said, a touch of hope in his voice.

"Is this true?" Faeoris asked, peering at Angst with a calculating look.

Angst held a hand out to Victoria. With a deep breath, she reluctantly took it. He could've kept her out now, Dulgirgraut seemed to create barriers on its own, but he let the adventure trickle through—unfortunately, more than he'd intended. Her eyes widened with surprise before darkening. She swung out, striking him in the jaw. Angst dropped to the ground, landing roughly on his backside. Victoria stormed away, cursing under her breath. Faeoris looked confused at this interaction, and was even more surprised at Tarness's laughter.

"That would mean it's true," Hector said with a satisfied grin, helping Angst to his feet.

"How did you swim to the bottom?" Faeoris asked, now more curious than ever. "How did you breathe?"

"You don't want to know. Let's just say I had help from a friend." Angst hated this, more than anything. His relation-ships…friendships with Moyra, Faeoris, and Victoria should've been mutually exclusive, but instead were becoming a jumbled mess. He shouldn't have cared, but did, and wasn't sure why. Maybe because he felt so defensive on Moyra's behalf and hated how everyone spoke about her. They were right, she could be dangerous, but she wasn't just some animal. She'd controlled herself with him, helped him by showing him what he needed to know, and even saved his life. Moyra was a friend, more than a friend, and the way everyone spoke about her put his teeth on edge. "Will you take us there?"

Faeoris studied him, looking him over from head to toe. She glanced at the giant sword that hovered nearby before returning with a steady gaze. "Yes," she finally said. "We will see you there safely, and I will stay to help."

"No, wait." He held up a hand. He couldn't stand putting one more person, one more friend in harm's way. No matter how strong and dangerous and indestructible that friend was. "It's going to be dangerous."

"Good," she said dismissively, walking over to the three un-conscious warriors, trying to kick them awake.

"I can't ask you to do this," Angst said, worry lacing his words. "You could die, Faeoris. Why do you even want to?"

She spun on her bare foot and looked at him with deadly sincerity. "That's what friends do."

* * * *

His jaw hurt. Tori's punch had landed hard. More mixed signals from his friend, who made him a naked sandwich, pushed him away, shared his dreams, and then punched him in the mouth. That last one wasn't mixed at all—she was jealous. As much as he wanted to mend things permanently, he wasn't even certain that was possible anymore. When he found her, he would tend to the wound, and hope it would last long enough to see them home.

The long trek down the steps in his armor should've tired him, but a constant stream of power and energy flowed from Dulgirgraut, and he wondered if he'd even need sleep. The question was immediately answered—he would, but not much. He sensed something about needing dreams more than sleep, and as the explanation became more complicated, he let his mind wander.

Faeoris had taken care of several things—gestures of friendship he could never repay. Berfemmian warriors returned Jarblech and her remaining crew back to their geode. She'd also sent some to search the ship wreckage for their armor, some of which was found. Angst had his suit and red cloak, but no bracers. Tarness was missing his pauldrons and shield, and Hector's was completely gone. His friend didn't find it funny when a muscular Berfemmian offered to trade sex for her chainmail skirt and top.

Angst reached the bottom of the long stairs and headed to the beach. He was early, but never earlier than Hector, who sat and watched the ocean. He looked almost naked and unprepared in his dark tunic and leather riding pants, like a cat that had been dunked in a bucket of water. His friend pointed down the shoreline without even turning his head to look. Curious. Angst set Dulgirgraut on its tip. The blade glowed softly and sang in his head. The song now filled him with confidence, which he would soon need.

There were hoof prints on the shoreline, and he followed them away from the meeting place. They dragged through the sand for a quarter mile before fading into lapping waves, and Angst's heart skipped a beat at the thought of Tori flying off and leaving him.

"I wouldn't do that," she said. "Well, I might think about it, but I didn't. I can't."

She sat with her legs crossed on the beach, carving pictures in the sand. Like Hector, she wouldn't look up to meet his eyes. She wore her tight leather riding pants, high boots, and chain Berfemmian top that looked nice from above. Her red cloak was in a crumpled ball behind her, and seemed to have been pummeled into place. Angst lowered himself awkwardly, attempting to sit in his black armor. He forced his legs to splay out to keep the armor from pinching anything, and leaned back on his hands. *Getting back up won't be fun*, he thought with a sigh, and Tori smirked.

"I don't believe you let her breathe for you," she said, not wasting a moment on preamble or customary flirting.

"What was I supposed to do, Tori?" he asked. "Not breathe?"

"*Yes!*" she said sharply, stabbing the stick into the sandy image of a fish she'd been drawing. The fish had a human-ish face.

"I didn't have a choice. You saw, and you know that." He tried not to sound like he was pleading. "Why are you so upset...again?"

She was now throwing fistfuls of sand on top of the stick in a furious attempt to bury it.

"I thought you were my champ..." She let the word trail off. "I thought you were my hero."

His heart wrenched—something she was incredibly good at. "I am," he said. "That hasn't changed. I have to be a hero for a lot of people. I'm pretty sure that's part of the job."

"But," she spoke very softly now, "you're starting to have feelings for her. For them."

"They're friends," he explained. "That's what happens when you go adventuring. You meet people, make friends. It's great!"

"Could you try to make less pretty friends?" she said.

"I'm not sure I know how." He grinned.

She threw a handful of sand in his face, which spilled off an air shield he didn't remember summoning.

Tori shook her head. "I take it back," she said. "You try too hard now. This must be how Heather feels."

"You're not Heather," he said.

They looked at each other. She was trying to get in. He wanted to let her, but was worn out by the constant hurt. Victoria was supposed to be his best friend, nothing else. This was supposed to be their adventure, probably the only one they would ever have. It shouldn't have been riddled with guilt or pain; it was supposed to be fun. She'd crossed the line, many times, and he'd let her because she was so…Tori. He was hungry for her attention, still, but for some reason hadn't expected the complications she'd discussed in their courtyard meetings to follow them all around Ehrde. He let this, all of it, trickle out of his thoughts.

Tori absorbed every ounce, but said nothing. She stood and brushed the sand from her butt, waggling it playfully, which made him smile. After shaking sand from her cloak, she put it on then offered him a hand. He took it, and as he began to stand, she let go. He rocked back to his rear in a noisy clatter. This made her smile.

"Our relationship is nothing like I have with anyone else," he said sincerely. "It never will be."

"Don't you forget it."

"Like you'd let me." He pushed himself up and stood, without accepting her hand a second time. "I'd die for you. You know that, right?"

"How about keeping me from dying?" she said with a gentle push. "That would be a better idea."

They walked the beach in silence on their way back to the meeting point. She felt closed off, friendly in a polite way, and he wished that magic could make it better. It was amazing at beating up monsters, pushing mountains around, and healing tiny cuts, but useless when it came to feelings. If he could just make it all better, if the relationship with just one of his 'girlfriends,' would come naturally, if *one* of them would completely understand them, he would have…he would just have…Heather. He thought about his wife, and her smile, and her understanding of all things Angst. For all their struggles, she might've been the only one who wanted him to be who he actually was. Angst.

They arrived to see Tarness, Dallow, and Hector talking with five Berfemmian, including Faeoris, who were all hovering overhead. Victoria turned her back on them with a grumble and began summoning her swifen.

"That's not necessary," Angst informed her. "Marisha is planning to fly you."

Tori flashed Angst a look filled with malicious clarity that silently screamed, "*If you think I'm letting that cute bitch fly me in there, you can jump off the cliff again!*" It came out more like, "No, thank you."

Angst held up his hands defensively and took a step back while she returned to her summoning. This reminded him of the many irrational arguments with Heather that he'd learned to just give into. "*Sure, it can be whatever color you want.*" "*No, I'm happy to wear the tunic from your mother.*" "*Of course I'd rather go to your friends' dinner than hang out with the guys.*" His focus returned, and he saw her mouth quiver, and her eyes becoming glassy.

"We can ride your swifen, Tori," he said.

"We don't have to." She took a deep breath and bit her lip.

"Are you kidding?" He pulled her into a hug. She tried pushing away, but he wouldn't let go. "It's my favorite way to fly." And he meant it.

She nodded and sniffed.

"Are we ready?" Faeoris interrupted from overhead. "Angst and I will take lead."

"Actually," he raised a finger, "I have a ride."

"I am no ride," Faeoris bit off each word.

"You've got to be kidding me," Angst muttered under his breath. He looked to the guys for support, but they were fighting laughter and avoiding eye contact.

Without further prompting, Victoria summoned her pink feathery unicorn. Its golden hooves and horn reflected brightly in the sunlight, and it stretched out its broad wings as if waking from a long slumber. Angst braced for scoffing and scorn from the Berfemmian warriors. Four of them landed around the creature, holding out hands to pet it. Their eyes weren't judgmental, they were wide with wonder.

Marisha seemed most excited. "This is a fine mount."

"Thank you!" Tori arched her back with pride and smiled at Hector and Tarness, who'd stopped shaking their heads just in time.

"We need to leave," Faeoris said tartly, apparently unamused by the attention Victoria and her unicorn were getting. "Does that thing even fly?"

"It does when I'm here," Angst boasted.

Tori's fists clenched as she flashed him a burning look.

"Huh," Faeoris said, her wings spreading wide and lifting her high into the air.

42

There was a hole in the ocean. They hovered far overhead, grouped in a circle, looking down at it. It was like one of the sinkholes approaching Unsel, but far larger than a mere mile across. This one could've engulfed the entire capital city, and Angst couldn't begin to fathom its size. Ten miles across? Maybe fifteen? Just the thought made him shake his head. The hole was surprisingly close to Angoria. Not close enough for him to swim to, but he could clearly see the cliff wall coastline leading up to a mountain peak.

"That's the tallest point in Angoria," Faeoris said, pointing at the mountain.

"It looks close enough to swim there," Tarness said. He looked uncomfortable in Marisha's grasp, and she looked a little tired from the load.

"You'd have to be a strong swimmer," Faeoris said. "And be able to dodge sharks and mermaids along the way."

"Are you sure it's down there?" Hector asked. His legs kicked at the air, desperate to seek ground. "I don't see a thing."

"We've never seen a dome, or a city," Faeoris said warily. She carried Hector effortlessly, gripping under his shoulders.

"It's there," Angst confirmed. "Let's get closer."

Victoria nodded, urging her swifen forward. Angst was impressed at how quickly she'd mastered flying, and glancing at his friends' discomfort, he was grateful for the ride.

"I don't mind being a ride," Victoria teased.

"Ha!" Angst laughed. "I'll remember that." He gave her bare stomach a squeeze. That was his Victoria, and she'd read him without trying.

His heart raced as they dove, once again amazed and excited. This was the adventure he'd wanted. Surrounded by his closest friends, facing an unknown, and experiencing things that no one else could. Dulgirgraut gave him a sense of confidence and security, so instead of being nervous, he was exhilarated. They hovered mere feet above surface level. It was stunning. The waterfall had formed a perfect circle, endlessly filling the cavernous hole. The drop must've been a mile or more. The watery spray refracted sunlight, surrounding them with rainbows. Tori reached out, running her fingers through the mist and colors. Dallow's eyes glowed brightly as he analyzed everything.

"I can't even begin to understand the spells involved. Not yet," he said to Angst's unanswered questions. His grin was ear to ear. "I'm guessing the water just goes back into the ocean, but the fact that it doesn't fill in is amazing."

"Hey," Hector yelled as Faeoris jerked him around. "Angst, look."

His friend pointed to a monstrous shadowy mass trailing the edge of the waterfall. It was the thing, the enormous creature that had destroyed their ship, the oldest living creature in Ehrde. Moyra had hated it so much that Angst gritted his teeth.

"You okay?" Victoria asked.

"I'd like to take a shot," he said, reaching for his sword.

"You can't, Angst," Faeoris said. She was flying right next to him. "It's not safe, even for you."

"We'll see," he grunted. Dulgirgraut warned him off, but he dismissed the sword. He cursed at the monster under his breath and tore his eyes away, looking deep into the hole. There was the barest reflection of light, as if off glass. A sheen that was almost hidden in the mists. He pointed to the center. "There. Let's go."

They moved in silent formation, spinning through the center

of the hole like a flock of giant birds. Within minutes, the top of the dome appeared, colossal and glassy. Half an orb in the middle of a hole in the ocean. It glistened with wetness, the mist and sunlight dancing across it like waterbugs over a lake. Dulgirgraut hummed a trickle of information, infusing him with a basic understanding of the spell that had created this dome. It wasn't enough, but when he asked for more, the foci tried teaching him the theories behind the combination of magic and air and water that had formed the dome. It was too much for Angst to fathom with his limited experience, so he wielded Dulgirgraut and slipped his leg over the swifen, letting himself drop to the dome.

"Angst, no!" Victoria shouted.

Angst landed with a moist thud. It was slick, and his feet immediately began to slide. He quickly set the tip of Dulgirgraut on the dome. It held firm, and his grip on the hilt kept him in place, barely.

"Wait," he called out. "Just wait. There's no footing, and we need to find a way in."

"We can't hover forever," Marisha said, her tone annoyed.

"How do we get in?" Faeoris asked.

"Good question," Angst shouted. "Dallow?"

His friend's eyes shone as he sought through the seemingly bottomless catalog of information in his mind. Unfortunately, sometimes, it had a bottom. Dallow shook his head. "Not a clue."

"You don't have a plan?" Faeoris asked.

"Plan? Plan." Angst smiled. "What is plan?"

Her expression showed her quite dissatisfied with his response.

"Mmkay," Angst said. He pushed down and found Dulgirgraut already anchored. Maybe he could inch the foci in further. His hands slid on Dulgirgraut's slick hilt, but the blade dug into the shield. There was give, but barely. He jumped up and tried to use momentum to push further. It wiggled more, inches more. With force and will, over and over, he tried stabbing the blade through the barrier, cursing in frustration. He kicked the foci and his legs slipped from under him. His grip failed, the back of his head smacked against the shield, and he began sliding down the side, quickly.

"Angst," Victoria called out, reaching for him.

"Let me go!" Hector demanded, trying to fight free of Faeoris's grip.

Faeoris threw Hector high into the air and dove after Angst, grasping his black armor and pulling him back in time to catch Hector. His mentor was pale as death, and even more silent. Angst's heart raced and his cheeks were red with embarrassment. He shook with fury. This just wasn't working, or not working fast enough.

"We should head back," Faeoris advised. "We need a better plan."

"But it's almost there," Angst said. "I'm making progress."

"Angst," Hector said consolingly. "This isn't working."

Faeoris held him over Dulgirgraut, urging him with a shake to pick it up. He placed a hand on the sword. It glowed brightly, but told him nothing. Angst jerked it free, like pulling arrows out of a target.

"Wait," Angst said, patting Faeoris's hand. Maybe Dulgirgraut wasn't telling him anything because he could figure it out himself. He pondered, looking at the notch in the barrier left behind by the foci. The words came to him slowly: it *was* just like pulling out an arrow. "Faeoris, how's your aim?"

* * * *

"What's he doing now?" Hector asked, clutching his chest as Faeoris deposited him on Tori's swifen. "I'm getting too old for this!"

Faeoris flew to Angst. He hugged her tight, whispering his plan into her ear.

"This is foolish," she said. "You'll die."

"Angst, no!" Tori cried out. She already knew.

"I won't die," he said firmly.

"Everyone back up, but not too far," Angst said, waving them away. "Stay away from that thing along the edge."

He pointed up, urging Faeoris higher and higher. As she flew, he consulted the foci. He needed his hands not to slip, he needed his armor not to shatter, and his bones not to crack. It would be nice if his brains didn't turn to mush on impact, too.

"This is a terrible idea," she said.

"Yup," he said, his ears thrumming from his beating heart. He swallowed hard. "You're just jealous. It's going to be fun."

"You're crazy," she said.

"Nope." He grinned. "I'm a hero. Now, as hard as you can."

Faeoris tossed him up and grabbed his feet. Like holding a child by their arms over the grass, she spun him about faster and faster. His guts pressed outward as he held Dulgirgraut forward and hoped he wouldn't heroically vomit. His arms and fingers throbbed from the pressure of her spin and his stomach went tight, but he didn't let go. The red glow surrounding his arm spread to cover his entire body. Faeoris spun and spun until it was too much even for her then let go.

Her aim was true, and like an arrow with the largest tip any-one in Ehrde had ever seen, Angst flew at the center of the dome. A human arrow. Dulgirgraut's power kept his body rigid; he didn't even feel the wind on his face, nor did his eyes water—but at some point in the journey, he screamed in panic or ex-citement or a madness that he would never be able to explain away. The sword struck the dome with a crack like a hundred lightning strikes, and a ten-foot section of dome exploded in-ward, shattering like a window.

"No, no, no!" Angst shouted as he kept flying through the dome and to the quickly approaching ground. He hadn't thought this part of it through and desperately pushed with air, slowing his descent. There was enough time to get Dulgirgraut away from his face and angle his body to land in a bellyflop on the cold stone. It was better than breaking his neck, Probably.

Angst lay on the hard ground, reconsidering his life decisions, and happy to breathe the little bit of air his lungs would allow.

CHAPTER FORTY TWO

Was he alive? Everything was numb. He heard busy shuffling all around, and he wiggled a foot. He did a mental check: there was breathing, he could wiggle his toes and fingers, his heart was racing—which meant it still beat in his chest. The shock of being the arrow was slowly subsiding, making way for waves of pain.

Tarness rolled him over. "His eyes are open, and blinking," he called out. He leaned forward and whispered, "You're an idiot. Don't ever do that again."

"I'm completely blind down here," Dallow said from above as Faeoris landed with him. He grumbled, "I hate this. And I hate him. Angst, what were you thinking?"

Angst's vision was fading in and out, and he concentrated on filling his lungs with air, which was forced out as Victoria landed on his chest. She kissed him and wet his cheeks with tears several times before whispering in his ear, "I hate you. I love you, but I hate you. I'm done with this adventure, I want to go home." She was shaking violently, and he was in no condition to hold her.

"That's everyone who could fit through," Hector said from above as Faeoris landed for the last time. "Are we interrupting his nap?"

"Really?" Victoria snapped. "How would you feel?"

Hector didn't answer.

Faeoris knelt next to him, her face pale and her lips trembling. "That was brave. You're an idiot, but a brave idiot."

He smelled blood and wondered if it was his before passing out.

* * * *

Angst awoke slowly to his friends' muffled voices. That stunt had taken so much out of him. His bones ached, but he wasn't so broken he couldn't sit up. Everything spun, and he felt Tori's small hand on his back propping him up. The exertion of forcing his way through the shield had left him famished. Everyone asked if he was okay, and he nodded reassuringly, though the nodding made him dizzy and nauseated. As he managed to focus, he saw Dallow, Tarness, Hector, Tori, and Faeoris sitting in a circle around him.

"Are you all okay?"

"Mostly," Tarness said, nodding to Faeoris.

Her arms were covered in blood, and the skin appeared flayed to the muscle in some parts. She held them close to her chest, out of sight except for the blood, which couldn't be hidden. She was pale and shaky.

"Come here." He waved her over. He'd healed Moyra, he could heal Faeoris.

She shook her head. He didn't feel like standing just yet, so, with a sigh, he crawled to her. She pushed away, kicking with her feet, but she didn't get far without the use of her arms. As he came close, and his vision cleared, he could see that her arms were far worse than he'd thought. They were stripped bare— skin was gone, muscle was missing, and in some spots, he could see bone. How was she even conscious?

"What happened?" Angst wheezed. "Where are the other Berfemmian?"

"The crack you created started to fill back in. There wasn't much time," Tarness said. "She pulled all of us in and flew us down, but she caught her arms helping Victoria squeeze through. Both of them could've been killed."

"I'll be fine," Faeoris snapped. She looked away from everyone, as if embarrassed for showing weakness.

Angst reached her feet and pulled himself to her waist until he hovered over her awkwardly. He smiled and pushed up onto his knees to straddle her. "Now you know how I felt in your bed." He winked, taking both her hands in his.

"My way would've been more fun," she said, jerking them away. "You're too tired for this."

"Now you're beginning to sound like my wife," he said, grappling with her to get a hold. She tried pulling her hands away again, but he gripped her wrists hard—harder than he'd meant to—and she cried out. "Stop fighting me!" he shouted.

The injury was bad, and he needed to know even more about

healing. Dulgirgraut provided him with just enough. It was more than using water, or magic, it was an actual spell that interwove elements in a way he hadn't expected. He'd been doing it the hard way, which was no surprise. He stared into her eyes and focused. A painful tingle of power crawled down his arms and into her hands. She attempted to pull back, but he held firm as muscle knitted over her bone and skin formed over her biceps and forearms. She grimaced, her eyes glassy but fierce. He *was* tired, and this wasn't easy, but he couldn't leave her like this. Holding his breath, he drew from whatever reserves he had deep down. Fresh skin crawled up her fingers, and missing nails grew back. The sight of it was amazing, the sound disgusting, but in the end, she was whole. Angst let out a gasp and rolled off her to collapse back to the ground.

"I still think you're a fool," she said, kissing his cheek. "Thank you."

"Anything for a kiss," he said, smiling to himself as he shut his eyes. It was nice behind his eyelids. Angst let his muscles relax one by one. Dulgirgraut was nearby, he could feel it, and…something else. Something distant, and quiet. It felt like Chryslaenor, or an echo of his old foci, but cold and dark. If he was right, maybe he could locate it.

"What were you thinking?" Hector asked. "Do you have a death wish?"

"What do you mean?" Angst said, not moving, keeping his eyes shut. It was still nice. "Did you have a better idea?"

"You couldn't have shared with the rest of us?" Hector asked.

"I felt rushed," Angst said. "Is there anything to eat?"

"You could've just thrown the sword," Hector snapped.

"No, not really," Angst replied, still face down on the pavement. "If the sword had gone through, and the hole had closed up before we followed, we'd have been stuck outside. No entrance, and no foci."

Hector grunted and paused a moment to think. "You can't tell me you thought all of that through."

"Angst, get up," Tori said before he could respond.

"Aww, mom," Angst replied.

"She's right." Tarness grabbed him under his arms and pulled him up.

"Oh, what now?" he griped.

"Looks like we found your mermaid's boyfriends," Tori said. "All of them."

43

Rookshire

Kala threw snow at Scar, and his little puppy jaws chomped as wildly as his tail wagged. They'd spent days rolling around in the thin layer of snow and leaves. They were both dirty enough to require baths every night, much to the frustration of her mother. Nikkola was very wary about bathing Scar, no matter how much Kala reassured her, but they'd truly become inseparable and Nikkola couldn't bear dirty floors, or that wet dog smell.

"What do we feed it…him?" her mom had asked.

"He likes horses," Kala said, and then laughed raucously at her mom's expression. "Come on, Scar, let's go find horsies!"

They'd begun exploring beyond the path to Mr. Angst's house. The path had become very boring, even with her pretty swifen. Near the house was a steep, rocky hill. He'd put a door in the hill that led downstairs to a room with shiny metals. It, too, was boring. So Kala and Scar had decided to walk around the hill, and he'd promised to protect her.

Now, though, it was getting cold, and dark, and while she told herself she definitely wasn't scared, it was probably time to go back before she got in trouble again. Scar whimpered.

"You're right, we should go home," she agreed. There were sounds in the distance, men talking. "What's that?"

Scar tore off in the opposite direction, but when she wouldn't

329

follow, he returned and then tried running in the opposite direction again, as if guiding her away. She could hear them nearby, and see the flickering of firelight. It was too curious not to inspect, so, despite Scar's whimpers, she inched forward quietly until she could see them. From the shadows, Kala watched Mr. Rook, Mr. Graloon, Mr. Jaden, and another man. They took turns holding what looked like a large, thick bracelet. She hid behind a tree and listened.

"Thanks for putting this together so quickly, Teedle," Rook said with a smile, patting the strong man on his shoulder. "Especially after making all that armor!"

"If this works, I'll take your thanks," he said. "But will it hold?"

"I can't make the metal any stronger," Jaden said. "That spell is used to harden armor, and it works. That's why it looks polished, like silver."

"Graloon?" Rook asked. "Do you think you can do it?"

The round man's eyes glowed gray. Other blue and red lights trickled down his fingers into the large bracelet. She'd never seen anyone do this before, and it looked even harder to understand than making the swifen.

"Done," he said roughly. "Not bad work, if I say so myself."

"Now, how do we lure the beast here?" Jaden asked. "I want to get back to Jadenville."

"Rookshire," Rook corrected him. Both men laughed.

That didn't sound right, and she took a nervous step back. There was a noisy crack as a stick broke, and the men spied her. She wanted to run, especially when Scar barked at them, but she knew how much trouble she would be in and fear froze her legs.

"Kala," Rook called. "Is that you?"

His long legs brought him close within seconds. The big man had a curious look on his face—his eyes flitting nervously to Scar, his smile a little too wide. It was the same smile her mom gave her before assigning chores. It wasn't real.

He knelt. "You're a long way from the path," he said warningly. "Your mother won't be pleased."

Her lip quivered, no matter how hard she tried to be brave. "Please don't tell," she said in a quiet voice.

"Our secret," he said. His voice was soft, and his smile became sincere. He looked at Scar again. "Would you like to see what we've been working on?"

She wanted nothing more than to run home, but she nodded, knowing she had to be polite. The lab pup whined, his tail between his legs as he followed closely. They approached the others to find them smiling as well. Graloon held out the bracelet, which was attached to a chain. She touched it then jerked her finger back. It was filled with his magic, and reminded her of the Wizard's Revenge. Her mom had taken her there once when running errands, and she'd seen how it was surrounded by magic. The bracelet was thick and not pretty, and she didn't understand.

Before she could stop him, Graloon bent over and slipped it over Scar's head. Graloon's eyes flashed brightly, and the oversized bracelet immediately shrank to fit around the pup's neck. It wasn't a bracelet; it was a collar.

"No!" she shouted, trying to pull it off.

Scar ran as far away as the chain would allow. It was fastened around an enormous tree and then into the stone of the rocky hill. The lab pup struggled against the collar, choking himself as he fought its restraint. He coughed loudly as he jerked and fell forward.

"You're hurting him!" Kala shouted, dropping to her knees beside the lab and attempting to get the collar off.

* * * *

Rook picked up Kala, pulling her away from the dog. Scar's eyes flashed a deep burgundy, and two more eyes appeared on the pup's forehead. Rook's heart raced. They had little time. Kala kicked and screamed as he took off.

"Run!" he shouted.

Seconds seemed to take minutes, even days, as the four men

sprinted away from the beast. Scar grew fast. Rook glanced over his shoulders to see muscle and skin bulge, fur merge to form vicious steel daggers, and more tails grow from its backside. The collar grew with him, just like Graloon's bar.

"Stop it!" Kala wailed. "He promised he wouldn't hurt me! He promised!"

Graloon slipped, falling on his large stomach with a groan. Teedle and Jaden both grabbed an arm and dragged him upright. He shouted in pain but limped forward.

Rook knew he needed to focus. He had to get the girl to safety—that was what this had all been about. To protect her, and the families who'd taken refuge. His feet began to slide as if running on ice, and he ran even harder.

The bark from the monster dog was ear-shattering and nerve-wracking.

"I think I just peed," Graloon called out.

"Is he coming after us?" Rook shouted.

"It's holding!" Teedle called out. "The collar and chain grew to fit."

"He's just trying to keep me safe!" Kala cried. "Please stop!"

"I'm not worried about the dog," Jaden said, ignoring the girl. "I'm worried about the bubbles."

Tiny crystalline orbs were forming at their feet, slowing their progress no matter how fast they ran. Rook saw something out the corner of his eye, and dared a glance. A squirrel caught in a bubble floated helplessly toward Scar.

"Duck!" Teedle called out.

Rook did, and a bear cried out overhead as it was carried toward the hungry beast. His heart ached and his lungs burned as he practically ran in place, barely inching forward. He was lifted off the ground and held Kala tight—his thoughts only of Janda. More than anything, he wanted to protect her.

"Here it comes!" Jaden shouted.

There was a popping sound, followed by another, and then a hundred more as Rook's footing became solid, and yet not solid. The ground was now made up of stone spikes, and he could already feel them digging into his boots as he launched forward. This was going to hurt. Stone quills ripped apart the hard leather soles with every step, shredding them like forks tearing paper. He wanted to scream as they penetrated to his feet, and warm, slick blood filled the remains of his boots. Graloon and Teedle cried out in pain, but he couldn't look back to see if they'd stopped. Rook watched as several rabbits fought against the confines of their orb, and he pressed Kala's face deep into his chest so she wouldn't see.

"This is the best you could come up with?" Rook asked.

"Yes," Jaden replied. "Almost there!"

Rook's knees wobbled from the pain and loss of blood. In the dusk of twilight, he saw the sheen of the pathway that led to Angst's home—an ugly haven of mismatched stone free of spikes and bubbles and magic. Rook clenched his teeth and, with his last ounce of strength, leaped. He rolled, bouncing hard off his shoulder to protect his precious package. Rook heard more grunts, and hoped that meant the others were safe.

When they were free from danger, when the bubbles were no longer a threat, when the quills no longer tore at their feet, they took a collective breath. Kala sobbed relentlessly, fighting Rook's protective hold and throwing a tantrum worthy of a dying element. Scar's tantrum sounded the equal to hers, yet a thousand times more frightening. Rook held her close, both to calm her and keep her from running off. He wanted to scream in pain—his feet had to be nothing but raw meat—but that wasn't his job at the moment. His job was to protect, and there was some satisfaction that they were all safe.

It was a hard-won and bittersweet victory. The girl was safe, they were all safe, but Scar didn't deserve this treatment. He'd been a hero, much like Angst and his friends, and Rook wished more than anything he knew how to help the pup. Rook looked at the others and saw the guilt in their eyes. They'd had no choice, but it felt wrong. He held Kala close, and when her tantrum became long sniffs and caught breaths, Rook could hear Scar, the puppy, crying out in the night for his lost friend.

44

Tarness held Angst up as he struggled to find footing on shaky legs. Light streamed into the city from high above, thin beams tickling the buildings that rose almost as tall as the dome. The buildings were pyramids of different shapes and heights, wide squares and rectangles stacked high like layered cakes. The city was enormous, far larger than Unsel, or any other he'd seen. It also felt wrong, like it was covered in stale shadows. A city like this should've been exciting and noisy. Granted, there were creatures all around them, but the only sound was their strained breathing and the shuffling of many feet. They were surrounded by ocean, but the air was desert dry, and smelled of old fish. This giant domed city might've contained life, but the city itself had died long ago.

"Describe them?" Dallow asked, his eyes brightly reading from the catalog of information in his mind. "How many?"

"They look like short mermaid-men," Tori said.

"Gargoyles," Angst corrected. "My mermaid doesn't look anything like this."

"Your mermaid?" she scoffed.

"Not now," Hector said in his gruff voice.

"Blue-green scales, large black eyes, fins behind their ears like gargoyles," Tarness continued for Tori. "But they look...deflated."

Dallow was shaking his head in frustration. "How many?" he

asked firmly.

The sunlight dimmed, hiding the distant mob in shadows and making the city feel much smaller.

"I can't tell," Hector grunted. He sniffed deeply, looked around, and hopped up to try to see farther. "Maybe dozens?"

A bright flash of light caught Angst's eye, and he spun around to see that Faeoris had spread her wings and was already hovering twenty feet above them. The light from her wings was like a deluge, making him wince. It created defining shadows along her muscular torso and reflected off her long boots and chainmail top as she slowly turned around to survey.

"Beautiful," Angst said.

"Yeah," Tori said to his surprise.

"Thank you," Faeoris said, landing next to them. She adjusted her stance for battle, and wielded a longsword. "There are hundreds, maybe thousands of the things. Why do they not attack?"

The crowd appeared agitated or nervous. Most hid from the light behind long, webbed fingers, while others waved it away like swatting at a fly.

"Yeah," Angst said. "They look like gargoyles."

"No, they look like *your* mermaid," Victoria corrected him.

"But they have legs, and the ear things," Angst said, putting hands behind his ears and flapping them. "I dunno, they're kinda greenish."

"Didn't Moyra say her people were trapped by that creature?" Tarness asked.

"Yeah, her story seems a little fishy," Tori said with a smirk.

"Very funny," Angst said, deadpan.

"I get the first hundred," Faeoris said, stretching out her new skin and freshly-knit muscles. Her flexing made Tarness smile broadly, and she winked at him.

The creatures in front tried to get away, pushing back as far as they could against the crowd, but there were too many. They looked sickly, tired, and the absolute opposite of threatening. Every single one of them appeared more exhausted with every breath drawn. Slits on their scrawny necks opened and closed rapidly, their scaly chests stretching taught to show ribs and distended bellies. He and Tori were the only ones not to have wielded a weapon. Faeoris nudged him.

"An-gst," he heard in his head.

"Wait," he said, holding up a hand.

"I hate waiting," Faeoris said, unwilling to lower her weapon.

"An-gst," echoed in his mind. He pulled himself from Tarness's grip and limped forward. *"An-gst,"* again, now from multiple voices. They became skittish as he hefted Dulgirgraut from the ground. He returned the foci to his back and inched closer. They backed away as much as they could, but it was a large crowd. A very large crowd. They had little room to maneuver. *"An-gst."*

"What is that?" Faeoris asked in an annoyed tone. Her hands shifted on the hilt of her longsword, and she adjusted her feet, which were wide apart and braced firmly on the ground.

He turned his head to see Hector wiggling a finger in his ear. Dallow's head was cocked to one side. Tori frowned at the crowd, her brows knitted in concentration.

"That's what Moyra calls me. An-gst." He struggled to mispronounce his name as she did.

"Oh, very cute," Tori sniped. "What does it mean?"

"I think it means we're safe," he said. "They think we're here to save them."

"I'm not here to save them," Faeoris said. "I'm here to keep you safe, and help find your friend."

He walked into the crowd with his hands out. The creatures pawed at his armor like starving children reaching for food, saying *"An-gst"* as they made contact.

"It's almost like they're worshipping him," Tarness whispered.

"Oh good. This won't go to his head or anything," Hector interjected.

"Have any of you seen Rose?" Dallow asked the crowd.

"Good idea," Angst said. Moyra had told him she saw pictures when he spoke, so maybe it would help to think about

Rose. He missed his friend, a lot, making it easy to picture her. He remembered her laughing at him, teasing him at the Wizard's Revenge. Angst thought of her pale, fair skin. He thought of her long, fine red hair, her curvy body, the way she walked funny when she found someone attractive, and her thin, stick arms that hit him frequently. He thought of all this and asked firmly, "Rose. Where is Rose?"

"No. No. No." The voices, hundreds of voices, rang in his head. *"No. No."*

Everyone covered their ears, dropping to the ground as if pelleted with a barrage of stones. There was the noisy patter of running as the crowd dispersed.

"No. No. No," they mentally shouted.

"Make it stop," Tarness grunted.

Angst sought Dulgirgraut for help. He was Al'eyrn again, bonded to the foci, and it should know. It did.

"Tori," he said aloud.

"What?" she shouted.

"You can fix this," he said.

"I can't," she said. "I don't know how."

"I do," he said, taking her hand.

"Oh," she said in a quiet voice as she absorbed what he'd learned from the foci.

Her eyes glowed bright pink as she bravely stood to face the onslaught. *"Silence!"* Angst heard in his mind, and all was quiet once again. He stood, no longer plagued by the little fish-men yelling in his head. His friends were shaking their heads, stunned and amazed at the same time. Tori's eyes still glowed bright pink, her hands pressed out as if telling everyone to stop.

"I don't hear them anymore," Angst said. "You can stop."

"It's gone because I'm still stopping it," she said. "I'll be done once they leave."

"You're powerful," Faeoris said, her thin eyebrows raised high.

"Don't forget it," Victoria said smugly.

"What did you do?" Hector asked.

"Tori can block out what she sees and hears in her mind," Angst explained. "She did that for all of us."

The creatures dispersed as quickly as they could, leaving Angst to wonder what about Rose had them so worried. It left him feeling cold, and he knew there wasn't much time. He was relieved that she was probably alive, but how safe could she truly be? Would she even be the same Rose? He saw his concern in Dallow's expression tenfold, and he went to him and gave him a brotherly hug.

"She's alive," he whispered. "Remember that."

Dallow nodded, the creases in his forehead easing, slightly.

When Victoria lowered her hands and the glow from her eyes abated, she stumbled back in exhaustion. Faeoris caught her in one arm, and held her up and out like she had someone else's baby and didn't know what to do. Tori shrugged herself free, mumbling a thanks, blushing brightly as if she'd fallen into the wrong arms.

A small handful of creatures remained in their dim view. They stood within a stone's throw, close but out of reach.

Angst held out both hands and approached them with cautious respect. "Can you help me?" he asked. "Can you help me find my friend Rose?"

Three of the creatures ran off, their arms flailing overhead, like crazed marionettes. It appeared that their fear of the dangerous Rose was too much for them, which made Angst chuckle. How frightening could his friend have become? The two remaining fish-men looked skittish, and nervous, but stood bravely. They wore the scantiest of disgusting, greasy leather loincloths that hung loosely from their hips. Broken copper chain armor covered their chests, and dented bronze weapons rested at their waists. Hands gripped his forearms and pulled him forward, urging him down a road. Tori shoved one of them off and held his hand firmly.

"Guard your thoughts," she whispered in his ear. "Make an air shield, or a wall, around them. Ask Dulgirgraut how to keep them out, like it sometimes keeps me out."

Tori's head whipped about, blond curls bouncing along her shoulders, her eyes wide in surprise.

"What?" he asked.

"That was fast," she said. "I already struggle to read you with Dulgirgraut, but I usually sense something. All of a sudden, it's like your mind is gone."

"It probably is." He smirked. "But I didn't really do anything." Angst glanced over his shoulder at the sword and frowned.

* * * *

After a long walk that painfully reminded Angst how big the city really was, they broached the barrier. The curse had cut off the edge of the city like a foci through monster. The invisible dome had clipped the tops of buildings and their rubble littered the streets. He could barely hear the constant rumble of the waterfall hovering over the edge of the city, a muffled drummer living in a neighbor's basement. The waterfall circling the city was hard to comprehend. He'd swum to the outside of the barrier with Moyra, and hadn't even sensed it. From above, it appeared to fall low along the bottom edges of the dome. Here, he could see it bubbling and storming overhead. He couldn't fathom if it was magic, illusion, or simply too much to understand.

One of the fish-men took his free hand and lifted it as high as it could before releasing him. Angst continued reaching up in that direction until his hand met the shield. Before he even thought to wield magic, his hand began to glow. Dulgirgraut again? The foci was becoming invasive, but maybe it called itself The Defender for a reason. He sensed power in the shield. It was like the shock he felt when he rubbed his feet on Meldusian carpet and touched Alloria on the arm. That shock, suppressed but constant. And, he felt something else.

"It's wet," Angst said in surprise.

"Why is it wet?" Dallow asked, his voice filled with concern.

Hector held his ear to the shield and tapped a crack the length of his arm with a long dagger. Faeoris placed her hands on it.

She licked the dampness from her palm then spat, looking as though she'd tasted bad meat.

"Salt," she said. "This is a leak."

"What could've done this?" Tarness asked.

"A foci," Dallow said hopefully. "But why isn't this one healing?"

"Good question," Angst replied. "Did the other one heal completely?"

Hector sniffed loudly, his long nose close to the crack. He sniffed again and scritched at the barrier with a fingernail. "Look, it's orange, like the Vex'kvette."

Angst could barely make out the faint splatter of dry orange crust, like someone had thrown a thimbleful of paint at the dome. "Why didn't I see that?"

"I'm here for a reason," Hector said with a wink.

"A lot of reasons," Angst replied.

Hector licked his finger.

"Eew," Victoria said, grimacing.

"Copper...like it's blood," Hector said. "And something else. Honey? Molasses?"

Faeoris wielded her longsword, jerking Angst behind her as she stared beyond the shield. Victoria sighed deeply and Tarness chuckled.

"What do you see?" Angst asked, placed a hand on Faeoris's shoulder.

She stared straight ahead, barely nodding.

"An-gst?" Moyra said in his mind.

He smiled in spite of himself. He stepped around Faeoris and reached out, pressing his hand flush to the dome. Thin, webbed fingers met his on the other side. Her beautiful face came into view, faint through the dim lights inside and the shield between them. Angst's smile widened. Tori socked him on the arm, but he ignored her, focusing on his new friend.

"Are you okay? Are you safe?" he said, thinking what he was saying so it would be clear.

"This is your creature?" Faeoris asked. "And she didn't eat

you?"

"We're close," he said distantly.

"You are brave," Faeoris acknowledged, sheathing her sword.

"He's something," Victoria said tartly.

"I was worried, when it attacked your ship." Moyra sounded guilty. *"I am sorry I left."*

"You don't need to apologize. You had to save yourself," he said. "And some new friends saved us."

"They are dangerous," she said fiercely, narrowing her eyes at Faeoris.

"She says the same about you," he replied. "I consider you both friends."

"Who is he talking to?" Dallow asked.

"His new girlfriend," Victoria snapped.

"Here?" Dallow asked. "Oh, on the other side. How did she find us?"

Angst did his best to ignore them.

Moyra glanced over her shoulder nervously. *"I have been coming back here, hoping to see you again, An-gst."* Her tail rocked back and forth in a mesmerizing dance, making her long blue hair sway from side to side, and giving teasing glimpses of her firm breasts. She smiled at his thoughts, and her tongue flicked the glass.

"Ugh. Gross," Victoria said sharply.

"No, not really," Tarness said, taking it all in.

"Is that her?" Moyra asked, her eyes narrow. *"Your princess."*

"Not mine," Angst mouthed quietly. "But that's her."

Victoria frowned, stepping closer to the barrier.

"She is not as pretty as you think," he heard in his mind, her voice but a whisper. *"Nice body but not her face. She would look much better without her face. And she looks tasty."* She licked her lips.

Angst sucked in his breath at the cattiness. "No, you promised."

"What did she say?" Victoria snapped.

Moyra stuck her tongue out playfully. *"I promise,"* Moyra said. *"I am better for you. She is using you, An-gst."*

"Of course she is," Angst said. "We all use each other. That's how it works."

Moyra's blue eyebrows frowned at this, her head tilting to one side thoughtfully.

"I don't trust her, but I agree with Tarness," Faeoris said. "She really is beautiful."

This made Moyra smile widely. *"I like that one."*

"So do I," Angst grinned. "She likes you," Angst said to Faeoris over his shoulder.

Faeoris eyed Moyra lustily.

The mermaid winked before her head jerked around. *"It is coming."*

"Leave," Angst yelled. "Now!"

"Be careful," she said. *"Save us, but do not die. Please!"*

"I will," Angst answered.

"I love you," she said in his mind, and then swam off so fast she almost blurred.

There was a loud sliding noise against the dome as dozens of tentacles dragged alongside. Angst gritted his teeth, letting angry minutes tick by before turning to his friends' shocked faces.

"Will she be okay?" Tarness asked.

Angst stared at Victoria. Her cheeks were red and her eyes filled with enough fiery anger to dry the ocean. She'd understood enough of the conversation to hate Moyra. Angst continued staring until Victoria rolled her eyes and sighed.

"I think she'll be fine," Angst answered.

"Why was she here?" Faeoris asked. "What does she want?"

"To make fish babies with Angst," Tori muttered.

"She wants the dome gone," Dallow answered. "She wants the curse lifted."

"Yes," one of the fish-men agreed. *"Yes, please."*

"Can you show us where Rose went?" Dallow asked hungrily, reaching out and grabbing at the creature's arm as if he could see.

Angst pulled Dallow's hand free and patted it.

"Dallow, we'll find her," Tarness said. "Are you okay?"

"I still have hope that maybe Rose can..." Dallow began.

"We all do," Angst agreed. "Save her, she fixes you, we save Unsel, and then retire. That's not asking for too much, is it?"

Dallow smiled and patted Angst's arm. Hector frowned at Angst as if worried he was giving Dallow too much hope, but Angst ignored him. Dallow, all of them, needed hope.

"Hey, you're doing better than I would," Angst said encouragingly.

"Yes, yes, I am." Dallow smirked. "Please don't go blind. It would be awful for the rest of us."

Everyone else chuckled. Angst was glad Dallow couldn't see his grimace.

"Pretend I'm winking," Dallow whispered.

"Sure," Angst said, trying his best to hide the guilt.

"What next?" Faeoris asked.

Angst paced, squeezing his hands fretfully. His stomach roiled from stress.

"What is it?" Tori asked, cattiness all but gone from her voice.

"It's too much," he said irritably. "I need to save Rose, find a way out while saving an entire race of people, and then keep Unsel from being destroyed by lunatic gargoyles and eaten by giant holes. Oh, and time is almost up. How much time do we have left, a week?"

"A few days," Dallow said, his voice stiff.

"That's what's bothering me." He felt dizzy, and his heart was racing. "How do I make a plan for all of that? How do I accomplish that in just a few days?"

"You don't," Tarness said. "We do, just like always. Just tell us what you need."

Angst stopped his useless pacing, closed his eyes, and took a deep, calming breath. Tarness and Faeoris towered over Hector, Dallow, and Victoria, as they all faced him, ready to accomplish the impossible. They had more faith in him than he did. It was enough to give him hope.

"I need to know more about this city," he said. "How did it get to the bottom of the ocean? What is this curse, and how do we remove it? There have to be books or a library—"

"On it," Dallow interrupted. He placed a hand on Hector's shoulder for guidance.

"We need books," Hector said loudly to one of the fish-men, as if yelling and speaking slowly would help. "B-O-O-K-S! All of them!"

The creature's eyes went wide and it rushed down a road. Hector led Dallow after him as quickly as they could follow.

"Let's try to regroup here in three hours," Angst called after them.

"What about me?" Tarness asked.

"You used to hunt with your dad," Angst remembered aloud. "Can you and Faeoris try to find Rose's trail? Maybe she could fly you around for a faster reconnaissance."

"Good idea," Tarness said gratefully.

Faeoris was already hovering overhead, looking for a place to grip Tarness before reaching under his armpits. "Ugh, you humans need handles," she said as they flew off.

"What about us?" Victoria asked, her lips pulled back and her eyes downcast.

"What Tarness said, just like always," he replied, an eyebrow raised high. "We're going to get into trouble."

45

ANduaut leaned against a decrepit pillar that strained to hold up the dusty old building. He cleaned beneath his fingernails with a thin shell broken from the exterior and shuddered at the thought that this would be the cleanest he could get. He was cold, and tired of this. He missed the warm sands of Vex'steppe almost as much as he missed EnDaer. Was this, somehow, punishment for killing his father?

"Where is she?" the man who called himself Vivek asked from a dark corner of the room.

ANduaut's heart skipped in surprise, and he turned to face the tall, ageless man. He bit back defensive words, all too aware of the power his sponsor wielded. "She is tending to her pet."

"You've done well, saving her." Vivek smiled as he tapped a long finger to his cheek. "You've earned her trust."

"Does that mean I can leave?" ANduaut asked.

"Would you like to leave the same way as EnDaer?" Vivek asked, reaching out to thump ANduaut's ruby ring with a knuckle.

ANduaut immediately placed his hands behind his back, remembering how the ring's destruction had cost EnDaer's life.

"What next?" he asked, hastily changing the subject.

"Bedding her would be wise," Vivek said. "But I suppose that's out of the question. Some charm would, at least, be something."

"This is a waste of time," ANduaut said with a frown. "How does this help my people? How does this make me their leader?"

Vivek grabbed both his shoulders and shook him with surprising strength, ending the brief attack with a sharp slap to his face. ANduaut covered his mouth and stepped back, undecided if he should fight or concede. He never seemed to make the right decision, and paid the price time and time again. He spun the ruby ring around his finger, a leash that kept him alive.

"You really are a weak-minded fool," Vivek snapped. "Have you seen that big, glowing stick she carries with her? She killed three times as many of those creatures as you did, and still had the strength to heal you."

"Yes," he said, "she is powerful."

"And if that power stood by you, supported you…" Vivek's voice was impatient. "Would that give you the spine you needed to lead?"

ANduaut slowly nodded in understanding. "Yes, I believe I could use her."

"You need her," Vivek said smoothly, "far more than she will ever need you."

"But why would she want to help me?" he asked.

"She's going through a few changes," Vivek explained. "They will help her bond, just as I did, with the others. She's alone and scared. Nothing a little love couldn't fix."

"Love?" ANduaut asked, and then his shoulders drooped in despair. "Oh."

"You can fake it… What's that?" Vivek stared off into the distance, his eyes wide with shock. "No!"

"What is it?" ANduaut asked, grabbing his staff and crouching in preparation.

"Another?" Vivek proclaimed in surprise. "There was only supposed to be one! Where are these all coming from?"

"Another what?" ANduaut said in frustration. "You aren't making any sense."

"Another foci!" Vivek placed a hand behind ANduaut's back. "It's too soon. Stop her from wielding it, before it's too late!" He pushed the confused man out the door.

* * * *

"Wait!" Rose called out. "We should let ANduaut know where we're going."

Gendel's thin shoulders dropped in surrender. The skinny creature paced back and forth, rubbing his oblong head and squinting dark eyes as he pondered. He looked so frustrated that Rose worried he might explode. She considered siphoning a teaspoon of his life so he would calm down, but wasn't convinced she could make herself stop. Even considering it brought a wave of hunger that made her stomach cramp.

"Fine, Creep...Gendel," she said, tapping her temple with an index finger. "Go ahead."

"You need to come and see now," Gendel thought in her mind. *"It will help save us."*

She searched the nearby rooms for the tribesman. ANduaut had been as conversational as her little friend, but there was something to be said about the silent type. Too many of them spoke too much. This one needed no words for her sake. He was so beautiful, and she shivered thinking about that sturdy jaw and chiseled muscles.

"Please." Gendel waved her to the door.

"Fine." She gave in, picking Chryslaenor up from the floor. "I'm sure he'll find us. I hope."

Gendel led her down a wide stone stairway covered in dimly glowing moss, pausing only briefly to survey the road before exiting the building. Rose was more cautious, still wary from their recent battle. Wouldn't the creatures be looking for revenge?

"No," Gendel answered in her mind. *"They are afraid of you and the man. They will not attack again."*

Rose shook her head irritably, the tinny sound of his high-pitched voice echoing between her ears. It was unnerving, and she yawned, stretching her jaw until she heard a pop. He studied her but remained quiet.

A glimmer of daylight provided a dramatic view of the vast city. Thin flickering beams reflected off tall shell-covered buildings that stretched higher than the castle in Unsel. They were passing an enormous building, like a rectangular pyramid. This city should've held thousands of people. So, what had happened? Had these fish-men killed everyone? That was impossible; they were practically helpless.

"So why haven't you tried to eat me?" she asked.

"You do not look that tasty," Gendel joked.

"Ha," Rose said in surprise. "I'm not, I promise."

"I need an ally," he explained. *"Not dinner."*

"An ally?" she asked. "For what?"

Gendel stopped and faced her, tilting his head to one side and crossing his arms.

"You're trapped in here," she said.

He nodded, spun about, and rushed forward.

"But the rest of your, uh, people," she prompted. "Why aren't they allies?"

"It has been a long time," his voice sounded upset, even in her head. *"They have lost their way."*

Chryslaenor sparked with noisy dark lightning as they reached a courtyard. In the center stood a monument she recognized all too well. Grime-encrusted and cracked, it was virtually identical to the one that Dulgirgraut and Chryslaenor had rested on.

"Not another one," she said with a sigh.

As she set Chryslaenor on the ground, the hilt seemed reluctant to release her hand, as if covered in cobwebs. Tiny bits of the black lightning bit her hand sharply. "Stop that!" she shouted, stomping on the flat of the blade to force it to the ground. She rubbed her hand, scowling at the sword's apparent tantrum. "I'll come back when you behave yourself."

Gendel's dark eyes were large as he watched the altercation, but he said nothing.

She approached the monument cautiously, as it was in bad

shape. The glowing moss had grown into cracks that splintered the marble like lightning painted onto canvas. Hand-sized chunks had given up their long tenure, falling from the stone to litter the ground. She circled until she had a better view, and that was when she saw them.

Two long-handled golden daggers rested atop the monument. They were identical, both the length of her arm, with three golden edges. The handles were long enough that she could imagine them connecting to form an odd sort of staff. The hilts of both daggers rested on the marble slab while u-shaped marble fixtures held the blades upward. If she'd found this on the surface, she would've wondered which constellations the daggers were pointing at. Down here, they were merely aimed at opposite ends of the dome.

She held her hand over the handle of one. No black lightning or angry bites. Rose already liked this foci better, if that was what it was. She blew dust off, and a chunk of marble broke free opposite her, its crash creating a cloud that made her cough.

Rose blew at the dust again until she could see Gendel, who nodded encouragingly. He raised his hand to indicate that she should lift a blade. Carefully, as if trying to pet a wild animal, she rested her hand on the hilt.

"*JORMBRINDER: THE EXCEPTION*," echoed in her mind.

She jerked back, and the dagger followed, stuck to her hand. It dropped to the floor, heavy as an anchor. A golden light surrounded the blade and crept up her arm, burning like fire.

"Get it off!" she screamed.

Chryslaenor was bigger, but it wasn't this heavy. Something was wrong. She tried lifting it, but was only able to drag it several inches. The golden glow burning her arm stopped at her elbow as it met a painful sleeve of black lightning. Her chest heaved as her arm went numb, and she felt the thirst for energy to fight this thing, to get it off.

The sword. She had to reach Chryslaenor. Jormbrinder became heavier with every movement. Each step was a battle as she reached for the giant sword.

"What have you done?" she shouted to Gendel.

"I am sorry!" he cried out in her mind. Gendel ran away as fast as his short legs would move. *"It was the only way."*

"He'll be the first one I eat." She grunted as her hand touched Chryslaenor's hilt. Rose didn't know if she screamed out loud or just in her head, but holding both blades at once drowned her body in such pain that the screams didn't last long.

46

"So, you're saying chicken means coward?" Faeoris asked, her tone befuddled. "I would never have guessed he was a coward."

"No, I don't mean it literally," Tarness said, trying to correct her gently. He didn't feel like being dropped. "When you were with him, I bet he didn't kiss you."

"He did not," she said irritably. "He said he couldn't."

"That's what I mean by chicken," Tarness said. The joke was completely lost on her. He wished they were back with the other Berfemmian. He was better at being 'forced' to mate than he was at flirting.

"Oh," Faeoris said, and it sounded like she understood.

They'd started at the center of the city and circled outward, flying over roving bands of fish creatures and dodging buildings and skyways. There was a lot to take in. Most cities looked the same, but not this one, and he wondered what kind of bars this place had, what kind of music they would play. Tarness loved big cities. In spite of his size, it was easy to get lost. People tended to forget just how enormous he was. He didn't feel so awkward.

"Um, is there any way to slow down?" he asked, embarrassed. "I'm having a hard time seeing anything at this speed."

"I'm not," Faeoris said shortly, not slowing. "Do you have a forever-mate, like Angst?"

"No," Tarness said, his voice low.

"Good," she replied.

"There is someone," he continued.

"Of course there is," she said with a sigh.

"I don't know if it's going to work, or even if she's interested," he went on. "She's Nordruaut, and I'm obviously not. We only met for a brief time, but there was something. It probably sounds silly."

"Yes," she said tartly, setting him down as she landed. "All you humans and your forever-mates are silly. And what does Angst see in that snooty child, anyway? She's using him, and he doesn't even know."

"Oh," Tarness said, suppressing his smile. "That's why you're angry."

"I'm never angry," she snapped.

Tarness tilted his head to one side and looked at her in disbelief.

"Fine, sometimes I get upset," she said with a huff. "But he would choose to bed with her and not with me? Am I so ugly to be dismissed like some…some friend?"

"You're not ugly," Tarness said, shaking his head. He sighed. "You should've heard Angst go on about you when we walked up the stairs. I'm sure he won't stop talking about you for months to come."

"Really?" she asked hopefully.

"I probably won't either," Tarness said. "You're gorgeous."

"Thanks," she said. "But that woman, how can she be a princess? She's so tiny, she couldn't even defend herself in a fight."

"Not that she should have to, being a princess and all," Tarness said, "but she could probably take me in a fight. Maybe even you."

"What?" Faeoris asked, mortally offended. "It's magic, isn't it? That's why he's chosen her as a mate?"

"She's not his mate," Tarness said with a laugh.

"But, how is she not?" Faeoris asked. "They are obviously connected."

"You know how he wouldn't kiss you? He won't kiss her, either," Tarness said. "They don't cross that line, they just jump on it a lot. Anyway, they're friends. About as close as friends should get. Too close, if you asked his true mate."

"Oh, they are *essent*," she said, looking high into the air. "Like my Marisha."

"*Essent?*" Tarness asked.

"They love each other, like friends and family," she explained. "Close like mates, but not lovers. *Essent.*"

"Yeah," Tarness agreed with a sigh. "That would be them. They get confused about it sometimes, but definitely not lovers."

"Good, because she's ugly," Faeoris said sharply, crossing her arms. "Don't you think she's ugly?"

"Uhhh," Tarness said, knowing there wasn't a right answer. He was so tired of discussing Angst's love life that this was only tolerable because Faeoris was beautiful and almost naked. She didn't appear offended by his attention, and he was grateful. "Why did you set us down here?"

Faeoris knelt, holding her hand over a pair of dusty footprints. Large ones that could've been from a fish-man's webbed feet, and smaller, human-like tracks.

"You saw that from up there?" Tarness asked. "Wow."

They jogged down the path, following the footprints until she placed a hand on his chest, stopping him like a wall. They could hear scuffling and the patter of feet. A fish-man ran up to them, his arms flailing over his head comically. He skidded to a stop, and looked at them both. The creature sported a sky blue oval on his forehead, like a birthmark.

"*I am sorry,*" they could hear in their minds as he ran past them.

"What was that about?" Tarness asked.

From around the corner, he heard the cry of a woman. Tarness recognized that voice.

"Rose?" he called out, running as fast as his thick legs would carry him.

It was farther than he'd thought, and he hoped Faeoris didn't notice how exhausted he already was. They jogged around a maze of alleyways until they found a square courtyard twenty feet across, surrounded by stone planters and benches. In the center stood a large, familiar monument. A dusty haze surrounded the stone slab, but he couldn't see anyone else.

"What?" Faeoris asked. "What is it?"

"Oh no," Tarness said, unable to keep the worry from his voice. "Not another one."

* * * *

"You don't even need me," Hector said encouragingly. "It's like you're not even blind."

"You are a terrible liar," Dallow laughed, gripping his arm tightly for guidance. "We'll find Rose and this nonsense can end."

"That's not why you want to find her," Hector said. "Aren't you married?"

"Barely," Dallow scoffed, stopping in his tracks. He faced Hector. "She moved out when I returned from Gressmore. I thought...I hoped she would come back."

"I'm sorry, Dallow," Hector said, placing a hand on the man's shoulders. "I didn't know. Maybe there's still a chance to fix things."

"With this?" Dallow tore off the kerchief.

Hector could've looked away—Dallow might not even have known—but he owed his friend respect for the scars he'd earned in battle. Dragonbreath had splattered across Dallow's face, searing a dark swath across his eyes like a raccoon mask. It had only happened weeks ago, but, surprisingly, the scars were almost completely gone. Dallow had been able to heal much. The eye sockets were now smooth skin that sank into empty holes. Far from grotesque, but still uncomfortable to look at, and his heart wrenched at the sight.

"She is a vain, cold-hearted bitch," Dallow spat. "And she would never tolerate this."

"Why didn't you say anything?" Hector asked.

"Because I didn't need a reminder of this," he said, pointing at his scars, "or that," he pointed to his wife, far away from them. "I needed an escape. I needed one of Angst's adventures. I needed to be a hero and forget about the disaster back home."

Dallow's chest heaved as he fought back the pain he'd held in for weeks, and Hector drew him in for a hug, patting his back.

"I can't even cry now," Dallow said, pulling back, wiping away nothing from his cheeks.

Hector didn't know what to say. This was far from his area of expertise, but he cared for his friend. "Now that Angst has made a connection with the sword, can't he heal you?"

"He tried," Dallow said forlornly, tying the kerchief back on. "Healing is complicated, and Dulgirgraut and I have tried to teach him, but for all he can do, his healing is limited to flesh wounds. Maybe broken bones."

"But Rose?" he asked.

"Maybe," Dallow said with a sigh. "But even if she can't, just to know she's alive and safe. Just to save her..."

Hector had never felt terribly close to Rose, and had always considered her one of many in Angst's bucket of companions. Even worse, he'd already written her off. As a friend, he, of course, wanted her to be alive. As a soldier, he knew she was dead, or lost to magic he didn't understand. But, there was no way he would tell Dallow this. In battle, hope was one of the most valuable assets.

"Then let's go save her," Hector said encouragingly.

Their odd-looking guide ran back down the road toward them and grabbed Hector and Dallow's hands.

"Books!" the creature thought to them.

"Finally," Dallow said as he followed.

Hector held the creature's hand with a firm grip to keep it from running too fast. It looked at him in annoyance then shuddered at Hector's dark gaze. They walked around corners and down narrow pathways between buildings until they reached an odd-looking cave-like hole gouged into the ground. Hector pulled sharply, stopping their progress to investigate. He knelt at the entrance, barely two bodies wide and equally as tall. He fingered the sandy dirt at its base.

"This is new," he said gruffly.

"What?" Dallow asked hurriedly. "I don't smell books."

"There's a fresh hole dug in the middle of the road. Big enough that it looks like a cave entrance," Hector explained. "It doesn't belong."

"No," the creature thought to them. *"No. Stay away. Stay far away. Come for books."*

Hector looked at the surrounding area, taking mental notes of their position before letting the creature lead them forward. Minutes passed as it led them along a dizzying path of sidewalks, making him wonder if the city wasn't better visited by the walkways far above. They stopped at two enormous doors that barred the entrance to a tall, impressive building. Stone columns rose all around them, and to the side of the doors hung a large, golden plaque with words etched in a language he didn't understand. The creature pointed at the doors, beating on the handle of one several times.

"Are we here?" Dallow asked excitedly. "Finally, a chance to be useful again."

"I think so," Hector said. "And stop that, you're always useful."

Both doors had handles that would've been impressive thousands of years ago—they seemed to be made for giants—but the brass fixtures were rough with corrosion, and Hector struggled with both of them to no avail.

"If this is a trap, or if there are no books in here, I will leave you in meaty pieces before you finish your next breath," he snapped at the little creature.

It ran off, screaming frightfully in their heads.

"What a creeper," Hector said under his breath.

"What is it?" Dallow asked.

"I can't get in," he replied.

"Let me try," Dallow reached out, and with Hector's help,

placed his hands on the handles. "Hmm, they're locked," he said with a grin.

Dallow's eyes were glowing white, which always took Hector aback. There was a loud clunk as the handles released, and Dallow shoved the doors inward. A rush of musty air made Hector cough and cover his mouth with one arm. Dallow breathed in deeply, as if he'd just found the best kitchen on Ehrde.

"Books," he said hungrily.

"Has to be," Hector agreed with a wince.

They walked into the pitch-black room, Hector guiding slowly. Dallow raised his staff and muttered something in a lost language. Bright light shone from the staff, illuminating the library. Rows and rows of shelves lined the room, and in the middle was a tall stack of books that would take a lifetime just to put away. It was a feast for the hungriest reader, enough to make even Hector gasp.

"Right?" Dallow said, his entire face now glowing in excitement. "I can feel them."

"You're going to love this place," he said.

He led his tall, thin friend to the pile in the center. Dallow sat, crossing his legs, and reached for a thick volume. His breath caught as he absorbed the book like a sponge. Hector picked one up and Dallow immediately slapped his hand as though he could see.

"These are so delicate, they'll turn to dust the minute you open them," he said, carefully taking the book away. "This is Acratic, but a dialect I barely recognize and, oh…"

"I'm going to go," Hector said, inching away. "I want to look around. You'll be okay?"

Dallow merely nodded, absorbing books faster than Angst could drink flasks of sweet wine.

"Should I come get you, or can you meet us back there in a couple hours?" Hector asked.

"Come find me tomorrow," Dallow said dismissively. "I won't be done in two hours."

"But…" Hector said worriedly.

"Hector, we lost everything in Gressmore Towers," he said firmly. "I won't let that happen again. Not for Rose, not for Ehrde. We need the full story of this place, like Angst requested."

Hector watched Dallow turn away, and knew he was lost to the world of knowledge. Hopefully, there was something within those pages that could help them, and Rose. He hurried out of the library and tried finding his way back to the hole. Something about it hadn't felt right and set his hackles on edge. He turned a corner and rushed down the path only to find a dead end. With a grunt, he returned to the main road and sought another path. He was adept at finding his way around woods and open areas, but may as well as have been blind in a new city. He rushed to find another blocked road, and cursed in frustration. How could anyone possibly find their way around this place? There were no recognizable signs, no sun or stars to provide direction, no smells or sounds that—

From around the corner, he heard a woman curse. He immediately recognized that voice.

"Rose?" he called out.

Hector ran at an all-out sprint, sliding around dusty corners like they were covered in ice. It was farther than he'd thought, and he drew two longswords from his back. He skidded to a halt as he entered a square courtyard twenty feet across, surrounded by stone planters and benches. In the center stood a large, familiar monument. Across the way, Tarness approached with Faeoris. and at the same time said. "Oh no, not another one."

47

"We need a way out," Angst said to the creature, the thought placed firmly in his head.

It started running away, but Angst held its bones, locking it to the ground. The little monster cried out, wailing in their heads. Victoria held her ears shut with her hands as if it that would block it out.

"Angst," she pleaded. "Please let it go."

So he did. It rubbed its knees, looking back at him with a bitter glare before sprinting off into the shadows.

"That didn't go well," he said, wiggling his finger in his ear.

"Yeah," she agreed. "Now what?"

"Not a clue," he said with a deep breath. "Scar was my guide initially, but he's not here. Can you see anything?"

"So, now I'm your dog?" she said, and he couldn't tell if she was offended or not.

"You know what I meant," he replied.

"I don't know, Angst," she said with a sigh. "Sometimes it works. Sometimes I can see. But down here, in this place, all I get are distant echoes. And that's only when your sword doesn't shut me out completely."

He held out a hand and she took it, her long eyelashes lowering in concentration. Angst looked at Tori's pretty face, admiring her full lips, the curve of her jaw, and the long blond curly hair she'd kept for him. It draped her shoulders and hung to the small of her back in a sexy, curled mass. It had been a long time since it smelled like strawberry, and he missed that. She opened her eyes and shook her head then stared at him quizzically.

"I figured you'd be looking at my boobs," she said. "I obviously can't read you right now."

"I just hadn't gotten there yet," he teased. "Let's circle the outside of the dome. I can't imagine the exit is in the middle."

They walked down a jagged road in silence, their crunchy footsteps echoing dryly between the nearby buildings and the shield. He didn't let go of her hand, and she didn't seem to mind. This place, with its still air and echoing walls and dark shadows, had to be the center of creepy in all Ehrde. The city was vast, far more than the needs of its current occupants. Angst felt it was larger still than Gressmore. How many mages had lived here? Was this place always underwater? What was it even called? For some reason, he felt a loss, like this city was another grave marker for more wielders.

"She's very pretty," Victoria said quietly, taking her hand back and rubbing it on her cloak.

"Who's that?" Angst asked.

"Never mind," she said through gritted teeth.

Victoria took the lead around a tall pile of rubble left by a building that had been sliced apart by the dome. The section of city they were exploring was made up of partial roads blocked by debris from building remains. He doubted the city had been built within a perfect circle, but couldn't help but be impressed that the dome only seemed to cut off buildings at the very edge. It would've required a powerful caster, maybe several, and a very accurate spell.

"Faeoris seems to like you, a lot," Victoria said.

"I like her, too," he said honestly. "She's amazing. I hope she sticks around for more adventures."

"Up above, I caught a glimpse of her future," she offered. "I think you'll know her for a very long time."

This made Angst smile. He really did like her, and wanted to get to know her better. Hopefully, Heather wouldn't mind that Faeoris didn't wear much. He certainly didn't.

"I think you two could be good friends," Angst suggested. "If you gave her a chance."

"I don't think that will happen," she said with a sigh.

"Oh?" Angst asked, trying to tease. "Is she too attractive?"

"Yes!" Tori said, sticking out her tongue. She said nothing else.

The exploration had continued in silence for ten incredibly long minutes when they came across a cave-sized hole. Dulgirgraut glowed warningly over his shoulder, and he wondered why. The hole certainly didn't belong with the rest of the architecture; it almost seemed fresh. It was large, large enough for two or three people to enter, and seemed to lead under the dome. He couldn't see anything else and took a cautious step down into it.

"Angst," she said quietly, holding onto his arm with both hands. "We need to stay away from there, please."

"Don't you think that—"

"No!" she said sharply.

"Oookay," he said, drawing out the word. "Are you seeing something?"

"Just a feeling," she said, pulling away.

"Where do we go next?" he asked.

He followed Tori, who was silent as death. He missed his friend. He missed their rapport and couldn't tell if he was just exhausted or if things were actually broken. They kept arguing and then putting everything back together, and he had no clue where they stood right now.

She led him back down the road they'd just walked, as if keeping him from danger. Tori stopped before a doorway and dragged him into a spacious room. Despite the broken tables and crumbling bar, it was a familiar sight. She'd found a tavern.

"Ha!" he said aloud.

"I thought this would make you smile," she said with a wide grin. "You did say we would get into trouble."

"This is where it usually starts," he said, taking her hands in his. He walked around her slowly, and she turned with him. "With a few drinks..."

"And then a few more," she said with a twinkle in her eye. She skipped every few steps. "And then we dance."

"And then you dance, or whatever that wiggle thing is you do," he said, leering mischievously. "I sort of sit there and gawk."

She shimmied delightfully, followed by a slow turn that made his too-sober heart skip a beat or two. Tori took steps toward him, got close, so very close he could've leaned forward and almost... She pulled away with smoldering eyes that melted him. They held hands, and she danced to silent music in the dim light of the foci, coming close yet staying out of reach. It was always enough to keep his attention, to keep him wanting more, but not too close, as if she were in a protective shell, a barrier he wouldn't even try to break. When he finally tired of the dance and wondered if it wasn't time to find their friends, she drew him in. The dance was over, the music that had never really been there was gone, and he looked down, and she looked up, and he remembered. He remembered how she'd ended their last dream, and he didn't know what to say or how to feel. He held her tighter, and—

"Angst," Hector said in an accusing tone.

It felt like he'd been caught by her parents, and he knew even before they pulled apart that Hector wasn't alone. He turned to face them with warm cheeks and a dry mouth. Hector looked at him with the disappointed gaze of a man who'd discovered you'd got his daughter pregnant. Tarness eyed him in disbelief, as if everything he'd said was lies. Faeoris was fury, her wings lighting the room as if she were ready to fly away.

"You said we couldn't do this," the Berfemmian snapped, her fingers digging into the rotting wood of the bar. "You are filled with lies, like all men."

"I agree," Tarness said, his voice heavy with disappointment.

"We just don't have time for this!" Hector yelled.

And his yells were joined by the others', including Tori's, as Angst stood in the middle like the failed director of a choir gone mad. His gut tensed to hear his friends' accusations, so infuriating he could barely contain the lump in his throat. When their words stopped making sense, and he was certain their shouts were about to crack open the protective dome, he screamed. *"Shut up!"*

They all fell silent, the disappointment in their eyes like daggers.

"This," he pointed at Tori, "is not lies. It's not deceit. It's none of your business!"

"I—" Faeoris said.

"Shut up," he snapped, unable to hold back a tear. "Hector doesn't like how I go about being a hero, Dulgirgraut hates being bonded with me, my most loyal friend accuses me of lying, and I can't take it."

"It's just—" Hector began. "You're just being so—"

"Angst?" he asked, crossing his arms and staring at his feet.

He sniffed deeply and began to pace. He could feel himself push away emotionally, close them off with every word. "I try every day, from the moment I wake to that reluctant moment I let go and finally fall asleep. I try to be happy, to be supportive, to be there for everyone. I try to do it right, all of it. I feel like I work insanely hard, harder than I should actually have to, but I can only do this the way I know how."

"You just don't understand," Hector said in frustration.

"Do *you*? I will never stop being Angst!" He slashed his hand in the air as he turned. "Even if I wanted to, I wouldn't know how! You, of all people, know that. You should all just do this without me. Or, maybe I should do it without you! Either way, figure out how to accept me, or stay behind next time!"

Angst stomped to the entrance, leaving behind chagrin and anger.

"Any questions?" Angst snapped over his shoulder.

He could feel their stares, but heard nothing as he stormed away.

* * * *

He sat beneath the crack, which was now longer than his forearm and occasionally dripped saltwater onto his chin. He didn't care. He was done with this adventure, and more than anything, he just wanted to sleep. He wanted to be with Heather, and he wanted to be away from all of this. Quite the heroic leader he'd turned out to be. He'd tried as hard as he could to be what everyone needed, but it felt like each of them wanted something else, someone else. How could he be what they wanted? How could he stop being Angst?

"What is wrong, An-gst?" He heard Moyra's beautiful voice in his head.

Angst looked around to see if she was somehow inside, and sighed when she wasn't. She was outside the curse, the protective dome that kept her out, and the ocean from flooding the city. He shifted to lie on his back with his head against the shield, and looked up. She swam outside, hovering beyond the dome like a dream. He reached up to the curse that divided them and smiled, in spite of himself. She was so incredible to look at, so fun. He shrugged and kept his hand on the shield. Moyra circled the crack several times, faster than Angst could believe, leaving behind a swirl of tiny bubbles that crept up the dome like spiders fleeing a nest. She rested her palm on the shield across from his.

"I miss you," she said.

"Yes," he agreed, his somber mood lightening.

"You should be over here," she said, and he thought he could see her blurred smile through the thick shield. *"So I can help you breathe."*

"I'd like that," he said, and he did like it. It was the most legitimate excuse for something else, and she didn't shy away. She never said he was too short, or too fat, or wanted him to be something else. It gave him strength.

"I am glad I did not eat you, hooman," she said.

He laughed out loud, even if she wasn't completely joking.

"Are you doing it?" she said, patting at the crack. *"Can you*

make it bigger?"

"I haven't figured it out yet." He sighed. "I'm missing something, and there are so many distractions that I can't concentrate."

She kissed the shield for a long moment, her full lips large and squishy. He missed her breathing, missed her swaying in his arms. She pressed her firm breasts against the shield, and he stared like a twelve-year-old.

"There," she said. *"Now you are only distracted by me."*

"My favorite distraction," he said, and couldn't help but smile.

"Why are you so upset?" she asked. *"Tell me."*

And so he did, relating as much as he could fit into a five-minute explanation. It was exhausting, but telling her about it made him feel better.

"You are silly," she said.

"What?" he asked with a frown.

"You are trying too hard to be what everyone else wants, hooman," she said. *"Be An-gst."*

"That...that actually makes sense," he said in surprise.

"Now save my people," she said, rapping on the spot with her knuckles then expanding her hand wide.

Before he could coax more from her, she jerked about as if something was behind her. Moyra kissed the barrier near his face before pulling away and swimming to freedom. Closely behind, the enormous tentacled beast squished against the barrier as it lumbered past. The crack spread noisily, growing another third in size. The water now dripped freely. Dulgirgraut glowed brightly, and Angst smoldered. His one moment of respite, his one break, scared away by this thing.

"Somehow, I'm going to rip you apart!" Angst snapped.

Dulgirgraut flickered like a candle in front of an open window.

He pushed himself up to stand, his mind suddenly clearer than it had been since doing the sealtian with Faeoris. He actually had the urge to do them now, which seemed to excite the sword, but he chose to pace. Angst walked through the adventure in his mind. Everything from Heather's kiss goodbye to yelling at his friends was clear as crystal. The only thing truly fuzzy was the dream he'd shared with Victoria. The one where Aerella had tried to tell him something important.

48

Angst returned to the decrepit inn with the tiniest spring in his step. Hector and Tarness had found two sturdy chairs and sat at a table in the middle of the room, chewing on hard bread and drinking water. Victoria and Faeoris sat cross legged on the floor in a corner, deep in a discussion Angst probably didn't want to know anything about. They looked up at his entrance and giggled. He walked straight to his boys and held out a hand to both of them. Without hesitation, they gripped forearms and briefly shook. Nothing else needed to be said.

"Where's Dallow?" Angst asked.

"He's in a library, a big one," Hector said with a smile. "He may never leave."

"Angst, we found something," Tarness said with a nod to Faeoris.

Tori and Faeoris walked over with mischievous grins.

Angst sighed deeply, just glad all seemed better.

"We found another foci," Tarness said.

"You're kidding!" he exclaimed. "Are you sure?"

"There was a dagger on a monument just like the one holding the swords," he said, pointing a thick finger at the one over Angst's shoulder.

"What did you do with it?" Angst asked excitedly.

"We left it alone," Hector confirmed, eyeing Faeoris accusingly.

"What?" she asked. "I didn't take it, yet. Nobody else is using it."

"I don't think you could lift it," Hector explained. "We can't."

"You should have let me try. I'm not human," she said proudly.

"I've noticed," Angst agreed. "Way too pretty."

Faeoris beamed, and he was amazed Tori wasn't upset. She merely nodded at the Berfemmian knowingly.

"I'd like to see this foci for myself," Angst said.

"There's something else," Hector said. "We may have heard Rose!"

"What?" Angst asked, surprised they hadn't shared this first.

"I heard a cry. It may have been her," he said. "We didn't actually see her."

"Faeoris and I followed a trail to a hole," Tarness said. "Kind of like a cave."

"Tori and I saw it too!" Angst said, more excited than before. "Let's go!"

"Let's not," Hector countered. "I checked in on Dallow while you were...away. He was brief, but asked us to wait."

"But..." Angst said.

"They're right," Tori agreed. "The feeling I get from that place, it's all wrong. It's dangerous."

"All the more reason to go now," he said firmly.

"Maybe we should have a better idea of what's actually going on," Tarness said. "Just this once."

"It's Rose, Angst," Hector said. "Dallow wouldn't ask to wait if it wasn't important."

Angst considered their options. He hated this. There was a chance Rose was alive. She was so close, and he could only imagine that she needed help. And another foci was nearby, in this city. Dulgirgraut buzzed in his head, warning him of everything but telling him nothing. He needed answers. He needed the missing puzzle piece, and he might know where to find it.

"Three hours," Angst said firmly.

"I told Dallow two," Hector agreed.

"That's perfect. He's always late," Angst said. "I need that time to figure something out."

"Oh?" Hector asked.

"The dream," he said. "The one Tori and I keep ending before it's done."

"Oh," Tori said quietly. "I was thinking of sharing a room with Faeoris."

"As amazing as that sounds," Angst said with a smirk, "we really need to finish this. Aerella said it was important."

Tori looked at Faeoris reluctantly. Their tall friend shrugged but said nothing else.

"You're welcome to join us," Angst suggested jokingly.

"I'm not really that tired," Faeoris said dryly.

* * * *

Victoria and Angst stood in the middle of a vast field. Wind blew waves of tall grass that leaned through the bottom of their translucent hands. Angst looked down and wiggled his toes. Blades of grass popped through, and he could just imagine them cool and sharp, scratching and tickling. The day was bright, and the sun baked the field with a warmth he longed to feel and let sink into his tired muscles. He breathed deep, only to smell nothing, not fresh air nor flowers.

"Every girl's dream," Victoria said, eyeing him up and down.

"That's me." Angst sniffled. "Didn't you know that already?"

A castle-sized boulder hurtled toward them, smashing onto the ground, ripping up dirt and brush with every tumble. They stood still, watching in awe as the small moon rolled through them, crashing past in a vicious hurry to wreak more damage.

"Dreams," he said calmly. "A nice change from actually being in danger."

"What am I wearing?" she asked.

"Upset that you aren't naked this time?" he asked.

She stuck out her tongue, frowning. They were dressed in the most unflattering of eggshell robes, draped lazily over their shoulders and hanging down to their sandal-adorned feet. With a grunting sound, she kicked off the ugly shoes and shook herself out of the robe. Underneath the robe was another, equally boring. Thong sandals once again appeared on her feet as though never removed.

"Magic," Angst explained.

"I can't change my outfit," Victoria said warily as she pulled her hair free from the robe to inspect it. It was straight and black, the way she'd worn it at the castle. "Why is this dream different?"

"It's my dream this time, a foci dream," he said. "And I didn't want any distractions to suddenly pull me out."

"Oh, so all of a sudden, I'm a distraction!" she shouted.

"You're always a distraction. My favorite distraction," Angst said gently. "I just wish you'd stop being angry at me."

"I'm not angry at you!" she yelled. She leaned into her words with her hands on her hips.

"We should figure this out now," he said. "All of it."

"I don't believe you kissed her." She crossed her arms.

"Who?" he asked.

"Alloria," she said, her voice filled with fury.

"She kissed me." He couldn't believe he was defending this again.

"What's the difference?" Victoria cried out. "You didn't pull back! You didn't try to stop her!"

"No...no, I didn't," Angst said defensively. "She's almost as pretty as you are, and I was flattered."

She continued staring him down.

"I'll admit, it was nice. I don't get that sort of attention from anyone," he said sadly. "But why would you care?"

"I just don't think it's appropriate when you're married," she said, brushing dark hair from her shoulders.

Angst's jaw dropped. "How can you even say that after this entire trip?" Angst asked. "Bathing naked in front of me, crawling into my bed, twice..."

"Not to mention," she said, her thin eyebrows frowning, "you kissing the fish."

He didn't say anything; his feelings for Moyra were complicated. His need for her wasn't just love or lust. He couldn't find a word to explain what she meant to him and hoped Tori could see through his lack of words. That relationship was something, Moyra was someone he could never have. She would never be his, but the feelings between them were so strong they'd numbed all his other pains. Maybe that was what had happened. Maybe he'd let this lovely, alien creature in to mask the guilt of leaving his wife at home rather than fixing their issues, or to hide the rift between him and Victoria and whatever their relationship was threatening to become. He couldn't deny his feelings for Moyra, but was it possible? Was there more to it? Maybe it was time to start facing these problems before it was too late.

"I did kiss her," he admitted. "Just like you kissed me."

A giant ball of fire and lava zoomed over their heads, crackling loudly. It crashed against a distant tornado that seemed to eat it. The tornado glowed with flames, spinning about in glorious madness until both disasters were past.

"Maybe we should pay attention to why we're here," she said, her voice rushed.

"We've got time," Angst said.

"You weren't supposed to remember," she said, refusing to make eye contact. "I didn't know what else to do."

"Right. Well, I do remember, now," he said, crossing his arms. "Why are you always so angry? Why do you push me and pull me? One day we're naked, the next day you're screaming, and the next kissing me in my dreams."

Tears dripped down her cheeks, and she held herself tightly.

"What do you want?" he asked.

"I want this, Angst," she said in the mousiest of voices. She turned to him, moving forward into that personal space she'd stayed far away from for so long. He didn't move back. "Ever since we met, I've wanted to go on adventures with you. I don't want it to stop. I don't want to be a princess anymore."

"That's all?" he asked.

"And I don't want to share," she said so quietly he almost didn't hear her.

"Oh." He didn't know what else to say.

Their relationship at the castle had been fun. Not only because he absolutely adored her, not only because she needed him, but they'd been getting away with something. It was like a tiny adventure, so when she'd joined them on the road, the adventure had become that much more exciting. It made everyone upset at them, but Angst had been so wrapped up in that excitement, in that fun, that he'd missed the obvious.

He'd always been dumb when it came to women. He could flirt and woo and tease, but when it came to knowing what they actually wanted, he was smart like a rock. And Tori? How easy it was to forget that she was only nineteen. He should've figured it out when he woke up to find Tori naked in his bed, or when she blatantly did things to make him jealous. She wore her hair just how Angst liked it, and tiny outfits that showed off all his favorite curves. He'd been too dense to pick it up. Evidently, he need to be smacked across his face with a sign, because never once would Angst have imagined that Victoria had fallen in love with him.

He would've loved to adventure with Tori forever, side by side with his best friend, especially if they could've gone back to having fun. But he'd never leave Heather—even on the bad days, the worst ones, he wouldn't even consider it. And that must've been the thought in his head, or the look on his face, when a tear trickled down her cheek.

"It's the great things about dreams," she said with a forced little laugh. "You can dream of all the stuff you want, even if it never happens."

"Like kissing a princess?" he asked with a wink.

"You wouldn't be the first one to dream of that," she said with a familiar smile.

"And when the dream is over?" he asked.

"You'll be a husband, and a dad, and my best friend," she

said, swallowing hard. "And I will try to be a good queen."

"You'll be an amazing queen," he said. He looked up to see her wearing his favorite smile and nodding…and something else. Not anger, nor sadness, but a kind of satisfaction. Her eyes were resolved, as if the last puzzle piece had been set in place, and he wondered if that meant everything would be all right.

"It does mean that," she said with a broad smile.

"About time!" he said with a grin. "Now, where is she?"

"Who?" Victoria asked.

"Aerella," he said. "She needs to explain why we keep coming here over and over again. I'm sick of this dream!"

"Me too!" she agreed.

Stone monoliths shot from the ground. A roaring wind cut into the stone, tearing it into tiny bits that created a blinding sandstorm. Years of erosion happened within seconds as the stones became pebbles and the winds subsided. And then, it stopped.

Thunder came, not from storms or earthquakes, but from hordes of creatures charging to the center of the field. They met in a crash loud enough to make Angst's teeth shake. It was a nightmare of destruction—Nordruaut killing Unsel soldiers, gamlin tearing through dragons, mages firing beams of light and fire at Berfemmian, Vex'steppe tribes battling Fulk'han, large mermen fighting cavastil birds.

They all fought each other. There weren't teams or sides or alliances. It was an endless dog pile of death upon death, none safe from the person or creature beside them. The elements waited like angry teachers, hovering over the field, arms crossed in high judgment. Angst looked around to see six watchers. He counted on his fingers then shook his head and counted again.

A gray man with scars on his arm and a giant Nordruaut with a long beard battled before them, blood flying through their ghostly image from a damaging swing.

"Angst, can we stop this? I think I'm going to be sick," Victoria said, her face pale. "What are you counting?"

"I thought there were five elements here," he said. "Earth,

Fire, Air, Water, and Magic." He pointed at each titan, ending at the tall beam of dark light.

"Right..." she said, her eyes followed his to the beam of white light shooting high up into the sky.

"Then what is that?" he asked.

The dark beam had moved to reach the white one, which flickered like a campfire. All heads turned to see it go out, followed closely by a blast that knocked everyone away. The ground shook so violently it began to blur, and the mountains shifted and flattened. There were screams of pain and a loud crunching of metal as the dream began fading out of existence before their eyes.

He looked at Tori.

"I swear, it isn't me this time," she said. "No kiss or anything!"

"What do we do?" Angst said fretfully. "Aerella's not here to tell us!"

He could barely see Tori now, and he was sweating with the effort of keeping the vision alive.

"She doesn't need to, Angst," Victoria said. "We already saw it. The Fulk'han and the gray men were both there. This isn't our past, Angst. This is our future!"

49

Rasaol and Jarle stood over the bodies of two Nordruaut. Another man and a woman had been finely carved and served to the snow. Their blood and entrails were frozen, and any footprints were lost to wind and drifts. This meant that Guldrich was far ahead. How could one injured Fulk'han do so much damage? The Nordruaut were the hunters, they were larger by half a body, and he was missing an arm. Jarle looked at Rasaol in dismay.

"How many more do we need to lose?" Jarle prodded. "Is this not proof enough that this entire endeavor was a mistake?"

"Mistake?" Niihlu approached, sheets of sloshy ice falling from his arms and covering the Nordruaut corpses. "More proof that he needed to be killed. But we did not need more proof, did we? Not after he killed her."

It was the end of the conversation for his old companion, and Niihlu marched off, looking for signs of a trail. Jarle sought wisdom from the king, hoping that Rasaol would speak reason. A tired shadow covered the man's face as he avoided making eye contact. He knew this was wrong, Jarle could feel it. There was an edge to this group as sharp as any axe. These Nordruaut no longer wanted to hunt for food or manage the land. The youngest in their party licked his lips as if thirsting to avenge their fallen comrades. Niihlu stared south, his eyes sharp as he sought a trail.

Rasaol, their king, seemed driven in an unnatural way, despite his exhaustion. It was as if a sickness had taken over them, and Jarle feared what they would wreak on Ehrde if set loose.

"Niihlu may be right," Rasaol said, peering at Jarle warily.

"We are hunters, old friend, not warriors," Jarle reminded his king. "This is not our way. Remember."

"We need to defend ourselves," Rasaol hissed. "That Fulk'han sneaks into Owenqua and kills our people! We can't let that rest."

"Yes, yes, we can," Jarle said.

"You would have us let this killer go free?" Niihlu asked, spinning on his heel, the enormous war axe raised high in anger. "After what he did to one of your own?"

"He survived judgment in battle," Jarle said, staring down Niihlu for the young man's failure. "I don't like it, but that is our way."

"I should have killed the monster," Niihlu growled.

"Yes," Jarle agreed. "As judgment in the challenge. You defeated him, but failed to kill him."

Rasaol moved quickly to keep Niihlu from swinging. He placed a hand on the young man's chest, but jerked it back as frost instantly covered it.

"Maybe there needs to be another challenge," Niihlu said hungrily.

"You see, my king. Do you see?" Jarle accused. "This is the champion you have chosen? Is this the path you have chosen, too?"

"Bah," Niihlu grunted, letting the axe fall. Soft snow hardened as the blade struck, shattering like ice under its weight.

Rasaol wouldn't answer, merely looking between Jarle and Niihlu. It was as if the man knew the right course of action, but was too far down the wrong path to turn around. Jarle shook his head and marched to his hairy bokeen mount.

"Where are you going?" Rasaol asked.

"I'm returning to Owenqua," Jarle called out over his shoulder. "I'm going to convince others of your foolishness, and put a stop to this before it's too late."

Without making contact, Rasaol held out a hand to keep Niihlu back. The young man was tense with indecision, his muscles ready to leap forward, but a sliver of respect for the king remained.

"Why do I not kill him as well?" Niihlu asked.

"Because we are going with him," Rasaol commanded. "Everyone, mount up."

"But the hunt! The kill?" Niihlu said, spit from his indignation frosting on his lips.

"You will get your chance, champion," Rasaol said calmingly. "But this is our one opportunity to blame Jarle for all of it."

* * * *

Unsel

Vars remembered being very young when his father, Vasil, was killed. It had been a friendly joust between Unsel and Melkier. He wasn't supposed to be there, but just had to see his dad win, and snuck under the risers to watch between legs. His father looked powerful on his dark steed, both wearing plate armor with gold leaves. He had the honor of carrying Princess Isabelle's kerchief, and waved it high to many cheers. The Melkier knight appeared almost as powerful, wearing rich colors of green and blue atop his pale mount. When the flag lowered, young Vars watched intently to see which lance struck first. The Melkier knight held his lance low, his father's was level to his opponent's chest. There was an odd moment of silence, either the anticipation of the crowd, or his focus blocking out all sound. He had to look back and forth quickly, unable to see both of them at the same time until the lance tips were close enough to scratch the horses' noses. There was a flash of blue light, and a sound so horrific he would never forget it. The crash of lance to armor, the squelching sound of blood, the whines of horses, and the screams.

Now that sound was all around him again, and it was unending. He opened his eyes, the memory of his father's death appearing between blinks, a reminder of why he was here. He swung his broadsword wide, the flat of the blade striking what remained of his gargoyle opponent. Thick oily fluid sprayed out as his sword swung through the creature. He watched it collapse into a green puddle that he kicked over the sinkhole ledge. Two men cried out from high overhead, and he blinked.

Young Vars had been watching his father joust ever since he could sneak out of the keep. He'd seen men die at the lance many times, and often thought the loser deserved death for being weak. He was used to death in its many forms. Vars had even seen a display of sparks as swords met. He'd never seen a flash of blue light, and knew what it had to be, even as he ran toward his father's body.

Vars opened his eyes to see two men, high in the air, their arms flailing. They were already lost, for it would be impossible to live through a fall from that distance. Even so, he watched with a morbid curiosity as one was caught between two gargoyle creatures. They drifted to each side of him, almost casually, both grabbing an arm and a leg. The gargoyles' feet met and then pushed away, quartering the man and ending his screams. Blink.

The Melkier soldier had been absolutely still, but Vasil twitched, his body holding onto life, which meant he'd won. Vars elbowed his way between the long legs of useless adults and dropped to his knees beside his father. The shaft of a lance protruded from Vasil's chest as if someone had planted a tree. Large men hovered over the body, fighting to remove the weapon. It had his father pinned to the ground like a specimen.

He opened his eyes and ran forward with his sword upright, as if preparing to slice the nearest gargoyle like bread. As he cut into the creature, the wound opened for but a second. The gargoyle was twice his size, and he'd seen them close their bodies around swords to hold them firm while killing their attacker. He leapt forward fast enough to land inside the creature as it tried to envelop him. Vars lifted the sword up into the monster's head and sliced through its back. The gargoyle spilt in half, dropping him to the ground. He jumped, spinning about while holding out his sword. Gargoyle remains spread wildly.

"I didn't command you to fall back," he shouted to nervous soldiers. "If an old man can kill these monsters, so can you." Blink.

"Son." Vasil gripped the back of young Vars's neck. His voice was barely perceptible through bubbles of blood.

"You won, Father," Vars answered.

Vasil blinked once in acknowledgement, as much of a smile as Vars had ever seen from the man. His legs had stopped moving altogether, but his chest and arms shuddered. The grip on his neck shook Vars painfully, but he didn't call out, even as the man pulled him forward.

"It was the magics killed me," Vasil gurgled. "Make it right, son."

Vars knew that men didn't always realize they were wielders, that the magic would come out in the direst of circumstances. Dangerous and uncontrolled like lightning from a storm. Wielding the magics could be every bit as frightening as the battle that aroused them. A soldier near the edge of the sinkhole shouted in surprise as yellow sparks flew from his hands and burned holes through his attacker. Vars sprinted toward them, his sword held high, and swung with all his might. The blade removed the virgin wielder's head from his body. His swing carried Vars around full circle to face the gargoyle, even as the sparks turned it into a thick mist. He blinked.

Vasil was lost to the magics, killed representing the country he'd loved. In later years, Queen Isabelle had suppressed magics like any good ruler, but not long after the birth of her daughter, she'd become soft. The laws opened enough to allow the tiniest bit of magic in, like welcoming a tiny spider into your house. Not only had Unsel been under constant threat by magic, but magic had killed his father, and his son. Isabelle had no longer been a fit leader when he'd killed her; she had deserved the justice he'd delivered. No man should outlive his son, and he almost hadn't. But in the name of his father, and his son, he'd agreed to the Dark Vivek's offer. He'd agreed to live.

Vars opened his eyes and looked over the ledge of the sink-hole. A giant, watery fist pounded in the depths far below the battleground, taking long minutes to pull free. A new hole would emerge within the hour, right beneath his feet. Brave men were losing their lives to enormous mystical gargoyles—maybe a third of Unsel's army had already been defeated by the beasts. In the hazy distance, he saw the great castle of Unsel. Maybe, with enough misdirection, he could destroy half of Unsel's army. More than he'd promised, and the least they deserved.

* * * *

"With Jaden, we've got twenty-one able wielders. We leave the two oldest, and the two youngest behind." Rook was pacing, dictating his thoughts to Janda, Nikkola, and Jaden. "When we arrive, we'll have ten wielders who can throw crap at the monsters. Five who can cast defensive spells. Two who can... I don't know, what can they do?"

"Simon can heal," Nikkola said hopefully.

"He's good with illness, a natural," Jaden said, his nasally tone disappointed. "I've been trying to teach him what I know of mending physical damage, but he's too afraid to cast and relies too much on instinct. Maybe the battle will break down that wall."

Rook merely nodded, grateful for Jaden's efforts but too distracted to acknowledge further. "And his brother?"

"I tried talking him out of coming," Janda said. "He's almost smaller than I am, and he doesn't talk... Well, not to people."

"He communes with animals," Jaden confirmed. "It's a rare gift, useful for information gathering, but I don't know what else he can do."

"At this point, I'll take what I can get," Rook said, trying to keep the disappointment from his voice. There just weren't enough to handle Vars and his soldiers, the gargoyles, and anything else they might meet on the way.

"What about Jackson?" Jaden asked. "She's got power to spare!"

"She's also sixteen," Rook said firmly, shaking his head. "I won't do it. She's too young."

"I've been fighting since before I was sixteen," Jaden disagreed.

"Where, Jaden?" Rook asked. "Fighting who?"

"I...I don't..." Jaden stared off into the distance, his eyes glassy and lost to memories impossible for him to grasp.

"If you've been fighting for that long, you know what war can do to children. Let's avoid that sort of exposure at all costs," Rook said finally. "She stays. Just in case something goes wrong, they'll need her here."

Jaden nodded reluctantly.

"We should group them, one defensive wielder with every two offensive wielders," Rook declared. "Jaden, Janda, and Nikkola with me, and one offensive wielder with the other two. Jaden, can you pair the others up? I think you have the best knowledge of whose spells would work well together."

"Sure," Jaden said, excitedly. "I—"

"But not the people," Janda interrupted. "Let my sister help. She knows who likes each other, and who doesn't."

"Right." Jaden grimaced. "But, I—"

"*Mom!*" Kala yelled from the entrance.

Nikkola stood, always attentive to her daughter's needs, especially now. Rook had noticed the worry hadn't left her face after they'd successfully restrained Scar. Her hands wrung out the air like a wet towel, nervously squeezing until Kala ran into her arms. She knelt beside her daughter and brushed long black hair from her round face.

"Mom," Kala said, her words high and fast. "Scar says it's time. Scar says you need to leave now!"

"What?" Rook asked, walking over to kneel by the girl.

"He's not upset anymore." Her eyes flashed blue and she stared off. "Scar's sorry he scared you, but you need to leave now. He's coming! Everything is coming!"

"Have you been out there?" Nikkola asked her daughter, grabbing her arm firmly. "I told you to stay away from that monster!"

Rook pulled Nikkola's hand from the girl's arm and pulled it away. He looked at Kala's eyes, focusing through the blue light to see the pupils, to see her sincerity. The young girl swallowed hard, her hands clenched in brave fists. She'd been out to see Scar, and knew she would get in trouble if she brought this message.

"It's going to be bad, Mr. Rook," she said sadly.

"I believe you," he said with a sigh. "Thank you, Kala, this was a very brave thing to do." He stood, his hand on the young girl's shoulder. "You heard her, it's time to go, now! Jaden, tell everyone to suit up. They have fifteen minutes."

"I should stay," Nikkola said.

"You should go," Kala disagreed, hugging her mom with all the ferocity a twelve-year-old could fit into a hug. "But please come back."

"Stay away from that monster," Nikkola said, pulling her daughter away to stare into her eyes. "Promise me."

"I promise," she said, looking at the ground.

"Let me see your fingers," she asked. "Are they crossed?"

"I'll go hide in our home," Kala called out, running between Jaden's legs as he rushed out the door.

"You're pale," Janda said to Nikkola. "Are you okay?"

"Kala's a bad liar," Nikkola said. "She's headed to that dog right now."

"And she's probably safer than the rest of us," Rook said.

50

A thudding finally woke Dallow. It was like a distant neighbor beating dust out of a rug. As he became more conscious, it sounded closer, steadier, like the wheels of a book cart rolling over tile. He was in a library, and that book cart would be better than other alternatives. But as the thudding became painful, Dallow realized it was the beating of a heart. His heart. It thrummed on the back of his skull like hooves clopping along hard stone. He lurched forward to vomit, but then remembered, books! He swallowed the acid down and returned to his bed of books, hoping his blocky mattress was the books-read pile. Dallow concentrated, trying to remember what had happened.

After hours of non-stop absorption, he'd read through hundreds of delicious books. He wished he could actually eat them, he was starving, and he had to pee, but both could wait. This brief moment of learning was the absolute best time he'd had on this adventure. It was the very thing he'd hoped for most. He'd absorbed old books in Gressmore Towers, but most of that was lost when Angst broke time. Returning that mage city to the past, as though they'd never found it, had forced two sets of memories to overlap. It was confusing to the others, and physically hurt all of them, but worst of all was the vast knowledge lost. This time, in this library, was making up for that and more.

His consumption of information within the books began slowly as he struggled to understand the unique dialect of Acratic. As he became more comfortable with it, his pace quickened. Some books couldn't be read at all, the years having turned the paper inside to dust. They were thrown toward the door, their pages hissing like sand on impact. The official read pile was stacked neatly to his left. To his right were books that needed to be kept and transferred to Unsel for other scholars. His friends might argue about the additional load, but after everything he'd sacrificed, they wouldn't argue much.

Without the use of his eyes, the process of sorting and stacking books took much longer than absorbing them. He reached for one that seemed to hover at an odd angle. He pulled the book, freeing it with a grotesque crunch that made him wince and wonder. With the book in his lap, he reached forward and grasped a bony arm covered in dusty cloth. He didn't bother pulling his hand back. What would be the point?

"You poor thing," Dallow said aloud. "I would guess your one consolation is dying in a pile of books. It's how I would want to die. I've never told anyone, they would think it crazy, but I bet you would understand."

He settled back, resting the hefty volume on his lap. He didn't dare open it for fear the pages would crumble to dust. "I hope you don't mind," he said to the corpse. "This book must be important for you to die with it in your hands. Maybe I can save what's in these pages."

His relationship with books was one few would understand. It was the pleasure of getting lost in a good story, those books with characters so relatable you missed them when you were finished reading. They were like friends or lovers, and he had the ability to visit with them whenever he wanted. Even tomes of reference and history books had their own personality that made them a pleasure to call on when he needed to remember something. Dallow couldn't have been more grateful for his gift, and smiled broadly when he placed both hands on the freed volume. With a deep breath, he drew the words in, absorbing them through his hands, along his arms, and into his head. Pages unfolded in his mind's eye like thoughts and ideas.

CHAPTER FIFTY

"No!" He jerked both hands away. Dallow scrambled to his feet, sliding on books as he reached for the nearby table. His throat constricted and his mouth dried. "It can't be you. Angst!" he called out, his voice shaky. "Hector!"

Nobody replied, not even an echo. His hands shook as he gripped the book and braced himself to absorb the rest.

"Oh no!" His heart leaped in his chest. "Please, no. I'm so sorry. I've got to tell them. I've got to let Angst know."

He took hurried steps forward, trying to remember his path here and cursing his blindness. His foot came down on a thick leather cover whose contents were dust. The binding slipped underfoot, he fell back, and his head met the table with a loud crack.

Dallow winced at the memory, and his heart raced. How long had he been unconscious? Minutes? Hours? He needed to get out of the library, find the others, and tell Angst. Everywhere he placed his foot was met with slippery covers and dusty piles. He couldn't afford to fall again. It was so frustrating, he wanted to throw the book in his hand.

"Dallow?" He heard Hector jogging toward him. "Eew. Look who you uncovered. She's not pretty."

"Don't," Dallow said darkly, letting go of the table and gripping his stomach. He was dizzy from the blow to his head, and wanted nothing more than to vomit. "I'll explain later, just get me out of here... We need to go."

"Are you sure?" Hector asked. "You look sick."

"Hit my head on the table rushing out to warn Angst," Dallow said, his voice unsteady.

"Warn Angst about what?" Hector asked.

"It's all been a lie," Dallow said. "The curse was put there to trap the mermen and separate them from the mermaids. That giant monster Angst wants to kill so badly? That thing isn't trying to kill the mermaids, it's working with them. It's waiting for the mermen to break free!"

"What?" Hector asked, helping Dallow over the pile of books. "How?"

"Jormbrinder," he said. "The foci can't be moved. It's the source of the curse. That foci is the only thing keeping the shield up!"

* * * *

"It looks like it's broken," Angst said, eyeing the single dagger that pointed upward at the dome. "Half is missing, and what's it pointing to?"

The monument holding the dagger was familiar, but ill kept, as if its time at the bottom of the ocean had prematurely aged it. The dagger, if that was what you would call it, had a long handle and a triangular golden blade. A fixture that could've held a second dagger was empty. He reached for the hilt.

"No, don't!" Tarness and Tori cried out.

Angst jerked his hand back in shock. He reached out again and they shouted once more. He kept doing it until they figured it out.

"You're a jerk," Tarness said.

"Well," he replied in frustration. "What are you two so afraid of?"

"Don't you remember last time, Angst?" Tarness asked, pointing a finger like an angry parent. "You almost died holding two of those things at once. Messing around in Gressmore Towers with Chryslaenor in one hand and Dulgirgraut in the other? I had to knock you senseless so they could sort you out."

"Oh yeah," he said, walking away to set Dulgirgraut down several feet away. "I completely forgot."

"Old people," Tori said to Faeoris with a sigh.

"Look, if it makes you feel better," Angst suggested, "stand on the other side of the monument. If you see any sign of trouble when I pick it up, you can knock me out again."

Tarness nodded and positioned himself.

"How is this even a plan?" Victoria asked.

"Shh," Faeoris said, moving to stand behind Angst. "I want to see this."

"Where are you going?" Angst asked her.

"Getting a better view," she explained, her weapon sheathed and hands at her sides.

Angst wiggled his butt, and she smacked it, making him jump. Dulgirgraut hummed warningly in his head, urging him not to proceed. He asked the blade why and merely saw an image of the city.

"Thanks, Dulgirgraut," he muttered under his breath. "Vague and useless, like always."

Without another word, Angst reached out to the long dagger, and Tarness punched him in the mouth. He flew back into Faeoris's arms. It hadn't been hard enough to knock Angst out, but he saw a few spots in front of his eyes. They cleared to reveal Faeoris sucking in her lips and trying not to laugh. The tip of his nose stung, and his eyes watered. Great, now he was crying in front of her.

"Whad was dat for?" Angst cried out.

"Sorry," Tarness said. "I was nervous."

Faeoris turned him around and inspected his face. "It's not broken.

"Id hurts," he said, sneezing several times until a clot of blood landed on the ground.

"See, you'll be fine, hero," she teased, turning him back around.

He sniffed deeply, wiping blood from his nose onto his tunic. He thought he heard Dulgirgraut laughing, but it was hard to tell through his ringing ears.

"You step back," Angst said, sniffling and waving Tarness away.

His friend took several steps back, looking decidedly sheepish.

"Shouldn't we at least wait for Hector and Dallow?" Tori asked.

Now that he was embarrassed and irritated, he didn't see the need to wait. "No," Angst said, placing a hand on the foci and lifting it.

"*JORMBRINDER: THE EXCEPTION*" rang in his mind

like a storm of bells. It was so noisy it almost hurt. There was resistance pulling the blade away from the monument. At first, it felt like tearing paper, but as it got further away it felt more like linen, and then leather, and finally wood. The litany of bells became louder, much louder than the shouts and warnings from his friends and Dulgirgraut. He felt his shoulders being shaken, but now he couldn't stop. This poor foci had been trapped here for thousands of years, it wanted out, and it was time to set it free. Without realizing it, he'd struggled until his hand and the blade were pointed at the ground. He could hear his friends clearly now, and saw that Dallow and Hector were back.

"Hey, just in time," he said. "You okay, Dallow? You don't look so good."

"You didn't do it already, did you?" his blind friend asked, worry apparent on his face.

"Do what?" Angst asked.

"The foci, Jormbrinder," he said hurriedly. "Don't pick it up!"

"I already did," Angst said. "See, I'm fine. It's not even a complete foci, just half. What could possibly go wrong now?"

"I hate you," Hector said, lowering his face to his hand.

There was a loud crack from high above, the sound a frozen lake makes when you're standing in the middle and it's a little too warm outside. The noise became louder, and they all looked up to watch a spiderweb spread across the dome, starting at their point of entry. It reached out, more noisy cracks that screeched and ground together. Water began dripping down like the gentlest of spring rains.

"Angst?" Tori yelled. "We need to get out!"

"I think I know where Rose is," he said loudly over the oncoming storm. "I can feel it now! She has the other half of the foci. We can follow her!"

"Fine, let's go," Hector said.

Angst hurried to Dulgirgraut and held out a hand. Remembering what had happened the last time he held two foci, he attempted to drop Jormbrinder before wielding his foci.

"Quit messing around, Angst," Hector snapped.

"I can't pick up Dulgirgraut," he said. "Because I can't let go of Jormbrinder. It's stuck!"

51

"You couldn't wait for five minutes!" Hector growled, shaking water out of his hair like a gray sheep dog.

"I waited ten!" Angst blinked water from his eyes as the sprinkle became a shower.

"He picked it up already?" Dallow cried out. "That's what was holding the shield up!"

"I sort of figured that out," Angst said. "How do I fix this? At least until we get out!"

"You don't, but at least we know where to find Rose." Dallow waved a hand to hurry them along, his other tightly gripping a book. "Angst, you're going to have to bring both."

"But..." he said, his words as reluctant as his muscles, remembering the waves of pain the last time he'd held two foci simultaneously.

"It's not a full foci," Dallow explained. "It's only half. There are supposed to be two daggers. And this foci...it's different."

"Everyone really can read my mind," Angst said in surprise.

"It's not that hard." Dallow smirked. His eyes were bright, squinting beneath the blue kerchief. "Trust me, Angst. I learned so much in that library. Let's use some of it."

Water was already rising above their ankles, as the city around them continued imploding. Angst looked up to see the hole in the dome, like a crack in a window from a stone he'd thrown. He hated to think who would admonish him for breaking a window that large. Daylight shone through freely, no longer filtered by the shield. The waterfall circling the dome shrank in diameter, creeping toward the rapidly widening hole in the dome's center. Noisy ocean frothed at the edges, pouring through the crack like the closing mouth of a rabid dog.

Aerella had once warned him not to wield another, giving him the impression that disaster of the worst kind would follow if he did. He'd thought she meant Dulgirgraut, but maybe she'd been talking about Jormbrinder all along. It was a mess, but certainly not a disaster, right? As he knelt beside Dulgirgraut, the blade glowed brightly and his hand shook over the hilt. His friends' faces were filled with apprehension. He listened for voices of warning, songs or shouts. His eyes met Victoria's.

"Do it," she said firmly.

Angst gripped Dulgirgraut's hilt. Jormbrinder's single blade sparked with a noisy pop, and a marble-sized ball of light shot up ten feet into the air before drifting slowly to their feet. It whistled as it fell and hissed on landing before dying in the water. Angst stood upright, looking at the blade, and then his friends. He closed his eyes and sighed in relief.

"Pretty," Faeoris acknowledged, nodding.

"Can we go now?" Hector said with a deep sigh.

"I still can't let go." Angst tried shaking the dagger off his hand, but it was reluctant to leave. After returning Dulgirgraut to his back, he was able to move the blade from hand to hand, but he couldn't set it down or throw it off.

"You and Jormbrinder are like the ends of a magnet," Dallow tried to explain, mouthing the words over the sheets of water cascading down around them. "Just put it somewhere out of the way. We'll figure it out later."

Angst rolled it along his arm and down his ribs until it clung to his hip, which was exactly where he would've put any three-foot-long triangular golden dagger. The flood of ocean was already knee high when they heard it: crashing sounds in the water. Not the random splashes of old buildings tumbling, or even the now-constant flow of water pouring in. This had a cadence, like horses or elephants crossing a rushing creek.

"Mermen!" Hector cried out, wielding two hooked swords.

Thousands of the little monsters ran toward them down a wide street. They crawled over each other like bees in a hive. An angry, hungry mob, with mouths full of long, thin teeth open wide in silent screams. Angst was sure his heart stopped, and had to remind himself to breathe. A quick glance at his friends showed they mirrored his fear—even Faeoris swallowed hard and gripped her sword tightly. It wasn't just the legion of creatures rushing toward them with their silent war cries. The mermen grew with every step. Like sponges dried out by their long entrapment, they soaked the ocean in with a thirst greater than the desert. Their muscles bulged, heads grew, torsos lengthened until most were larger than Tarness. Their charge quickened when they were at full height—seven feet of angry muscle, desperate for revenge and, by the look of their bared teeth, hungry for blood. Even before Hector could launch into the air, Faeoris spread her wings and flew forward. She picked up the nearest merman and spun him around at a nauseating speed before tossing him at others. Five fell into the water on impact and didn't get back up.

"I don't understand," Angst said, grabbing Dulgirgraut. "We saved them. It was an accident, but still, we freed them."

"Angst," Dallow said, placing a hand on his shoulder. "We need to leave."

"No," Angst cried out. His heart felt as if someone had squeezed it, and his throat was dry. "They shouldn't be attacking! Did she lie to me? I thought—"

"Angst." Tori pulled him to face her. "We need to get to the cave. Once you picked up that dagger, some blocks went away. I'm starting to see our futures more clearly. We won't make it if we stay."

"Jormbrinder the Exception," Dallow explained. "It works differently than the others. I read—"

"Not now, Dallow," she said. "Angst, it's going to be dangerous, but it's the only way. We have to go."

He nodded, but didn't really listen. Everything was numb, his hands shook slightly, and he had that empty feeling you get from a loved one's death or a breakup caused by betrayal. He barely noticed Tarness rush forward and call out for Hector and Faeoris to retreat. Tori hooked an arm around his and Faeoris grabbed his other arm. Together they pulled him down a street. He just stared at the water, his feet dragging along the ground. Moyra loved him, she'd said so, and he'd felt it. He'd been so sure their relationship was different. Faeoris and Tori dragged him around a corner. The water was now waist high and they slowed, each step a chore. Tarness and Hector killed any creature within arm's reach. Everyone took turns shouting at him, Tori slapped him, but he just didn't care.

The darkness and pain in his mind overwhelmed him, until he heard it. The sound was like someone had picked up the ocean and dropped it. They all looked up to see the giant creature, still outside the dome but pressed against the remaining shield. Dozens of hairy feelers reached through as if trying to widen the crack, pull the beast in, or both. They stopped for a brief moment, stunned by its enormity, the unfathomable size of the oldest creature in Ehrde. Angst stood, wielding a glowing Dulgirgraut, and pointed it at the monster.

"Angst," Dallow said. "I know what it is. It cannot be killed."

"You mean it hasn't been killed," he said bitterly.

"Even if you could, it would only end in our deaths," Dallow pleaded. "We have to get out. We have to save Rose."

Pain washed over him, along with a thirst for revenge, a hunger to understand. He looked at Dallow and nodded, burying as much of it as he could. "For Rose."

"We'll have to swim for it," Tori said.

Something gripped his ankle, and he drove Dulgirgraut straight down before anything could bite. A merman's body floated up, surrounded by dark, cloudy water. Its body was pulled aside to make room for the next attacker.

"Everyone down there," he yelled. "I'll hold them off."

"We both will," Faeoris said with a wicked grin.

Nobody argued. The water showering them had reached the bottom of their ribs and would be over their heads in minutes. Angst glanced up. Half the monster's body was now inside the city. Maybe, if he held out long enough, he would have his chance. Other creatures were diving through the hole—distant, tiny bodies. Were the mermaids coming to attack too? His attention returned to the mob of mermen. He reached out to feel for their bones, to hold them in place. With Dulgirgraut, he should've been able to stop hundreds, but could only find the nearest dozen. His foci distantly informed him that Jormbrinder was muffling everything, but he'd already figured that out.

"Go, now!" he shouted. It was like standing under a waterfall. When he lowered his head to take in deep gulps of air, salt water poured over his ears and around his mouth.

Tori took the lead, followed closely by Hector, who swam with Dallow. Faeoris was in a berserker rage, her longsword shredding every merman with such ferocity Angst couldn't help but shudder. He called for her, but she wouldn't stop. His new friend screamed a battle cry he didn't understand and cut a merman in half at his chest. He was in awe of her raw strength, and her fury. Her mouth was pulled back in a grimace that was hard to distinguish from a grin.

Angst struggled to wield air, but couldn't even form an entire bubble around her. Instead, he wrapped it around her waist and chest, like hugging her from behind, and with a lurch, jerked her back toward him. She landed beside him with a great splash, her face covered in blood, and her teeth bared in rage. He could tell that she fought every urge to kill him for pulling her out of the battle. Hers was a wild sort of beauty, a fierceness that was exciting and dangerous, and the sight of her created a crack in his shroud of pain. She shook her head at his gawking, but couldn't help but smirk.

"Go," he pleaded. "Please!"

"Only with you," she said firmly.

With a nod, he sheathed Dulgirgraut on his back and took a deep breath to follow her. They both dove in, fighting the waves and a shifting current to gain momentum. There was just enough light from the opening above to see the cave entrance. She was a natural swimmer, her long legs kicking fast. Those legs in front of him and the monsters behind were all the encouragement Angst needed to try to keep up. Faeoris turned around to look back, checking on him constantly as they progressed. He was desperate to breathe; Moyra had spoiled him. The dim light ahead almost eased his racing heart and aching lungs. He nodded at Faeoris, urging her to swim on. As she kicked faster, webbed hands wrapped around his ankle. His body jerked back, and he cried out, losing the last of his precious air.

52

Unsel

The wielders were forced to slow as they approached the castle, weaving through a mass evacuation. A chaotic jumble of frightened people converged on them, carrying everything from crying babies, to confused pets, to armfuls of valuables, all hurrying away from the castle as quickly as they could, like animals fleeing a forest fire. Rook hadn't expected this, and it was arduous moving through the crowds. He wanted to hurry—that was the whole point of riding the swifen—but he didn't want to injure the people they were supposed to protect. Rook ran a hand through his light, curly hair, trying hard not to pull it out. These people should've left weeks ago under the safety of an escort.

Where was the plan? Sure, Alloria was hoping Angst and his friends would make it back before the sinkholes and gargoyles arrived, but that hope hung by a spider's thread. What if they didn't make it back in time, or battled with something even worse, or were dead? Alloria wasn't a leader, she was a burden on the crown.

The earthquakes were only minutes apart when the group finally reached the castle grounds. With every shake, stone fell from the castle walls as if it were shedding rocky tears. This was his home, his castle, and it made him furious. He looked around at the nervous wielders, a dozen men and women of all ages, uncomfortable in their new mage armor, each holding a different sort of fear in their eyes.

"They need to hear something," Janda whispered over her shoulder, her red hair brushing his face. "From their leader...from you."

"Right," he said with a sigh.

Rook was too upset, too distracted to be an inspiration. He dismounted Janda's lioness swifen and could almost feel all their eyes follow him. He made eye contact with each of them, looking for something. What he saw was death. It was that moment before battle he hated most, a rush of concern that some of his soldiers wouldn't make it. One, several, maybe all of them, and there was nothing he could do about it. Their training had been almost nonexistent, and none had fought in armor. Rook already felt he'd failed them, and wished nothing more than to die in their places, or even better, for nobody to die. He met each gaze and hoped his worry didn't show. None had the veteran reserve of old warriors, nor the fiery determination of young soldiers. They barely had hope, and were drawing it from him with a leech's hunger.

He took a deep breath to speak when a quake knocked him off his feet. He scrambled from under a swifen, but couldn't stand. His teeth rattled, his head hurt, and he wondered if the earth beneath him would ever stop its violent rocking. He called out for Janda, but couldn't hear his own voice over the thundering crack. It sounded like a mountain splitting in two, a landslide that didn't end until the shaking stopped. Rook wanted to vomit, lie still, and maybe vomit some more. Shakily, he looked at Janda, who'd remained on her lioness swifen.

"On it," she said in reply to his look. She raced toward the noise, her mount charging down the empty street.

"That's not what I wanted," he called after her, too late. He'd just wanted to know that she was safe.

"I'll back her up," Jaden said and was soon on her tail.

Behind him, Rook heard whimpers and cries, but turned away. He didn't know what to tell them, too distracted by his own concern. She returned at a breakneck pace, sliding to a stop on the snowy ground. Janda leaped from her mount and into his embrace. She was crying uncontrollably, her pale complexion sheet white. Jaden arrived, his face drawn and his eyes stunned.

"What is it?" Rook asked. "Are you okay?"

"It's the castle," she said with a loud sniff. She buried her face in his shoulder.

"The west side of the castle is completely gone," Jaden said, his nasally voice quiet. "Everything has collapsed into a sink-hole."

Rook took a moment to hold Janda close as she sniffed her composure back. She stood straight, squaring her shoulders and nodding toward the others. They were in far worse shape—those not crying were pale with fear, some visibly shaking. How could they move forward like this? He didn't know what to say. Soldiers weren't supposed to cry; this was the time to be cold, and distant. This was when a soldier dug deep for strength and bravery. He looked at the pale old man and Janda's sister, Nikkola, who were fighting back tears, and that was when it struck him—they weren't soldiers. They were people fighting to save their homes, fighting for a better future. A life they'd only, barely, tasted. In spite of years of repression by the Unsel bureaucracy, they were giving their lives for their nation. These wielders, these volunteers, weren't soldiers, they were patriots. They thrived on hope, and there was no better hope than a hero.

Rook reached out, gripping shoulders, pulling some in for hugs, wiping tears away with his thumb. They needed to hurry, but they wouldn't even be able to defend themselves in this state. After making a connection with each of them, he beckoned them closer. Jaden stood aside until Janda drew the young man in, and all the wielders huddled together around Rook. A human break from the cold and the chaos.

"A long time ago," Rook began, "it wasn't only legal to wield magic, it was encouraged. Wielders were the heroes, and they were called zyn'ights. They wore armor just like yours, just like Angst's, and they protected Unsel from the monsters. The monsters left, the magic was hidden away, and foolishly, Unsel forgot. Zyn'ights became myths, legends, almost lost forever, until Angst."

He saw proud smiles, and heads nodding. Janda gripped his arm encouragingly.

"All his life, Angst wanted to be that hero, to be a knight for Unsel. The queen was not a fan, and I'm sure we've all heard the reasons." There were several chuckles and shoulders relaxed. "Angst trained with soldiers when he was young, so Queen Isabelle hid him away in the cellar. He got old, like we all do. Too old to be a knight, too old to run off and be a hero. And when the monsters came back, he could've stayed in that cellar, but he didn't. Angst wielded that giant sword, and he fought like it mattered."

He pulled back from the group a little, his voice becoming louder.

"From Fulk'han to Unsel, he fought the monsters, even giving up his sword to save us," he said, louder still. "And the queen tried to hide him away again, giving him land far away from the castle, where our homes are now. That still didn't stop him! The monsters came again, destroying our coast. Not many know this, but Angst was dying. Giving up that sword almost killed him, but he knew the monsters were coming, and so he went to get another sword."

The wielders looked at each other with surprise and wonder.

"He did this because he believes in Unsel, because he believes in your future, and because he is a hero," Rook shouted. "And just like the last time monsters attacked Unsel, the last time you fought to defend your homes, Angst will race through this city to save the day! He's coming. I swear to you, he's coming!"

Several younger wielders muttered "yes" under their breaths. The old ones nodded firmly, their eyes wide with hope. Even Janda was caught up in the moment, her face beaming with pride.

"We're going to be right there with him! Protecting this castle and protecting Unsel! You're going to show Unsel what it means to be a zyn'ight again," he said firmly. "And when we see Angst and our true queen coming, we're going to clear a path!"

* * * *

"Are you sure this is a good idea?" Maarja asked, her low voice panicked after the longest quake yet. "We told Heather we would protect her."

"There is nobody left to protect her from," Jintorich squeaked. "The castle is the last place a pregnant human should be, right?"

"Right," Maarja said, not completely convinced. She struggled to keep up with her friend's short legs; her own felt shaky and weak. "But shouldn't we have at least seen her home?"

Jintorich jumped to one side as a stone fell from the ceiling. He bounced off a wall and rolled to one knee, his staff held out in front of him. She was amazed at his perceptiveness—he'd moved faster than she would've thought possible from a danger he couldn't have seen. The little Meldusian led her to a wide hallway before stopping. She stood upright and stretched, breathing in deeply. He looked around, his hands held out as though sensing the air and the earth.

"The wife of Angst said she was safe, and that we were needed in battle," he said with wide eyes. "And I believe her."

"I was convinced too. But now that we're away, I remember how she influenced Jaden," Maarja said. "I don't know if she encouraged us—"

"Maarja, Jintorich!" Rook called.

Eighteen men and women approached, all wearing armor similar to Angst's, except theirs shone silver. Strong breastplates protected their chests, dangling with chainmail that covered lazy bellies. Much of their armor appeared pointless. Wide gaps behind arms and legs made it lighter and wide open to attack.

They looked more like a stew of random vegetables than a troupe of hardened warriors. Old men, young women, boys, and girls, filled with a rush of bravado hiding a deeper fear. They couldn't do this alone.

"Young Rook," Jintorich said, sounding pleased. "How may we be at your service?"

"These wielders are going to clear a path for Angst," Rook said. "They'll fight the gargoyles so he can stop the sinkholes!"

Maarja could sense he wasn't being completely honest. His mouth was tight, he swallowed hard, and looked away from his 'soldiers.'

"Are you sure?" she asked.

"I believe in Angst," he said firmly, and that wasn't a lie.

Jintorich faced her with his curious black eyes, whisking light eyebrow hairs over his bulging forehead as he nodded. She wanted more answers, but knew enough not to question a leader at the heady edge of battle with a following so tenuous. She couldn't read her little friend's mind, she barely understood him at times, but she did understand the smirk that rose up his cheek.

"That sounds fun," Maarja said with a smile that made several step back. "We shall join you in battle!"

"This is not your fight," Rook said. "You should seek safety."

"We are allies," Jintorich said, squeaking with conviction. "Your fight is ours."

Maarja nodded once.

Rook's eyebrows rose and his eyes widened, but he nodded in appreciation. "The west side of the castle has been destroyed by sinkholes, we are headed there now."

"Then lead us," Maarja said. "We will fight together."

* * * *

The shaking had stopped, and with an unceremonious grunt, Heather crawled out from under Princess Victoria's vanity. Jagged splinters from a toppled bookshelf spread across the floor, mingling with glass from a broken mirror. She walked across the room, careful to avoid the rubble left behind by the quake. The air was filled with a haze of dust. She coughed and wiped it from her face, only to feel the dampness of tears. Heather feared what the violence of that earthquake had done to her baby. She waited, her lip trembling, until she felt movement, a lot of it.

"I'm sorry," she said to her belly, rubbing it in relief. "Were you napping?"

Heather laughed at herself as she wiped tears away. What a mess she must be, with frazzled graying hair, pregnant belly, dusty clothes, and tear-streaked face. She brushed off her forest green dress and tried pushing her hair back into something more manageable. The vanity mirror had split in half, making an ugly gap in her reflection, right across her oversized belly. She sighed at the image and assured herself the princess's mirror must be cursed to make Heather appear so much older.

She made her way to the entrance of the room. The frame pinched the door, which could only be shoved wide enough to let a thin man through. She peeked out into the hallway to see that the corridor was abandoned and wondered if that nap had really been worth it. Especially since she hadn't finished sleeping—earthquakes were the least fun alarm ever. She jumped with a start as a nearby tapestry tore in its listing frame, ripping noisily until it fell into a mottled heap. Dusty stones crumbled from a spot in the ceiling like a tiny fountain, as if the castle were barely able to keep together.

There was no 'sucking in your gut' when pregnant, and she gasped for breath, lifting her belly protectively as she broached the doorway. It hurt, doorframe splinters scratching her stomach deep enough to draw blood. She cursed loudly as her bellybutton caught on something sharp, forcing her to jerk past the obstruction. With a whimper and a wheeze, Heather squeezed through. There should've been cheering at the miracle—she had just saved herself. Instead, the empty hallway echoed with the distant sounds of battle, and something else. A faint voice, a muffled whisper nearby. She peered up and down the wide hall to find that the only open door led to the queen's chamber.

Heather marched to it, not caring about the noise since she'd practically made birthing cries getting out of Victoria's room.

"What was that?" said a dusty voice.

"Nothing," Alloria said. "It's a mess out there, and you're wasting my time!"

"Don't speak to me that way, mortal," the other voice hissed and crackled. "Or I will burn you."

"You can't kill me," she said. "Not as long as he has my ring."

There was a loud roar like wind through a bonfire and light blazed through the doorway.

"Are you done?" Alloria snapped. "What do you want? I'm in a hurry."

"He is not what you think," the high voice said irritably.

"Angst?" she asked.

"Not the Al'eyrn," he said. "The one who calls himself Vivek. He tricks you."

"He saved me," Alloria replied, her words rushed. "That's all that matters."

"He will be your death," the voice hissed.

"I died long ago," she said sadly. "You only have one more chance to make your offer."

"Kill Angst," he commanded. "Kill the wielder, and I will be your ally."

"You will be my ally?" Alloria scoffed. "That's it?"

"Your ally with an army of dragons," he replied.

"And all I have to do is kill Angst?" she asked.

Heather pushed into the room. "This entire time, I just may have been hating the wrong princess."

53

Hector helped Faeoris, pulling her out of the murky depths by her hand. Light glistened off her scale-armored top and bare midriff; she was the only one who didn't look like a drowned rat. She gasped for air, but jerked her hand free to turn around and wade back in to her waist.

Faeoris put her head into the water and looked around. "Angst," she called, noisy bubbles forming around her face. She pulled her head out.

"He's coming," Tori said, her voice filled with worry. "I know it. I see it."

Faeoris shot her a look that would've knocked a grown man onto his back.

"I promise, he's coming," Tori said quietly. "Just be ready to help them."

As a group, they stepped back to keep above the rising water. One step, two steps, and then three. The cave stretched up, far beyond the dim glow from Dallow's staff. The distant sounds of havoc came from the darkness above. Angry thunder, crashing, screams, and unnatural crackling noises. Between each attack, there was silence and the sound of close breaths and echoing drips that counted down the moments Angst was gone.

"I'm going back in," Faeoris announced.

"All that's left is ocean," Dallow said, his eyes glowing white. "The waterfall has completely collapsed."

"You'd be going to your death," Victoria said.

"And if you really loved him," she said, "you'd be going with me."

Faeoris took a deep breath and bent over, only to jerk upright. A distant, silvery reflection swam up the cave toward them. She stepped back with her sword at the ready.

"Make room," they all heard Moyra say in their minds. *"Help me!"*

"I'll kill her!" Faeoris cried.

"No, don't," Tori said. "She just saved him, and she's keeping him alive."

Tarness shoved Faeoris aside to reach them, splashing with each step. Just as he had on the pirate ship, Tarness lifted them both with a grunt and pulled them from the waters. Angst's arms hung lifeless, one dragging Dulgirgraut listlessly. His eyes were shut, but his chest moved as Moyra continued breathing for him. Angry cuts bled freely along her sides and back.

"I do not know if he is breathing on his own," Moyra said, her voice quivering.

"Dallow," Hector urged. "She's pretty cut up. Can you heal them?"

"Like you wouldn't believe," Dallow said, a white aura shining brightly around his hands.

* * * *

Angst woke, coughing out water and taking in desperate gulps of air. His eyes opened to blurry spots of dim light, the familiar sounds of his friends, and the beautiful face of Moyra. He lay in her arms, exhausted, hurting, and helpless as a babe. His own breathing became easier as he watched ugly wounds on her face and neck close. Together, they become whole, healed, and he looked over his shoulder to see Dallow's proud face. His old friend clapped his hands together, pleased with his accomplishment. Angst would have to remember to thank him later, and ask what he'd learned about healing at the library. It must've been a lot, and he was sure to get an earful. Dallow deserved at least that.

Mermen had gotten him at the last second, the clawed hands dragging him down, his mouth filling with water instead of air. Through the panic, he'd known they would go after Faeoris next, and then the others. His lungs were already lost, half-filled with ocean. He'd been too scared and too weak to wield, so he'd flailed as best he could. He'd swung wildly with the sword as the mermen jerked back, staying out of reach, playing with their food. But, as he began to fade, she had come. Moyra rushed in, a fury of teeth and claws. She struck, fast as a barracuda, rending flesh and muscle with her shark-like teeth. She killed every merman waiting for Angst to die, and he'd passed out in a cloud of their blood.

"I should kill her," Faeoris said.

Moyra faced Faeoris with a look that said, do what you must. She bowed her head submissively, her shoulders drooping, and Angst could feel her heart race like a hummingbird. He lifted her chin with his thumb and forefinger. She stared at him, her eyes dark as the ocean at midnight, and filled with sadness and guilt. Moyra still held him protectively, reluctant to let go, and he knew he'd been right. She did love him.

"No," Angst replied gently, his voice low and scratchy. He felt like his heart was being ripped out, but maybe it helped, just a little, knowing he wasn't alone. "She risked everything to save me."

"But, she used you. She lied," Tori said. "This was all her fault. You said so!"

"No. No, it wasn't." He continued staring into Moyra's eyes until she rested a webbed hand on his cheek and his eyes shut. "We may never know everything that went into play to make this happen. I won't judge, I don't want that job. Do you?" He looked back at them. "Do any of you?"

All eyes turned away from his stern gaze.

She'd hurt him, and he was upset, and his heart was…well, it just wasn't right. Something inside told him this would be it, that he would never see her again. "Won't they come after you for helping me?"

"They are all dead," she said. *"Everyone nearby, all of them. I would not let them hurt you."*

"Thank you," Angst said.

"I am sorry," she said. *"I love you. I will make this right."*

"What do you mean?" he asked. She still held him, and as his strength returned, he started feeling embarrassed in her arms, but didn't think it was the right time to get up.

"There is one more thing you need to know, An-gst," she said. *"They are going to Unsel."*

"What?" he said, rolling off to kneel beside her in the water.

"They are of Water. We are her creatures. They can swim to Unsel now," she said. *"All of them."*

The cold from the water crept into his veins. Realization struck him with the force of his head being split in two. This had been Water's plan all along, and he hadn't seen any of it. The sinkholes weren't tearing their way through Unsel countryside just to destroy the castle. The sinkholes were a path, a waterway that connected the ocean straight to the castle. Not only was his home under attack by sinkholes and gargoyles, but soon by mermaids, mermen, and that giant monster.

"I am sorry, An-gst. I am so sorry." She shimmied into the water, wiggling out of Tarness's grasp.

"This isn't your fault, Moyra," he said. "There's no way all of this could be your fault."

"I will make this right," she said, diving into the cave and swimming away.

"No, please don't," he said to her.

"I am going to stop them!" she said, her voice distant and determined. *"I will be a hero, just like you."*

"There's nothing you can do! This isn't your fault!" Angst cried out in his mind. "Please come back. I..."

The cave was silent. Angst stood and turned around to face his friends. The looks on their faces said everything. It was at that moment he realized that he hadn't called out in his mind, he

407

had said it all out loud.

To his surprise, just like a best friend should, Victoria came to him. She wrapped her arms around him and gave him the most loving, understanding hug he'd ever needed. It was far, far more than he deserved, and, more than anything, he just wanted to weep on his friend's shoulder.

"You should've let me kill her," Faeoris said coldly, her sword sheathed and her arms crossed.

A thunderous sound echoed through the cavern, and Angst let out a sigh. He balled up all the remorse and pain, all the worry and fear, the guilt and anger, and used it to push forward. It was the only energy he had left. He pulled away from Tori, thanking her with a nod.

"There are other battles to fight," he said. "And we're going to go finish this now."

54

Dulgirgraut didn't make Angst invulnerable. He felt pain. All of it. The physical pain brought on by rampaging monsters, and the emotional pain that was his constant companion. He'd always known that pain drove him, that a certain amount of hurt was needed to push forward, to push beyond what he would normally be capable of. Right now, he felt very driven.

Angst's left hand was pinched painfully in Victoria's death grip, but he couldn't bring himself to ask her to loosen her hold. He'd dragged her through a nightmare, and he worried about her safety and even her sanity. A sore hand was a small price.

"I'm fine, Angst," she said between rapid breaths, almost hyperventilating.

"I'm not," Tarness said, close behind. "I wish someone would hold my hand."

Victoria flashed him a terse smile. Tarness winked, but his face showed the worry he suffered with the others. As they walked up the endless stairway, an uncomfortable electricity crept through their arms and into their skulls. Not only did it lift hairs, it pulled at skin. There was a buzz, a hum that rattled Angst's teeth. It was a creepy, malignant energy that made him want to run back down into the watery depths below and swim for freedom.

"We can probably slow down," Hector said, baring his teeth to the energy. "The water's stopped rising, and we've been hiking uphill for hours."

"We must be above sea level by now," Dallow said, out of breath, his hand on Hector's shoulder for guidance, a soggy book jammed under his armpit.

Everyone was soaked from head to toe. Victoria and Dallow shivered violently, Hector was paler than normal, Tarness had goosebumps, and Faeoris's brave face contradicted her wide, worried eyes. Victoria shook her head, wordlessly letting Angst know that they shouldn't stop. He let go of Tori's hand, and she frowned in concern.

"Just for a second, I promise," he said.

At his urging, Dulgirgraut glowed bright red, and, with more effort than it normally would've taken, thanks to Jormbrinder, the cave warmed. He eyed the single dagger stuck to his hip like a thorn in his side, dampening everything he tried to do with magic. Even communication with Dulgirgraut seemed muffled. How could he fight whatever was ahead under these conditions? Distant bangs and shouts echoed throughout their chamber, beating against the cave walls like rows of drums. His teeth chattered and his gut wrenched. There had to be a way to draw more power from the sword, or get rid of Jormbrinder.

"I know everyone is tired. It feels like we've been hiking up this cave forever," Angst said with a conviction he didn't feel. "Take a minute to breathe then we're going to carry on, because I can feel it, we're almost there."

"Are your adventures always like this?" Faeoris asked, looking at Angst intently. "My heart is racing, I feel..."

"Anxious?" he asked. "Excited?"

"That's it," she said, unable to stand still, bouncing on her toes like a runner before a race.

"Always." He nodded.

"Good," she said with a wicked little smirk. "I like it."

"Angst, we have to keep going," Victoria pleaded. "We only have a short window for everything to happen right."

"We're only stopping for a moment so I can think. Chryslaenor is close, I can feel it, but that's not all. There is...power ahead that I don't understand, and all I can get from Dulgirgraut is that we should leave. Jormbrinder isn't exactly a big helper." Angst took in a breath of thick cave air before sighing deeply. Victoria took his hand once more, gripping tightly. "I don't know if I can keep everyone safe. We're coming up on something powerful, and you don't all have one of these things to protect you. If it gets hairy in there, I need you to find a way out."

"We won't leave you!" Victoria promised.

"Agreed," Faeoris said, crossing her arms.

"Yes, you will!" Angst said sternly to both of them.

"Yes, we will," Hector agreed, his wolf-like gaze staring down anyone who disagreed. "I'll make sure everyone is out safely."

Angst nodded in gratitude.

Victoria looked at Angst then back at Hector. She chewed nervously on a lock of blond hair, and it was obvious she was unhappy with both of them.

"I don't approve," Faeoris stated firmly.

"Agreed," Victoria said with a nod. "There has to be a way we can stay together."

"I'm open to suggestions," Angst said with a smirk. "Your Majesties."

Victoria's shoulders dropped and Faeoris looked at him with wary, calculating eyes. Neither of them answered.

"Keep going," Victoria eventually said in frustration.

They continued, walking slowly up the cave passage within the glow of Dulgirgraut. The cave walls narrowed, forcing them into single file. Tarness and Faeoris crouched low, often shifting sideways as they approached turns and thin corridors. Angst held the giant sword out before him with one hand and held Victoria's hand with the other. They continued creeping upward, until the noise became louder, more frightening, and the energy palpable.

"Chryslaenor," Angst whispered. "Finally."

Victoria gripped even tighter, making his knuckles pop. The

way before them was bright, and Angst willed Dulgirgraut's reddish glow to fade. Even through Jormbrinder's dampening haze, Angst could sense the power in the air around them. It was hard to fathom the enormous amounts of magic being wielded. The energy made his jaw ache, as if there were too many teeth in his mouth. Someone was shouting in a language he couldn't understand over the roars of crashing waves and strange whooshing sounds. It seemed they were approaching madness. Over the noise of the battle came the faint sound of a woman's pained grunting. Rose. She sounded like she was fighting something, which meant she was alive. Angst took careful steps forward, listening intently.

The walls of the cavern entrance gave way, and Angst inched toward a corner. He pulled free from Victoria's grip, and she immediately held onto his shoulder so they peek around together.

The small cave path opened to an enormous room ten times larger than the maiden's courtyard, two training grounds, or even a field massive enough to produce grain for every family in the castle of Unsel. Twenty-foot marble statues, the size of elements, stood along the walls. Each statue was a different, horrific monster that strained to hold up an arched ceiling. A hundred yards away, at the opposite end of the room, titans battled. Water and Air clashed with storm and sea, throwing tornado at tsunami. Angst and Tori ducked their heads nervously as they tried to avoid being noticed between the attacks.

The cave floor was made of ten-foot square, pale marble tiles. Dust covered the tiles except for a footprint path that led to a stone slab. Rose lay prone on that table, Chryslaenor hovering over her horizontally. Black lightning spewed from the blade, biting along the edges of her arms and legs. She twitched at each lightning strike, but otherwise appeared asleep, or dead. A large diamond-shaped dagger—the other half of Jormbrinder—rested at her side, reflecting the light from the battle off its golden edges. Beside her stood a seven-foot tall bald man, his brow furrowed and his eyes shut in concentration as he mouthed words. He held his arms out, his fingers spread wide and aimed at the hovering sword.

"Do you see anything?" Faeoris asked loudly.

Everyone jumped, but no one seemed to notice, and they all relaxed.

"Everything," Angst said. "Dulgirgraut says a man is trying to force Rose to bond with Chryslaenor."

"She'll die!" Dallow said angrily.

"I won't let that happen," Angst said, placing a hand on his friend's shoulder. "I promise."

"What are you going to do?" Hector asked.

The last time he'd fought an element, he'd lost. Fire had thrown a sun at them, and he hadn't been able to wield enough magic to fight back. Now they faced two elements throwing unfathomable power back and forth like a giant food fight. How could he possibly defend against both of them when Jormbrinder muffled his ability to wield? He needed his magic now more than ever, just to save Rose, but he couldn't just pull Chryslaenor free. Holding both swords had almost killed him at Gressmore, and now he had a third foci to consider. A third foci that dampened magic.

"I have an idea," Angst stated, licking his dry lips. "I'm not sure it will work, and I don't know if I can protect everyone." Angst sought Hector, his old mentor, his friend, and gripped the man's shoulder. "You keep them safe, no matter what I do," Angst said firmly. "Do you understand?"

Hector nodded, his old, gray eyes skeptical.

"That goes for all of you," Angst said to Tarness, Dallow, and Faeoris.

Victoria's eyes were glazed over with a vision. "Angst." She looked tense, her shoulders hunched. "There's a chance you'll die. A good chance."

"Again?" He smirked, but then noticed Faeoris's very serious face.

"Don't die," Faeoris said, more of a command than a concern.

"I promise."

Suddenly, Victoria reached up, gripping his neck to pull him in for a kiss. He turned his face to the side at the last moment, and her lips landed firmly on his cheek. She jerked back in surprise. He looked at her blushing face and smiled fondly.

"Chicken," Tarness teased.

"Really?" Angst asked with a wink. "Watch this."

He shoved the surprised princess back into Hector's arms, wielded Dulgirgraut, and jogged around the corner. He wanted to blur to Rose, but with Jormbrinder's "help," he might just blur into a wall or rush in at a snail's pace. Instead, Angst jogged as fast as his armor would allow. He wasn't even halfway to Rose when he heard a voice like a thundering waterfall.

"Angst!" Water stormed.

He spun about to see the element of Water raise a hand toward him, shards of ice flying from her palm. Considering that they were titans, shards really meant stalactites large enough to destroy small dragons. He kept running.

"Yes," Air hissed.

Angst felt a change in the air that made his ears pop. He brushed most of the missiles aside like waving away falling leaves.

"With me, wielder!" Air cried. "We can destroy her together!"

Dulgirgraut shielded him before he even thought the spell, deflecting small icebergs, though tiny bits got through, pelting his cheek. Angst skidded to a halt, momentarily distracted by Air's assault on Water. It was foolish, but how do you not stop to look at a natural disaster, to take a moment and witness the tornado racing toward you, to stand in awe at a tidal wave? Especially when they were both happening in the same room! Thin tornadoes bored into Water like worms into soil. A surge of waves formed from nothing, crashing into Air and knocking him back. Both elements returned their focus to the battle at hand.

"Help me!" Air called out to Angst.

He looked at the elements, and wondered for a second if it would be best to join forces against Water, to help Air succeed where he'd failed alone. He turned to look at Rose and the tall man weaving magic he didn't understand, pouring it into her.

"Angst," Faeoris cried. "Run!"

Without another word, Angst ran toward Rose and Chryslaenor. It felt like he was moving in slow motion, but he managed one step, two steps then something sharp struck his jaw, forcing him from his path. Dulgirgraut left his hand as he landed on his side and rolled to a crashing stop against a stone wall. There was no pause for breath as a kick to his ribs sent him flying ten feet into the air. He landed in the arms of a man who caught his shoulders and rammed him against the wall, knocking all sense and breath away. Dulgirgraut sang off key, and stars flashed before his eyes.

His attacker paused to smile smugly, looking down on Angst with distaste, with his muscular dark arm reared back. Fists pummeled so hard and fast, it was as if he were armored in a pillow case. One landed against the chainmail under his chest plate with a noisy crack. It was suddenly hard to breathe, and Angst fought to retain consciousness.

55

Bright lights shone in Angst's eyes as Faeoris landed behind the man. She gripped him by the shoulders and picked him up, flinging him high overhead, making him cry out in surprise. He crashed hard on a shoulder against the corner of Rose's table.

When he pushed himself up, he looked at Faeoris. "You!" he said accusingly. "You bitch! I already turned you away once!"

"Are you okay?" she asked Angst, helping him up.

"No," he wheezed, feeling every year he'd lived. "Who is he?"

"ANduaut of Vex'steppe," she said.

"*That* guy?" Angst remembered her tale from the night they'd stayed up talking.

She merely nodded.

"Did you come back to be rejected again?" he screamed. "This time, you need to die!"

"Don't die," Angst wheezed.

"I promise." She nodded.

"And beat him senseless," Angst said with a nod.

ANduaut sprinted toward her, running faster than any mere man. His eyes were wild, maniacal, and spittle dripped from his lips. He'd picked up a long staff with daggers on each end, and spun it expertly, a whirlwind of vicious steel. Faeoris stood as still as death. When ANduaut was a foot away, she reached out in a blur and clutched his throat. His feet slid out from under him while his head remained in place. There was a sickening gurgle as he choked in her grip.

"There's a reason Berfemmian are feared more than the Vex'steppe tribes," she said solemnly. Faeoris stood over him, her long legs spread in a fighting stance, one hand on a hip and the other held out like a sword at a man's throat.

Angst shuddered. So much strength, so much anger in such a beautiful package.

She looked down at Angst with keen eyes. "Run, my friend. Run!"

She slammed ANduaut to the ground with one arm, and his staff flew out of his hand. Faeoris picked him up, lifted him high, and slammed him down again. Her knee landed hard in his groin, and he squeaked. He covered his face with his arms as she struck, each driving blow hard enough to make her hair bounce from the shock. His forearms split open and blood sprayed. Angst tore his eyes away and pushed himself up. Faeoris would be fine. More than fine.

He wanted to run heroically and leap onto the sacrificial table like a graceful antelope. Instead, he lumbered forward in an old man jog. It was hard to breathe—his ribs weren't right and his armor and cloak weighed heavy. The fear and excitement in his mind warred with the labored thumping of his heart. He had the sudden urge to lie down and rest, to sleep a thousand years, but she needed him. They all needed him. He crawled onto the table and, with a grunt, pushed himself to stand over Rose. He looked up, staring at Chryslaenor as though nothing else in the room existed.

"What are you doing?" Hector called out. "Leave that thing alone!"

"Let me go," Victoria said, squirming in Hector's grip. "He shouldn't be alone!"

"Faeoris," Tarness shouted. "Get out of there."

"He's a fool," Hector cried out. "It almost killed him last time."

"No!" Water yelled, aiming her hands at Angst once again.

"Yes!" Air replied, redoubling his efforts and forcing Water to defend herself. "Distract her while I kill her!"

"You are a silly mortal," the tall, bald man warned. "You can't wield another foci!"

ANduaut flew across the room like a tiny rock tossed down a hallway. Faeoris stood strong, her high boots and scale armor shining, and a wicked, hungry grin on her mouth.

Angst took a deep breath and blocked out everything in the room. He blocked the sounds of the elements battling. He blocked the cries of ANduaut as Faeoris beat the life out of him. Blocked the old man's threats and warnings and Victoria's desperate sobs. He even blocked Dulgirgraut begging him to stop. All so he could listen. He could hear this foci, his foci, Chryslaenor. It was the faintest of songs, but Angst remembered it well, and as he focused, he could feel his sword shrouded in something dark and forbidding. Slippery like the statues of people covered in stone that attacked them at Camfeld, or the lake that tried to suck in Victoria. A sickeningly sweet smell made him want to gag.

Chryslaenor wanted free from this darkness, and Angst wanted his sword back. He raised his hand, fighting through the black lightning and dark shadows to reach the blue light hidden within. Angst could feel his friend with his mind. The sword struggled against Magic. It was tired and ready to give in, but Angst wouldn't let it. Dulgirgraut couldn't stop him; the foci was held back by Jormbrinder still at his hip. It tried. It fought, and so did Chryslaenor. Neither sword wanted to be joined together like this.

"I'm almost done!" the bald man yelled. He reached out and thick bolts of black lightning struck Rose's body, making her scream in pain. "You can't do this!"

"I thought you were bluffing! This will kill you," Air warned. "Help me instead!"

"You can't wield another," he heard Aerella whisper.

Dulgirgraut glowed bright red in his left hand. Chryslaenor was just within reach. He turned his head to face his friends.

Faeoris had returned to stand with them, and her face, all their faces were filled with worry.

"Don't do this," Victoria cried out. "Angst, I love you!"

"Hey," he said. "I've got this."

With a deep breath, Angst faced the sword and wrapped his hand around the hilt. Black lightning instantly surrounded him, biting and stinging his flesh like a thousand bees in a windstorm. The pain reached deep, and it felt like his insides were being ripped apart. Angst was struck by a moment of doubt. Had he made a mistake? Was this it? Was he finally going to die? To leave Heather to be a mother to their child alone?

He didn't have a choice. Rose would die, Victoria could die, Unsel could be destroyed...so many depended on this. Dulgirgraut vibrated in his left hand as he gripped Chryslaenor with his right.

An impossible jumble of people, elements, foci, creatures screamed in his mind. Angst wanted to pull away. The red surge of Dulgirgraut's cloud attacked both Chryslaenor's blue lightning and the black lightning of Magic. Chryslaenor continued to defend against itself against the darkness of Magic, while simultaneously attacking Dulgirgraut. They were like aged siblings brimming with hate, battling each other without reason. Magic spewed black lightning at everyone and everything in a desperate attempt to fight. Jormbrinder clung to his side, a silent void siphoning a little of everything.

The first time Angst had held Chryslaenor at Unsel, and later Dulgirgraut in Gressmore Towers, he wasn't Al'eyrn. He hadn't truly bonded to any foci. Now he was bonded to Dulgirgraut, and with every ounce of will, he struggled to bond again with Chryslaenor. His flesh burned, his head pounded, his heart raced. It felt as though his skin couldn't contain the power and was ready to peel from his bones. Dulgirgraut had filled the place in his mind left behind by Chryslaenor, finally finding peace with the help of Faeoris and her sealtian. Now he struggled to force his old sword to occupy the same place. It was like cramming two square pegs into the same round hole. They hated it, and so did he.

The second half of Jormbrinder lying beside Rose shot like an arrow. It struck ANduaut in the eye, tearing away part of the man's forehead and flipping him over like a coin. The tribesman lay on the ground, his muscles jerking like a dying animal.

"Yes!" Faeoris said vindictively, and then looked about guiltily. "What?"

The twin brother swords despised each other, but they hated the darkness more. Their rivalry was temporary, brief, and together they began to fight off the dark lightning. The raw power flowing through Angst was unforgiving. Pain, physical and mental, poured through him. He wanted more than anything to let go. Yet if he did, Rose, Victoria, Faeoris, and all his friends would die. Why did it always have to be so hard? Fury crept up from deep inside, and his jaw set. Angst was tired of elements, of foci, of magics he didn't understand, and it made him so upset, he began to shake.

"That's enough!" he said in his mind, his will bearing down on the swords. "You are both mine!"

* * * *

"Why is he screaming?" Victoria begged. "Please make it stop. Please pull him away."

"This fight isn't for us." Hector grunted as he struggled to hold her in place.

"She's right," Faeoris said, taking a step forward. "He needs his friends."

"He's saving his friends," Tarness said, standing in her way. "All of us."

* * * *

"You are both mine!" Angst shouted. "Now!"

There was a loud pop as the black lightning flashed out of existence and the tall man was thrown to the ground as if knocked from his feet. The room became deafeningly quiet and all eyes turned to Angst. The red glow of Dulgirgraut darkened, as did Chryslaenor's blue lightning. Air and Water lowered their arms and turned to face the human bonded with two foci. The tall man sat up, his eyes wide and face gaunt.

"I did it," Angst called out, his teeth chattering. It felt like he held two lightning rods that were being struck simultaneously. The hairs on his neck and arms prickled unnaturally. "They're both mine!"

Jormbrinder fell from his waist, landing on the stone floor with a metallic clunk.

"Ouch!" he cried as he felt a sting. "What was that?"

A thin glowing crack opened on Angst's forearm, deep enough that a light shone up from his bone and through his armor. He grimaced as another appeared on his other arm. The foci flooded his brain with information, too much, too fast. He buckled as light poured from burgeoning cracks in his chest and crept up his face. He felt like a shattered mirror, the fractures in his skin glowing and throbbing brightly. Jormbrinder no longer dampened the magic, possibly burned out from all it had absorbed during the bonding. Angst was unable to contain the power, and it was finding a way out.

"You can't control it, Angst. You have destroyed yourself, your friends, everything," crowed the tall man. "It's over."

The cracks hurt like open wounds filling with acid, and he wanted to scream. Grotesque splits in the metal and his skin grew in size, exposing more light. Blue lightning crawled along his arms and legs while fissures in his chest and face leaked power, like a volcano ready to erupt. The glow became brighter with every passing moment. He swallowed hard and opened his eyes.

"Oh, really?" Angst asked maniacally.

"You're going to die, Angst!" the tall man yelled. "Finally!"

"Then I'm taking you all with me!" Angst roared.

* * * *

421

"*No!*" Victoria yelled. "Please, no. It wasn't supposed to happen like this."

"I can see him, so clearly," Dallow said in amazement. "Everyone down!"

"He's going to explode!" Victoria clawed at Hector and Tarness, frantic to break free of their hold.

"Is there anything we can do for him?" Hector yelled desperately. "Anything at all?"

Before Dallow could answer, Victoria stopped struggling and turned to Hector. "No," she said, tears streaming down her face.

Hector stared at her for a brief moment. "Fall back!" he yelled. "Faeoris, hurry!"

* * * *

It was euphoria and pain. Memories and thoughts and power flowed through his mind like an endless waterfall. His strength was gone, as was his capacity for reason. The twin swords embraced and battled, and he was their catalyst. Their battlefield. His muscles clenched and his stomach churned. Angst didn't want to die, but more than anything, he wanted his friends to live. He wanted them safe. Thinking about Victoria, and Moyra, and finally, Heather, gave him the final bit of strength he needed to keep it restrained.

"Are you clear? Are you safe?" Angst yelled in an unnaturally deep voice that echoed through the cavern.

"I'm safe, Angst. I promise," Victoria said from far away.

"Me too!" Faeoris shouted. "All of us!"

"Die," Angst said bitterly to the elements.

"No!" the old man, Air, and Water cried out simultaneously.

He set it all in motion. In the moment just before he let go, Rose's cool hands gripped his ankles. Power. Power flowed through every fiber of his body, looking for any means of escape. It poured out the cracks in his skin, some of it flowing into Rose. She screamed. He screamed. It felt like a thousand, thousand suns. With the knowledge that his friends were safe, Angst let his shoulders drop and with one last sigh, stopped holding it in.

56

Scar lay on his side as he howled and cried and scratched at the air. With tears streaming uncontrollably down Kala's cheeks, she sniffed loudly. She was trying to be brave for her friend, but she felt so helpless. He was big again, tall like the mountain he was tethered to, and he wouldn't have grown so much if he could've helped it. Colors of magic flowed through him like the brightest rainbow. He was frightening like the sun and beautiful like a storm. She took a deep breath and willed herself not to be scared.

Kala carefully stepped forward. Scar didn't seem to notice as he rolled on his back, his whimpers ringing in her ears. There were no scary bubbles or helpless animals floating to feed him, but he was a giant and frightening. Her favorite puppy was covered in steel daggers, and with his three tails and six eyes, he couldn't help but be scary. In spite of this, she knew he was still Scar. He just didn't remember, yet.

Scar pushed at the collar with two of his six paws, his loud coughing blowing away dead leaves and dust. He scrambled to his paws and leaped forward, making rocks bigger than her jump like they'd been surprised. Still, she inched forward. He was so scary, but she loved him so much.

His monstrous head whipped about to face her, and his enormous steel-covered nose, almost the size of her entire body, huffing out clouds of steam in the cold winter air. She held her hand out and turned her head away. Her eyes squeezed shut, her hand shook, and she couldn't stop her teeth from chattering. She wanted to scream, but the sound caught in her throat. The monster dog's nose sniffed deeply enough to draw in her long black hair. Scar yelped in pain, and the quake knocked her down.

Kala rolled to her knees, getting her rust-colored leggings even muddier. She crawled forward once again. His eyes were barely open, and his leg twitched as if he were dreaming. She placed a hand on his muzzle, pulling back as the sharp edges pricked her. Her hand was cut, but it only stung like a rose thorn. Kala reached out again, carefully, and tried petting him.

"It's okay, Scar," she said. "I'm here."

With a shuddering sigh, Scar shrank like a melting ice cube. Six eyes became two, four tails became one, harsh blades split into fine puppy hairs. The lab's tiny body showed no signs of life. She placed her hand on his full belly and shook it gently. Scar remained still. She petted him frantically but nothing happened. He wasn't breathing. She grabbed him by the scruff of his neck and dragged him to her lap.

"Please, Scar," she pleaded. "Please! You're my best friend! Get up! Get up!"

She lowered her face, pressing her cheek against the lap pup's soft fur, sobbing loudly. Her friend wasn't breathing, he wasn't moving, he wasn't playing with her. It was so unfair. She hated it. Now she was scared.

"Please," she whispered.

* * * *

Unsel

Rook led the seventeen wielders, Maarja, and Jintorich through the castle to the west side. It was deserted, save for the occasional frantic maid or page scrambling to find safe passage. The hallways were strewn with rubble. The group jogged around destroyed furniture, small fires from toppled lanterns, and piles of stone from collapsed walls. The air smelled like oil, smoke,

424

and dust from old tapestries hanging by threads. Throats dried and eyes widened in trepidation as the sounds of battle became louder with every step.

Their race to the unknown stopped before the closed door of the maiden's courtyard. Thick beams of sunlight shone through holes in the wall surrounding the tall wooden door. This had to be it, yet he hesitated. His heart raced and sweat beaded his brow. Not only did he worry over the lives of those in his charge, he'd never been through these doors; it simply wasn't allowed.

"What is it, Butter?" Janda asked, resting a hand on his outstretched arm.

He didn't want to admit the truth, so instead faced the wielders. "You can do this, all of you. Steel yourselves!"

With a deep breath, he turned and opened the door. The cool light of winter illuminated a scene that didn't seem real. Half the maiden's courtyard was simply gone. The marble floor stretched out twenty feet before them, only to end abruptly at a cliff, like a cracker broken in half. Looking from left to right, Rook could see that this wing of the castle had not fared well. The sinkhole had taken a round, toothy bite, eating away a third of the west side, creating a U-shaped inlet, like a cove in a lake. Walls had fallen away on either side of the courtyard, leaving a rubble-strewn path that stretched across the entire side of the castle like an ugly stone porch. The remaining ruins were now wide open to attack.

Along the newly-formed veranda, enormous gargoyle creatures battled helpless Unsel soldiers. Teams of soldiers attacked their nigh-invulnerable opponents, but their blows were as effective as punching a giant tree trunk. Unsel was losing—he counted more piles of mangled bodies than actual fighters. Not only were the gargoyles almost impossible to kill, Rook couldn't begin to fathom how many there were. Maybe hundreds? They glided through the air in flocks, taking turns plucking apart armored men and women. Many stood along the cliff ledge with arms crossed. And only one man seemed to be having any success. A hundred yards away, Vars leaped into the body of a gargoyle before splitting it in two. How could he do that without the aid of magic?

Jaden screamed in pain, dropping to his knees and squeezing his head as if to keep everything in. His eyes bulged unnaturally, and blood gushed from his nose and ears. Rook knelt by the young man, looking for a head wound and scoping the area for an attacker or hurled weapon, yet saw nothing.

"Jaden, what is it?" Rook asked. "What happened to you?"

"Angst has another," he said, spit flying from his lips. He sounded mad, and rolled from side to side as if every muscle were cramping. He stopped, grabbing Rook's shoulders and pulling him close. "I came back to stop him, to keep him from destroying Ehrde! I remember...I remember everything!" He slumped back, unmoving.

Rook checked to make sure Jaden's heart still beat and then waved Simon, the young healer, over. "Drag him away from the battle. Keep him alive."

"I...I don't know if I can," the skinny man stuttered, his eyes wild with fear.

"Just do it!" Rook barked.

"No!" Janda cried out. She was pointing at Vars.

Rook turned in time to watch Vars cut the head off an Unsel soldier. The orange sparks spewing from the soldier had burned a gargoyle to smoke, and the sparks followed him over the cliff's edge as Vars kicked the body into the sinkhole. Rook's jaw set in fury at the traitor, and he squeezed the hilt of his sword.

"Make a path for Angst," Rook cried out. "I'm going to start with Vars!"

* * * *

Dozens of candles around the room burned like stars, and the woodless fireplace before Alloria blazed like a bonfire. Heather approached slowly, awestruck, circling the young woman with her fists raised defensively. Clad from neck to toe in black leather armor that gleamed in the firelight, and with a red cloak slung across her shoulders, Alloria no longer appeared sickly or tired. Her thin hair was once again a full mass of gorgeous light brown curls that draped over her shoulders and far down her back. Her eyebrows arched in the very embodiment of cunning, and her full lips pulled back in an ironic smirk.

"Your husband is safe, Heather," Alloria said sharply. "My champion is coming!"

Heather side-stepped for a better view. The fire felt intense enough to heat the castle. The ten-foot marble hearth opened to a wide fireplace framed by a white stone archway. The beauty of the fireplace would've been enough to leave her awestruck, if it weren't for the burning face inside. The bonfire had eyes like rocks in lava, and a mouth that billowed dark smoke with every breath. It filled the entirety of the fireplace, and made the room feel hotter than summer.

"His wife," the fiery head spoke thoughtfully.

"Did you hear me?" Alloria asked, returning her gaze to the blazing visage. "I won't kill Angst, and neither will you. Now leave, or I will call for Vivek!"

In a rush of air, the fire simply vanished, and the candles burned out, until the only remaining light was the stingy beams from the window.

Something hurt, deep inside Heather's belly. Everything cramped so hard she didn't remember dropping to her knees. It felt like a thousand wasps stinging to escape, and she looked down to see her stomach grossly distended. Alloria was suddenly at her side, kneeling beside her, holding her body.

"What's wrong with you?" Alloria snapped. "I don't have time for this."

"Don't kill him," Heather pleaded, choking out the words.

"Don't be stupid," she said. "I don't think I could if I wanted to... Eew."

Heather screamed in pain as a battle raged inside her. She placed her hands on her churning belly, on the tiny bumps and bulges pushing against her skin. Her legs were damp, and her leggings red with blood. Her head throbbed. So much pain.

Bright lights swam in front of her eyes, and she thought of Angst as everything went dark.

57

"Angst?" Victoria called out. She coughed, brushing bits of stone and rubble out of her blond curls. "Anyone?"

"I'm here," Hector said between coughs, pushing himself up to his knees.

Tarness stood, freeing Dallow from his protective hold. He wiped blood from his cuts before dusting off his friend.

"Yup," Faeoris confirmed, already standing. "I think. What was that? Is Angst okay?"

"We're alive. That's a good sign, right?" Tarness asked hopefully.

"Always," Hector answered.

The sun peeked brightly through high, rolling clouds of white fluff. Their lungs were rewarded with clean, fresh air. A cool breeze slowly brushed away the dust and smoke. All was silent.

"What happened to the cave?" Tarness asked, looking around.

"That explains why I can see again," Dallow said, pressing the memndus stone against his temple. "We're on top of a mountain. Part of a mountain anyway, overlooking Faeoris's home."

"I'm going ahead to check," Hector said gruffly, pulling a broadsword and shield from behind him. "Wait here."

He made his way around the remaining wall, Faeoris following closely. He looked back at her in annoyance but said nothing. She swooped forward, flying ahead.

"The top of the mountain is completely gone!" Hector said in disbelief. "Is that...? By the Vivek... Victoria, everyone, get up here!"

Tori scrambled over stone rubble to stand beside Hector. She gasped when she saw Angst, still standing over Rose, with Dulgirgraut in one hand, and Chryslaenor in the other. Angst held the two giant foci aloft, both pointed up at the sky. He looked into the distance, as though lost in thought. Fissures of red and blue glowed through his skin like fresh lava diving into a rushing creek. A red glow hovered around Dulgirgraut, and blue lightning snapped and popped around Chryslaenor like an on-coming storm.

Rose let go of his leg and unsteadily pushed herself up to a sitting position. Her eyes wide in shock, she shakily brushed tangled red hair from her shoulders. "The hunger, it's gone!" Rose hugged his calf, tears streaming down her cheeks. "Angst, you did it! I'm finally free!"

Angst swung his two foci about, angling them smoothly behind him, setting both to rest between his shoulders. The enormous twin blades set into place with an audible click, hovering behind his back as if sheathed in two invisible scabbards. He dropped to one knee, lifting a tired Rose, and embracing her tight.

"I swear, I'm fine, Angst," Rose said dryly, patting his back in a barely hug.

"Shut up," Angst said, continuing to hold her. "I was so worried. I've missed you so much!"

Everyone walked to the stone bench and waited patiently. Angst finally let go and hopped off the stone table, grabbed Victoria, and drew her into a hug. Faeoris wrapped her arms around them both, picking them up. She held them tightly, and looked as if she fought tears before releasing them and straightening out her armor.

"My turn," Dallow said, reaching out to Rose.

Rose stared at the bandage around his eyes with worry. Before she could ask, Dallow kissed her firmly on the mouth. Rose, slightly dumbfounded, returned Dallow's kiss before pulling away. She ran her hand gently along the kerchief of Dallow's blindfold, and then roughly through his blond hair.

"What happened?" she asked. "Are you okay?"

"I am now," Dallow said sincerely.

Tarness grabbed Hector in a bear hug and gripped tight.

"What was that for?" Hector wheezed in surprise.

"I didn't want to feel left out!" Tarness said with a broad smile.

Rose pushed Dallow away, tearing her eyes from the blindfold to look at Angst. He still held Victoria as though they'd barely made it.

"Would you two stop it?" Rose said. "I'm going to throw up."

Angst reluctantly let go, ending their embrace with a wink and a triumphant grin.

"I'm ready to retire," Rose said, sounding exhausted.

"I thought I was the old one." Angst looked at her with a raised eyebrow.

"You are," Rose said coolly. She looked Victoria up and down, clearly disapproving of the Berfemmian armor. "This is a new look. Angst must love it." She laughed.

"Of course he does." Victoria grinned, ignoring the cattiness.

"Who's this?" Rose asked wryly, thumbing at Faeoris as she eyed the scantily-clad warrior.

"My new friend," Angst said, beaming.

"Why am I not surprised?" she replied dryly.

"I do have excellent taste in friends," Angst said proudly. "Meet Faeoris."

"Hi." Rose nodded curtly, and Faeoris returned the gesture. "The, um, this armor isn't a new requirement for being friends?"

"That's an option?" Angst said hopefully.

"No." Rose stamped out his hope like a campfire.

"What's that?" Tarness interrupted, pointing at the spot where the bald man had stood.

"Describe it?" Dallow asked.

"It's a dark, shimmering hole in the air," Hector explained, "surrounded by floating black dots."

"It sounds like a portal," Dallow proclaimed excitedly. "I'm having a hard time seeing it from above. Can you see where it goes?"

"No, it's blacker than me," Tarness proclaimed.

"Wait," Hector said. "You're black?"

"Very funny," Tarness said.

"That's...odd," Dallow stated.

"Hey, look at this!" Faeoris was holding half of Jormbrinder, her arm stretched out and a satisfied smile on her face. She swung it and stabbed at the air.

"You can pick it up?" Angst asked in excitement. "Do you hear music? Is it talking to you?"

Faeoris put her ear against the golden blade, her eyes wide with wonder. "Yes. Yes, I think it says I should keep it."

Rose burst out laughing. "I like her."

Faeoris picked up the second blade, which was apparently no longer weighed down by magic. She flipped it in the air, expertly catching the handle. She beamed with pride at her new trophy as she strolled back over to them.

"May I?" Dallow asked. He set what remained of his book down and reached out.

"Do I get it back?" Faeoris said, her gaze wary.

"I promise," Dallow said, beckoning with his fingers.

He took the blade and grunted. The tip immediately landed on the ground, but he was able to hold the handle aloft. "It's heavy," he said through gritted teeth, "but it's not acting like a foci anymore."

"From the moment I picked that thing up, it dampened every ounce of magic I could wield. Like a sponge," Angst said. "Maybe it was too much for Jormbrinder to handle. Serves it right."

"Your bonding must have purged Rose from whatever that man was doing," Dallow explained. "And both Jormbrinder and Rose siphoning off power is probably what kept you alive!"

"Good thing I was here," Rose said, yawning nonchalantly. "Saving your ass, once again."

"Saving each other," he corrected proudly. "Don't make me hug you again."

She slugged him with one of her thin arms, and he feigned pain. Dallow returned the dagger to Faeoris, who looked for a place to sheath it. Tarness handed her a satchel that was almost deep enough to carry them. She threw the leather strap over her shoulder, part of both dagger handles sticking out awkwardly.

"I guess this will work," she said with a nod.

"I'll tie them down," Tarness offered. "We can get a proper sheath made in Unsel."

"Unsel!" Angst said, as if remembering. "We need to get there, now!"

"How are you going to do that?" Rose asked. "Can you fly all of a sudden?"

"Victoria," Angst said, placing his hands on her shoulders as he looked at the ground in concentration. "Summon your swifen."

"What?" Rose asked in shock.

Victoria nodded at Angst, and together they summoned her swifen, just as they had before fighting the giant dragon. The two swords glowed brightly, and within seconds, Victoria's swifen appeared. The unicorn was covered in pink feathers, and its golden hooves and horn shone in the sunlight.

"You have got to be kidding me," Rose said in exasperation.

Angst dropped his hands from Victoria's shoulder to her hands. With a loud whoosh, bright pink wings spread wide. The unicorn pranced and whinnied in anticipation, its wings flapping. Victoria pulled her hands free and clapped uncontrollably.

"Really?" Rose continued. "Since when does she wield magic?"

"She is a seer," Dallow explained.

"A seer?" Rose was already in a mood.

"She can glimpse the future, see the past, see the now. I'm pretty sure she also reads minds," he said. "She sees."

"Whatever." Rose made eye contact with Faeoris and both women shook their heads in disapproval at the brightly-colored swifen.

Victoria pulled Rose gently aside to whisper in her ear. "Don't let me die," she whispered. "You're the only one who'll be able to save me. You're the only one who can save us all."

"What?" Rose said aloud, her eyes wide with shock. "What are you even talking about? I'm done being a hero. That's his job!"

"Please," Victoria pleaded. "Angst can't know or he won't get through this. Please remember."

"Can't know what?" Rose snapped. "That didn't even make any sense."

"Tori, we need to go!" Angst mounted the swifen with bravado and power, pulling Victoria aloft to join him. "I'm sorry, Rose. We'll catch up soon."

"Okay," Rose said, a befuddled look on her face.

"How will you get off this rock?" Angst asked Dallow.

"We'll be fine," Dallow replied. "I have an idea."

"Faeoris?" Angst asked.

"I'm with you!" she said, her wings of light spread wide.

"Really?" Rose asked, sardonically.

Faeoris smirked at her and gave a half-shrug before lifting into the air.

"I've been away too long," Rose said with a sigh. "Everyone is naked...has wings... I feel a little cheated."

With a nod and a wink at his friends, Angst and Victoria flew off on her unicorn, Faeoris following closely behind.

* * * *

"Ugh, I hate her," Rose said, exasperated, when Angst and his companions had flown out of earshot. "They make me want to vomit."

"Jealous much?" Dallow asked, his forehead scrunching.

"And the new one? Where does he keep finding them?" Rose practically meowed. "It's just gross. They're both so much younger, and I... Never mind."

"I know what you mean," Hector said, patting her on the back. "Good to have you back."

"So good to be back, Hector," she replied gratefully.

"So, what's your idea?" Tarness asked Dallow. His thick brows furrowed so deeply, he looked furious. "Is there any way we can get to Unsel in time to help Angst?"

"Is the portal still there?" Dallow asked hopefully, kneeling to pick up the book, which was dripping from their swim.

"Yeah, there's a hole in the air, if that's what you mean," Tarness stated warily. "And it looks hungry."

"Please bring me closer." Dallow held out his hand.

"Are you going to tell me what happened?" Rose asked, grabbing his hand.

He clung onto her desperately as she led him to the black hole. It hovered inches from the ground and buzzed with energy. Dallow reached out his free hand, not quite touching the emptiness. He closed his hand as if squeezing a ball.

"Later," he said, his voice rough.

"I think the tall man passed through that thing," Tarness advised. "He was carrying the dead guy who attacked Angst."

"That's okay," Dallow said agreeably. "From what I learned at that library, with the way these things work, we should be able to go anywhere we want."

"So we could beat Angst to Unsel?" Hector asked excitedly, rubbing his thumb along the scar on his chin. "I'd love that."

"It's possible," Dallow said. "Everyone hold hands and follow me through. I'll try to concentrate on the Wizard's Revenge."

"Why are you wincing?" Rose asked.

"I'm concentrating," Dallow explained. "I just absorbed a lot at the library. There was so much to know, so many places, and...never mind. I'm sure we will be fine." His eyes glowed brightly behind his bandage.

"Everyone take a hand," he said. "We need to stay together."

Rose held onto Dallow's hand and reached for Hector, who reluctantly held onto Tarness's.

"After the hug, I'm starting to wonder if you don't like me," Tarness taunted.

"I hate hugging," Hector replied dryly.

"Right?" Rose agreed.

The blind man led his friends into the empty, dark hole, each of them disappearing as they passed through the shadowy circle.

"Why is this portal so cold?" Tarness, the last one through, asked.

58

The two foci were playing king of the hill in Angst's mind, and it felt like the winner was driving a chisel into his brain. At least their bickering was no longer physically violent; they seemed to understand the danger around them and that they needed their host alive, if not alert. But they used Angst's head to slap each other around like kids on a playground. Chryslaenor flooded his thoughts with an image of a victorious battle, only to have it replaced by a duelist wielding Dulgirgraut, handily defeating Chryslaenor. Images coursed back and forth, victory after victory. Angst tried distracting them by asking questions, but that only made it worse. Chryslaenor wanted to kill the mermen, Dulgirgraut wanted to fly ahead to Unsel and shore up defenses, and neither wanted to fight the monster.

"Angst," Victoria screeched, probably not for the first time. "Look!"

The unicorn glided, skimming a mere fifty-feet over the ocean, pacing the shadowy figure beneath the water's surface. Cold, moist air blasted their faces, and he breathed deep, seeking calm, but finding none. He could see thousands of mermaids and mermen swimming alongside the creature like a school of angry fish. Several mermen stood atop the beast behind a larger one, who'd apparently taken lead. Angst looked ahead to see the coastal inlet created by the first sinkhole. The foci vied for his attention again, but he noticed Tori hyperventilating. She

437

gripped the reins so tightly, her white-knuckled hands shook.

"Relax, before you pass out," Angst yelled over the wind.

He tried putting his hand on hers in a calming gesture, and the swifen wavered as though losing balance.

Angst immediately let go. "Never mind," he yelled. "You're doing great!"

He looked back over his shoulder to see the thin curvy figure of Faeoris flying nearby, her colorful wings flapping gently and then gliding on the air currents. It was a stunning sight as she appeared suspended on strings. She smiled at him and winked before nodding in the direction of the monster. Angst looked down and saw glimpses of shadow that darted below the surface so quickly, they were barely able to keep up with the beast. He couldn't begin to understand how such an enormous creature could move so fast. Angst wanted a better look, but every time they got closer, a long tentacle shot out of the water to swat at them.

"It's gaining speed," Angst pressed. "Can you go faster?"

"Aren't you making her fly?" Victoria snapped. "You've got two of those things now, can't you throw one at it?"

The foci didn't think her suggestion was funny as both struggled for dominance over his bond. Angst constantly had to will the swords to stop, beg them to help with this crisis at hand, and worry about everything Al'eyrn later. He felt like a toy being fought over by toddlers, one they didn't mind breaking. He wanted to attack the monster, and reached out to both with his mind, wondering what sort of spell they could help him put together. It was like two streams pouring into one river as the reply flooded back.

"Angst, are you still with me?!" Victoria yelled.

"Yeah, they just aren't being much help." Angst replied.

"I can tell. What I'm able to read is a mess!" Tori said. "What about asking for something simple, like one of Dallow's fireballs!"

"Good idea. I'll try," Angst shouted.

Dulgirgraut was first to answer, and immediately Angst understood how it was done. Chryslaenor also had an idea, and Angst struggled to fit the odd puzzle shapes together. He could see the glow of both swords over his shoulders, both hungry to be the catalyst. Without knowing how to aim with the two enormous swords simultaneously, he chose Chryslaenor. He pointed the tip down at the ocean, trying to angle the blade so the wind didn't drag him off the swifen. In spite of only using one sword, both prepared as he called forth the spell.

"Get ready to veer left so I can aim!" Angst bellowed then muttered under his breath in Acratic, wishing he understood what the words meant. The buildup of power made the hairs on his arms rise and his teeth chatter. Just as it became too much to keep in, he yelled, "Now!"

The flying pink unicorn veered left, and Angst let loose the spell. A ball of blue flame shot from Chryslaenor, surrounded by crackling halos of lighting. He immediately blocked the heat with an air shield, encompassing Angst, Victoria, and Faeoris. The fireball spell had created a beautiful mess that thundered constantly in its descent. It was large, larger than his house, and merpeople leaped off the monster's back at its approach. Angst, Tori, and Faeoris watched in amazement as the fireball smashed into the water, directly on top of the creature, engulfing its dark, watery form. There was a deafening, bubbly roar followed by a whooshing sound, as water evaporated in the blue flames. The fireball had forged a path through the ocean, creating a channel that soon filled with water.

Victoria pulled back on the reins so the swifen would hover in one spot.

Faeoris placed her hand on Angst's shoulder. "How... What did you do?"

"I don't have a clue," Angst replied, just as stunned. He returned Chryslaenor to his back and scratched his graying head.

"Is it dead?" Victoria asked impatiently.

"What could possibly live through that?" Angst stared on.

"You didn't really just say that, did you?" Faeoris sighed.

"He does that." Victoria grunted.

"Get closer," Angst commanded.

Victoria looked back over her shoulder.

"Please," he said. "Faeoris, please stay back. No need for all of us to be in danger."

"Yeah, just your best friend," Victoria muttered.

Faeoris nodded once but still followed close, either defiant or oblivious to his commands. Victoria urged her swifen toward the ocean until they were five feet from the choppy surface. Pale green and red ooze bubbled up with chunks of flesh. Dozens of small shadows swarmed a larger one, like bees surrounding a hive. They were too big to be fish and too small to be whales.

"Angst, fly higher," Faeoris called.

A living island rose from the ocean, and waves twenty feet high shot from the gigantic dark figure, parting over its pale green skin. Victoria screamed, and Angst beckoned her to pull back and fly higher as half the monster's body bent horrifically, rising out of the water. The giant mass struck the air shield with such force it shattered like glass, the impact throwing them up into the sky. He lost his seat on Tori's swifen, and kicked helplessly as he flew up higher and higher, far over great masses of clouds. The air became unbearably cold, his lungs burned, and he gasped for breath. His head pulsed from the creature's blow, and Angst squeezed his temples, trying to contain the throbbing. How hard had that thing hit them?

"Too fast, too high," Angst wheezed out in panic. "Tori! Faeoris!"

The bright blue sky and white clouds darkened. As everything became black, he saw spots before his eyes. Then he realized they weren't spots, they were stars, and Angst looked up to see the night sky.

"This isn't right," he gasped to himself. "How can it be night?" Then he began to fall.

59

Unsel

Sparks flew as swords crashed together, notching both blades as they struggled for dominance. Rook was younger, and stronger, but Vars was a statue, unflinching. This close, Rook could see he was missing an ear. A quick glance down revealed several missing fingers, and he stood at an odd angle, as though compensating for a bad foot or leg. The man was old, broken, yet strong as a bull. Vars pulled back, circling him, his eyes darting quickly as he sought an opening.

"You killed that soldier," Rook accused. "One of our own! He trusted you to lead him, and you cut off his head."

"I saved Unsel from another wielder," Vars spat. "This country is cursed with them! They are far worse than these green beasts."

Vars swung in a wide arc, forcing Rook to leap back. Rook pressed forward to drive his sword into the old man's neck, but Vars swatted it away. Vars sliced in a backhand, and Rook blocked, pushing the blade down. He drove up with the butt of his hilt, smashing Vars in the mouth. Blood sprayed onto Rook's face; it was cold. Vars bared his teeth, now framed in blood. Rook cut in a downward arc, his blade deflecting off of the old man's leaf-embroidered plate armor.

"They don't make armor like this anymore," Vars said. His blade struck Rook's leg, the same spot damaged by the gargoyles.

"What are you?" Rook cried out. "You're too old to be this strong."

"I'm justice," Vars cried. "I'm the one who will cleanse Unsel. I started with the crown, and I'll kill every last man, woman, and child that wields or sides with them."

"You killed them?" Rook said, incredulous. The blood drained from his face. "You killed Queen Isabelle and the Captain Guard?"

"What choice did I have?" Vars said, his eyes wild, spittle foaming at his mouth. "They harbored and supported wielders, even making magic legal. Can't you see? Those inflicted with the magics do nothing but rain destruction on everyone! They're the ones who killed my son."

"You idiot! You can't win this fight without them," Rook declared. "Your army will be torn to pieces. Our army! Nobody will be left!"

"Sometimes you have to start from scratch," Vars replied with a wicked grin.

"Traitor!" Rook called, attacking with renewed vigor. He swung down, again and again, chopping down against Vars's sword.

Vars backed away from the onslaught, shaken by the younger man's blows. His sword began to lean toward his face as his hold weakened. Rook sensed victory until the old man looked toward the sinkhole and laughed. Even if Vars were insane, what could possibly be so funny? He leaned back and kicked Vars in the chest, knocking him to the ground. Rook turned his head and almost dropped his sword.

A monster as wide as the sinkhole rose from the chasm, its slimy thick green-gray hide covered with creatures. Even from this distance, Rook could tell the beast's passengers were bigger than any soldier in Unsel, maybe even the size of Tarness. They looked like large, walking fish. Bluish scale covered their legs and arms, fins jutted from their backs, and some had wide, webbed ears that looked like the gargoyles'. Fish people? With legs?

The sounds of battle silenced as the newest challenge approached. Everyone paused to stare in horror as the massive creature slowed like a ship coming into harbor. Water sloshed over the edge of the maiden's courtyard floor, pushed up and over by the creature's mass.

The tallest fish creature stepped off the giant monster and stood a stone's throw away from Rook. He set his pike down as if claiming this territory. He was different from the others—an oblong circle of blue stood out on his forehead. He opened his mouth, baring rows and rows of thin, shark teeth that made Rook shudder and tighten his grip on his sword. No words came out, but gargoyles landed with noisy thuds beside him. They were obviously on the same side.

"Wielders," Rook shouted. "To me!"

He glanced at Vars, who was leaning back on his elbows and laughing maniacally. He didn't want to kill Vars like this, but it was time to finish him and move on. Blood spattered as he drove his blade in below the breastplate, the grotesque squishing and gurgling sound lingering in his ears. The old man kept laughing, even after Rook twisted the blade. Vars gripped the end with his shaky, gauntleted hand and forced it out of his chest. As Rook lifted his weapon to strike again, he heard a resounding thud beside him, followed by a second, and then a third. Three gargoyles flanked him and didn't hesitate in their attack. He swung out defensively as a large, green hand filled his vision.

* * * *

Janda watched Rook run toward Vars, his thick muscles gleaming in the sunlight as he raised his sword. Janda sighed for the briefest second, grateful for her catch. They needed to hurry up and make babies...right after they survived this. She shook her head and immediately noticed six gargoyles advancing, gliding toward them in a V formation, like a flock of birds.

"Before we make a path for Angst, we need to make one for

my boyfriend!" she called out, pointing her hand at the nearest one. Flames shot from her fingers, engulfing a gargoyle. The monster didn't burn; he boiled. Bubbles formed beneath the surface of its body, coming faster and faster like a tea kettle that finally blew. The gargoyle exploded, steamy ooze landing in dark pools before disintegrating into smoke. Before she could throw another burst of flame, Unsel soldiers attacked her flank. "You fools!" she called out. "Fight the gargoyles, not us!"

"Wielders die first," the nearest one said, raising his axe.

Then the soldiers began to disappear, all of them dropping through a black portal in the ground. The old man, Andec, stood beside her, his outstretched arm surrounded by a cloudy darkness. Sweat trickled from his forehead and his hand shook with the effort of his will.

"Where did you send them?" she asked.

"To the dungeons," he grumbled. "Where they belong."

More soldiers faced them, but now seemed hesitant to attack, in spite of Vars barking orders. Rook closed in on his target, but more gargoyles were swarming overhead and five still stood between them.

"I can't do this alone," Janda ordered.

"I join you in battle!" Maarja roared. The large Nordruaut rushed forward, grabbed a gargoyle by the leg and swung him around like a weapon.

"Woo hoo!" Jintorich cried, leaping off a broken pillar. He struck a gargoyle with his staff. A flash of light made Janda wince, and the gargoyle was gone. The small Meldusian sprinted after Maarja on his tiny legs.

Simon's brother, Sean, walked past her calmly. The only wielder to refuse armor, he was dressed instead in loose-fitting brown linen robes. He had unruly black hair, and his gaunt, tanned features seemed malnourished. Without a word, Sean lifted his hands in the air, as though trying to hug the sun. He threw his head back, his long black mane flopping wildly. Nothing happened as a gargoyle landed before him with a smirk on its face.

"Someone get him out of there!" Janda commanded.

"Just wait," Simon said, placing a hand on her arm. "My brother is fine."

"Where's Jaden?" she asked. "We need him!"

"He's alive, but unconscious," Simon replied. "I dragged him back into the hallway. I even healed a cut from his fall!"

"Good job," she said, unable to keep the worry from her voice. "But what about your brother?"

"It's the animals," he explained. "They help Sean."

The nearest gargoyles covered their heads and ducked as a massive dark cloud approached. At first, it looked like a wave of small birds migrating, but as they closed in, Janda could see how much bigger they actually were. Similar to the cavastil birds that had attacked Unsel, scores of almost human-sized bats, with furry bodies and black leathery wings, descended on the gargoyles, diving into the monsters like statues of wet clay.

Rook's path was clear, and he swung down at Vars again. Janda wanted to watch her man in action, but had fighting of her own to do. Soldiers who attacked from her left were either teleported to safety or slid on summoned sheets of ice to crash into distant walls. Dark ovals of power shot over her shoulder, as Nikkola blasted a gargoyle out of existence. Hope swept through Janda as other wielders stepped forward, bravely attacking with weather and light and darkness, whatever they could throw or defend with. It was almost fun, the rush of battle filling her as she began counting how many of the giant beasts she'd destroyed in balls of fire. Some of the dying gargoyle remains landed on others, making the creatures grow in size, but they were still no match for the onslaught of magical power assaulting them. She took a deep breath and sighed. She would live through this, marry Rook, and make babies. Lots and lots of babies.

"Janda!" Nikkola grabbed her shoulder. Her sister patted it hurriedly and pointed toward Rook.

Three gargoyles landed between her boyfriend and the cliff. Vars was already lying on his back, almost defeated. Rook could finish the old man, but there was no way he could defend against the monsters. She ran.

60

Angst flailed in panic as he fell toward the clouds. Water streamed from his eyes, and his cheeks pulled back mercilessly in the wind. He didn't know how to fly, nor did his foci. He could try slowing himself like he did when diving through the dome, but that had still hurt, a lot. It would be much worse at this height, even if he did land in the ocean. Just his luck to fall from the stars and land in a feeding frenzy of hungry mermen.

Angst jerked to a stop with a frightened yelp, his armor digging painfully into his armpits. Faeoris had reached through the towering blade hilts with one hand to grab the back of his armored chest piece. She strained at the awkward position, holding him several feet over billowing clouds.

"This isn't as easy as it looks," Faeoris grunted in his ear, throwing him up a foot to reach under his arms for a better hold.

"Y-you caught me!" Angst stuttered, unable to slow his breathing.

"That's what friends do, right?" she asked.

"You're a good friend," he said, patting her hand and wishing they were on the ground.

"Now the sex?" she asked.

"What?" he choked out.

She had done it again; he was at a loss for words. Faeoris laughed so much he thought she would drop him. He couldn't help but shake his head and smile before coming to his senses. In the panic from the fall and the relief of being caught, he'd lost track of his best friend.

"Where's Victoria?" Angst looked around. "Did you catch her too?"

"We were all thrown in different directions. I couldn't catch both of you, Angst." She didn't sound apologetic. "Can't she fly?"

"Not without me," Angst said in panic. "We've got to find her!"

There was the sound of rushing wind as the clouds roiled and rolled. Great pink wings pierced the cloud veil, lifting a very determined princess above them. Her teeth were set in a grimace of concentration, and her eyes and hands glowed bright pink. She was drenched, her hair matted, and her eyes filled with fury. The unicorn's wings brushed away cloud vapor for a clear view of an angry young princess.

"I'm fine," she grumbled.

"You did it!" Angst said in amazement. "I knew you could fly on your own! How did you—"

"I made it," she said, glaring at Faeoris. "That's all that matters."

"I'm impressed," Faeoris said with a nod. "Most would've died from a fall like that."

"That's not how I'm going to die," Victoria said with conviction. She nodded to Angst. "Hop on."

Faeoris didn't fly Angst to the unicorn, and he didn't know what to say, as if his tongue were caught between their glares.

"He's safer with me," Faeoris said before diving through the clouds.

Angst was certain he heard Victoria scream, "Bitch", but it was hard to tell with the wind rushing in his ears. He actually preferred to be on a mount, to have something underneath him, but was in no position to argue. He couldn't believe how fast they flew, as if racing away from Tori. He glanced over to see the unicorn flanking them closely. They approached the water, and he saw no sign of the beast below.

Victoria drew her swifen directly in front of Faeoris. Angst hung there, feeling more like a sack of old potatoes than a hero. Maybe he could swim for it?

"Give him to me now!" Victoria commanded. He'd rarely seen her so upset. Her pale cheeks flushed to her ears.

"After I'm convinced you know what you're doing," Faeoris said with a *tsk*.

She flew around Tori, rushing to the coast. Angst's legs dangled freely in the wind as she held onto the openings under the armpits of his chest armor. She shot up into the air with Tori on her heels then dove steeply enough that his stomach lurched. Tori yelled a battle cry. They were wasting time, and he worried that, in spite of Faeoris's strength, her grasp might slip. They'd gotten along so well in the domed city, this had to be concentrated frustration, and he needed it to end.

He could make out the remnants of Cliffview in the distance. Water's first attack had eroded the foundation of the old city until it had fallen into the ocean, taking all the people living there to their deaths. It was tragic that they'd been killed well before their time, and it made him angry. Water had kept tearing away at earth until an enormous sinkhole formed, and then another, creating an enormous river that led to Unsel.

"Land over there." He pointed at the cliff's edge, where the inlet met the first sinkhole.

"There isn't time for this!" Faeoris argued.

"Exactly!" Angst yelled over the wind.

She swooped low and placed Angst down roughly. He dropped to his knees and fell to his side. There was no heroic rolling with two giant swords on your back. The unicorn swifen landed closely behind.

"I'm sorry," Faeoris said, "it's just—"

"Shush," Victoria said, stomping forward to offer Angst a hand up.

"Don't you shush me," Faeoris snapped. "You're the one who dropped him in the first place!"

Before Angst could get solid footing, Victoria let go to shake a fist at Faeoris, who looked ready to snap it off. Angst rolled to his stomach as they continued bickering and pushed himself up, his knees and hands sinking deep into the mud.

"The monster isn't at Unsel yet," he said, standing with a grunt and shaking mud off his hands. "But she's got to be close."

"She?" Victoria asked sharply.

"Only a woman would be that angry and bitter," he said to both of them with the most sincere face he could put on.

As if on cue, the women's backs snapped into a sharp arch, and they crossed their arms and raised their eyebrows. Both began cursing vehemently until they saw the smug look on his face.

"Finally," Angst said. "You two are teaming up instead of arguing at each other like kids."

They looked at each other warily. Angst gave them a moment until Faeoris shrugged and Victoria's eyes flickered to the ground.

"You're friends," he said. "We're all friends. Old, new, it doesn't matter. I need you working together, or we're going to fail."

There was a long moment of hesitation; neither would apologize or admit to being wrong.

"Tori?" he said, feeling like an admonishing parent.

"Yeah…" She nodded, half rolling her eyes.

"Faeoris?" he prodded.

"Fine," she said with a grimace.

The two women looked at each other and nodded.

"You really should kiss," he said. "It would make you feel better."

Faeoris rolled her eyes, but smiled. Tori looked for a place to slug him; her eyes said he'd get it later.

"Where did the mud come from?" Faeoris asked. "I would've expected snow or ice."

"Ever get in a bathtub that's too full?" Angst asked. "The monster swam through here, and the wake washed up over the edge."

"Dallow would be proud," Victoria acknowledged.

"That thing must be enormous." Faeoris's eyes were wide. "The water looks far away from here."

Angst swallowed hard. "We need to go." He jerked his head toward Victoria's swifen. "We have to do this my way. No bickering."

"We don't bicker." Victoria winked at Faeoris.

Faeoris smirked back. As Angst struggled to mount the swifen, Faeoris grabbed hold and, in spite of his protests, flew him above the steed and dropped him behind Victoria.

"I'm assuming we are in a hurry?" Faeoris asked. "You are old and slow."

"Isn't he?" Victoria agreed.

"Thanks," he grumbled. "Let's go."

The three took off, flying along the path of the sinkholes.

"Faster," Angst said to Victoria.

She grunted, but the swifen sped up.

"Faster," he shouted.

"I can't," she protested. "I can't fly faster."

"Nor can I," Faeoris called over his shoulder.

"Yes! Yes, we can!" Angst yelled. "Faeoris, hold on to me!"

He felt a tug on his back as she gripped the hilt of both blades. His eyes glowed red and his arms shone blue as he placed his hands on Victoria's shoulders. The swords sang in his head, for once not fighting. Instead, they created a harmony of power that flowed through Angst and into Victoria. She whimpered but didn't resist as they rushed forward at incredible speed. Within seconds, the ground below became a blur and leagues of land flashed by.

"Steer gently," he urged Victoria, his voice raspy with the effort of wielding.

She nodded and they began to veer right, following the water. Faeoris cried out, but Angst didn't slow.

"Are you okay?" he called.

"This is amazing!" the Berfemmian shouted. "I've never had so much fun!"

"It hurts, Angst," Victoria muttered, trying not to be overheard.

"Almost there." Angst continued filtering power from the swords through Victoria and into her swifen. His eyes watered in the cold wind, and he could see streams of tears along Victoria's cheek.

"I see it!" Faeoris screamed in his ear.

They were half a mile from the castle. Carefully, Angst slowly cut off the power until it was a mere trickle. Blue and red smoke hissed from Victoria's hands as they descended. The battle was more frightening than he'd prepared for. There were scores of gargoyles, either gliding through the air in v-shaped formations or guarding the edge of the sinkhole. As they approached, he could make out mermen and mermaids fighting humans. Soldiers fighting wielders. Fireballs and portals being thrown like snowballs. Men tossed into the air by gargoyles or torn apart by tentacles. And the castle...

"My castle!" Victoria screamed in fury.

The sinkholes, or the monster, or the battle had demolished a third or more of the castle, tearing away walls to leave the west side exposed. Something about the scene looked familiar to Angst, but there was too much going on for his brain to place it.

"Where do we even begin?" Tori asked.

Angst and Faeoris looked at each other and shrugged. He squeezed his eyes shut, concentrating hard, and reaching out as far as he could.

"What are you doing?" Faeoris asked.

"Calling in reinforcements," he said, his eyes glowing brightly.

"That's great," Tori said fretfully, tugging at her blond curls. "What about us?"

"I'll see what I can do about that thing." He pointed at the mammoth creature a hundred yards below them. "Wielders and soldiers are fighting each other instead of the gargoyles and the merpeople. They need to pull it together or they'll be annihilated. They need their queen, Tori."

CHAPTER SIXTY

"I..." She swallowed hard. "Fine. I can do this."

"I know you can." He nodded and squeezed her waist. "Faeoris, are you okay?"

The Befemmian's face was strained with effort, and for the first time, Angst saw a bead of sweat drip from her forehead.

"They're getting heavy," she grunted, pulling the satchel from over her shoulder.

"What?" Angst said in exasperation. "Maybe the foci didn't die. Maybe it was just knocked out! Get them to the ground before you get hurt."

"I'll clear a path for Her Majesty," she said excitedly. "Die well!"

"How about, 'don't die!'?" he said, watching Faeoris practically stumble in the air with her load. He redirected his concern for Faeoris to Tori. "What's wrong?"

"All that power you pushed through me to get here faster, it was almost too much." Victoria sounded worried. "Is it always like that for you?"

"It is now," he said sincerely.

"What have you become?" she asked, her shoulders tensing.

"Let's find out." He kissed her on the cheek and dismounted the swifen, falling to the giant monster.

61

The sound was like thunder that didn't end, loud enough to wake old men and sleeping babes. The clamor became a rumble as families of wielders peeked out from their homes to see if it was safe. It had to be safe, danger was far, far away from Angst's home. Nowhere near the domed chatlen Jaden had created.

The rumble came closer, shaking the ground more and more violently by the second. Pebbles and stones hopped around like water in hot grease. The families scrambled nervously to the larger, central chatlen, with cooking forks and knives, with tenderizers and hatchets. The two youngest wielders and two oldest, who'd reluctantly stayed behind, now fought their fear as they stood guard at the edge of town. Their hands shook and their auras flickered like candles in the wind.

Onlookers covered their ears, expecting to see a herd of wild bears or a regiment of soldiers on steeds of war. In the bright of day, they saw a steely blur approach, its enormous shadow eclipsing the town as it passed. Some would later describe it as a nightmare, with its many red eyes and bladed tails. Others would call it a sign of hope, that for once they weren't the ones being attacked. All would say that the thundering silver blur racing to Unsel with speed and determination was a breath-taking sight. And they feared for its target.

And amidst it all, those with the best hearing swore they could make out the smallest cry of excitement.

CHAPTER SIXTY ONE

* * * *

Faeoris's arms shook as she shifted her grip on the satchel. She wasn't used to this; nothing had ever been heavy for her. She slowed her descent and knew there were only moments before she couldn't hold her beautiful daggers any longer. Faeoris hated giving them up. It felt like she was being cheated of something she'd rightfully earned, and it made her furious. That anger wouldn't go to waste once she located the perfect spot. There were so many creatures fighting below. Mermen and mermaids had teamed up with the gargoyles to fight soldiers, but the soldiers were fighting the wrong battle. The fools were attacking the human wielders.

There was the occasional scream as tentacles snatched bodies and split them asunder. The giant creature had pressed up to the center of the castle ledge, where merpeople positioned themselves to attack, which was perfect, to Faeoris's thinking. She held onto the dagger handles, spinning like she had with Angst over the dome. She grunted with the effort of momentum until the foci became too heavy, and let go. The satchel of foci daggers crashed into the castle floor with a bellowing clang. The impact threw bodies into the castle walls, and part of the ledge crumbled into the sea below, taking several gargoyles with it.

"Yes!" she shouted.

Tentacles shot up from the ocean, giving Faeoris the briefest of seconds to wield her longsword. She swung, slicing one and dodging another before a third struck her back, launching her toward the battle.

* * * *

Rook heard Vars move behind him and knew he was trapped. He'd lost to these creatures before, and thought desperately of Janda. He hoped she knew how much he loved her. He braced for the blow as the gargoyle's large, green fist swung down, and then flinched at the heat of fire. It must've been what the sun felt like.

Streams of flame shot from Janda's outstretched hands as she stormed forward. The silver plate armor around her forearms glowed bright red from the encompassing heat, almost matching her wild red hair and glowing red eyes. She was a beautiful force, and he needed to marry her, once they survived this.

Her pace slowed as the three gargoyles bubbled and burst. Hot liquid singed Rook's face, making him cry out in pain. It didn't matter. She was alive, he was alive, and she had saved him. She smiled broadly as he reached out to her.

"I love you," he declared proudly.

"Rook!" she shouted, shoving him aside.

She was much smaller, but her momentum propelled him several feet over as Vars's blade lunged forward. It pierced her chainmail, driving into her gut with a rip and a crack. He twisted maliciously, pulling up as she gurgled, helpless to the steel. The fire in her hands went out, and with one last glance at Rook, her eyes went dark.

Vars pulled the blade free and stepped back to admire his kill. Janda dropped to the ground, as still as death. Rook partially knelt, desperate to hold her, to love her back to life. His blood ran cold and his lip quivered as he realized she was already gone. It had happened before he'd had the chance to tell her just how much he loved her. She needed to hear those words over and over again. She deserved that and more. He cried out in anguish and his hands shook with rage. The pain in his leg, the pain from the fresh burns were all gone. Rook felt only hate.

"Exactly how I feel about wielder filth," Vars said, spitting on the ground beside her.

Rook was lost to a berserker rage, his vision a red haze of anger as he roared like an animal. Before Vars could even lift his sword, Rook spun around and began chopping. He smashed into the solid plate of Vars's sword arm, striking again and again with uncontained fury. Vars cried out in pain and surprise as his armor dented and split. He tried pushing Rook back, but a wildness had imbued the young man with strength that couldn't be stopped. Blood spewed from the old man's arm as Rook continued to chop until it was cut free. There was a sickening thud, as Vars's arm fell to the ground.

Vars laughed, madness ringing in the sound. "You haven't figured it out, have you?" He held up his other hand, a red ruby ring shining brightly in the sunlight. "I can't be killed!"

Rook ignored the crazy words and condescension. He saw only the opening in the old man's defenses. With the arm gone, his ribs were unshielded, a good place to strike next. Rook chopped and chopped, the man's laughter driving him even harder. He looked up to see Vars's pale white face leaned back, his eyes wide with a madness that matched Rook's. Over Vars's shoulder, Rook caught sight of a young woman in dark leathers with long, honey blond hair. She was hopping up and down, as if cheering him on. Alloria. What was she doing here?

There was an explosion from behind, and the body of a fish man plowed into him. Rook was thrown forward, landing on his chest, the wind knocked out of him. His ears rang, but he knew he had to get up. He pushed himself to all fours and then to one knee.

The cold steel that entered his side pierced his lung and drove through his heart. Rook couldn't breathe as all strength left him and he dropped his sword. Rook didn't understand. It was so wrong; Vars deserved to die. He grasped helplessly for the dagger Vars had shoved between his ribs, but was too weak to free it, and collapsed to the ground. Air rushed from his lungs as Vars kicked him over. Rook could only stare up at the old man with the missing arm, feeling helpless as life escaped him. Vars pressed a foot to his chest and leaned forward, pulling his weapon free. Rook could only blink.

"I'll kill every single one of you," Vars shouted. "Just like you killed my son."

62

Angst wasn't breathless from the flying or the falling. He wasn't winded from the solid landing on the back of an island-sized monster, or the battle raging all around him. He wasn't dazed from some random blow to the head snuck between the two giant foci, and his jaw hadn't been knocked loose by a gargoyle's attack. He was awestruck that Moyra was here, walking toward him on two long, slender legs.

Sunlight shimmered off the light blue scale that covered the outer half of her thighs and calves. In spite of the chaos surrounding them, Angst gawked as one leg sinuously moved in front of the other. Her hips swayed like waves on the sea, and it took strength to lift his gaze from those lovely legs and long torso and bare breasts to see her full, beautiful smile and large black eyes. Even as a mermaid, she was exotic. As something more human, she was possibly the most beautiful creature he'd ever seen. So much had changed—her eyes were no longer filled with desperate hunger, and she could now walk on her own legs. All this made him wonder what else her people had suffered under the curse.

Angst walked to her slowly. He swung Chryslaenor without looking, slapping aside a gargoyle like a fly. She shoved away a merman, who slipped on the creature underfoot and fell into the sinkhole. From the corner of his eye, Angst saw another merman leap toward him, only to crash into the flat of Dulgirgraut and crumple into a heap.

Her eyes locked on his intently as she approached. Angst set both swords to hover behind his back as they met. They looked into each other's eyes, and she pulled him in for a hug. He worried that his armor would be cold for her, but she didn't seem to mind. She placed her cheek against his.

"You did it, An-gst," she said in his mind. *"You freed my people, just like I knew you would."*

"Yeah," he said, at a loss for words. He had done what he'd set out to do, for once, even if it was by accident. It was almost freeing, in a way. "I'm glad you're safe. That was the most important thing to me."

She looked up at him with those larger-than-human dark eyes, and he melted. So alien, and so honest, and so filled with—

"You were right," she said, sounding a little sad.

"That's not something I hear often." He smirked. He created an air shield in time to deflect a thrown Unsel soldier.

"I love you, hooman," she replied. *"I really do. It is not supposed to be this. I cannot, we cannot..."* Her voice trailed off.

"You do?" he asked, hopefully. His heart raced and his mouth went dry.

Moyra merely turned away, as if ashamed. Angst took her chin in his fingers and gently pulled her to face him. They were so, very, close. Her eyes were sad, and in his heart of hearts, he knew there could be nothing more than this moment. He felt the ache of loss. More than anything, he wanted to share, to tell her how he felt. He wanted to explain that the hunger that had overwhelmed her wasn't hers alone. He wanted to find a place that they could be...something. To be whatever they were. A mermaid and a hooman and...and... And he swallowed very hard.

Angst had chosen to be a hero. This was what he'd always wanted, what he'd dreamed. He was married. And Moyra deserved to be happy. She deserved much more than he had to offer.

"I..." His voice caught. The longer they stood there, the more it hurt. He forced himself to swallow through the lump in his throat, stood tall, braced his shoulders, and said, "I would do anything for a friend."

She lowered her head and squeezed her eyes shut, her thick blue brows hanging low. Angst could feel her in his mind, and his response had been like a physical blow. He brushed a tangle of fine blue hair over her ear. In spite of his words, he was still thoroughly drawn in by Moyra's beauty and her presence. If she could stay in his life, Angst would even settle for friendship, though it would only hurt her in the end. It was selfish, but he couldn't control what he felt. His hand was on her cheek when she looked up. Her eyes understood, but—

"Thank you," she said. *"How can I thank you?"*

"You said you were going to try to stop this," he pleaded. "Please do something! There's no reason our people should fight."

"I chased them and killed as many as I could!" she said proudly.

"Would you try asking?" Angst said calmly.

"I'll try," Moyra shut her eyes and frowned. *"I told them not to kill hoomans."*

He nodded gratefully and pulled her in close.

"An-gst," she said, her voice quavering in his mind. *"If we cannot... I must go."*

"That's it?" Angst asked and felt his cheeks flush. It sounded like he was asking for a reward. "I mean, I get to see you again, right?"

"You said...you thought...we cannot," she said.

She looked sad, almost guilty, but he nodded in understanding. Their worlds were so different, and so far removed. How could they possibly be anything? He knew this, and yet his heart still ached. He faked strength he didn't feel. "No eating people, okay?"

"I will try," she said, her eyes mischievous.

Angst sighed because he knew she was serious. "Thank you."

She looked at him curiously.

"I was a little lost, a lot lost, and you gave me purpose. That's a generous gift."

She pouted and turned away. Her head lowered, she took a step. Angst sighed, reluctant to go into battle with a heavy heart. Moyra spun about and launched into his arms. She pressed her lips to his, her thin tongue flicking inside his mouth.

"One last breath shared." Her words echoed in his mind.

Her cheeks, wet with tears, pressed against his own. She didn't want this to end and neither did he. Chaos and war reigned around them. He felt a thousand eyes glance their way, but didn't care. He needed this moment, needed her, and knew she felt the same. There was no insecurity, no heroics, nothing but the passion of two beings who'd found each other in the midst of everything wrong. With every bit of him, he was reluctant to let go of this moment.

She slowly pulled away from his lips and his racing heart. Angst continued holding her hands as he stepped back for one last look at his beautiful mermaid. He longed for her, in all ways possible. She'd briefly filled that hole in his life. Moyra was the adventure. Exotic and beautiful, she was wrong in all the right ways. It was a singular moment that he would appreciate forever. How could he be so lucky?

"I...I love you, silly hooman," she said hopefully.

"I..." he started to reply. *"Moyra, I..."*

Moyra screamed as she was wrenched from his hands. The wail in his mind made him wince as he watched her rise into the air. Angst reached for his swords, looking for tentacles to cut off but found none. She hovered there, writhing and fighting as her arms splayed apart and her fingers spread. Her panicked eyes sought Angst's, desperate for him to be the hero.

"What do I do?" he pleaded to the swords.

A flood of information from both weapons filled him with theories and ideas, each vying with the other to provide empty answers, but neither had experienced anything like this.

Angst leaped to tackle her, hoping to free Moyra from her invisible confines. He bounced off an unseen barrier and was thrown roughly, flipping over onto his chest. He pushed himself up, only to watch in horror as water drained from her fingers, from her toes. It flowed out like a fountain, as it had with Tamara. She deflated, her skin tightening to her skeleton as all fluid left her body. Her breathing began to labor, her body shrank, and she continued to scream in his mind. It was all of his nightmares, and his mind recoiled into a cold, dark place.

"No," he cried out. "Please, no..."

"An-gst, you are my hero," Moyra pleaded in his mind, her voice scratchy. *"Save me!"*

"Moyra," he pleaded. "I lo—"

It was done. The husk of her remains fell into a pile of scale and bones. Angst stood still. He'd dropped a sword and covered his mouth with a shaking hand. Tears streamed down his cheeks. The water drawn from Moyra joined a stream flowing from the sinkhole to create a small water spout. The watery tornado grew in size until it formed into the shape of a woman, and Water stood before him. She was the same titanic height as Earth, and sloshed noisily as she pressed forward. An evil, satisfied grin spread across her fluid face.

"Why?" Angst croaked, his voice thick with mourning. The swords were in his hands, though he didn't remember wielding them. They provided no information, no song; they merely hummed with a dangerous power that made his bones rattle. He felt cold and distant from everything around him.

"So you could experience what you did to me," Water said in a gurgly voice.

63

The effort required to control her swifen was more than Tori had wanted to admit to Angst. With his help, the creature flew on its own and she could steer it like a ship, albeit a ship that could barely turn. Now, it reacted to her every movement, and she felt like she was learning all over again. She looked down, and whatever Faeoris had done had cleared out a section of the maiden's courtyard, like clearing off place settings at a dinner table with a broadsword.

Victoria veered the unicorn downward, patting it encouragingly. It landed on the outcrop, and she looked around with a sad sort of bitterness. Her courtyard, their courtyard, the place she'd met Angst, was torn in two. It broke her heart. This was her castle, and she hadn't been here to save it. Resolve filled her, a cold strength that kept her from mourning the loss of life and property. Mourning would be for later; now was the time for vengeance.

She dismounted, petting the summoned creature thankfully before dismissing it. Wielders and soldiers alike stared in slack-jawed silence. An old man shouted to attack, but none did. Judging by their surprised stares, they knew who she was, but looked to each other for guidance. They now knew the princess could wield magic, and she sensed their resentment for her leaving. Tori felt respect, fear, awe, but also uncertainty. She also saw Vars.

The old man, who she barely recognized as Sir Ivan's father, stood over the body of Rook, a friend of Angst's. She rushed to Rook, her red cloak flapping behind her, and knelt beside the young soldier.

"My queen," Rook said in a weak voice.

He was close to death, and Victoria touched his cheek. She saw in her mind what had happened. In that brief moment of his remaining life, she knew him. She knew his love for Janda, the future they should've had, the many children they would've had. He would've led the wielders to become zyn'ights, her mage corps, defending the realm from unknown forces. He could've gone on to become one of her generals, one of her closest advisors, and her friend. In her heart, she knew that he'd stood for right, and he loved his queen. She lowered her head, tears leaking down her cheek.

"You saved us with these wielders," she said in a raspy voice, "and you and Janda will be avenged. And I promise, forever, you will be honored in my court." The tiniest light of pride appeared in his eyes as they were lost to death.

She saw clearly, more now than ever in her life. Her vision wasn't clouded by remorse, nor foci, nor Angst. Victoria had been forced to wield like never before, summoning her swifen to fly on her own. It was a newfound strength, a pinpoint of clarity. Her vision was pink from her suddenly-glowing eyes. She saw all those around her, felt their lives and knew them. There was nothing lost to her as she knew their greatest hopes and darkest fears, the path this could be, that she would make.

"Wielder!" Vars cried, striking down.

As fast as thought, Queen Victoria drew her long, thin swords and blocked the attack. She rolled over Rook's corpse and swung with her other sword, slapping Vars across the face and cutting his cheek. She sliced his wrist before ducking from another one-armed attack. Tori leaped into the air and kicked his face. He stumbled back as she landed and kicked his groin. He grunted.

"I won't be defeated by one of your kind," he cried out.

She said nothing, ducking another wild swing.

"You can't kill me!" he said.

"You're already dead," she said calmly. "But I'm going to make it hurt before sending you back."

She dodged his blows, slicing at his face and wrist. Tori avoided striking his armor but punctured his every opening with the quickness of a wasp. In her mind's eye, she could see Faeoris, a Nordruaut, and a Meldusian keeping the gargoyles and merpeople away. Soldiers, and wielders, were starting to cheer, and she was even more driven than before. He lifted the sword to defend a blow, and she saw the ring. A red ruby shone from his finger, identical to the one hanging from Angst's neck, identical to Alloria's, and she knew.

"You see," he said, bloody spit flecking his mouth. "No matter how much damage you do, I still survive."

"Gross," she said, as the spittle landed on her chest. "I'm done with you."

As she swung down with all her might, he reached up to block her blow. The hilt of Victoria's sword struck the ring, shattering it.

"No," he cried out.

"For Rook," she said. "For Janda."

A vortex of dark color swirled behind him, like the portal they'd left at the cave, but this one seemed hungry. Hair flapped around her face as the wind was sucked into the darkness. He cried out, reaching for her, for anything as his body bent. She heard a crack as he was folded like paper, his bones snapping to fit into the darkness as it shrank. His body continued to crack, the metal of his old armor creaking noisily as pieces of him were jerked through. Victoria watched coldly as Vars disappeared into nothing, and the vortex flashed out of existence with a noisy pop.

Cheers surrounded her, and she spun on her heel to see soldiers and wielders kneeling at her feet. Faeoris bowed her head respectfully. The Nordruaut and Meldusian knelt to a queen. She shook with rage.

"That is enough!" she shouted. Everyone looked up. "We are at war! All of us! Together!"

Everyone stood, looking at each other in surprise.

"We fight as one!" she cried, lifting a sword high into the air. "Soldiers and knights, wielders and friends, we will defend Unsel together!"

Most cheered, and none argued as they braced themselves for another round of battle. A skinny young man with wild hair and clad in dark robes pressed through the crowd.

"But how?" he asked. "How can we fight all of this?"

Even as he uttered the words, he stepped back in wonder when the ground rippled as if a stone had been dropped into a pond. A body popped out in front of him with hard, spiky fur and a human-like face. Gamlin jumped out of the ground as if it were water, each looking at Victoria. Angst had called for reinforcements, and seeing them made her shoulders drop. Several soldiers and wielders drew arms or stepped back until a small one hopped onto her hand.

"We brought help," she said, looking at the creature.

It nodded at her with a grin, and she threw it at a gargoyle. It bored partly into the creature's chest along with several others and then the gamlin shook like dogs after a bath. The gargoyle's eyes widened in shock as it exploded into gooey pieces. Without a backward glance, the gamlin dove back into the ground.

"Now I task you all," she commanded, "go save Unsel!"

64

Water knelt to inspect Moyra's remains, rubbing several scales between her large, fluid fingers. She flicked them away as if they were sticky and disgusting. The element stood, towering over Angst, her knees rising higher than his eyes. Unlike Earth in her toga, Water was nude, though without definition. She was curvy, with the suggestion of short, tightly curled hair, but no hint of fine distinction. She placed her hands on her hips like an angry parent.

"Why?" he cried out as he stared at the small pile of scales. His heart ached, but everything else was numb.

"It's called revenge, Angst," she said, crossing her arms. "You chased Magic through the countryside, and Johnis, my love, was killed in your wake of madness. I thought it only fair to take something of yours for the pain you dealt me."

"I'm sorry," he said quietly, kneeling before the remains. "I couldn't stop it. I couldn't stop Magic."

"And that's your excuse?" she asked, nonplussed.

"I was trying to save people," he replied. He felt like he'd been slapped in the face.

"You just can't help yourself, can you? You have to be a hero, no matter the cost," she admonished. "That's what made this so delicious, Element of Humans. I led you to a challenge you couldn't refuse, the opportunity to be a hero once again."

"Your people," he began. "I set them free."

"Moyra deceived you to save my people," she explained. "They'd been cursed long ago. The men were imprisoned in that mage city, left to die. That dome trapped them, separated them from the women so there could be no love, no children. They were kept from me and forced to live apart forever."

"And I freed them. Wasn't that enough?" he demanded.

"No! You needed to feel the pain I felt, but more," she went on. "She never loved you. She lied to you, Angst." Water leaned forward, a wicked frown on her face. "Oh, how that must sting."

"I..." Angst clenched his fists, staring down at the remaining scale as it blew away in the cold wind.

"I wanted you to lose someone you cared for, but I could only hope to get lucky enough that you would actually love her."

Angst's head snapped up.

"But it's worse, isn't it?" she taunted. "She betrayed you! Using you to free the mermen, and now they're killing your people! What a hero you turned out to be!"

"No," he cried out.

"Oh, and you destroyed Air in the cave when you bonded with a second foci." She crossed her arms. "I think I may be winning this war again."

"All this destruction, all this death, all because of something Magic did?" He screamed so loud his throat hurt. "And her! Why her? She's one of your people."

"Was one of my people." Her icy voice was filled with bitterness. "Now you know what I went through."

Angst wiped tears from his cheeks. She was smiling, almost reveling in his pain until he started to chuckle. It grew louder until it was outright laughter. Her watery face frowned.

* * * *

Victoria pulled her blade from a mermaid's chest, and took a step toward Angst. He was in more pain than she'd ever felt.

"He needs me," she said out loud.

"Of course he needs us," Faeoris agreed, fighting by her side.

CHAPTER SIXTY FOUR

"Let's go!"

Victoria tore her eyes from him and looked up at the sky. Clouds were rolling in much faster than they should have, framed by flashes of blue and red lightning. She shivered at the power and electricity filling the air until Faeoris placed a hand on her shoulder and drew her sword, her bright wings spread wide.

"No," Victoria said firmly.

"What?" Faeoris snapped. She punched a merman beside her, releasing pent up frustration. There was a loud crack as he flew into the air.

"I believe in him," she said confidently. "He's got this."

* * * *

"No, you did it wrong," Angst said, catching his breath. "You miscalculated so badly. You're an idiot!"

"What?" She raised her arms and waterspouts grew from her hands up into the newly-formed clouds. "I'm not wrong! I'm Water, and I always win!"

"You're wrong about her. Moyra wasn't a betrayer. She was a hero," he said firmly. "She did what she had to and freed her people. She sacrificed herself so they would live."

"Moyra still lied to you," Water argued.

"She said she loved me, she saved me, even after her people were free," Angst declared. "What does that mean?"

"It means she was a fool!" Water spat.

"No. It means you are a fool," Angst said.

"I'm done with your insults—"

"What happened when Johnis was killed?" he asked, his voice as frigid as her own. "What happened when your love was murdered?"

"I just told you," she said with a frown. "I sought revenge."

"Exactly." He leaped forward, plunging Chryslaenor into the element's belly.

Lightning struck from the nearest dark cloud like hungry blue fingers reaching for Angst and pouring into his blade. She instantly froze to become a giant icy statue, protecting herself from damage, just as he'd seen in his dreams. Just as he'd witnessed the night she attacked the ship. Cold covered his sword in frost, biting into his grip. She held Chryslaenor with both hands, smirking at Angst as though he annoyed her. She was ice now, as cold and solid as a lake in winter. Her movements slowed, slivers cracking away as she bent over to scold him.

"Fool!" she spat, shards of icicles splaying with every word. "No mortal has ever killed an element with a foci!"

"Try two!" he roared, driving Dulgirgraut deep into her chest, the blades now buried a foot apart between her sternum and midriff.

"I'm not a human. This isn't a body." She laughed. "I can leave this behind when I want and... Wait, I can... I said, I can... No!"

Red lightning now joined the blue, striking Angst, pouring through both weapons. He drew in so much power that it burned as hotly as his aching heart, but he no longer cared. He poured the anguish of Moyra's death into both swords. He drew in the hurt, the guilt, the overwhelming failure, and forced it all into the foci. A bright pinpoint of light flashed inside Water, hovering evenly between the two swords. Angst roared as he forced the flat of both blades closer, ripping through her icy body.

"*No!* You can't!" She tried pulling back. "I'm Water! No human can do this!"

"I'm no longer just human! You made me this!" he said through gritted teeth. "I'm the element Human. I'm the element of Life!"

She laid her hands on his shoulders and began drawing water from Angst's body. He could feel himself weaken as liquid trickled out his fingers, but he wasn't sure if his scream was from pain or anger. Chunks of ice shot out, and the light between the swords became brighter as they closed, so bright he squeezed his eyes shut. With a final burst of rage and power, he roared, and forced the foci together.

Light flashed as the swords met. Water screamed as her body exploded into shards of ice, shooting outward. The flash burned his hands and face before he could raise an air shield; his armor felt so cold it was hot. He blinked a bright spot from his eyes and tried looking around. Everything within twenty yards was gone. Gargoyles, fish people, soldiers, all of them obliterated by the silent flash created by the twin blades, and no sign of the element.

Angst was furious. Vanquishing Water wasn't enough of a fight to quench his hunger for revenge. She'd killed Moyra. More than anything, he'd wanted to punish Water for what she'd done, but she was gone. He lifted Chryslaenor and struck at the giant creature below his feet. Smashing down with Dulgirgraut and then Chryslaenor, he pummeled the monster with his swords. He screamed in anguish as he let his fury out on the oldest creature in Ehrde.

* * * *

Everyone had stopped fighting, their attention on the battle between Water and Angst. Gargoyles, merpeople, and humans now watched in stunned silence as he continued smashing and swinging. Blue lightning struck the creature, and blinding flashes of red made them all turn away. Green bits of ooze splattered his armor and weapons. It went on for long minutes until he slowed. Angst lowered his weapons and dropped to his knees, weeping into his hands.

"Bring me to him," Victoria commanded Faeoris, knowing it would take longer to summon her swifen. "Now."

"Finally!" Faeoris said, as she reached around Victoria.

Angst screamed in pain, and they jerked their heads up to see Angst being lifted into the air by the creature's tentacles, his body listless.

* * * *

The first lash was like a wasp sting, but the size of his leg. Two more attached to his armor, trying to drill into his flesh like

471

teeth, but Angst stopped them short of penetrating his skin. The creature shook him in frustration. His brain rattled painfully in his skull, and he saw the familiar stars of faint. He was too distraught to attack but refused to completely give in. Two tentacles let go, the largest reeling back with a jerk. It threw him with such force that the crowd below him gasped.

* * * *

A deafening noise shook their eardrums painfully; it sounded like a bark but was too loud to be from just any dog. Victoria and Faeoris spun about to face it, the Berfemmian's fingers digging painfully into Tori's arms when it appeared.

Scar, the giant monster dog with too many eyes, shiny steel fur, and now bigger than ever, leaped over a broken castle wall and grabbed Angst out of the air in his wide jaws. The enormous metal-coated lab landed at the opposite side of their battleground.

He pranced over to Tori, casually knocking over any creature in his way. Soldiers screamed as they flew into the air, merpeople were cut to shreds, and gargoyles exploded at the touch of his tail, which wagged with every step.

He stopped before her, his three metallic tails scraping noisily on the ground. His six glowing eyes made Scar appear vicious. Her jaw agape and arms held outward, Victoria inched forward. She heard Faeoris's breath catch as Tori held out a trusting hand.

"Good dog, good Scar," she said with a quiver in her voice. "Oh!"

The small head of a young girl with long black hair popped around the shoulder of the dog. She'd apparently found a spot, or one had been made for her, nestled comfortably between sharp steel blades.

"Hi," she said, "I'm Kala!"

"Um, hi," Victoria replied.

"Scar," the girl said primly. "Release."

Scar regurgitated Angst, letting him roll off his drooly

tongue.

"Good boy!" Kala said, patting his neck.

* * * *

Angst dripped off the giant dog's tongue in a jangled mess, a wreck of dark dented armor, wet gray hair, sad eyes, and flushed cheeks. He coughed and gasped. Everything hurt from his body to his heart. He looked up at Victoria and grinned.

"Hi," Angst said, his voice raspy. He let go of his two foci and pushed himself up to sitting.

"Hi." Victoria looked ready to laugh, kneeling and patting his gooey shoulder. "Are you okay?"

"No, not even a little," he said quietly, fighting every urge to start bawling. They remained that way for long minutes.

Finally, Angst took Faeoris's offered hand and stood. He needed more—a hug from his best friend would've been a great bandage. But before he could reach out, Jaden tackled the princess in an embrace that screamed of marriage and children and every bit of future. Her eyes were closed, Jaden's embrace was true. Their lips locked.

Angst turned from them to watch the oldest creature in Ehrde slowly swim away, as if his attack had meant nothing. He felt like an utter failure. Gargoyles swarmed after the creature, fleeing the castle in flocks. Mermen and mermaids dove into the ocean as if on show, soldiers of Unsel watching in awe, letting all of them part without further chase.

He dismissed the gamlin but urged them to stay close. They dove back into the ground, only a small one remaining near Victoria. It seemed they weren't all completely his, after all.

A merman approached Angst and stared at him. He was different than the others, a blue oval almost seemed inked on his forehead. Angst hated everything, and wanted to kill this creature, chase after the green monster and destroy it, along with anything else that mouthed off. But he was exhausted, and he hurt. The merman just stood there, watching Angst with large black eyes, looking him up and down, his weapon sheathed.

"You loved her, hooman?" Angst heard in his mind.

Angst could only swallow, unable to fight back tears at the still-raw wound. He said nothing.

"You saved us," he said.

"We don't have to be enemies." Angst choked.

"Maybe," the merman said. *"Tell Rose that Gendel...Creeper...is sorry."* He nodded once and patted Angst on the chest with his webbed fingers as though that would fix everything.

The merman leaped off the ledge, diving into the castle's new ocean view, and swam away. Gone was the monster Angst couldn't defeat, and the gargoyles, and Water. But Moyra's people were free, and safe, and he could only hope they weren't new enemies.

When he thought his heart couldn't hurt anymore, he looked down to see Rook and Janda's bodies lying next to each other, their hands touching. Angst knelt beside them to check for life. He felt nothing but cold, and in spite of his great power, there wasn't anything his two foci could do to help. He closed their eyelids out of respect and looked up to see the desperate eyes of other magic wielders, several of whom were weeping. He nodded to them once but had nothing heroic to say.

Angst pushed down a guilty longing for Moyra. Knowing she was dead because of him was far, far worse than knowing she was lost to him, swimming around somewhere in the ocean. Her eggs, her babies floated at the bottom of the sea, alive and untended, and there was nothing he could do but wonder. He looked around and saw the dismayed eyes of a short, odd-looking creature, and Maarja. Saw Tori in the arms of a man he couldn't stand. Saw the ruins of Unsel, of the maiden's courtyard, and the bodies of Janda and Rook. Faeoris looked at him sadly, helpless. His other friends were nowhere to be found. He felt more alone than ever.

"Where's my wife?"

65

A bitter, medicinal smell numbed her nostrils as she wrenched her eyes open. They fluttered as the room swam into view. She awoke to see Angst speaking with the physician, Nynette. It had to be a dream. Not only was he in the room, but he was smiling. A silly, child-like smile stretched from ear to ear. His eyes looked wet from tears, and without warning, he embraced the physician. Nynette's eyes went wide, and her nose turned away as if Angst stank.

"I almost die, and you're already hugging another woman," she said huskily, her voice scratchy from screaming.

Angst rushed to her side and kissed her. It was long, dry, and full of love. Blood and muck caked his cheeks. He smelled of sweat, iron, and battle, and tasted of...fish? He pulled away to bury his face in her chest and hug as much of her as possible, digging his fingers between her back and the down mattress. She petted his gray, thinning hair and breathed his scent in deeply as he sobbed. She didn't care why; she was overwhelmed by the fact that he was finally back in her arms.

"It's okay, Angst," she said soothingly. "I'm okay." She grabbed her belly and felt around. "Wait, I am okay, right?"

The physician nodded and smiled. "A little bruised, but that's nothing like the pain you'll feel during childbirth."

"Awesome." Heather gently pushed Angst from his hug to look at his face. "It's so good to see you."

475

"You too." Angst ran his fingers through her graying brown curls. "I'm sorry I've been gone for so long, but I'm back, and I'm healthy again. Everything is fine now. Better than fine."

"What do you mean?" Heather frowned. "What happened to me? I thought I was going to lose the baby. Are you sure she's all right?"

"She?" Angst smiled wryly before turning his head, nodding at the physician. "You should tell her."

"Tell me what?" Heather strained to push herself up to a sitting position.

"Well...I'm sorry, I don't know where to start," the physician said quickly, red blotches of blush on her pale face. "I've never been wrong about this sort of thing before. Even after your last examination, I could've sworn..."

"Sworn what?" Heather's voice became louder. "What is it?"

"I guess I should say congratulations," the physician said encouragingly. "You and Angst are having twins!"

Heather covered her mouth with both hands as she gasped. Her eyes sought Angst, who nodded. He looked proud, but tears poured freely down his face. "Oh. Oh, Angst."

"I know!" Angst dove in for another hug.

"After all these years," she sobbed. "I'd given up hope of having just one." His cheek was pressed against hers; it was so comforting to have him home. "And now you're back, and safe, and we'll have babies and be a family. It's everything I've wanted."

She took in deep breaths and squeezed tears from her eyes. With her free hand, she wiped away bleariness to see bright lights over his shoulder. Two giant swords hovered horizontally at the entrance to her room. Not one sword, not just Chryslaenor. Two. A dark red hue shone around Dulgirgraut while Chryslaenor glowed bright blue, both swords resting on their tip by the doorway, as if guarding the entrance with the same pride she saw in her husband.

"Angst?" Heather pushed away, looking from the swords to him. "What did you do?"

66

Several days later, Faeoris found Angst in the middle of numerous domed buildings, admiring a large statue with a Nordruaut woman, a small, odd-looking man, and a pretty brunette with curly hair. A young girl with long black hair chased a lab pup, giggling as it pounced on a gamlin that dove into the ground for safety. Angst's two great foci stood nearby, hovering on their tips. After she landed, Angst immediately gave her a hug before introducing her to Maarja, Jintorich, and Heather. Maarja inspected her with untrusting eyes but said nothing. He also tried introducing her to Kala and Scar, who were too busy chasing after a gamlin to be bothered.

"Am I interrupting?" Faeoris asked.

"Never," he replied.

She looked up at the statue, lifting her hand to shade her eyes. The white marble man and woman were easily three times her height. The female had wild hair and a fierce disposition, and the male featured broad shoulders, muscular arms, and short curly hair. Both looked proudly toward Unsel. The statue was beautiful, and the couple looked like they belonged together.

"Who are they?" Faeoris asked. "Do they lead this city?"

"Dear friends, lost to this war," Angst said, covering his mouth with his hand. "Rook led the wielders safely here. We've invited them to stay, and thought it appropriate if he and Janda watched over them. We're calling this place Rookshire."

"That's beautiful," Faeoris said, swallowing hard at the sentiment. She could hear Heather clearing her throat and thought it best to stay quiet for a moment.

"Did you have any luck?" Angst finally asked.

"None," she said, and his face drooped with disappointment. "I'm sorry. I tried to find them. I flew all the way back home, circled the entire area with Marisha. There's no sign of them at all."

"It's not your fault," Angst said. "If it's anyone's, it's mine. I'm sure my friends will make it back safely. They probably just took a different route."

"What about Princess Alloria?" the Meldusian squeaked. "Has she been found?"

Faeoris merely shrugged, not knowing who the woman was, nor caring. She looked to Angst, who was pacing.

"Alloria is key to understanding what's going on," Angst said, wringing his hands behind his back. "She could be dangerous."

"That little thing?" Maarja asked in surprise.

"Heh, well, I'm not even sure that little thing is human anymore," he said, pulling the ruby ring from the chain around his neck. "Nicadilia and Crloc both wore these. Alloria and Vars too, and when the ring was destroyed, he supposedly died. Didn't the tribesman you beat down in the cavern have one?"

"ANduaut," Faeoris said, gritting her teeth. "I wish I could beat him again and… Wait." She vaguely remembered something from the fight. "Wasn't he with someone?"

"There was a tall, bald man casting spells on Rose," Angst said.

"That's it!" She thumped him on the chest, making him cough. "That's the bastard who killed my mother! He offered us rings, and she refused. How could I not see that?"

"It sounds like there was a lot going on," Jintorich interjected.

"This one man is infiltrating all the kingdoms?" Angst asked. "Why?"

"Or maybe a better question is, who?" Jintorich said. "Who would have such power to control life and death?"

"Why don't you destroy that thing?" Faeoris pointed at the ruby ring. "That might get rid of her."

"It's our only link to Alloria," he said, tucking it back in protectively. "If we can use it to find her, we can discover what's really going on. When my friends get back, we should—"

"Angst," Heather said in a firm voice. "Your promise?"

"Right," he said, shoving his hands into his jerkin pockets.

"What is it?" Faeoris said, instantly annoyed at his change in mood. "What promise?"

"Heather is due, with twins now," Angst said, but his smile seemed forced. "Her pregnancy was apparently affected by bonding with both swords. The physician said she could give birth any day now. I need to be here."

"Pfft." Faeoris waved at the air as though trying to swat away his bad idea. "She doesn't need a man to give birth. Your job is done!"

"No, Faeoris, it's not that simple," he tried to explain. "As I was just telling Jintorich and Maarja, I have to stop. I've completely failed at being a hero. All I've done is gotten friends maimed or killed. You saw Dallow, and now Rook and Janda." His voice caught. "Queen Isabelle and the Captain Guard murdered, and how many soldiers and wielders lost their lives? These things have made me dangerous," he said, pointing at the swords.

"What are you saying?" she asked in frustration.

"I promised Heather, and I'm going to tell Victoria," Angst said firmly. "I'm done adventuring. I'm done being a hero."

67

Epilogue One

Melkier

Dusty looked about nervously, sniffing back his winter cold vigorously. He lifted a hand to wipe his nose and then yelped from the pinch of cold shackles holding his wrists back.

"Should we bathe it first?" asked a guard, nodding at Dusty.

"No time," replied the second.

The chamber doors opened to the Melkier throne room, and the guards pushed the man through roughly. The room looked disheveled from the recent attack. Stone debris and bits of pale yellow and light blue flag lay in forgotten heaps throughout the hall. A sizeable crack had opened in the middle of the room, partially eating the throne.

To the left of the throne sat Queen Nicadilia, and beside her stood a very short man. Dusty couldn't help but notice the queen eyeing the man's stubby legs.

He'd never been within a stone's throw of royalty and swallowed hard, fighting back bile and tasting blood in his mouth from his recent attempt to escape. He felt a blow to the back of his leg and fell to a knee before the throne.

"There's no need for that," the queen said. "Please rise."

He stood but looked down at the stone floor.

"Look at your queen when she addresses you," the stubby snapped.

The queen sat tall in her throne, her posture tense. Long blond hair framed her pale face. Her cheeks appeared sucked in, outlining her jaw with dark shadows, and her blue eyes bulged in a way that screamed of crazy. Nicadilia stared down her sneer at him.

The queen nodded toward the back of the room. He turned his head and sobbed aloud with relief. His wife and children were sitting nervously at a table covered with food. None of them ate, but instead stared at him anxiously. They were tucked in neatly to the squares insets of the Melkier table. They appeared well tended to, and completely trapped. Trapped, but alive. He sniffed loudly before facing the queen.

"Show me," she commanded.

"Pardon, Your Grace?" Dusty asked.

"Show me what you do." She waved a finger, making a circle in the air. "Your...your magics."

"I..." He was at a loss for words and thought. Was it a trap? Would he be cut down again? He was going to deny her, but the stubby man's grimace told him otherwise. He sighed deeply; it was illegal, but the queen commanded it. What choice did he have?

There was a crunching sound, followed by a noisy ping of metal as his shackles flew free.

"You do...handle stone," she said hungrily. "Quite well, it would seem."

She stood and took several steps, running her fingers across his rocky body.

"Is that wise, Your Grace?" the stubby man asked.

"He's not going to harm me, Crloc," she said, still looking only at him. "Are you?"

He glanced at his family, shaking his head in compliance.

"Are you covered in stone, or do you turn to stone?" she asked.

"I'm really not sure, Your Majesty," he replied, his voice now like the grinding of gravel.

"That's fine. You still manipulate earth somehow, and that's all that matters." She walked up the stairs. "Did you see the destruction wrought by Unsel on our doorstep? Did you see my kingdom laid waste?"

"Yes, Your Highness." He'd been devastated. So many lives lost, so many friends gone. "It was Unsel?"

"It was," Crloc said solemnly.

"They disarmed us," Nicadilia said. "Killed my father and ran off into the night."

"Why am I here?" Dusty asked. "How can I help?"

"We have a choice, Dusty," she said. "We can cower, or we can fight. Melkier weapons and armor were once imbued with dragon bone, making our soldiers almost invulnerable to fire and magic. Unsel stole that from us, and our weapons once again became useless metal. We need you to repair our weapons and armor, make them strong again."

"How can I do that?" he asked. "That's not how I use magic."

"We have methods to help you learn," she said.

"And my family?" he asked.

"The safety of your family, of all Melkier, is in your hands," Nicadilia said warningly, her eyes boring into him.

He looked back at his family with every apology he could fit into a glance. His wife held hands with their children, tears down each cheek, but remained quiet. She nodded vehemently.

"What's to keep it from happening again?" he asked. "What's to keep Unsel from taking away our protection?"

"We have a new source of material," Crloc said. "Not just the bones of any dragon, but bones from the mother of all dragons."

* * * *

Vex'steppe

Three men of ages, young, middle, and old, sat at the corners of a large tent. Long staffs with daggers at both ends rested in their laps. Leathers barely covered their fit, muscular physiques.

Their disapproving eyes missed nothing.

"This is the best I could do," Vivek stated. "All things considered, much more than you deserve, and better than I expected."

ANduaut sat up to the gasps of everyone in the tent. The front left side of his forehead was gone. The entire corner, from his eye socket to the middle of his head, was caved in. Fresh pink skin had grown over the indentation, and he blinked one eye rapidly, looking around the room.

"He is lost," said the middle-aged man.

"Gone," said the older man. "How can he lead us? He must be blind and dumb."

"You judge too quickly," replied the Vivek. "Just wait."

"We are not fools," said the younger man. He moved closer, placing a hand on the dent in ANduaut's head. "It's magics keeping him alive, nothing el— I... Urk."

ANduaut stood abruptly, grabbing the man's throat. He squeezed until there was a pop, and the man hung limp in his hand. He stood, walked to his father's stadauf, and picked it up. He held it, swinging it around several times before slicing the throat of the older man. The old man grasped at the wound, and as he fell, ANduaut rested the blade against the throat of the Vivek. He leaned forward to the remaining man, his sinewy muscles taut and ready to pounce.

"Will you follow?" he asked briskly.

"To?" the middle-aged man asked, looking at the other bodies nervously.

"Victory," ANduaut replied, his voice cold and distant.

"Yes, my Iroquia!" he replied abruptly. "All of us. All of your tribes!"

ANduaut pulled his two-bladed staff from the Vivek's throat and stood. He walked out of the tent to hordes of tribesmen, each resting on their knees, waiting to learn their future. Silence fell as they looked at their new leader, frightened and awed by his deformation. The middle-aged man and Vivek crawled out of the cloth tent. The man dropped down and lowered his head to

ANduaut in respect. ANduaut raised his staff high to the cheers of all tribesman.

"Much better than I expected," Vivek muttered to himself.

* * * *

Rohjek

Guldrich left the Nordruaut furs behind as he crossed the border to Rohjek. The sight of this land left his mouth dry. The Vex'kvette had wreaked havoc randomly throughout Unsel, reaching out with its hungry orange fingers, changing or killing everything in its path. But this, this was far worse devastation. As far as he could see, the ground was hot and dry, as if from a long summer's drought, but in the middle of a wet winter. The air above was cold to his shoulders, but the ground below was a seething heat, and he sweated profusely.

How could he possibly survive this? He had fought Nordruaut weaklings, struggled through freezing cold and snow, had his arm cut off, only to be besieged by hunger and thirst. For the first time in his life, he wanted to give up. Only sleep and rest, for a thousand years or longer, would quench his exhaustion. Where was this champion the bitch had promised? He was on a fool's journey and was only driven to live because he wanted so badly to wrap his hands around her beautiful neck.

Days passed, maybe weeks, as he trudged through this new wasteland of heat and desolation. He wanted to collapse, but his new body wouldn't let him die. He spent his time wondering what could have happened to this place. Was it all like this? Had the capital been destroyed? What could have burned the entire nation?

Guldrich crested a hill, and saw down into a ravine that looked ravaged by the Vex'kvette. The ground was parched and dead, like all of Rohjek, but he could smell the sickeningly sweet residue of honey and molasses. He wanted to vomit, but only tasted bile. There was a shape at the bottom of the ravine, and he stumbled to it, hoping it was something to eat.

A hand the size of his torso stuck out from the dried earth.

"I seem to be too late, my champion," he said. "You're already dead, like I should be."

He kicked the giant hand in frustration, and it grabbed his leg.

* * * *

Nordruaut

"Shame has befallen us," Jarle began as he paced. "Our moment of greatness, of proof, is lost to the thirst."

He tried drawing them in, making eye contact with every leader of eastern Nordruaut standing in a circle around Owenqua. They stared at him with non-committal eyes.

"Few remember this story, so listen as I tell my tale," he said and several heads nodded in acknowledgement. "In the beginning, the Nordruaut were like humans, and we hungered like them. We were a greedy, covetous people, always thirsting for more. More land, more things. It was a pit with no bottom!"

Jarle knelt in his leather loincloth, swinging his arm horizontally in a slicing movement. His skin dripped with sweat from the nearby fire.

"A noble race of beings lived on our borders," he said dramatically. "The Mendahir were neighbors and friends who lived close to nature. They were tricked into an alliance with the Angorians. The Nordruaut wanted their lands, and when that alliance fell apart we watched the Mendahir perish. We stood by as all of them were killed."

The faces were still cold, and he didn't understand their distance.

"It was as if the Nordruaut destroyed them, an entire race of creatures, a unique people lost but for ghosts," he said sadly. "When we realized that, when we came to our senses, we tried following their path. We decided to become caretakers of Ehrde, living in congruity with nature, seeking greater balance with living things. We threw away our want, our desire, for something much better."

"And that's why we let spies and villains kill our people," Niihlu interrupted. He stepped into the circle unwelcomed. Several gasped at his impetuousness. "Too long have we sat idle, waiting for our enemies to have their due. War is coming, and we will not be its victim."

"No, not its victim. We can be its better," Jarle said. "Our passion is for the hunt, not for the drums of war. Not for killing. We have strength and power now. Do we use it for conquest, or do we use it to become better?"

"We use it to defend ourselves against a world coming to war," Niihlu said. "And you are too old and naïve to see this."

"Then let us decide here by vote," Jarle stated. "Who will stand for peace? Who will stand for Ehrde? Be brave and stand with me!"

Moments passed, and none did.

"It seems you stand alone," Rasaol stated, walking out of the circle.

"That is unfortunate," Jarle replied, lowering his head. "The west will not be with you in this."

"We need a unified Nordruaut," Rasaol commanded.

"The west will not war with Ehrde," Jarle said.

"Then you will war with the east," Rasaol said sadly. "Until we are one."

"You may kill me now," Jarle said, his heart wrenching in pain at the loss he knew was coming.

"No," Rasaol said, holding up a hand to stop Niihlu's approach. "Speak to your leaders in the west. We will give our sisters and brothers the respect they are due. They will decide to march with us, or there will be war."

Jarle approached Rasaol and placed his hands on the man's shoulders. He lowered his head in despair and muttered, "I know what they will say, and I fear for all Nordruaut."

68

Epilogue Two

Like stalwart guardians, Dulgirgraut and Chryslaenor rested on their tips at both sides of the main entrance to Victoria's chamber. The red aura of Dulgirgraut and the blue glow of Chryslaenor was comforting, and Angst hoped that, for a brief moment, they would get to enjoy some privacy and safety. Weeks had passed since the battle. He felt out of sorts and out of place in Victoria's bedroom. The last time he had stumbled into this room, it had been a mess, a mistake that seemed a lifetime ago. Now, she felt much older, and the bright pastel colors of her room no longer seemed to fit the woman standing before him. It was as though she had returned to her childhood home after being away for many years. Despite its great size, her bedroom felt smallish, and he looked at her forlornly from across the room.

"Yes, that's exactly how I feel," Victoria said, turning away from the window.

"You've gotten better at that," Angst confirmed with a wry smile. "Even after I bonded with both foci, you can still read my thoughts."

"You don't mind, do you?" she asked. "I mean, I can't do that with everyone, but with you, it just seems to happen now. At least when you let me."

"I don't mind, Tori," Angst stated sincerely. "What else is

there to hide?"

Victoria giggled then looked at Angst. Her thin brows furrowed, and the corners of her pouty mouth pulled back. She walked toward him. Her white gown flowed regally behind her, almost glowing in its majesty.

"There isn't a little something to hide, Angst?" she asked, stepping too close.

It was that game she had played to make him uncomfortable when she was younger, mere months ago. Rather than stepping back, Angst pressed forward and embraced Victoria, not as a friend but something more than a friend. He cared for her so much, he felt so much love for her, that an embrace hardly seemed enough. Angst felt sorrow, a loss for this moment that was temporary and fleeting. Their adventure was over, the last month had been a lifetime, more than he could have ever asked, everything he had ever wanted with her. And when he thought this, Victoria held on even tighter, clasping the back of his tunic, gripping it tightly with her little fists. He couldn't hear her crying, but his shirt was nevertheless wet.

Angst felt a catch in his throat as he was struck by the realization that he would have to share her. She would be in demand by her entire kingdom, as well as by others. Once again there would be boys. Jaden, or the Jadens of the world, would be vying for her attention, and he would have to patiently wait his turn. He would wait, Victoria meant that much to him, but his deepest insecurity made him wonder if he meant that much to her. They were more than friends, yet far, far less than lovers, and as always, it was complicated to keep that balance. He had lost so much, first Moyra, and now...

At this, she started to pull away. "It doesn't have to be over, Angst." Victoria said, pulling back only a little.

"I don't want it to be over, Tori," Angst said, more pleadingly than he had intended. "But I can't ask for more, nor do I have more to offer. Tonight, you take the crown. Unsel needs you, and there is no way you can leave again. I wouldn't consider taking you away. It's just—"

Victoria pressed her finger to Angst's lips to shush him. "I love you, Angst, you know that," she said quietly. "You're my best friend. I trust you. I can tell you anything. You will always keep me safe and will fight the world to be there for me. It feels like you've already started."

Angst nodded, not knowing what to say or how to share his feelings. He pulled her hand away from his face and held it.

"You make me feel important in a way different than being queen. You make me feel special. You love me unconditionally," Victoria said in a whisper. "You deserve more than I will ever be able to offer you."

Victoria drew away from him, walking to stand between her bed and the servant's entrance. Light reflected off her golden hair and her long white gown. Angst was certain it was one of the most beautiful sights he would ever see. He gawked, unashamed, even when she blushed. He was proud that his friend was so beautiful in his eyes, even as a part of him hurt to know that this was all, that she wasn't completely his. He turned to look out the window, sighing deep in his personal anguish.

"You've kept your hair blond," Angst said wryly.

"You like that, don't you?" Victoria asked.

Angst nodded but was otherwise quiet.

"Please, Angst," Victoria asked. "Don't you have anything to say?"

"Do I have to say it out loud?" he pleaded. "You already know—"

"It's nice to hear," she replied hopefully. "Don't be a chicken."

Angst smirked at the taunt Tarness had used throughout their adventure. She had taken steps back, so very far out of arm's reach now that not even their fingers would touch. He steeled himself to answer.

"I love you so much," Angst said in a deep, raspy voice. "I love you and everything about you. I will always try to be here for you, to be everything you need. This last month...I don't know what to say but thank you. It's almost everything I've ever wanted. I want more, but friendship is all I have to offer."

Now Angst heard a catch in her breathing, as though she were gathering her strength. It sounded as if this was as hard for her as it was for him. He felt like they were breaking things and parting ways forever. That nothing would be the same once this meeting was done.

"It doesn't have to be over, Angst, not completely," the princess said. "It's already better than I visioned it to be. I don't want it to be over."

"I don't understand," Angst said firmly, clenching his fist. "What do you mean? Better than you visioned? I don't understand." He continued staring out the window in frustration; it felt like she was teasing him, and prolonging the inevitable. A cool breeze made him shiver.

"You're right. It won't ever be like our adventure. But we don't have to be apart. I still... I want you..." Victoria took a deep breath. "I want you to be my—"

There was a sloppy wet sound, a sad sound, an angry sound that made Angst spin about. One of Jormbrinder's large triangular blades pierced Victoria's stomach. She was grasping the point of the blade with both hands, looking at Angst in panic. Slick, hot blood covered the end of the foci and dripped to the floor.

"No!" he cried out.

Angst blurred to Victoria, catching her before she fell to her knees. He held his princess as she slowly lay back in his arms. She gripped the blade in one hand and held Angst's face with the other. Her blood was warm on his cheek. Her eyes were wide in shock and fear and death; her face paled as her breaths grew increasingly short. He would heal her. He could do it with two foci! He gripped the back of the dagger and drew in every bit of knowledge the foci would impart to him. The dagger was stuck; he couldn't pull it free.

"I love you, Angst." Victoria coughed weakly. "I love you."

Angst looked over his shoulder. Alloria stood with one hand covered in thick, crimson blood and the other holding the second blade of Jormbrinder. She seemed in shock, as though surprised by what she had done. Her hand, her entire body, shook violently. She looked at Victoria and then at Angst with sorrow-filled eyes. Tears streamed down her cheeks.

"Angst," Alloria said pleadingly, her face contorted in anguish. "Angst, I'm sorry. I'm so sorry." And in a blur, she was gone.

Angst scrambled around his princess, tripping over his own feet to reach Dulgirgraut. The twin foci were still glowing. They hadn't been glowing in honor of him and his princess, but in warning. He had failed again, but for the last time. He would set things right. Drawing Dulgirgraut, he looked at Tori on her knees, the long golden blade of Jormbrinder through her chest, and decided.

He walked to the center of the room, and with every ounce of resolve and fury, slammed the foci into the ground, calling forth the great spell. "At all cost!"

About the Author

David J. Pedersen is a native of Racine, WI who resides in his home town Kansas City, MO. He received a Bachelor of Arts degree in Philosophy from the University of Wisconsin - Madison. He has worked in sales, management, retail, video and film production, and IT. David has run 2 marathons, climbed several 14,000 foot mountains and marched in Thee University of Wisconsin Marching Band. He is a geek and a fanboy that enjoys carousing, picking on his wife and kids, playing video games, and slowly muddling through his next novel.

To learn more about David and his writing please visit his blog:

www.gotangst.com

Angst and his friends return in the sequel:

Burning with Angst

Available now!